PRAISE FOR THE

N Y X I A TRIAD

"*The 100* meets *Illuminae* in this
high-octane sci-fi thriller." —*Bustle*

"*Nyxia* grabs you from the first line
and never lets go." —Marie Lu,
#1 *New York Times* bestselling author

"Brilliant concept meets stellar execution
in this fast-paced deep-space adventure. I was
hooked from page one." —Victoria Schwab,
#1 *New York Times* bestselling author

"We've got our Katniss and Tris and Ender
and Thomas and all the other teens that kick a lot
of ass in pursuit of a goal . . . and now we have
Emmett." —Nic Stone, *New York Times*
bestselling author of *Dear Martin*

"Fans of the Hunger Games and the Maze Runner
series will enjoy this series opener." —*SLJ*

"Both curious and suspicious at every turn,
[Emmett] is an ideal narrator, and a sequel
can't come soon enough." —*The Bulletin*

"Emmett's self-deprecation, wit, and ability to see the good in others will keep readers riveted and eager for the next volume in this planned trilogy." —*Publishers Weekly*

"Nyxia seems to have a mind of its own, but its mystery will carry over into the sequel, which cannot come soon enough." —*VOYA*

"Impossible to forget. Impossible to put down. This wonderfully diverse epic is an utterly thrilling binge-worthy treat." —Jay Coles, author of *Tyler Johnson Was Here*

"An engrossing premise that explodes to life in Reintgen's imaginative debut. Highly recommended!" —Jason M. Hough, *New York Times* bestselling author of the Dire Earth Cycle

"Sleek, fast, and action-packed, this is a thrilling new take on space adventure. I got to the end and instantly wanted more." —Stefan Bachmann, author of the internationally acclaimed *The Peculiar*

"With a vivid cast of characters, relentless pacing, and layers of mystery, Reintgen hits all the right buttons to craft an addictive page-turner." —Fonda Lee, author of *Zeroboxer* and *Exo*

NYXIA
UNLEASHED

THE NYXIA TRIAD

— Book 2 —

SCOTT REINTGEN

EMBER

Text copyright © 2018 by Scott Reintgen
Cover art copyright © 2018 by Heiko Klug

Ember and the E colophon are registered trademarks
of Penguin Random House LLC.

Visit us on the Web! GetUnderlined.com

Educators and librarians, for a variety of teaching tools,
visit us at RHTeachersLibrarians.com

The Library of Congress has cataloged the hardcover edition of this work as
follows:
Name: Reintgen, Scott, author.
Title: Nyxia unleashed / Scott Reintgen.
Description: First edition. | New York: Crown, [2018] | Series: The nyxia
triad ; 2 | Summary: Emmett Atwater and the other Genesis spaceship
survivors are caught between Babel and the indigenous Adamite population
when they are sent to extract nyxia, the most valuable material in the universe.
Identifiers: LCCN 2018010155 | ISBN 978-0-399-55683-8 (hardback) |
ISBN 978-0-399-55685-2 (epub)
Subjects: CYAC: Conduct of life—Fiction. | Mines and mineral resources—
Fiction. | Life on other planets—Fiction. | Science fiction.
Classification: LCC PZ7.1.R4554 Nx 2017 | DDC [Fic]—dc23

ISBN 978-0-399-55686-9 (pbk.)

Printed in the United States of America
10 9 8 7 6 5 4 3
First Ember Edition 2019

FOR MOMMA.

I fell in love with books while tucked under the covers listening to you read. Your voice built bridges to other worlds. I still find them sometimes, like majestic ruins, and can only marvel at how many ways you gave me to pursue my passions. So this world, this story? I've built it for you.

Love, Scott

PART I

THE ADAMITES

CHAPTER 1

THE FALLEN

Emmett Atwater

Fallen angels were cast down to Earth and became demons. When Babel casts us out, it's in fire and blood and steel. As the descent begins, I hold on to one truth: I am more than what they would make of me.

It takes thirty seconds for the silence of space to give way as I break through Eden's atmosphere. It sounds like giant fists hammering the sides of the pod. Metal screams, and I start shouting every cuss word I know. The porthole windows dazzle: bright purple slashes and golden hooks against black backdrops. The patterns start to turn my stomach, so I close my eyes.

A snarl and a snap, then I get a nice gut shot as the drags deploy. Flame-resistant chutes explode overhead. My velocity cuts to nothing, but my heart rate's still spiking when the entire console flashes red. I lean forward and catch a glimpse of dark nothing before the pod drives, hammerstruck, into Eden's surface.

"Landing sequence complete."

I groan at the android voice. Grid lights flash from the console. They trace the contours of my body before winking out. My holographic avatar appears in the air. Burns on my lower back. The cut on my shoulder from Roathy's blade is a thin red slash. There are a few speckled internal stresses, but nothing with exclamation points.

"You require medical attention."

"You think? Let me out of the pod."

"Exodus Sequence confirmed."

The porthole windows are covered in mud, but that doesn't stop the walls from peeling back like the wings of a great metallic insect. Sweat-soaked, I stagger out beneath the hatches and take my first steps on a foreign planet. Turn and search, turn and search. I'm alone.

My launch pod flashes red beacon lights, but I see no answer on the dark horizon. Behind me are vague, mountain-like rises. Ahead, a strangled valley thick with trees and creeks.

I look up, blink, and look again. Two moons loom in the starless night. Their combined light creates the illusion of a bright, snowy evening. Every branch is pale-painted, every creek a whitewashed echo. I look back up. One moon is bigger and brighter, its surface marred by a series of bloody scars. The other moon is dime-to-quarter of the first. Hanging in the sky, they look like a pair of mismatched eyes set in a dark, endless face.

The moons watch me stumble to the nearest creek and plunge my hands in elbow-deep. A rippling shiver runs up my spine and sharpens the senses. My hands shake as I wash Roathy's blood away. I scrub dark streaks from my suit, rinse my face, and try to forget the broken boys Babel wanted to bury in the stars.

I left Roathy alive, but what about Bilal? The others?

Shivering, I stumble back to the pod and hoist my knapsack over a shoulder. There's nothing else to do but walk, find the others. Did something go wrong with my landing? Or did Babel lie about this too? The need to see another human face dominates every thought. I can't fathom the idea of sleeping alone on an alien planet. So I climb the nearest hill. And after that, another. My strides are light and long in Eden's lower gravity.

At the top of the next hill, I look back. My pod's beacon glows red, but there's still no sign of the others. I stare down at the strangled valley, brightened by both moons, and realize it's empty. The creek shuffles through the hills. A breeze clacks branches together like spears, but I don't see any animals. No birds fluttering between branches or fish leaping out of creeks.

Anxious, I press on to the next hill, and the next, and the next.

Finally I reach an overlook that connects to the other valleys. They honeycomb darkly out, each of them beaconless. I have no idea where the rest of the crew might have landed, or if they landed at all.

In the gloom, I look for a sign. A hole dug into a hillside or a tree snapped by a falling spacecraft. Anything. The landscape stares back, and a fear takes shape, nestling in the darkest corner of my mind: I'm alone.

Then a flicker. Bright orange against the pale moonlight. Not a pod beacon, but a fire. It's no more than a speck, but

I strain my eyes, scared to lose the sight. It flickers again, a bright flash, and then someone brandishes the torch like a flag. The movement's so human, so hopeful, that a ragged breath escapes my lungs.

I'm not alone. The others are here.

The way isn't easy, but I cut across the face of the valley, trying not to lose sight of the fire. I'm forced down a pair of steep hills and into the forest. I splash my way through ankle-deep creeks and finally plunge through the low branches.

They're waiting. Four faces washed in flame.

Morning stands apart. She's holding a crude and crooked branch tipped with fire. I don't know who she expected, but the sight of me dismisses some dark fear. There's something fierce about the way she tosses the branch back onto the pile and crosses the distance. I can barely get my hands out as she wraps me in a hug, head pressed to my chest like it belongs there.

Over her shoulder, though, I get my first good look at the others.

They look like the survivors of an apocalypse, not explorers knocking on the door of a new world. Azima's eyes are dark. She's wearing her ceremonial bracelet for the first time in months, and I understand why. Out here, anything that feels like home is a good thing. Jaime rests his head in her lap. I almost confuse it for something romantic until I see the wound. An angry red marks him from rib to gut. It's already stitched up, but that doesn't make it look any less nightmarish. His pale knuckles are painted with dried blood.

My heart breaks. For him, for whoever they made him

fight. The sight puts an end to my theory that Jaime was ever special or different. Babel's broken him just like the rest of us. My mind jumps to Bilal. Is my friend alive or dead? Was he put in Jaime's launch room? Anton sits nearby too. The little Russian's eyes look completely lost. What did Babel do to us?

Morning slides out of my grasp. She takes a deep and steadying breath, like for one second she was breathing me instead of air, before turning back to the others.

"We should get moving," she announces. "Our supply location is nearby."

"Moving?" Azima asks quietly. "Look at our boys. We need rest. We need sleep."

Morning considers that. "Does anyone feel like sleeping?"

Anton looks up. "I can't sleep. Not now."

Morning's eyes flick to me. "Can you sleep? After what happened?"

I realize she knows. She knows what Babel did, what they wanted us to do. If I close my eyes, I can still see Roathy on the other side of my barrier, begging to go down to Eden. It takes about two seconds to figure out *how* she might know.

"You?" I ask, stunned. "They made you fight?"

Her expression hardens. My question just confirms her guess. Now she knows what Babel tried to do to me, to them. "No," she says. "I didn't have to fight. It was in the captain's instructions. The computer told me to *monitor my team*. It said that some of you *experienced additional testing*. After Anton landed . . . he told me what happened."

My laugh is harsh and short. " 'Additional testing.' That's what they called it?"

Morning nods. "I'm sorry. None of you should've ever had to go through that."

There's silence, a crackle of flame, deeper silence.

I ask, "So we just keep moving?"

Morning nods again. "The walk will tire us out. No point sitting here if we can't sleep. Babel's instructions say the supply center is by far the safest place to be. The other crews will be heading to the same center from their landing sites. I want to get us to a secure location as soon as possible. But let's get things straight: all we have is each other. Babel's up there plotting. The Adamites will have their own plans. Starting right now, we depend on each other. We fight for each other. Everyone got that?"

There are nods all around, but no one gets to their feet. Jaime pinches his eyes shut in pain. His perfect hair is slicked back with water. Azima gently rubs his shoulder like that will help. Only Anton looks up, his expression slanted and dark in spite of the firelight.

"We need to get all our shit out on the table now," he says. "I don't want grudges."

Wind slashes through the valley. Our circle grows cold with his words.

"I killed Bilal," he says.

There's only shame in his voice, but blood still pulses in my neck and through my arms and up my throat. I don't remember moving, but Morning has me by one arm. Azima's up too, holding me by the other. I'm dragging the two of them slowly forward.

Anton stares back, eyes dead stone, face colorless.

"I didn't want to kill him. He was in the room. Waiting

there. They didn't even tell me. He did, though. He said they were going to let him go to Eden if he killed me. Babel wanted us to prove ourselves, one last time." Tears streak down Anton's face, pooling along the rim of his nyxian mask. "I wanted him to at least fight me. Just fight me. I shouted at him. I pushed him. He just sat there. Refused to do it. He stepped to the side and told me to go. I didn't know what else to do. I . . . I went. The room vacuumed after. . . ."

I sink to my knees. My whole body trembles. Azima loosens her grip, but Morning holds on, and thank God she does, because I almost collapse into the flames. I want to rage. I want to hate. But Anton? The broken boy who was forced to kill my friend? He's a sword in the hands of Bilal's true killers. He's nothing. I remember Isadora's final look. The hatred that burned its way from her pod to mine. I realize she must think that I killed Roathy.

But I didn't. And Anton didn't really kill Bilal.

It was Babel. It always comes back to Babel.

"Roathy," I say. "They tried to make me kill Roathy."

"Tried?" Morning asks.

"I used nyxia to seal him in the room and launched."

Anton's eyes snap up. "God help me. Why didn't I think of that?"

I don't have any answers. All I can do is look away. Morning's hand tightens on my shoulder. I hear Azima hiss a string of curses. Everyone looks at Jaime next. The bloody knuckles and the gut wound are their own answers to the question, but he still says the name.

"Brett. I killed Brett."

I always thought something about Jaime was wrong, that

he was Babel's favorite for some reason. I started to realize that was a lie on *Genesis 11*. The photograph of his family, the way Jaime acted toward me. I couldn't keep seeing him as wrong. Babel is just confirming that truth. He wasn't spared. No one was. The Adamites think Babel is sending a group of innocent children. They couldn't be more wrong.

Anton stands. I want to hate him, but it feels useless. How can I honor Bilal through hate? The boy who refused to kill for what he wanted. The boy who was better than us, than all of this.

"Remember him," I whisper. "Be better than they want you to be. Don't let them win."

He gives a nod as he wipes the dirt and the tears from his face. He glances over at Morning. "The other fight," he says, like he's realizing it for the first time. "Loche and Alex."

"Alex would have won," Morning says.

Anton shakes his head sadly. "You don't know that."

There's silence for a few seconds. Grief takes over Anton again. I remember how inseparable they were aboard the ship. I have no comfort to offer. Not with my best friend already confirmed dead. Anton lowers his eyes.

"It won't end there," I say. "They're going to try to kill us too."

"They still need us," Morning replies. "But yeah, after we hit their mining quotas, I'm assuming they'll try to get rid of us. We can use that knowledge against them. For now we keep up appearances, fathom? We mine nyxia, we earn our keep, and we *always* remember who Babel really is. On *Genesis 12* my team had a saying: shoulder to shoulder."

"Shoulder to shoulder," Anton repeats.

"No gaps in the line," Morning explains. "We stand together or not at all."

The group nods their approval. I can't help asking, "You have a plan?"

"A couple. Let's get moving."

I walk over and offer a hand to Jaime. He looks at it for a second, then takes it. A bloody peace offering. A reminder that we're not that different. Azima and I take turns helping him walk. If the wound was any deeper, he'd probably be dead right now.

Morning leads us into wilderness. At first she walks up front. But a few minutes in, she falls back so that she's walking with me. She wears her hair in a dark braid over one shoulder. I can tell her mind is racing: the creased forehead, the restless hands, the clenched jaw.

She's so tough, but the weight of all of this is threatening to bury her.

We walk together, shoulders touching, like we're walking home from school on a normal day. But that's not reality. Reality is a new world. Reality is two moons hanging in the sky, bright and beckoning. Reality is what we're leaving behind as we move through an empty forest and out into a world that feels full of ghosts.

CHAPTER 2

A NEW WORLD

Emmett Atwater

As we walk, Morning slips each of us a food ration and a new gadget from Babel. She wasn't supposed to give them to us until we reached our first supply station, but she's smart enough to see that we need them. Too much time alone with our thoughts could be a bad thing right now. It helps that the scouters are a choice piece of tech.

Black nanoplastic suctions to the skin just above our nyxian language converters. The piece extends over a cheekbone and in front of one eye, ending in a tinted, transparent rectangle. I've only ever seen stuff like this in old anime shows. But there's nothing old about the scouters. A thought from my brain cycles the screen through different settings: night vision, satellite maps, even a point-and-click database for identifying random objects in the environment around us.

Our first taste of something alien comes from the surrounding forest. Azima points out that every tree has a slight lean to it. We realize it's because every single leaf is reaching out, curling in the air, grasping for the nearest moon.

"That happened to mi abuelita's houseplant," Morning says. "But with sunlight."

It gives the trees an imbalanced look, like they're being blown off course by a permanent western wind. Our surroundings have been so quiet that the first snap of branches sounds like a gunshot. Morning signals for our formation to tighten as the distant sounds draw closer. Her eyes look dark and serious above her nyxian mask. A huge section of the forest on our right fills with shadowed movement.

"Weapons out," Morning commands. "Be ready for anything."

Manipulations fracture the air. I pull my nyxian knuckles on. It takes about thirty seconds for the shaking branches to close on our location. I'm expecting something straight Jurassic, but the movement's coming from above.

We catch glimpses of flocking, winged creatures. Their swinging limbs aren't birdlike, though. They're more like feathered monkeys, sharp-clawed and strangely limber.

My scouter lands on one of them, and the word *clipper* pings into the corner of my vision. A thought will bring up a prepared description of them, but I'm a little busy staring as an entire pack swings overhead. Morning's the first to snap into motion.

"Let's keep moving."

"Are you sure they're not a threat?" Jaime asks through gritted teeth.

I glance over. Morning's eyes are unfocused. She's clearly reading the description I decided to skip. "It says they like shiny objects, but thankfully, they don't eat meat."

As one we start to move. We keep our formation tight

as the clippers swing overhead, clearly curious but keeping their distance too. I watch as Morning fishes something out of one pocket. She holds up a quarter, pinched between her thumb and forefinger.

"Should I give them my lucky coin?"

Anton smirks. "Didn't you read the sign back there? It said no feeding the ducks."

Morning waves the coin. "But I always ignore those signs."

Before I can even make fun of her for *having* a lucky coin, one of the clippers comes sweeping down. I know how quick Morning is—her reactions were godlike in our duels—but the creature's even faster. She stumbles back empty-handed as the thing bounds off with its prize. Half the pack gives chase, but the rest of them stick to following us.

"Great," Anton says. "Now the other ducks are hungry."

A few of the clippers grow bolder. They swing into plain sight, baring filed teeth and beating chests and flashing bright wings. We're never in actual danger, but Azima has to hide her bracelet, and one clipper makes a swipe for Anton's watch. We're actually enjoying the distraction when one of the lead clippers lets out a hiss. The rest of the pack pauses, all dangling from branches, waiting for an order.

We've reached the edge of the forest, I realize.

An empty plain waits ahead. And as one the clippers start to vanish. We watch them move back through the forest. Their departure is so quiet I almost feel like we imagined them.

"Right," Anton whispers. "That's not scary as hell."

We all pause on the threshold. The waiting landscape

looks just like what we saw in the mining simulations. An oppressive wall of mist in every direction. Grass-knobbed hillsides rising like graves. Little creeks darting this way and that, snake-tonguing through it all.

Morning nods. "Well, we can't go over it. . . ."

Azima looks up excitedly, like she always does when she's in on a joke.

"Can't go under it!" she exclaims.

"Have to go through it," Jaime finishes.

I smack his shoulder. "You skipped a part."

He shrugs. "The last part is the only part that matters."

Anton stares at us in confusion. "What is this? What are you talking about?"

"Going on a Bear Hunt," Morning answers. "You never read that book?"

Anton shakes his head. "We had more knives than books."

Morning rolls her eyes. "Great. We'll let the one with the knives go first."

"With pleasure," Anton replies.

He starts into the mist and we follow. The deeper we go, the more otherworldly Eden becomes. Even on the rare trip to Lake Michigan, I've never seen a place so empty of anything human. The grass crunches stiffly beneath our feet. Every now and again, ash from our heavier steps puffs out like smoke. The hills boast only a few plants, and all of them have the same skyward reach as the forest, like hands folded in prayer to the distant moons.

It looks like the moons have shifted in the sky, like they're on the verge of collision. I watch them for a while before realizing that quiet has snaked its way back through the group. I glance back and find Morning trailing the group silently.

"Hey, you want in on a little bet?" I ask. "Just to keep things interesting."

She cocks her head curiously. "What's the bet?"

"Our first alien sighting."

Anton laughs from up front. "Alien sighting? We're the aliens."

Morning notices what I notice. No one in the group has their head bowed now. Even Azima and Jaime are glancing over, wondering about the Adamites and when we'll see them and what they'll be like. It won't erase what Babel did to us, but it's a step in the right direction.

She nods at me. "I'll take that bet. But you remember I don't lose, right?"

"She really doesn't," Anton says grumpily.

I look around, trying to involve everyone. "Any takers?"

Everyone's in. Azima goes long shot, guessing it will be a full week before we see an Adamite. Anton throws his dart down on three days, and Jaime snags the hour window after his. Everyone laughs when I take the hour right before Anton's choice, squeezing the timing of his guess airtight. The Russian laughs loudest. "You're a pair of pisspots."

Morning goes last. "A day and a half from now," she says. "Early. A few hours after dawn."

The way she says the words makes them sound like prophecy. Anton reaches over and taps her scouter. "You have a captain setting, don't you? Some kind of radar for Adamites?"

"I don't cheat. I just win."

Anton shakes his head. My mind flashes back to Morning's score, nearly double what Longwei posted aboard *Genesis 11*. All we knew about their crew in the beginning was what we saw on those scoreboards. It's easy sometimes to forget that they came through space on an entirely different spaceship, manned by different astronauts, with different highs and lows. Did Morning ever get put into the med unit like me? Did Anton ever feel like an outcast? How did they become such a tight-knit family? It all has me curious.

"You didn't really win every competition," I say. "That's not possible."

Morning throws me a raised eyebrow. "I lost a handful of times in the Rabbit Room. Omar beat me twice in the pit. Oh, and one time this *punk* tackled me off a boat and into the water."

Azima glances back. "Emmett's leap! That was *amazing*."

Morning winks. "Doesn't make him less of a punk."

We keep walking. Whatever spooked the clippers hasn't made an appearance. Our maps show we're halfway across a basin that's marked by crooked creeks. I'm still not sure I could sleep, but Morning's plan is working. I'm getting tired, body-worn. If I can reach a point of complete physical exhaustion, maybe my body will turn my brain off for me.

I want to file the whole day under *N* for *Never Again*.

Anton clears his throat. "Azima, I hope you won't think me forward, but you have a great deal of distracting black marks on your . . . suit."

Azima glances back, cursing. "It's from my landing. One of the tanks busted."

Anton's mask hides his grin, but I can still hear it in his voice.

"Just let me know if you need my assistance."

She strides off to the nearest creek and turns back to throw a rude gesture at Anton before leaning down to wash the grime away. We all hear the faint, agitated moan. Before I can figure out what it is or where it's coming from, everything around Azima distorts.

The air looks like a corrupted file, a ring of broken pixels. The water splashes upward and four birds take flight. They're sleek things, no bigger than hawks, and their wings shiver black to white and back again. They were cloaking, I realize. Floating invisibly on the water.

Azima looks back, eyes wide and bright above her nyxian mask.

We all start to laugh at her, but the laughter dies when a grating shriek sounds above us. Our eyes swing up to the birds. Their formation breaks. But before they can scatter, *it* comes spiraling out of the mist. A pair of massive black wings snaps wide. A grotesquely human-looking body contorts, and the creature somehow snatches all four fleeing birds midflight. My scouter throws the name *eradakan* into the corner of my vision.

Wingbeats stir the hip-high grass. The eradakan hovers above, opening a gigantic beak and letting loose another deep-throated screech. I shiver as it looks down at us with all four of its eyes. Two set into an arrow-shaped head and two center-set in the rippling muscles of its chest. Eyes wide, the creature slams the first bird down its gullet and we hear the bones crunch.

"Let's go," Morning hisses. "Nyxia at the ready. Azima with Jaime."

We're all still backpedaling when the eradakan lands. The creature's attention dances between us and its current meal, like it's considering whether or not we're worth the chase.

Before we can fully turn, the landscape behind it starts to *move*.

Dark shoulders slouch and roll. I stumble as what I thought was a hill glides with deadly grace over the plain. The name *century* pings in my scouter. Moonlight avoids the creature's scaled back. It prowls behind the distracted eradakan. I've never seen anything so big move with such terrifying silence. In old movies, creatures that size shake the ground to announce their coming. Buildings and cars get destroyed; cities burn.

The silence defies some natural law. We all watch the century rise to its full height and descend on the distracted eradakan. I catch a moonlit glimpse of rows and rows of teeth before the predator drags its new meal back into shadow.

Dying shrieks chase us through the hills. We don't need Morning to sound the command. Basic instinct creates as much distance as possible between us and the feeding ground. I shake my head at Babel's name for this world: Eden. If this is the same mythical garden, I don't think Adam and Eve were cast out. More likely they were eaten first.

Distance eases my nerves. Morning keeps us moving at a good clip for about thirty minutes. No one tells jokes. Sweat runs down our faces, but we all know this is nothing compared to the Rabbit Room. In the lighter gravity, I could run for days.

When Morning finally pauses, it isn't for rest; it's to listen.

We each hunch down onto a knee, breathing quietly. I glance over at Jaime. He's wheezing, and his wound's ripped open a little. The blood's soaking through his uniform. Azima holds a rag to the thing, trying to stop it. This isn't exactly the welcome we expected on Eden.

No one speaks as Morning listens for a few minutes, then gets us moving again. We run together. We should have known Eden would be dangerous after Babel's training. The Rabbit Room and the pit should have prepared us. Running and fighting and fending off the wild—those weren't random tests. But I don't remember anything this big and deadly-looking in the simulators.

It's almost dawn. One of the two moons is starting to fade. The other one—with its bright red scars—still hangs stubbornly in the sky. Morning orders us to walk. Our pace has left us just a few kilometers south of the rendezvous point. It's hard to tell through the fog, but either a forest or a swamp separates us from the marked location.

Jaime's the first one to break the silence of our heavy breathing. I think it's a good sign he's able to speak at all. "Are we really not going to talk about what happened back there? That was like live footage of a *Planet Eden* episode."

"I have a feeling we're not at the top of this food chain," Anton adds.

Jaime nods. "That first thing looked like a dragon."

"No scales," Morning says, like she's a dragon expert. I shoot her a funny look, and she shrugs into laughter. "I don't know. I'm just saying, it didn't have scales."

"It didn't breathe fire, either," I say. "Dead giveaway."

Morning laughs. Jaime looks back long enough to make himself wince.

"The other one," he grunts. "The century. That was the biggest animal I've ever seen."

Anton smirks back at him. "Where are you from?"

"Switzerland."

The Russian wags a knowing finger. "In Russia we're accustomed to monsters. The seas are full of leviathans. They're all twice the size of that thing, and they eat the children who behave badly."

That has Azima raising one eyebrow. "How are you still here, then?"

Anton slides a knife up from his hip. Light flashes across nyxian black before he tucks it back in. "A sharp knife is a boy's best friend."

I think about the century's massive, rolling shoulders.

"You're going to need a bigger knife."

Ahead, sunrise breaks over the plains. Just an orange streak that blossoms and scatters the mist. I was expecting something dramatic, but it looks like any sunrise over any forest on earth.

As the fog clears, we get our first glimpse of the next valley. There's another forest on our left. The trees are thick, wide trunks pressed together at chaotic angles. Moss hangs between them like party lights. Our eyes are drawn beyond, though. Sunlight catches metal and glass.

Buildings.

"We're here," Morning says. "Foundry."

CHAPTER 3

FOUNDRY

Emmett Atwater

It's like Babel didn't want to be outdone. It's not enough to show us the miracle of another world, not enough to let us witness dueling moons and deadly creatures. Babel's compound is a reminder: they intend to carve their initials on this world one way or another.

A pair of towers command the rolling hills. Diamond-shaped windows spiral up the nearest and tallest building. The panes are checkered, a pattern that exchanges glass for moss all the way up. The tower has to be at least four stories tall. I notice that the top of it sheers diagonally. The effect makes the building look unfinished, like a false and majestic ruin.

The second building is a more proper silo. It reminds me of the solar stacks on the outskirts of Detroit. A basic gray cylinder with the top carved like a massive funnel.

There's clearly an underground too. I see reinforced doors plugged into hillsides and half-buried greenhouses flanking the natural creeks. Morning's title for the place is confirmed on my scouter as the word *Foundry* blinks into one corner.

"Hell of a supply center," I say.

Azima points. "Look how extensive the gardens are. It reminds me of Nairobi. Before I left, they'd started major conversions of all the skyscrapers, sustainable gardens in every nook and cranny. Politicians wanted it to be the next landscape city."

"Well," Anton says, "I am very proud of our employers for being so conscientious about their role in sustaining Eden's plant life. I've no doubt their intentions in making this a better world are entirely selfless."

Morning rises from a crouch. "Who's running the place?"

"That would be me."

The proximity of the voice makes our whole group jump. Jaime stumbles back into Azima. Anton's knife just about teleports into his right hand. Morning is even quicker, both hatchets out as she places herself between us and the interloper. A response catches in her throat, though. She looks as shocked as we do, because the speaker is *our* age.

A year or two older, maybe, but young. He has blond hair, pale skin, and a few centimeters on me. The height's deceptive, though, because he looks thin enough that a good breeze might take him with it. The dark suit he's wearing displays the Babel towers on one sleeve. He has both slender hands held up innocently, but the effect isn't helped by the pistol holstered at his hip.

"Corporal Kit Gander, at your service."

He double taps the name on his uniform, like it means anything to us.

"What are you doing out here?" Morning asks.

"At Foundry?"

"Here," Morning explains. "On a foreign planet no human is supposed to be on."

"Section two of the Interstellar Contract. Babel got the hookup to build three of these stations on the continent known as Grimgarden. Which is where you landed. The contract stipulated that a marine would be sent down to man each station." He gestures to himself. "And you know, I actually *watched* the negotiations go down. It was like watching the signing of the Treaty of Versailles or something. . . ." He frowns at Morning. "Can I lower my hands yet?"

Morning glances back at us before putting away her hatchets. Kit's hands go down too, and the transformation happens in the hottest of seconds. He stumbles forward like we're all just best friends catching up after school. "Come on. There's a path this way."

We trail him uneasily. I can tell Morning still has her guard up. Probably she's trying to figure out how this kid got the jump on her. The thought makes me smile as Kit starts flooding us with answers to questions we haven't even thought about asking yet.

"I had you pinged on my radar at the kilometer barrier. I know I should have followed protocol, but I couldn't resist coming to get a look. I've been down here for a few months now, and the only person I've seen is West. He's not exactly a talker, either."

"West?" Morning echoes.

Kit nods. "West runs Myriad Station. About two hundred kilometers north of here. To the northeast of him, Rahili is in charge of Ophelia Station. We didn't get to name them or anything, but I'm glad I ended up with Foundry. Always thought it sounded kind of badass."

I try not to laugh when Anton rolls his eyes back at us. Kit's too excited to notice.

"You'll get to visit each station," he explains. "Foundry's your first stop. We're outfitted to host three mining crews. You've got bunks, showers, rations . . . the works, really. It's home for your first leg down here. Each crew will head off to a mining site, work the day, and then rally to home base at night. I'll pack you up and ship you to Myriad after we exhaust the area."

Morning's the first to ask the obvious question. "Why'd they send you? You're kinda . . ."

"Young?" Kit guesses. "And what, you're all a bunch of veterans? That's what the contract required. The Adamites demanded that Babel's three youngest employees man the stations. Kind of like that old-school ward thing that medieval kings did, you know? If the treaty goes south, the Adamites come in and take us back to their capital, I guess. We're basically the first interstellar hostages. It's awesome."

Kit's talk carries us down the slope and toward the towers. I'm still eyeing Morning as we make our way. Clearly, she didn't expect to find someone down here, especially not someone like him. I can't get a read on what she's thinking. At least we don't have Defoe brooding over our efforts. Still, I'm kind of annoyed by Kit's presence. The more he rambles on, the more I realize he has no idea who Babel really is or what they've put us through.

". . . kind of a space brat, I guess. Spent more time out

here than on Earth, but anyway. How about you? How was your first night on Eden? A success?"

"We were almost eaten a few times," Anton remarks. "Does that count?"

"Really? Is that . . ." He points at Jaime's wound. "Something *did* that?"

Jaime returns a dark stare. "No. This happened during my launch sequence."

Kit frowns before darting back to the other topic. "There are some *serious* preds down here. The Adamites did their best to clear the area out, but push one species out and another one comes sliding in. I knew Babel would jettison you during the best atmospheric window or whatever, but landing at night? Brutal. Everything down here hunts by moonlight. So what'd you see? Any everhounds? I'm dying to catch a glimpse of one."

"We saw a century," I answer. "An eradakan. A pack of clippers too."

Kit shakes his head in disbelief. "Been here four months, and I didn't know there *were* centuries on this continent. You know how rare they are? Was it big? Must have been huge."

Morning throws out a rough estimate. The rest of us are walking, stiff and silent. Anton's staring at the kid like he's from a different time period, but Jaime's hands are shaking with anger. I shoot him a quick *keep it together* look, and he just clenches his jaw even tighter. Kit's small talk is important. We need to learn as much as we can about Babel, and he seems like the type who will keep talking as long as there's someone with a pulse nearby. But there's still the fact that he thinks this is all *fun*, like this is all just a *game*. I thought that once too.

As the tower's entrance comes into view, Kit pulls back his right sleeve. I realize for the first time that only that hand is gloved—and that the glove is anything but normal. A white nexus is implanted in the palm. The same neurofibers Babel used for our mining simulation stretch to each finger before suctioning tight to the skin on his wrist.

With a lazy backhand, he casts a digital interface into thin air.

It's like a floating computer screen. The projection has a series of blue-tinted applications, tabs, and icons. We all stare as Kit double taps a button here, shuffles an object there. Another backhand sends the display spiraling back out of existence.

There's an answering grind of metal. Overhead, windows open at Kit's command. A series of solar panels to our right start to rotate. Finally the front doors of the tower gape open.

Kit lowers his hand and realizes we're all staring.

"What?" he asks. "It's standard tech. Didn't Babel have this on their ships?"

Morning nods. "They did. One day we'll stop being so surprised by it."

"Understandable," Kit replies. He starts through the doors but glances back at Jaime as he goes. "All right. Let's get you down to the med bay. The other two squads are still a few hours out, so you can pick your hive first. This central space is shared by all three units. The hives are your personal space. A little pro tip: Hive-1 has the sunrise views. If you're looking for blackout sleep, though, go with Hive-3. Sun doesn't really hit until late afternoon."

Inside, the tower's almost hollow. Sunlight casts down from the windows, filling the entire structure with bright light. A pair of black staircases curl up and around the tower walls like a helix, crisscrossing to form a catwalk every twenty meters. The main floor is decorated with cushions and mismatched rugs. All the furniture is nyxian, but rough workmanship. The kind of half-formed manipulations we did in early training sessions.

"It's not much," Kit says. "But make yourselves at home."

Jaime looks uncomfortable as he follows Kit toward the med bay. Morning slings a pack over one shoulder and marches in the direction of the first hive. She's about halfway there when she realizes none of us have budged. "What?" she asks, turning back. "No sunrises?"

Anton just shakes his head. Azima wags a finger.

"You're my queen down here," she admits. "But *sleep* is still my god."

Morning glances at me. "Et tu, Brute?"

"Two words: blackout curtains."

Morning slides back our way and rolls her eyes. "Hive-3 it is."

We follow a path that takes us out of the tower, underground twenty paces, and into a connected building with gentler lighting. Half the roof and an entire wall are made of glass. "This is one of the buildings we saw," Azima says. "I thought they were greenhouses."

The other half of the hive looks more like a bunker. Nyxian walls separate rooms that could double as fallout shelters. They're arranged in a circle, honeycombing out for effect.

"Like a hive," Anton remarks. "So very clever, Babel."

Morning glances back the way we came. Kit's voice echoes, but it's growing distant.

"Remember the plan," Morning says. "We get work done and we keep our eyes open. I wouldn't reveal much to Kit. He seems harmless, but he's with Babel, end of story."

"So anything we say to him, he'll relay to Babel?" Azima asks.

Anton shakes his head. "Not just to Kit. I would assume anything you say inside this building has a chance to reach Babel, including this conversation. So let's stick to small talk until we know how things work down here."

Morning nods. "Rest first, talk later."

Anton chooses the first room, tosses his bag in one corner, and slams the door shut. Azima wanders off to explore the rest of the hive. Morning gives me a long look, the same stare she gave me the night I visited her room in space. She glances around once, making sure no one can hear us, before asking, "Do you want to be alone?"

I shake my head. "Nah."

"Let me settle in," she says. "Just a minute."

She moves to the room on the far right. I take the room next to hers. I set my knapsack down in one corner and sit on the edge of the bunk. The room's mostly dark, with the only light leaking in from the hallway. It's the first time I've been alone since the landing, and I was too panicked then to think about anything but finding the others. Now I have a second to wrestle with everything that's gone down. Roathy's hate chases me through space. Isadora's final look echoes. And Bilal . . .

Babel killed him.

Babel *killed* him.

A dark part of me thinks that that was always the danger of letting them in. First Kaya and now Bilal. I made them a part of me, I housed them like organs, and Babel decided to rip out the pieces I let myself need the most. In those hollow spaces, hate wants in; hate is already growing.

Morning opens the door. She looks exhausted, but one glance in my direction has her crossing the room. She kneels beside me. "Emmett," she says. "Are you okay?"

"I'm fine."

She frowns. "You're not fine, Emmett."

"Really, it's nothing. I'm fine."

"Emmett," she repeats carefully. "You're not fine."

I glance around the room. For some reason, the whole place looks colorless. Even Morning's face seems like a faded portrait. "Seriously, I'm good."

I've never seen Morning look so heartbroken. "You're crying, Emmett."

"I'm okay. I don't . . . I'm not . . ."

"Come here."

She sits down on the bed next to me. The only safe place is her arms. I lean that way and let my head fall into her lap. Morning strokes my hair, the way Pops always did for Moms. It takes about a minute for my senses to come raging back. My eyes are thick with tears.

"They took them from me. Bilal. Kaya. They took them from me."

Morning whispers softly. The graze of her fingertips against my head is the only thing that keeps me from fading to dust. At school I learned to be tough. I learned that real men only cry at funerals. Friends—and sometimes teachers—taught me to keep my emotions out of life's equations. It was Pops who poked holes in that theory. Sometimes he would cry when Moms had her bad days. He never apologized for a single tear. Neither will I.

Morning holds me. When I close my eyes, Bilal smiles down out of the dark. I can't bear looking at him, though. So I move off into dreams or nightmares or both. I know I'll have to say goodbye, one of these days, but not yet, not now.

CHAPTER 4

A DYSFUNCTIONAL FAMILY

Emmett Atwater

I wake up to raised voices. I reach for Morning, but she's gone. The room's dark. I can't tell if that's because it's night or because I slept through to the next morning. The voices continue to echo down into Hive-3 until I'm on my feet, stumbling toward the sound.

Our hive is empty, but in the tunnel I spy someone leaning against the wall that connects the underground to the tower. It takes a few seconds to place Katsu's bulky frame. As soon as he spots me, he pushes off the wall and wraps me in an unexpected hug.

"I thought you were going to sleep through your own trial," he says.

"Trial?" I side-eye him. "What trial?"

"Let's just say you've caused some controversy."

Beyond him, two voices volley back and forth. I finally recognize that Morning's is one of them. The other one is Parvin's. She might be a head shorter than Morning, but she's not remotely intimidated. I remember Parvin as a strategical mastermind in the Waterway. She and Morning would always consult as they took in a new course. Like Jazzy, she doesn't usually break under pressure. The argument has heat rising along Morning's neck and her cheeks, but Parvin is a perfect picture of calm. She adjusts her nyxian-framed glasses—clearly a parting gift from Babel— before delivering a reply.

"We deserve to know what happened," she says.

"I told you what happened," Morning flings back. "You're just gonna ignore the fact that Babel did this? Seriously? And it wasn't just Emmett and Roathy. Anton, Jaime, Alex . . . they all had to fight. Connect the dots, Parvin. None of them *wanted* to do this."

As I step out into the light, the entire room goes quiet.

Everyone's here. The other squads must have arrived while I was sleeping. And it's pretty clear that they've already taken sides. Anton's spinning a knife in circles on the nearest tabletop with a lazy finger. Golden-curled Alex perches on the same chair. He's tapping out a drummer's rhythm on Anton's shoulder. They look as inseparable as they did up in space. I expected Alex to look more scarred after what Babel put him through, but the relief of being at Anton's side must be keeping the damage at bay.

Azima is standing behind Morning in clear support. She's buried her hands in her hips, like she finds this entire argument exhausting.

There are three neutral parties too. Omar looms against one wall. He's the biggest person in the room, but I can see him tapping his arm nervously, like he can't stand the idea of two close friends fighting. Longwei and Jazzy sit in front of him, neutral judges of an entertaining tennis match. I almost nod over to them before remembering that the entire room's staring at me, waiting.

My accusers stand in support behind Parvin. For some reason, their nyxian masks make them look even angrier. Ida's glare is a cold wind. Noor folds her arms, face full of disapproval within the perfect circle of her hijab. Holly actually cracks her knuckles like we're about to box. But their glares are nothing compared to the sight of Isadora.

She stares at me like some horrible queen. I notice that the tight fabric of her suit has stretched. She sets a gentle, protective hand beneath her stomach as she walks forward. The gesture ends me. It's not possible. How is it possible? I think back to the conversation I overheard on the Tower Space Station. Roathy and Isadora's frustrated argument.

It wasn't just an argument between lovers.

It was an argument between soon-to-be parents.

Parvin steps aside as Isadora takes two strides forward. She's careful to let the entire room see her, see the child she's carrying, as her eyes lock on mine.

"I want to hear you say it. Now that you know what you took from me, Emmett, I want to hear you *say* it. Tell me you killed him. Say the words."

The accusation strikes like lightning. The following thunder almost drowns out my thoughts. If the room is a storm, we're standing center, clear against the chaos.

"They put him in the room with me," I say. "They wanted us to fight. Roathy—he almost killed me. But I left him, Isadora. I used nyxia to seal him in. I left him in that room *alive*."

She hesitates, but only for a second. The brief softness steels over.

"Liar," she spits. "He told me what Babel said. He told me there was only one way out. He—he promised me he would win. But you're here instead. I know what that means."

Her nyxian sleeve blurs into the shape of a spear. I take an instinctual step back as the substance responds to her anger. Morning slides between us, though. Her own nyxia forms into that deadly pair of hatchets. The rest of the room braces for impact. Anton's knife is the only thing moving as it spins around and around.

Isadora considers Morning, then me. It's clear she doesn't believe a word I've said.

"Keep him," she says. "For now. One day, though, I will claim him."

I can almost feel the anger pulsing through Morning. I try to make my feet move, to say the right thing to calm her down, but everything feels numb. Omar crosses the room in two strides. He sets his massive hand on Morning's shoulder to stop her from doing something she'll regret. The whole room feels like it's ready to explode when Kit comes barreling in from the opposite hallway.

"Incoming!" he shouts. "Put on your game faces! The Adamite emissaries have arrived. This is going to be one of history's—" It takes him two seconds to pick up on the energy of the room. He holds both hands up in an innocent gesture. "But take your time or whatever. History can wait. I'll be outside."

He ducks through the entryway, and it's like the ticking bomb stops at the very last second. Morning turns, angrily shrugging Omar away. Everyone moves like startled birds, preparing to go outside, but the attention from Morning and Isadora pins me in place. Isadora's eyes are dark with promise. Morning's are lost somewhere between fury and fear.

Morning takes a deep, calming breath and says, "I'll take point. We need this to go well."

"Then with all due respect," Parvin cuts in, "you're not the right person. Not right now. You can take back the lead when you've cooled off."

Morning starts to snap something, but realizes she's just proving Parvin right.

"Fine," she says. "Parvin takes point."

Our new leader adjusts her glasses and slides calmly forward.

"Come on," she says. "Let's go meet an alien species."

There's an awkward second as the group calibrates to their new commander. Some move toward the entryway. Ida is whispering furiously with Isadora. Holly turns a lock of red hair around one finger, listening to their argument, always so quiet.

Katsu comes forward and slaps my back. "Who's having fun?"

Morning cuts in my direction. She takes her place at my side, grinding her teeth, as the entire group files outside after Parvin. Isadora follows, chin raised. Morning broods beside me. I've never seen her this way. I don't know how to calm her down.

"So I catch heat for saving Roathy's life," I point out. "But Ida wasn't exactly shooting daggers at Alex over Loche. Isn't that what Alex being here means? That he killed Loche?"

Morning takes a steadying breath. "Ida doesn't know which room Loche was in. She doesn't know who killed him. I'll make sure Anton and Jaime keep their mouths shut. It's hard enough keeping one of you alive; we don't need to throw another target on Alex's back."

There's a second where we just stand there, breathing in the unfairness of it all. Babel's sins are starting to count against us. "He's alive. Roathy's alive. We could ask Babel for proof."

"If he's actually alive," she says. "How do you know Babel didn't just kill him after you left him there?"

The question catches me off guard. I realize she's right. I really have no clue.

"I don't know what to do," she admits. "If she really decides to come for you, I—I can't just hurt her, Emmett. Not with a baby. I don't know what to do. . . ."

There's an excited shout from outside.

"You've got my back. I've got your back. That's enough for now."

She shakes her head, like that's too simple, like she needs to have a *real* plan.

"My big takeaway from all of this, though, is that you clearly like me a lot."

She smacks my arm. "Lurch."

Outside, the entire group waits in a line. I lead Morning carefully to the opposite side of where Isadora is standing. Parvin's waiting at center, a few steps ahead of us. I glance over at Morning and can tell she's still hot with it all. "Didn't mean to get you demoted."

She forces a smile. "Parvin will do fine."

Dust swirls on the distant plain. Beneath the clouds, four black spheres speed in our direction. Electrical charges crackle between them, flashing every few seconds like horizontal lightning. They're still a few thousand meters away, but covering ground quickly.

"Hey," Morning whispers. "What was my guess? The second day after dawn?"

I look up at the sky and realize she was spot the hell on. "Not bad."

She raises an eyebrow. "I'll collect my prize later."

My eyes flick back to the approaching spheres. All four begin to unwind, black shards peeling open like the petals of a flower. Each vessel gapes open wide enough for their riders to come walking right out onto the plain. I can hear Azima laughing.

Anton glances down the line. "What's so funny?"

"I just realized my breath smells like a nightmare," she says. "Anyone have gum?"

The joke cuts straight through the tension. We all laugh, because the thought is so absurd. Forget that this might be the most important moment in human history, in our lives. The four figures continue their approach. From a distance they look like men, but we know they're not.

"Adamites," Jazzy says, farther down the line. "This is actually happening, y'all."

Parvin glances back at us. "Shoulder to shoulder."

Mostly Genesis 12 members repeat the phrase. We all watch as the black spheres twist through the air. They reform around the approaching party, dressing each Adamite in dark capes with walking sticks or armor. It's not hard to see how effortlessly they're manipulating the nyxia. It's quite an opening performance.

I can't stop my mind from flashing back to the first video that Babel showed us. The welcoming parties of our two species. I remember the obscuring flashes of black, the dismembered marines. I can hear the tortured Adamite that Kaya and I found imprisoned in the belly of the ship too. The pulse of anger that shouldered forward before he killed her. We're here again, on the edge of something that's so much bigger than ourselves.

We all take our places. We try to stand tall.

"No pressure, Parvin," Katsu calls. "Just our lives hanging in the balance."

"I was captain of the debate team," Parvin answers. "This will be a walk in the park."

The Adamites are one hundred meters away. I realize how little we know about them. Only what Babel's told us, and that's never been much. All we have in this moment is the hope that Babel didn't lie about this too. I imagine Defoe watching the scene unfold through some camera on the outskirts of Foundry. Does he know what is about to happen? Do any of them?

The Adamites have a leader too. He strides ahead of the others, chin held high. I guess some things are just universal. All of them look well dressed in their tight-fitting fabrics. Sunlight shimmers off silver buttons and decorative rings. It's clear they've come in their finest. Only one of the four wears a weapon on his hip. I'm not stupid enough to think that makes him the dangerous one. All of them are dangerous. The first Adamite we encountered was bound

hand and foot to a wall, and he still killed Kaya. The last
thing I notice is that all four of them are male. I want to
jump to a few conclusions about that, but the sample size is
too small.

I take a steadying breath as they come to a stop just
twenty meters away.

"Welcome, Genesis," the leader says. "May we speak?"

I'm surprised to hear them call us by that name. It's the
way I've started thinking about us, almost a way to distin-
guish us from Babel. Parvin takes a decisive step forward.

"We would be honored."

His face breaks into a wide smile. It's unashamed delight. He looks at the others, gesturing excitedly, and they
look recklessly happy. One of them gives a nervous laugh.
We are welcome. We are wanted and long-expected. The
emotion that echoes through each face is so powerful that
it's almost like we're watching actors in a play.

Their leader begins. "I am Thesis of the First Ring, the
appointed spokesman of the Daughters. I speak on behalf of
all Sevenset." He allows us time to process, but the words
don't mean much. I snagged his name and his title and
that's it. He's the messenger. "May my brothers introduce
themselves?"

Parvin nods. "Please do."

Aside from Thesis, the Adamites are all barrel-chested. I
can see lines of muscle beneath every stretch of fabric. Their
eyes are wide set too. Full of color, but not all the paintings
are as striking as the rest. One looks like he has a galaxy of
colors implanted in his irises. Another stares back mud pits.
Their skin's so tan that it verges on gold. Each wears his hair

high and swept away from his forehead. They've buzzed the sides so that their sweeps look dramatic and startling.

As the first one steps forward, I notice the nyxian implants. They all have shards of it grafted into their skin. My mind flashes back to the captive aboard *Genesis 11*. I can picture the nyxia set into his knees and elbows. Each Adamite wears his implant in a different place.

"I'm Beckway of the Seventh Ring."

He looks younger than the others. His hair is pulled into a topknot, and nyxian implants cover each of his knuckles. Not someone I'd like to get in a fight with.

"I am Bally of the Third Ring." He's the one with eyes that look like captured galaxies. Nyxian implants are set into each temple. "It is an honor."

The final Adamite has a voice so soft that we all lean forward to hear him. Nyxian stones are planted into the skin around one mud-colored eye, circling in the shape of a bull's-eye. It's hard to think about anything but how badass it looks.

"And I am Speaker of the Second Ring. The Daughter's Sword."

Again, not sure what that means, but it sounds as badass as he looks. Their leader—Thesis—steps forward again. I notice he's the least warrior-like. It has me wondering what the power structures are in their world. Maybe he's their version of a politician or something?

"Well met," he says. "Now, please tell us why you are here."

I see Parvin's shoulders go rigid. The question is direct, almost rude, but they're different people with different customs. Parvin looks like she's tracing back through the handful of details Babel gave us about the Adamites during our studies. I try to remind myself that, in their eyes, we're visitors from a foreign planet. Maybe even hostile visitors, considering all they have to measure us by is Babel.

Parvin recovers quickly. "We've come to Eden by your invitation. We are emissaries. A bridge between our people and yours." She holds up a piece of nyxia. "And we've been asked to mine this substance. Our employers expect us to work on their behalf."

It's hard to read all the reactions, and they're subtle as hell. Beckway's fist tightens before he smiles. Bally and Speaker exchange delighted nods. I watch and wait, and let out a breath when Thesis responds with enthusiasm.

"We are honored. Though, may I make a slight correction?"

"Of course," Parvin replies.

"You called our world Eden. We've heard Babel representatives call our home by that name. But you cannot be wise if you do not call things by their right names, do you agree?"

"I do agree."

He gestures up to the sky, like the word is written there. "Our relationship to the two moons dictates our identity. The larger moon is Magness. For now that means that our world is known as Magnia. But the system's rotations will bring the smaller moon—Glacius—closer in a few years. When that happens, we will call our world Glacia. In another fifty years from then, we'll call ourselves Magnia again. And so on and so on."

Parvin nods. "Magness and Glacius. They sound beautiful."

Thesis smiles wider, but for the first time it looks forced.

"We are honored to fulfill this contract. Babel has delivered you to our world as agreed, and your presence will be a brightness to our people. To see children again, to have you in our homes and walking through our streets, that will bring back a lost kind of paradise. All of you are here to restore a world our people have forgotten."

For the first time, I feel the *weight* on this side of the equation. I've always understood Babel's reasons. More money, more nyxia, more power. That makes all the sense in the world, but I never thought about what the Adamites got out of the deal. It always seemed like we were an entertaining sideshow. A permission granted to Babel so the Adamites could witness a miracle they've lost. For the first time, it feels like more than that. Thesis and the others are looking at us like we've come to *save* them. I file it away under *D* for *Dig Deeper.*

"And in exchange," Thesis continues, "you will have twenty-one days to work as Babel has requested before your visit to Sevenset, and another one hundred days after your visit. Mine the substance. Take it with you. It will not hurt us to see some of it go. For now I will leave you these three escorts: Speaker, Bally, and Beckway. We would not risk your lives by leaving you unattended. As you may know, Magnia is not always a friendly world."

The Adamites exchange grins at that.

Thesis says, "Grimgarden is our *safest* continent. Assigned hunting parties worked to make this section of our world even safer prior to your arrival. We know, however, that your kind are not familiar with the ways of our creatures. I offer these escorts to see you safely through your tasks and eventually lead you to Sevenset's gates.

"Not only are these three of our most respected warriors, but they've been trained in our histories as well. As you travel through Grimgarden, they will tell you our stories, give you a deeper understanding of our people. Is this suitable?"

All three of our offered guardians wait with trembling excitement. Their faces light up with smiles that are so wide they almost look fake. Again, I'm left feeling strange about it all. We mean even more to them than we thought we did. That could be very good, or very bad.

Parvin is quick to accept their offer, because what else can she say? These were Babel's terms; this is Babel's arrangement. Reject the offer and we risk offending the welcoming party. And our main plan is to play nice, mine nyxia, keep our eyes open. Eventually we'll have to fight back against Babel. It's not hard to see that the Adamites might be our best possible ally.

"Good," Thesis says. "I do not doubt that Babel would like you to take advantage of every hour. I will await your presence in Sevenset. I leave these escorts at your disposal. We hope that this will be the first step in a long and meaningful partnership."

Parvin reaches out her hand. The gesture has me leaning in to get a better look. Do the Adamites even shake hands? Thesis considers the handshake, but holds out both of his hands instead, bunching them into fists. He sets them both a few centimeters apart.

"This is our way," he explains. "One fist for each moon."

Parvin reaches out and bumps her fists into his.

We all watch as Thesis crosses one hand under the other and holds the fists out again, twisted now. "And the second symbolizes a permanent agreement. One for both worlds, no matter how the moons might change. It's a promise between peoples."

Parvin daps him up again, and the entire group lets out a held breath.

Our negotiations have already gone about a hundred times better than anything Babel has managed in the last two decades. All three of our guardians come smiling forward. We watch Thesis summon the nyxia from his shoulders and bracelets. The material blooms out and encircles him. Up close the vehicle looks about the size of a motorcycle. I spy a final, satisfied look on the emissary's face before nyxia swallows him whole.

We watch him launch into motion and pick up speed before he's reduced to a black speck on the distant plain. Speaker turns to us. "Now, shall we teach you the ways of our people?"

CHAPTER 5

THE WAYS OF OUR PEOPLE

Emmett Atwater

It takes Kit about two seconds to remind us that Babel's shadow hangs over everything. He steps out front so he's nice and visible before lifting both hands to get everyone's attention.

"Time to start digging," he announces. "I'm going to have the trucks pull around. One for each unit. The locations of your assigned mines are on the map. You'll mine until an hour before sundown, then head back here. Don't stay out there at night, okay? I'll let you all decide which escort will go with which crew."

Rolling back one sleeve, Kit brings up the digital inter-face that controls Foundry. There's a distant rumble of gates opening and engines starting up. Morning signals for our crew to join us off to one side. As the other groups form ranks, I catch another glimpse of Isadora. She's clenching her jaw so hard it looks like it's made of steel.

I try to shake off the bad vibes and focus on the task ahead.

Bally ends up joining Katsu's crew. I'm not surprised to see that Katsu somehow already has the Adamite shaking with laughter. And Beckway's in an animated conversation with Parvin, which leaves us Speaker. We introduce ourselves and he repeats each of our names, rolling syllables over his tongue and smiling at the way they sound. It's like he's discovered fire or snow for the first time. But our first exchange gets swallowed by the sound of the approaching trucks.

Three pristine mining vehicles come rolling out of underground storage. It's a little overwhelming to remember that this is the first time we've ever actually seen them in person. Everything on *Genesis 11* was simulation. Kit directs the trucks in a straight line so they're ready to be boarded and taken out to the mining sites. Azima sets a dark hand on the nearest wheel. It has her entire forearm vibrating. She turns back, eyes bright above her mask.

"It's real!" she shouts. "I call riding in the back."

Anton slides quietly between Morning and me. He wraps an arm around our shoulders and lowers his voice to a whisper. "Not meaning to break up the *lovely* couple, but I was wondering if I might ride up front with Morning. I have a few things I'd like to discuss."

"Couple?" Morning asks, smiling. "I must have missed all those times Emmett took me out to dinner on the Tower Space Station. . . ."

I throw her a raised eyebrow. "Let me check out a few Adamite restaurants on Yelp and get back to you, all right?"

She laughs at that before nodding. "Be careful back there."

Speaker waits awkwardly off to the side. I nod back to

Morning before walking over to join him. "Let's ride in the back, Speaker. You can give me the unofficial tour."

The truck is broken up into three parts. Morning and Anton climb into the driver's hatch and sit down in front of an intricate nest of high-tech panels and switches. There's the birdlike drill squatting behind it, and the open loading bed bringing up the rear.

We all climb up, carefully skirting the miniature rover that's roosting there. A series of black straps runs along the base of the loading bed. I demonstrate putting my feet in so that Speaker gets the idea. The last thing we need is for Morning to hit a bump and send our escort flying out of the truck. Wouldn't exactly be the most diplomatic beginning.

Longwei sits in the driver's seat of the truck right behind us. Azima blows him a kiss and he shakes his head, blushing. Jaime sits beside her, all patched up, the blood cleaned from his uniform. When Kit gives the signal, the whole truck heaves back into motion.

Speaker's eyes are quick to take in everything we're doing. We stand together like farmhands, green hills rolling by, everything burned gold by the rising sun.

"Hey, Speaker, so what can you tell us about your people? We're not exactly well versed in Adamite culture. Babel only had so much to pass on to us."

He smiles at me. "Your first lesson will be easy. We are not called Adamites."

I stare at him for a second. "But that's—"

"What Babel has always told you." He nods knowingly. "It is an odd habit of theirs. Naming what already has a name. We have overlooked it for decades, but if you truly want to know us, then we should begin with a proper foundation. Our people are known as the Imago."

Imago. It's not hard to link the name back to Magnia and Magness. It's a strong-sounding name, and a long look at Speaker has me feeling it's a far better fit. It doesn't surprise me that Babel's out here playing the role of colonizer, slapping labels on the originals and pretending they created it all in the first place. It's pretty standard procedure for folks like them.

"I like that. The Imago." I trace back through our grand introductions, searching for another topic. "And you're from the Second Ring, right?"

He smiles politely. "Yes, Emmett."

"Is where you're from important? You all said it in your introductions."

"Yes. I live on the Second Ring. It identifies me to other Imago and to you. It is a way of showing how I am esteemed by my people."

I nod. "So the Second Ring is good?"

Speaker's brown eyes narrow playfully. "It is better than the Third."

"But worse than the First," Jaime guesses. "And there are seven total rings."

"The farther out, the lower the status?" I ask.

"For the most part," Speaker answers. "The outer rings usually have less esteem than the inner rings, with the Seventh as an exception. It borders the continents and acts as a barrier against the dangers of our world. Those who live on the Seventh are often warriors of great standing. Some believe their status is above the Second and below the First, but it's not a universally accepted view."

On the ship, we studied maps and landscapes and fuzzy satellite photographs, but every word from Speaker is a new lesson on the Adamite—no, the Imago—people. Babel didn't teach us about a ranking system, or a ring in Sevenset dedicated to the military. Either they didn't know or they didn't want us to know. I can't help imagining my neighborhood in Detroit as the Sixth Ring with a little bit of the Seventh thrown in. We might be the lowest of the low, but we're fighters too. Always have been.

I find myself eyeing the nyxian bull's-eye grafted in a spiral around Speaker's eye.

"I noticed your markings," I say, gesturing to them. "What are they?"

His fingers trace over the spot idly, like he's forgotten it's there. "We have them implanted at birth. They are a reminder of all who have come before us."

A thousand questions come to mind, but I don't ask any of them. He says the words with such respect that I feel it'd be rude to ask more, like interviewing someone at a funeral. Instead I lean back and watch clouds blot out the sun.

Magnia. It's a beautiful world. I don't have to close my eyes for it to feel a little like home, a little like Earth. We drive in silence for a while before Speaker points west. The trees at the edge of the forest shake and bend. I can just make out flashes of bronze moving from branch to branch. "Clippers, right?" I ask. "We saw a pack of them last night."

"They are one of a select number of remaining pack species in our world."

Azima perks up at that. "Strange. Most of the animals in our world work in packs."

"Our scientists think once it was so," Speaker admits. "The theory is that originally there was only a single moon in the sky. Fossil records show that pack species dominated that era, but the creation of our second moon changed how those systems functioned."

The words *scientist* and *theory* drum through me. Listening to Speaker is forcing me to dismiss the image Babel gave us of them. I always pictured a tribe of wanderers, powerful and primitive people. I expected strange religions or bizarre clothing. Speaker is offering us a glimpse of more.

"The moons?" Azima asks curiously. "The moons changed the *animals*?"

Speaker gestures up. Overnight, both moons have shifted again.

"Glacius and Magness provide a great deal of light. Their frantic dance with our world almost guarantees the light of one, if not both, at all times." His eyes linger for a long time on the faded outlines of each moon. "Their constant attention encouraged *changes*."

"Evolution," Jaime says from the other side of the truck. "Animals had to adapt."

Speaker nods now. "More light meant more camouflage and poison among the smallest creatures, heightened senses and strength among the largest. Inevitably, creatures were forced into relationships. If they work together over a number of generations, we call them *forged*."

"The eradakan," I say, thinking now. "It had two sets of eyes."

"Because it is two separate creatures," Speaker answers. It's clear he's thinking hard about how to phrase what he wants to say next. "Nature has forced two skill sets to work in harmony. Often, the change happens when a greater enemy enters their territory. The two work together so that they might survive."

"Symbiotic relationships," Jaime says thoughtfully. "That's kind of cool."

"The erada have notoriously vulnerable stomachs," Speaker explains. "Once, they were easy to kill with a well-aimed spear. Their bond with the akana offered a new protection. The body of an akana is scaled, but it's also slow. The erada offers speed and flight. The akana offers defense. Together, the two have a better chance at survival."

Jaime shakes his head. "Except when a century comes hunting."

Speaker's eyes widen. "You saw a century?"

We all nod, and he's so shocked that he actually covers his mouth. I can see the nyxian implant around his eye quivering with movement. "You are lucky to be alive."

"It was huge," I say. "What two animals make a century?"

He shakes his head. "Not two. One. A prime."

The word sends goose bumps down my arm. "Prime?"

"There are twenty-three prime species. Predators that are dangerous enough to survive on their own. They rely on nothing but their own power, or speed, or ingenuity. They are the most dangerous creatures that exist in our world. Scientists have tracked their movements as often as possible. It's better for our people to simply avoid their migratory patterns."

"Great," Jaime says. "Glad we found one on our first night."

Speaker smiles. "Fortunately, there are only two prime species in all of Grimgarden."

I nod. "What's the other one?"

"We call ourselves the Imago."

We all stare for a second, and then Speaker throws back his head with wild laughter. It's so untamed and unexpected that we all laugh with him as our truck thunders over the hills.

CHAPTER 6

DIG

Emmett Atwater

Our first dig site is nestled in the southern corner of another sprawling plain. On the scouter map, it looks like a little claw dug into the underbelly of a forest that grows wider as it moves west. The ping on our map emits from a silver capsule that's plunged into the ground just outside the mining site. The chrome top of the buried device sits perfectly flush with the earth. There are a series of unmarked buttons and a glowing green dot to indicate the deposit on our radar.

Speaker watches with fascination as the survey process begins. A dark cloud of drones sweeps out from beneath the truck, scanning the terrain all around us. As they work, digital imaging etches itself onto the captain's screen. Morning eyes the layout carefully, marking gas pockets and alternative routes into the heart of the mine. As I watch her work, I can tell that talking to Anton has lifted her spirits. Maybe they've got a plan brewing.

"Okay," Morning announces, "I'll run the show from the

truck. When we get nyxia on the surface, I'll show everyone how we manipulate it for crating. Let's split up tasks."

Azima raises a hand. "I helped with the conveyor shaft."

Morning nods. "Anton will go with you. Follow his lead: we always set up two shafts. It's tricky, but if we do it right, we drain the mine twice as fast."

She glances between Jaime and me. "What about you two?"

We both answer. "Jackjack."

Morning considers us. "I'd rather not have you in the drill right now, Jaime. Let's get that wound healed up first. You'll help manipulate the product in preparation for shipment. Emmett, you're on as the jackjack for now. Pull your weight or I'll bench you."

I raise an eyebrow. "Damn, Captain."

"Captain is right," she says, smiling. "Let's pit this peach."

It takes about five minutes to get the drill set up, two minutes to climb inside, and one more minute for my world to be reduced to jaw-jarring vibration. Voices squawk over the comm, but I'm too focused on the descent. Two hundred meters down into darkness. The drill tip bites into stone, spitting smoke and gutting a path to our collection point.

On my monitor, Anton and Azima's progress on the conveyor shaft is marked by a thin, diagonal streak of blue. Morning buzzes directives, but right now my only job is to dive and hold tight as my hands burn and blister, even with the protective gloves on. Gas pockets dance on the screen as we disturb the nyxian deposit. I realize it's probably never been touched before.

It used to take Longwei an hour to dive this far. Now, I realize why. When his hands started to hurt, he would let go of the grips. Let go and the drill keeps spinning, but it doesn't keep diving. In this, at least, I'm stronger than him.

I hit my depth and Morning retracts the drill. The drill tracks with the weighted supports on the surface, gliding back up through the initial carnage of my dive. When I'm back up top, I pop the hatch so cool air can rush in. There's still too much heat flooding up from the hole for it to make much of a difference, though. Morning stands by the captain's console and flashes me a thumbs-up. Speaker stands beside her, watching everything curiously. About ten minutes later I hear her voice pipe through the comm.

"Shafts are ready. You're on again, Emmett."

I slip back into the cockpit. A second later, the two side drills extend. One drill had the world rattling. Two feels like earthquakes inside earthquakes. I adjust my grips on the silver joysticks, and metal whirrs as my chair leans back, my legs extending. Silver foot panels blink with light, and I punch my feet against them. Darkness devours the windows as I reach my first depth. The drills hiss and catch on the nyxian walls, rag-dolling me until they find a balance.

Nyxia shatters, tumbling down the first shaft and into the collection area. The pulses light up, and I strike into the heart of the rock. I can't help smiling because this still feels like a video game that I'm pretty damn good at. My steady work keeps nyxia raining down in constant streams. The drill is fifty meters deep when the screen flashes its first warning. Red circles churn along the edges of my tunnel.

Gas pockets.

"See that, Morning?" I ask.

"You're fine," she says. "Keep both drills rolling."

I miss a few pulses as I stare at the red discoloration. I only blew up twice in simulations, but one time will do the trick in real life. "Who are you going to boss around if I explode?"

"Someone else, I guess," she says, and I can almost see the smirk. "Just trust me."

I do trust her. The drill digs down. Ten meters. Five meters. I give the wall right above it a good pulse, grit my teeth as rock rains, and watch the red blotches flutter on my screen. I brace myself, but the gas retreats, finding deeper spaces between the stones. I let out a ragged breath and keep things moving. Morning's laugh sounds in my ear.

"You really think I'm bossy?"

"Oh, the worst," I say, smiling.

Anton adds, "I've always seen you as a female version of Napoleon."

"Too tall," Jaime disagrees.

Morning actually groans. "Not to mention he was a tyrant, Anton! At least make me a hero from Mexican history, like one of the Adelitas or something."

"She should be compared to a queen," Azima pipes in. "Like Cleopatra."

"Actually, I'd take Cleopatra," Morning replies. Everyone laughs at that.

Three hours later, I'm bone-tired, but the mine's done. I admire the rows and rows of manipulated nyxia stacked in the truck bed. I don't even want to guess how many millions of dollars it translates into. My boots are puddled with sweat, and my hands are hating me. Morning calls us all out to clean up and find a place to go for a swim.

She pulls aside Speaker first, though. "Are we okay to wash up? Or is it too dangerous?"

"We prepared for your coming," Speaker replies. "Hunting parties were sent through the areas between your established bases. We thinned out the more dangerous species, or at least forced their migratory patterns elsewhere."

"So it's safe?" Morning asks.

"Safe enough," Speaker replies. "The nearest creek isn't large enough for our most dangerous breeds, either. I believe you will be fine."

Morning pings the creek in question and we all head out. It's a brave new world, but the boys head over one hill as the girls go down another. Speaker stands awkwardly back by the truck. The Imago probably didn't give him any protocol for how to handle bath time.

We strip down to underwear and splash around a creek that's barely knee-high. I've never felt anything so good in my life. Long after I've washed the grime from my face and hands, I lie belly up, staring at clouds that remind me so much of home it hurts.

Anton gargles water and sprays it out like a fountain statue. Jaime sits off to one side, hair slicked back and pale shoulders hunched. The scene looks so normal, so human. It's almost enough to forget that each of us was asked to kill someone just forty-eight hours ago.

One look at Jaime or Anton is enough to see the truth. Babel's betrayal isn't done digging under our skin. Maybe it's a good thing, I think. Maybe resistance will be easier. Babel's shown us too many of their cards to pretend they're something else now.

Jaime runs a hand over the water. We've been quiet for a while, but I can tell he's working up the courage to say something. This is the first time I've really looked at him since landing. It's easy to forget how close he was to dying.

He hasn't forgotten. "I hate them," he finally says. "I really hate them."

I exchange a glance with Anton. "Yeah," I answer. "Me too."

Anton just leans back in the water and points a middle finger skyward. Jaime squints up through the clouds like he can actually see the station orbiting. Anger fills his voice.

"It's not fair. They set the rules and I followed the rules and I won. That should have been the end of it. It wasn't fair that they put Brett in the room with me and . . ." As he talks, his hands ball into fists. "I haven't been able to sleep. They broke their promise and made me a murderer. None of it is fair. And now? I'm going to do everything I can to bury them."

He glances back at us nervously, like maybe he sounds extreme. But Anton stands up and slaps Jaime's bare shoulder with affection. "I was worried before," he says. "I thought you were just another broken boy we needed to look after. But you're not. You're a weapon. Babel put you through the fire and you survived. They shouldn't have made us this way. They'll regret how sharp we are now that we're aimed at them."

Anton offers a hand to help Jaime up. The three of us walk back to the truck, and Anton's words echo and build, louder and louder, until they're in my chest like a song.

We're weapons. They made us this way.

And we're coming for them.

CHAPTER 7

ORBITING

Emmett Atwater

Morning keeps us moving. We pack up the dig site, load our truck back up, and leave behind a crater. Looking down into the gaping cavern, I feel a little sick to my stomach. We've been on the Imago's planet for twenty-four hours and we're already shredding it.

But this is our plan. We're going to go from one site to the next, gathering enough nyxia to send back to Babel as we wait out their next move. It feels wrong, really, to just accept their next betrayal. There's just not much we can do besides play nice until we figure out our options.

I glance back at the loaded stacks of nyxia and remember Defoe's presentation at our first meeting. *Each of those black dots is worth somewhere in the realm of two billion dollars.* Each mine. Worth billions. The idea of that much money is disorienting.

We move on to the second mine, and it's a nightmare.

Arrival time gives us about three hours to work. Gas pockets are shifting so much beneath the surface, though, that the computer system can't even find a good origin point. Morning maps out the movements for thirty minutes before picking a proper setup.

One of the conveyor tunnels collapses on our first attempt, so Anton and Azima end up moving the rover to the opposite side and starting over. There's an hour's worth of delays as we wait for the underground shifting of gas to stop. Time feels like it's moving slower than the sweat on my visor. Speaker noted our efficiency on the first mine. I wonder if he's monitoring our failures during the second.

"All right," Morning calls. "You're clear for now, Emmett. I'm gonna go down the conveyor shaft to fix a jammed line. Jaime's got eyes on you, all right?"

"Got it," I say, firing the drill up again. We've only sheared away three or four meters from the main shaft. I haven't built a rhythm at all today, so I miss pulses and feel groggy the deeper I go. Jaime calls out another pressure shift, and I kill the drill, frustrated and sweating. I'm about to vent my frustrations when an explosion tears through the underground.

A deep grumbling follows. I hear a single, violent shriek through the comm. Rocks shift all around me. My eyes dart to the scanner, the windows. I've got no visuals at all.

"What the hell was that?" I ask. "Is everyone all right?"

Jaime responds from up top. "Conveyor shaft collapsed again."

Then Anton is shouting. "Morning! Are you there, Morning?"

There's no response. Only Anton's heavy breathing, a grunt.

"She was in there!" Anton shouts. "Jaime, can you see anything on the screen?"

We're all asterisks on the computer. Panicking, I make the count.

Four. Only four of us.

"Negative," Jaime answers. "Right before it happened, her asterisk vanished."

"Shit," Anton says. "Get over here now."

I have no idea what's going on above, but I can see the comet streak of our conveyor shafts on the screen. I'm about fifty meters above the end of the tunnel. On the screen, it looks like a black claw has slashed the shaft in two. Morning's in there somewhere.

There is nothing to think about. There is no decision to make. There is only my body moving toward hers.

I unstrap from my chair. In a side compartment of the drill casing, I find the emergency supplies. Rope, oxygen tanks, and a ton of gauze. I attach everything to my suit's utility belt and hook the rope carabiner to the top of the drill. We all learned this in the simulator, but it takes a few extra seconds to make my nervous hands repeat the steps I practiced. I hook the rope under my arms and around my waist, cinch it tight, and give a tug. It holds.

Slowly I lower myself over the lip of the drill. I avoid the extended claws, knowing they'd burn through suit and skin with a touch. Down into heat, into the hole I've been carving for hours. Darkness swallows me. I flick on my shoulder light, and a bright beam spotlights the wall. I take it slow, knowing a fall and a broken neck won't help Morning.

Voices pipe through as I descend. A curse from Anton. A question from Azima. Every word colored with fear.

Morning had us download digital reads of the mine before we started. Blinking, I pull up the map on my scouter. I've lowered myself just above the conveyor shaft, but I still can't see the mouth of the tunnel. Below, nyxia glitters in chaotic piles. Another meter and my feet find empty air. Reaching down, I trace the lip of the conveyor shaft with a hand. It takes a little twist to lower myself inside.

I detach the rope, and my shoulder light flashes up an undisturbed tunnel. God, it's small. Hardly big enough to walk down. I crouch forward, heat knifing through my suit and turning my stomach. Red spots leap across my vision. The map shows gas pockets gathering in the second shaft, some ten meters beneath my hands and knees. I steady my breathing and keep crawling forward. Morning is the only thought in my head. I have to find Morning.

Finally the light lands on shattered rocks. Charred air and twisted stone. I shovel what I can behind me and come to the largest pile of nyxian rubble, all strewn around a dark form.

"Emmett," Jaime's voice sounds over the comm. "You've got red sneaking up on you."

"Copy that." My hands dig frantically at the stones. Even with my suit and triple-thick gloves, it's like plucking pieces of meat from a sizzling grill with bare hands. I'm halfway to the dark bulge beneath the rocks when Jaime pipes in again.

"We moved too much down there," he says. "It's going to release. I'm pulling the drill."

I grunt, knowing my rope will get pulled with it. Knowing it's too late to crawl back that direction anyway. The only way out now is forward. Gritting my teeth, I slide rocks away until I've unearthed a dark sphere of stone. I crouch over it. It isn't a shard like the rest; it's smooth as a tomb and cold as a creek. I lower a shoulder, trying to wedge it out.

Nothing happens. I glance back down the tunnel and hear a click. The massive sphere unfolds in circular strips, peeling away from the center like an orange. The dark casing slides back, and Morning smiles out at me.

"You came for me," she says. "You shouldn't have."

Relief thunders in my chest. "You're alive."

She takes my hand and crawls out of the shell. With a manipulation, she draws the protective cocoon back into the form of her nyxian jacket. She must have thrown it over herself just before the tunnel collapsed. We're still trapped between a rock pile and the creeping gases behind us, though. On my scouter, red dots are blossoming. I think back to all the times I died in the simulations. We have less than two minutes. "You have a plan, right?"

Morning flips on her comm. "Retract the drill. Move the truck. Everyone out of the tunnels. We're coming up." She turns her attention to the pile of nyxia. "These pieces are all shattered. So it's not one big piece anymore, right?"

I stare at the pile. "We don't have time to manipulate all of them."

"No," Morning says. "Not even close. But we can do all the loosened pieces at once."

My panic doubles. "That's not possible."

"Do you trust me?" she asks.

Red curls to life in my readout, fighting for open air. Pressure will release, and pretty soon it won't matter whether I trust her or not. "Let's do it."

"All right, it's like what we did on the Waterway ships. You would feed Longwei energy, right? Add your strength to his to move faster?" She waits for me to nod. "It's kind of like that, but we're going to make a circle. I'm pushing energy to you as you push it to me. I'm receiving energy from you as you receive it from me. Make sense?"

"Yeah, yeah, I got it. And then what?"

"Once we have it moving," she says, "we'll take on the pile of stones. Imagine *dust*."

Morning digs through the pile and finds the largest chunk she can. She sets it between us and meets my eyes. The stone resists my first grasping effort. I take a breath, focus my mind, and reach for it again. Our connection clicks to life. I can feel Morning across the nyxian link. Slowly I start to push some of my energy forward, through the stone, in her direction.

It's answered immediately on her end. She's pushing energy to me, and I can feel it pulsing; the hairs on the back of my neck rise as a circle starts to form. Push and pull. Energy that's moving in a constant circle and gaining momentum. It's a use of nyxia I never learned aboard *Genesis 11*. It takes about ten seconds to establish a rhythm, churning in the air around us. It almost feels like the power is orbiting us, forming a new center of gravity.

Morning nods toward the pile and we turn, our steps in perfect harmony.

I think about Defoe showing off on the ship. The way he manipulated the massive slab of nyxia into squares and cylinders and pyramids, so quick it looked like child's play. I know the pile in front of us is five times bigger, and full of shattered, shapeless pieces. An impossibility, but as the energy turning between us reaches a peak, I know we're strong enough.

"You guys need to get out *now*," Jaime pipes through the comm.

As one, we reach out. Our feet dig into matching stances. Even her breathing is completely in tune with mine. One breath, two breaths, three. We begin.

The force inside all that nyxia almost takes control. It's more powerful than anything I ever felt on the ship. Dark faces come rushing forward, a strength that smacks into us like the warning wave of a tsunami. But together we stand our ground. We shoulder back the grasping hands in the substance, and our power cracks like a whip.

My eyesight flickers as every piece blocking our path grinds, shudders, and pulverizes. Dust fills the shaft, and it's only sheer luck that we stumble toward one another. My remaining energy is a thin, dying thing. Morning is smaller than me, more staggered by the weight of all that power. I catch her arm and drape it over one shoulder. "Hold your breath."

We stumble forward like firemen. Coughing and blinded, I force a path through the slanting shafts of falling powder and dust. Our efforts almost run us right into Anton.

"How the hell did you do that?" he asks. "All that nyxia just crumbled to dust."

"Get her other side!" I shout. "We have to get out."

He snakes past us and adds his strength to mine. We lurch forward, crouched and tripping over ourselves. Speaker stands guard at the entrance. He moves aside as we pour out, falling into the dirt and taking great gasps of fresh air. Behind us, explosions rip through the ground.

I turn in time to see Speaker manipulating nyxia, sealing both conveyor shafts. Everything shakes and quivers. Jaime's driving the truck toward us. Behind him we see a snaking tongue of fire sear the air. It almost looks fake, a Hollywood explosion. Black smoke circles everything. Wind disfigures the perfect edges. We watch dark shapes writhe in the air.

No one says anything for a long time.

It's Speaker who finally breaks the silence.

"I'm starting to believe your species lives more exciting lives than ours."

Even Morning laughs as smoke colors the sky.

CHAPTER 8

SURPRISES AND MISTAKES

Emmett Atwater

Everyone is eager to pack up and head back to Foundry after that.

As we do, Morning comes up with seven new procedural rules for mining the shafts, even though she's the only one who was breaking them in the first place. She laughs and leads us like nothing happened. Maybe I'm the only one who can see the change.

There's a gentleness she offers only to me.

I've seen this side of her before, but only in glimpses. A shared song as we looked down on Magnia for the first time. The quiet whispers before we fell asleep in her room. The hug she gave me after landing safely. But something about the way she looks at me now feels more permanent.

It fills me with a light that I thought Babel took from me. It's the first sign on a long road back to something good. As our truck cruises through foreign valleys—all full of fading light—I can almost feel Bilal's and Kaya's spirits urging me to hold on to this first ray of hope.

Kit greets us at the edge of Foundry. We climb out of the truck and circle to the back as he counts the payload. "How'd we do?" Anton asks. "Were we good boys and girls today?"

"Pulled more than the other crews," Kit says, still scanning the rows with his enhanced glove. "Longwei will be pissed. He's been hounding me about the totals. I keep telling him there's not a scoreboard down here, but he won't listen. I'm surprised by your numbers, though. This is a lot of nyxia to pull from just one mine."

"That's because we pitted two," Anton replies. "Try and keep up, rookie."

Kit raises one eyebrow. "Impressive. I'll take it from here. The truck will get retooled and you'll be ready to roll tomorrow morning. We're setting a great pace."

I can't help but notice the word *we*. Kit really thinks we're all one pristine unit, working together for some common Babel good. He thinks this is actually our team of choice.

"When will you send up the first shipment of nyxia?" Anton asks.

Kit's scrolling through an interface, eyeing numbers in some kind of spreadsheet. Morning flashes Anton a quick look. He returns it with a calm *I've got this* gesture. Thankfully, Kit's too distracted to notice the exchange.

"Maybe day five?" Kit replies. "The silo has to reach capacity before we send up a shipment, but I can't wait to hit the launch button. It's like science class on steroids."

Anton just nods like he's not really *that* interested. I catch another look between him and Morning, but when I raise an eyebrow, Morning just shakes her head. I feel a little flash of jealousy. I want to be in on the plan. I want to be her go-to. But at least they *have* a plan. Deep down, I know she's just being smart, not wanting to risk letting Babel in on the secret.

The sun's almost set, and Foundry's lights have flickered on. Overhead, the two moons have rotated slightly. I trace the red veins on Magness's surface, trying to memorize their pattern.

"You must excuse me," Speaker says. "The Interstellar Contract asks that we stay outside the boundaries of the base. I must join my brothers, but I look forward to more time with you."

Azima waves back. Jaime offers a little salute.

I nod his way. "Take it easy, Speak."

He smiles at the nickname before heading out. Morning drifts to my side as the whole group approaches Foundry's open entryway. Her voice isn't louder than a whisper.

"Remember to be careful. Isadora isn't going to forget about you."

"You got my back, though, right?"

She nods. "And I owe you one for saving me down in the tunnel. Just don't try to cash in that favor anytime soon, yeah?"

"Wasn't exactly planning on trading life-threatening situations with you."

Morning smiles. "We might not have much choice down here."

Azima and Jaime lead us into the tower. I can already hear Katsu's laugh dominating the shared space. The group is slouched around a circular table in the middle of the room. I search the gathering for Isadora and breathe a sigh of relief when I don't find those rigid shoulders, that dark stare, the familiar crowned-eight tattoo.

Anton eyes the group before saying, "I need to get my beauty sleep."

He walks toward Hive-3 with purpose. Maybe he's going to work on whatever plan they have brewing. Azima moves in the opposite direction, charmed forward by all the noise. A roar from Katsu's crew lures the rest of us in too. "Seriously?" Katsu complains. "This is unreal!"

It's a surprise to find one of the Imago with them after Speaker just said they couldn't come inside. It's a bigger surprise to find Longwei sitting down with the group, playing cards.

And then the surprise to end all surprises: Longwei's actually *smiling*.

He made such a habit of avoiding us on *Genesis 11* that seeing him deal a hand of cards feels like sighting a mirage. Jazzy plucks up a single card before waving at us.

"Come on over, y'all," she says. "Ever play forehead stud?"

Alex has his golden curls pushed back by a headband. He grins and makes the name of the game clear by slapping a card against his forehead: two of diamonds. Noor adjusts her black hijab and does the same, flashing the queen of spades. We stand around the table and watch as the others follow suit, everyone but Longwei.

"We wanted to teach Bally how to play," Katsu explains. "The sooner he knows which cards are which, the sooner I can start winning money off of him."

Bally holds a nine of clubs to his forehead. "If we were

playing for money, so far all of it would be in Longwei's pockets. I spent all day with him and he didn't say a single word. But offer a little competition and he transforms into *this*."

We glance that way and find Longwei with a playful hand hovering over his unturned card. Everyone waits in anticipation as he locks eyes with Bally.

"Are you worried I'll have the highest card again?" he asks.

Bally frowns. "It seems statistically unlikely."

Longwei lifts the card slowly to his forehead. We all lean forward, and the table erupts when the ace of spades appears. Alex actually stumbles to his feet and shakes Longwei by the shoulders, like he just scored the winning goal in a soccer game or something. I laugh when Longwei presses the card in and it sticks to his forehead. He raises both hands in triumph.

Bally nods before standing. "I think it is time for me to return to our camp before I get in trouble because Katsu forced me to come inside. Tomorrow I will teach you some of our games. We will see if your luck holds, Longwei."

Longwei dips his head in acknowledgment. The card flutters down to the table.

"I look forward to it, Bally."

The others lean back in their chairs as Bally exits. Katsu kicks his feet up on the table. I claim the seat across from him. Morning eyes the room again and—when she's satisfied Isadora isn't a present threat—decides to join us.

"Your dig go all right?" I ask. "No issues?"

Katsu shrugs. "Same old stuff. Dig a hole. Grab the nyxia. Blah, blah, blah."

"It went well," Noor chimes in. "Katsu's a good leader."

He waves the comment away. "So . . . you haven't figured it out yet?" He nods over to Longwei and the others. "I told you. I knew they wouldn't figure it out. The game was a distraction, but still . . . Morning, the proclaimed genius of *Genesis 12,* even she must bow before my eternal wit and wisdom and cunning."

Their group exchanges smiles. It takes me about two seconds to *finally* notice what's so different about all of them. Their smiles. I can actually see their full smiles.

"You're not wearing your masks."

"Emmett rings the obvious bell first." Katsu grins. "But now let's head into the uncharted territory where dwell the *real* mysteries. How the hell can you understand what I'm saying?"

I stare at them, completely lost. Morning reaches for her mask and pulls it off.

"You can understand me?" she asks. "Without the mask?"

Katsu just smiles. "We figured it out during our dig."

"I don't get it," I say. "How's that possible? Are you—I mean, you don't speak English?"

"And you don't speak Japanese," he replies. "Yet here we are, having a conversation with each other."

Noor's face brightens. "It's *weird,* isn't it?"

Jazzy leans forward like it's the juiciest piece of gossip. "Here's my theory: Those masks? They retrained our *brains,* y'all. Maybe we just know things now. Like—I don't know—

like there was dormant knowledge that's woken up or something."

"Or there is another explanation," Longwei suggests. "It only works with *spoken* language. I wrote down a few Chinese characters, and the others couldn't understand them."

I slide my mask off, but Katsu waves abruptly. "Emmett, actually, we've had requests that you keep yours on. Longwei and I remember how bad your breath smelled most mornings."

Longwei shoots him a look, shocked to be implicated. I fling my mask at Katsu, and he barely manages to deflect it away. "I was just kidding, man!" he shouts. "Come on! You could have knocked a tooth out of this beautiful smile of mine."

The surprise and joy of the moment is swallowed by chaos near Foundry's entrance. My entire body goes rigid. Morning rises to her feet, but it's not Isadora. We can hear voices shouting as a press of bodies fills the doorway.

"Incoming!" Kit shouts. "Get her down to the med unit!"

Omar's carrying the front half of a stretcher. Parvin and Ida are hefting the back end. It takes a few seconds to realize that Holly is sprawled out and unconscious. Isadora trails the group, followed closely by the three Imago escorts. Speaker's expression is full of horror.

"What the hell happened?" Morning shouts.

"Too much nyxia," Omar calls back. "She accidentally manipulated a piece that was still connected to the rest of the mine. It pushed back and she went down hard."

Speaker presses forward. "You need to let one of us attend to her."

The triage team marches through the living space to the back of the tower. Holly's always been pale, with a scatter of freckles on both cheeks, but now she looks downright ghostly. Morning starts to follow before realizing there are too many bodies crowding around too narrow a hallway. And there's nothing we can do; we're not doctors.

Katsu hisses a curse. The others crowd around, heads bowed, as Kit guides the team down into the med bay. I almost jump when I realize Isadora's standing a few feet to my left. She throws me a dark look before raising her hands innocently, like the accident has called to life a temporary truce. I nod back and the whole group takes seats, waiting for word from below.

Morning sits beside me. She sets a hand over mine, and I realize for the first time that it's been shaking. We've lost too many people already. I've had one eye on Isadora and one eye in the rearview mirror, just counting all the ways Babel has wronged us. It was easy to forget how vulnerable we are down here. The creatures stalking the plain. Morning's accident in the tunnels. And now this.

"She's going to make it," Morning says softly. "She *has* to make it."

CHAPTER 9

GRIPPED

Emmett Atwater

Real tragedy always brings silence with it. A few people pace, but most of us sit our fears on elbows, waiting for the would-be doctors to surface with their diagnosis. Everything about the moment feels a little too close to home. The insomnia of waiting rooms, the sterile halls of hospitals. Morning and I exchange a few glances, knowing how close we were to being the ones brought home on a stretcher. It's so quiet for so long that Morning's whisper startles me.

"We launched right before my birthday," she says. "Missed it by a few days."

I glance back at her. "Yeah?"

"It was my quinceañera."

"I've been to one of those. For this girl from school. It's a huge party, right?"

Morning nods. "It represents the transition from childhood to womanhood. You wear a pretty dress and go to mass and your whole family is there. The way we do it up in our neighborhood, it's like one big block party. Mi abuelita was furious I was going to miss it."

Her eyes are still locked on the spot where Holly vanished.

"Did you see how young Holly looked?" Morning shakes her head. "Knocked out like that . . . She's just a kid. We're all supposed to be kids. I might not be wearing the pretty dress, but I know I'm not a child anymore. After all this? None of us are."

I lean back on the cushion so our shoulders are pressed together. I'm searching for the right words, but what she's wrestling with is what I've been wrestling with since Kaya died. I spent a long time weighing who deserved how much blame. Was it my fault or was it Babel's fault? At the end of the day, though, what mattered was that Kaya was gone.

"Mi abuelita always says you get one of two worlds. You either get the world you hope for or the world you fear. When my name was on the top of the scoreboard, I thought all my dreams were coming true. I was gonna go back and change the world. But the longer we're out here . . . I'm not sure what kind of world I'm getting. We can't keep losing people. I can't—I can't lose you. I can't lose them."

Before I can respond, Speaker emerges. My heart sinks as I take in the posture of his shoulders and the look on his face. I've seen Pops look like that coming out of doctor visits as Moms got worse and worse. Which is why it's a surprise to see Holly stride out behind him. The sight of her walking like nothing happened pulls the rest of us to our feet. The other Genesis members trail her, but their faces aren't excited or relieved.

They look just as horrified as Speaker. I don't get it until I lock eyes with Holly.

We didn't speak all that much on the ship, but there's something intimate about standing across from someone and trading punches. There are details you memorize as the adrenaline kicks in, as you dip shoulders and throw jabs. Holly's eyes were *green*. A light color like mint.

Now they're black.

"Holly?" Morning's voice trembles. "What happened to her?"

Speaker shakes his head. "She was Gripped by the substance."

As we watch, Speaker stops walking. Holly pauses at the exact same moment. She looks over at him like she's waiting for a command. Something about that look and those eyes feels worse than death. "Gripped?" Morning echoes.

"To the Eternal Tasks. She will be . . . compelled," Speaker explains. "Compelled to perform useful tasks. Preparing meals, cleaning rooms, fixing broken equipment."

None of us have forgotten Babel's experiments in space. I can still see the line of nyxian objects, each one slightly bigger than the next. Every time the substance cut us away from the present, pulled us down with greedy hands, was this what it was trying to do?

"Eternal Tasks?" Morning echoes.

Speaker nods. "If we cannot free her, she will work in this world and the next."

The entire group flinches at that. I'm not sure where everyone else stands on the afterlife, but the idea of Holly working mindlessly to her death—and maybe beyond—has me completely shook.

"But you can fix her?" I ask desperately. "Right, Speak? There has to be . . ."

I let the sentence trail off as Holly lifts her head. We all watch as she turns mechanically and marches toward the kitchen. The group stumbles that way, keeping an eye on her as she reaches the cabinets. She takes up the nearest rag and starts wiping down the counter.

"Damn," I whisper. "This is so messed up."

Speaker shakes his head. "I am sorry. We didn't expect—it's very uncommon. Babel told us that you would be trained in manipulating nyxia. It was a point of emphasis in our negotiations. As outsiders, you're more vulnerable to the substance's pull. We made it very clear that there are limitations you must learn if you're to come here. We warned Babel."

"She made a mistake," Omar says. "I saw it happen. Just manipulated the wrong thing."

Morning's eyes sweep back to Speaker. "So what are you saying? That she's stuck like this? That doesn't work for us, Speaker. That person in there isn't Holly."

"She is fortunate to be alive," Speaker replies. "The Gripped are a crucial part of our society, but it is a process that's usually done with great care and guidance. I am amazed that she survived. There are ways to bring her back, but those methods are difficult. We should be able to treat her when we reach Sevenset."

"So take her now," I suggest, earning a few looks. "Treat her now."

Speaker exchanges a look with the other Imago. The three of them come to a silent understanding before he responds. "We have to honor the treaty. She'll receive treatment, but only after Babel receives what we promised them. She's not in danger if she waits. You will just have to make sure she doesn't exert too much energy. She will only eat and drink if she is ordered to do so."

Morning looks frustrated by that answer. So does the rest of the group. In the kitchen, Holly's finished wiping down the counters and has started sorting through the cabinets, making sure everything is in order.

Speaker offers an apologetic look. "It would be irresponsible of me to not use this moment to warn the rest of you. Proceed with caution. Nyxia is a complex substance. I am hopeful for Holly's recovery—I do think there are ways for my people to restore her—but it will not be without difficulty. Please be as careful as possible when you work with the substance."

Morning nods a concession. "We fathom. It's late. Let's get some sleep. I'll stay with Holly for the first shift."

Parvin waves her off. "I'm her captain. She was my responsibility—is my responsibility. We'll set up a rotation with our group until she falls asleep." The thought has Parvin frowning. She looks in Speaker's direction. "She will sleep, won't she?"

He gives a nod. "Less than most, but yes, she will sleep."

The Imago excuse themselves after that. I can hear them whispering together, clearly imagining this as a blow to the first week of negotiations. The rest of the group disperses too. Morning tries to say good night to Holly, but she ignores

Morning as she restacks bowls in the upper cabinet. We cross back to Hive-3, and there's an undeniable grief hanging in the air.

Anton and Jaime are already in their rooms, doors closed, probably sleeping. Today should have been a day of wonder and exploration. A day to remind us all that we're still here and we're still fighting, even after everything Babel's done. I saved Morning in the tunnel earlier. I discovered I can speak languages I have no business knowing. This new world's been full of miracles, but there are nightmares waiting for us here too.

As I drift off to sleep, my dreams ignore the joys and victories of the day. I dream of Holly's pitch-black eyes. I dream of Roathy standing behind the nyxian barrier I created, but this time Isadora is standing with him. She raises a hand that's covered in green-black smoke.

The two of them come for me, and there's nothing I can do.

CHAPTER 10

BEHIND THE CURTAIN

―――――

Emmett Atwater

There's a second where dream becomes reality. I wake to darkness. There's a hiss for quiet, a figure hovering nearby, a dread in my chest that somehow Isadora has come for me . . .

. . . but it's Jaime. Jaime's in my room, crouched at the foot of my bed, and he's holding the side of his rib cage where the wound is. "Emmett. I need to go down to the med bay."

My heart pounds with relief. I sit up, half-asleep, and start pulling my suit on. Jaime stands, but the motion costs him something. He lets out a muted grunt before limping to the door.

"Here," I say, zipping up my suit. "I got you."

With one of his arms draped over my shoulder, I move us through the door and out into Hive-3. At this hour, only a handful of lights have been left on. The far end of the common room is sheathed in darkness. The tunnel that leads back to the tower proper is a nest of shadows too. I stare that way, Jaime draped over one side, and find myself hesitating.

"Isadora went to bed," Jaime says, reading my fears. "I didn't see her out there."

I offer him a tight nod and get us moving again. Jaime's words don't stop me from reaching for the nyxia in my left pocket. I link my mind to it, like letting a mental hand hover over the handle of a holstered gun, just in case. There's no sign of Isadora in the common room, though. Only Holly and Parvin. Holly's asleep on one of the couches. Parvin's sitting up at the opposite end, and she's dozed off too. A single overhead light throws shadows in every direction. Jaime winces again, and I move him in the direction I saw them take Holly earlier.

There, beneath the upward winding staircases, is a narrow ramp. It runs down thirty meters before hairpinning, thirty more meters, another turn. A cracked door offers us a sliver of light. Jaime nods us inside. "So what . . . it just started bleeding again?" I ask.

"I think I popped one of the stitches," he says. "I just need some bandages."

The bright interior reminds me of the ship, the time I spent in the med unit because of Jaime. It wasn't his fault, not really. All he did was accidentally punch a sword through my gut.

Three gurneys are arranged in a half circle. There's a sink built into one corner, and stacks of medical supplies are sectioned into a makeshift shelving system. I'm eyeing the rows and rows of equipment when Jaime shuts the door.

"Over there," he says. "Second row on the far left."

I'm barely awake as I fumble through the rows and pull

down a stack of bandages. A glance shows that Jaime's exhausted. He looks like he hasn't slept since landing.

"How you holding up, man?"

Jaime shrugs his shirt overhead and starts picking at the current bandage. He grits his teeth and pulls the thing off with a solid rip. "I'm fine. Everything is fine."

"You sleeping?"

He stares at me for a second. "I keep having nightmares."

I cross the room, nodding. "About Brett."

It takes a few seconds for me to blink the sleep away. I stand there, eyeing the wound. Blood has dried along the center section, but everything else looks normal. Jaime takes a deep breath. "I was always a good kid. I followed the rules. That's what you do where I come from. You follow the rules. If the crosswalk says don't walk, you don't walk. If it says you can only hunt during this season, you only hunt during that season. We're taught that if you follow the rules, you'll succeed—that's how life is supposed to work. Babel took the rules away. I don't know what to feel right now. It's like they showed me the worst of who I am."

I nod my understanding. I'm starting to see the difference between the two of us. It's not that I'm not mad. I haven't forgotten what Babel did to us. It's just that this has happened to me before. I'm used to a world that sells me a lie and pretends it's the truth. It's clear that, poor or not, Jaime never had someone do him this way. All the anger that's burning inside him used to burn inside me. Until my grandmother taught me how to file things away.

But Jaime has no system for tracking this pain. It's too new to him.

"Can you see anything?" Jaime asks. "Did one of the stitches open up?"

I inspect the wound again and shake my head. "You're good. I think you just tugged at some of the skin between. New bandage should do the trick."

He takes a piece of gauze and dabs at the wound. After a few seconds, he leans back and nods. "Get it on as tight as you can."

"Dr. Atwater at your service," I say, lining up the bandage. It's easy work, and I take a step back when it's done. Jaime smooths the edges before pulling his shirt back on. I'm standing there, thinking about what my Pops would say to me if I was in Jaime's shoes, when something catches my eye. Jaime's seated on the far left gurney. There are two others. On the floor next to the middle one, I see a series of scuff marks.

It's the same detail I noticed aboard *Genesis 11*. The kind of detail that's just a little bit off, because down here in a brand-new med bay, why would there be scuff marks at all?

Curiosity drags me to the spot. Definitely scuff marks. A ton of them too. Someone's been visiting this exact location over and over. Jaime's finished pulling his jacket back on. He looks over, confused. "What are you doing?'

"This spot . . ." I shove the gurney aside. The overhead light plays tricks on the surface of the tiles. For a second, it looks like there's nothing, and I feel like I'm making it all up. I run a finger along the floor, though, and it snags. Finding one edge brings out the whole outline.

A trapdoor.

I trace a finger along the edges until it snags again. A little digging pops up a latch.

"Secret room," I say.

Jaime offers me a dark look. "Of course they have a secret room."

I lean down and give the latch a solid tug. The entire panel gapes open. There's a hole leading down into the dark. We need to investigate. We need to see what Babel's hiding, even if this is just a route leading out to safety. But standing there on the threshold reminds me of the moment before Kaya and I entered Babel's torture chamber.

We were curious. We did too much digging. I side-eye Jaime.

"We have to go inside," he says.

"We really don't."

He shakes his head. "We can't beat them if we don't know what game they're playing."

I stare over at him. It's the kind of thing PJ would say. Jaime takes one look at me before lowering himself into the dark. I stand there, staring after him, and know that he's changed. On the ship he never led the way in anything. He was a middle-of-the-pack performer from day one. Babel pushed him too far when they put Brett in the same escape pod as him. They activated some quiet part of Jaime that's always been there. He's becoming someone who takes *action.*

"Damn it."

I crawl in after him. It's a narrow tunnel. Dark too, but Jaime's movement sets off a motion light about twenty meters ahead. I force myself to not think about tight spaces, about being buried alive. Thankfully, the journey's not long. Jaime reaches the end of the tunnel and we're facing a door with a hatch-wheel handle. He gives it two spins and then pulls.

I'm not ready for what waits behind the door. I should have known. We all should have suspected. Babel has masks for their masks. Curtains behind their curtains.

The room is full of marines.

Individual capsules run along the walls, framed by nyxia, hanging with flawless precision. Each capsule is fronted by glass casing, slightly fogged by frost. A different face stares down from each chamber. Women and men. Light skin and dark. All tagged with the Babel emblem of a looming tower. I take a second to file this under *C* for *Conspiracy.*

When I exhale for the first time, my breath mists in the air. It's almost freezing in here. Jaime moves forward until he's standing beside a central console. Blue light runs between the glowing numbers of a keypad. He eyes it for a second before looking back up at the faces.

"How many of them are there?" Jaime asks.

"Maybe thirty on each side? More?"

Jaime looks up into the face of a sturdy-looking marine. He has thin, graying hair and a small scar just above one eyebrow. "They're all asleep."

"It's like in comic books," I say. "Cryogenic chambers."

"Just waiting to be activated," Jaime says, glancing back at the console.

"Babel built them into the base. Right under the Imago's noses."

The sound of an echoing click has us both whipping around. Kit stands by the entrance, pistol raised like a professional gunslinger, eyes dead-set on us.

CHAPTER 11

THE BACKUP PLAN

Emmett Atwater

Kit steps inside the hidden room, eyes turning the scene over. It takes him about two seconds to realize we're the ones responsible for the breach. My heart hammers in my chest.

But Kit's shoulders relax. He lowers the weapon and sets it back in the holster.

"Oh," he says, smiling. "It's just you."

Jaime and I exchange a glance as he comes sliding forward, gesturing to the walls around us. "Pretty cool, isn't it? Babel never ceases to amaze."

I glance Jaime's way again. He's a mix of confusion and anger. Clearly, he doesn't know how to approach this new development. I decide to take the reins.

"Like something from an episode of the *Illuminauts,* man. Never seen anything like it."

Kit's eyes widen. "You're not going to believe this, but that's all I've been watching down here. Just finished season seven. You know, the one where they go back in time to find the captain?"

"You've got access to your Neverland account down here?"

Kit smiles at that. "We're not *that* advanced. I just chose a few uploads before launching. They knew I'd be alone down here. I've been binge-watching it for a while. You guys want to catch a few episodes?"

I gesture back to the walls, to the sleeping marines.

"Why watch it when you're living it?"

Kit smiles even wider. "Fair enough. Yeah, I come down here and visit them every few days. They're the closest thing to company I've had at the base."

Jaime finally summons the courage to ask the obvious question, the one that's digging under our skin. "Why are they here? I mean, why send us if they have marines?"

"Just a backup plan," Kit replies. "You know, if things go south. All I have to do is type in the right code and the marines activate. It takes six hours for them to fully recover from the freeze, but after that? They're ready to rock and roll."

"Cool," I say, lying through my teeth. The frozen battalion isn't *cool*. It's just one more sign of Babel's true intentions. "So what happens if nothing goes wrong?"

Kit shrugs. "Nothing. We ship them back into space and wake them up there. Like I said, they're just the backup plan. If something happens, would you rather be on your own down here, or have seventy trained marines rallying for a rescue mission?"

Jaime glances my way before nodding. "It's smart."

"Right?" Kit waves us deeper into the chamber. "Come here. This is the best part."

Our footsteps echo. The ghostly faces watch us pass. A shiver runs down my spine as Kit stops us in front of one of the last marines. He has a narrow face, high cheekbones, and a wash of blond hair. There's something eerily familiar about him.

"Who is he?" Jaime asks. "A commander or something?"

Kit nods up at the marine. "He's my dad."

I stare at the sleeping soldier in disbelief. "Your dad?"

"I told you guys," Kit replies. "I'm a space brat. Spent almost my whole life out here. Dad and Mom are both with Babel. He's a lieutenant. She's a techie on the space station. Bugs the hell out of her that we're both down here. Says she doesn't like us in the line of fire."

Kit seems to realize he's been rambling. I watch his eyes trail to the floor before he shrugs his shoulders again. "We should get back. Don't want to throw off the environment down here. I'd hate for my dad to melt because we were dicking around."

He leads us back through the chamber and up the tunnel. I stay quiet, because at least seven different truths are hammering their way into me. Babel's plans are bigger than we imagined. Kit might think these marines are some final option that won't get activated, but Babel's too smart for that. My guess is they have more marines—maybe one more batch at each of their other bases.

They're already on Imago soil. They're already making preparations.

War is coming.

And then there's Kit. He's just a kid like us. His dad's down here. His mom is up in space. I keep wanting to slap the toxic-waste symbol on Babel and call them what they are: a poison. It's easy to forget that some of their employees have no clue what's really happening. Maybe the marines do. Maybe they don't. At the end of the day, Defoe and Requin are the real enemies. More and more it's feeling like a cut-the-head-off-the-snake situation.

"We're going to keep tonight between us," Kit says as we pull ourselves up into the med bay. "I really don't care that you were down there, but some of the Babel higher-ups might. I'll keep it out of my reports if you don't talk to everyone else about it. We definitely can't risk the Adamites finding out about any of this."

"Tell the Adamites?" I ask, smiling. "We're smarter than that."

Kit nods again. "You guys want to watch some *Illuminauts*?"

"Honestly, I'm trying to go back to sleep," I reply. "Bad enough I had this clown waking me up to play doctor." Jaime shoots me a well-timed middle finger. "I might hit you up later, though, if it's an open invitation. I never finished the series."

"Sounds good." Kit runs a hand through his thick blond hair. "I'll let you two clean up down here. Sleep well."

He slides back into the hallway. Jaime turns to me, ready to say something, but I silence him with a look. We put everything back in its proper place before moving through the silent tower. The common room is empty now. Parvin and Holly must have found their way back to their rooms. I shiver a little, thinking about those empty eyes. The thought links back to the frozen marines. There's too much happening, too many pieces spinning out of our control.

We've just made it back to the hive when more movement has us jumping. Anton's door opens, and someone way too tall to be Anton slips out. We both stumble back until stray light flashes over Alex's face. He nods at the two of us as he walks past.

"Hey," he says. "Night owls, huh?"

He doesn't stop to chat. I stare after him. My first thought jumps right to what Anton and Morning have been brewing. I can't help feeling a little jealous as I watch Alex stroll back through the dark corridors. He's in on their plan, but not me? The idea has me scowling.

"What was he doing down here?" Jaime asks.

I shrug it off, remembering I've got my own secrets now. "Not sure."

Instead of separating, Jaime and I agree to go to his room. It's not hard to piece together Babel's plans with a clue this big. Jaime states the obvious: "They want more than nyxia."

All the pieces are starting to click neatly into place.

"They want to get rid of the Imago," I whisper. "They want the whole *planet.*"

CHAPTER 12

A JEWEL

Emmett Atwater

We're the last team to leave on the second day. Morning lets us sleep in, a reward for pitting two mines in the time it took the other groups to complete one. I was half expecting Holly to be roaming around Foundry fixing windows or something, but Kit informs us that she went obediently with her crew to work the mines. Her unexpected transformation still hangs over the place. I imagine everyone's going to be a little more cautious out at the work sites today.

There's some small relief in walking around Foundry without Isadora waiting in every shadow. But now there are other shadows, other games being played. Jaime and I agreed to keep quiet for now, especially inside Foundry. We need to fill Morning and the rest of the crew in on what's happening as soon as possible, but we're also not sure how much we can share in front of Speaker. What if the Imago find out and cut us off entirely? Or maybe they'll decide we deserve the same treatment as Babel's first landing party.

As we make our way to the truck, I pull Morning aside.

"Hey. Last night, Alex was in Anton's room. He's in on the plan?"

Morning considers our surroundings, clearly weighing the possibility of being monitored.

"Let's talk about this later."

"But why involve him and not me?"

Morning frowns before realization hits. She starts laughing.

"You already solved your own riddle. Alex was leaving Anton's room."

"Right," I reply. "After discussing the plan?"

She rolls her eyes. "You really didn't notice? Up in space? Anton and Alex."

"Anton and Alex . . ."

"Are together. They like each other."

My mind traces back through details. The fear and grief on Anton's face the night we landed. The relaxed look the two of them wore when they safely reunited in Foundry. Really, I can't remember a time that the two of them weren't together up in space.

"I feel like a lurch now."

"Subject change?" Morning suggests.

I nod at her, thankful for an out. "How about what we did down in the mine? How the hell did you learn to do that?"

Morning shrugs. "Not much to talk about there. I figured it out about twenty days into the competition: the substance responds to a circular movement. I have no idea why."

Jaime leans out of the truck. I realize the rest of the team has already loaded up.

"When you two finish flirting, I'd like to actually get going," he snarks.

We table the talk for now. The third mine has us heading due east. I retreat to the back of the truck, joining Speaker and the others, and our lessons in Imago culture continue. We learn a little about everything. The nearest moon, Magness, is volcanic. Speaker explains that children make a game out of memorizing the changing patterns in the red veins.

"At least, when there were children," he adds sadly.

He's impossibly patient with us, answering every question. I like that he doesn't just give the bare-bones explanations. He actually teaches us, and his only request is that we teach him in return. When he asks, I have a hard time explaining where I live.

"It's a big city," I say. "With everyone stacked right on top of each other."

"And it's called Detroit?"

I nod. "Motown. The D. I lived there my whole life."

"And you said it's like the Sixth Ring?" he asks.

Of all the comparisons, this one makes the most sense to Speaker. The city of Sevenset. We studied it on *Genesis 11*, but Speaker's descriptions have worked to fill in the missing gaps in our education. The Imago first built the seven rings for protection. A wall-inside-a-wall-inside-a-wall kind of thing. The outer ring grazes three of the world's five continents, but the inner rings were built over the sea, spread across hundreds of kilometers. Each consecutive ring has a smaller diameter until you arrive at the Sanctum, which sits

at center. Speaker informs us that 95 percent of the Imago
live in Sevenset.

Hearing that number reminds me: Babel's main plan is
attack. If they can expose Sevenset, they're exposing almost
the entire population. The game we're playing matters more
than I realized. It takes a few minutes to refocus on the present, on the now.

Speaker explains that, over time, the rings transformed
into a ranking system when their duo of queens—the
Daughters—moved the throne permanently to the Sanctum. He doesn't say it directly, but there are enough clues
to connect the dots: there aren't many women left in their
world. Babel told us they'd stopped reproducing. Is the lack
of women the reason why?

"When the queens consolidated power, proximity to the
Sanctum became one of our most valuable commodities,"
Speaker explains. "I was born on the Fourth Ring. It has
taken most of my life to earn my place on the Second. One
must earn his way forward."

It's a surprise to hear him describe the lower rings with
such disdain. Never mind that he came from there and grew
up there. His words about the Sixth Ring leave me annoyed,
even a little cold.

"You know the place I live is like your Sixth Ring," I
explain. "Except all of Detroit isn't separated by rings. The
people from the different rings all live near each other. And
they walk down the street and see people from every ring.
If you go downtown, everyone mixes together."

Speaker considers that. "Sometimes a person visits another ring, but they cannot live there. So in Detroit they live in harmony? The honored and the dishonored? Together?"

"Not really," I say, picturing the suits and sunglasses on every street corner. "No, not really at all. I guess we do live on different rings, but we're so close we have to pretend like we don't. Kids in class would talk about vacations sometimes."

Speaker frowns. "Vacations?"

"Vacations . . . it's like time off from work. You go to nice places and stuff? My family couldn't exactly afford too many of those, you know? I guess where I come from, you can go your whole life just sticking to people in your ring. And leaving other people to talk to the people in their ring. But I promise you one thing, my neighborhood doesn't have any first-ringers, and it's always been that way."

"But you can change that, Emmett," Speaker says confidently. "As with my people, your people move from ring to ring. You can return as a member of the third or even the first."

"That's why I came. Babel offered to take me all the way from sixth to first."

Speaker gasps. "Then you must be excited to go home. To take a new place."

I nod half-heartedly. "If we make it back. You saw what happened to Holly."

Speaker frowns. "An accident. I promise you, Emmett, as I have promised the others: we will do *everything* in our power to restore Holly. I am hopeful she will recover."

His eyes roam the distant hills. Hoping for a distraction,

I ask Azima to tell Speaker about where she grew up. Her face lights up as she describes her family, her younger cousins, and her selfless mother. She describes market tables stacked with passion fruit, cafes that trade in smoke and laughter. I know my corners of Detroit, but it's clear that Azima was and still is the very definition of an explorer. There's not a stone in her old city that she's left unturned.

Jaime describes his home too. Zermatt. A valley town in Switzerland that sits in the shadow of the Matterhorn. Orderly streets, cold winters, roaming tourists. He spends all his time talking about how things *work* there, all the rules and structure that make the whole place tick like a well-tuned clock. I can tell Babel's betrayal is still gutting him. They've rewritten the rules, and Jaime can't wrap his mind around the fact that they'll do whatever they want to do.

We arrive at the mine as Speaker asks Anton about his home. The Russian doesn't answer. He just shakes his head, hops down from the truck, and starts the survey process.

Morning distracts us by describing San Jose. She likes the city, but spent all her time in the parks outside it. She describes trees like most people describe their friends. Embarrassed, she digs in a pocket and holds up a smooth stone for us to see.

"It's from my favorite waterfall," she says. "This spot in Alum Rock Park. I couldn't resist bringing a little bit of home with me."

I love learning about Morning, but thinking about home feels like trying to hold on to the wind. Will we ever get back? And when we do, what happens then? I can't help thinking about the possibilities as the third mine gets charted, as our drill digs down three hundred meters.

I decide to bury the harder questions with it.

We spend hours pitting the thing. Nyxia rains down through the tunnel, then gets gathered up the conveyor shafts and repackaged for manipulation. We don't break any records, but that's because everyone's a little cautious after Holly's accident. I'm enjoying the mindless work when Morning calls me back to the surface.

I climb down off the drill and find the others already gathered by the truck's monitor. There's a voice patching through the comm system. Morning's playing with switches, testing this and that, until finally she gets an image to appear. Parvin's face fills the screen. We didn't even know there was a way to talk to the other crews. She looks exhausted and worried.

"It's Beckway," Parvin crackles. "He left."

Speaker was standing a polite distance away, but the announcement has him rushing over. He looks like he's struggling to find something diplomatic to say, and failing.

"Why would he leave?"

"He didn't tell us," Parvin answers, shaking her head. "He disappeared an hour ago. He took Isadora and Ida with him. They're gone, Morning."

Morning's eyes flick my way. Isadora has made one thing perfectly clear. There's one person she wants to punish. Morning nods over at Anton, and he slips away from the group, circling the grounds. I notice he's carrying both knives at the ready.

"Who are Isadora and Ida? Why them?" Speaker inter-rupts. "Beckway's task was to care for your entire group. There are only a few reasons he would have left some of you vulnerable in favor of protecting others."

Parvin sighs. "Isadora is pregnant."

There's a moment where Speaker's facial features remain completely motionless. I watch as he processes the infor-mation, linking it to Beckway's actions, then moving into the territory of his own response. It's not the first time that I feel like I'm watching an actor pick an emotion for his next scene. When Speaker finally finds the right words, they come stumbling out.

"Can you not see both moons?" A massive smile splits his face. "She is with child."

Jaime shrugs. "And that's . . . exciting?"

"I cannot imagine our people being more excited about anything. Long have we discussed your arrival with excite-ment. But a child? A child would be a jewel in the eyes of our people."

A jewel. The thought has me grinding teeth. Now I know why she left, what she's doing. Isadora might not have per-formed well in the standings, but I *know* she's smart. Maybe she weighed the odds of fighting past Morning and realized she had no chance on her own. That first night, she swayed some of the Genesis crew, but not all of them.

That left one possible option unexplored: the Imago. What happens if they really value the child this much? What status will Isadora be given?

". . . I'm unfamiliar with human birth cycles. Is the child likely to be born here?"

Azima nods to Speaker. "She looked like she was already halfway there."

Speaker can't contain his excitement. "You understand what this means to our people? To host such a miracle would restore hope to even the lowest of our kind. This is a great sign of what is to come and a great sign of the hope you offer us. It makes sense to me that Beckway would escort her to Sevenset. He should have called for a replacement first, but if Isadora was insisting to be taken to the capital? It was the right decision. Her health is paramount."

Parvin's been listening attentively. Now she pipes back in.

"So you'll take her, but not Holly?"

Speaker swallows before answering. "Forgive me, but it is a different situation. Holly will not benefit from quicker treatment. Our remedy for her will work or it will not, regardless of the time she receives it. But Isadora? A pregnancy?"

He's so excited he doesn't even have the words to go on. Parvin turns her attention back to us. "Makes sense. Be careful, Morning. You know what she wants. I've talked to her about Emmett. In her mind, all of this ends in blood."

I start to respond, but what can I say? Until we show her Roathy, alive and unharmed, she'll be working to put me in the ground. I knew she'd come for me, but I never imagined she'd come with the weight and blessing of the Imago people behind her.

Anton comes back around the truck. "It's all clear. No one in range of our guns."

Morning nods, turning back to Parvin. "Are you heading back to Foundry?"

"No other choice," Parvin says. "It's just the three of us, and I have to keep an eye on Holly the whole time."

"Have you let Katsu's team know?" Morning asks. "I don't like the idea of them not knowing what's going on, especially if they could be in danger."

Parvin shakes her head. "I'll link you through to him. We need to get moving."

"Copy that," Morning says. "Be safe."

The screen blinks back to blueprints of the mine. Morning sweeps forward and swipes to a new screen. A little message appears from Parvin. Morning double taps the link and buzzes through to Katsu's squad. It takes about a minute or so, but the display finally patches video footage onto our screen. We get a live feed of a familiar, fog-laced landscape.

Our call's been accepted, but the screen is empty.

"Where are they?" I ask.

Fog swirls, and Morning covers her mouth, gasping. The others crowd around, and we see what she does: dark forms everywhere. Morning taps the screen, and the shot zooms in on the nearest body. Katsu. My friend stares lifelessly at the screen, all his humor erased in death. A streak of blood runs from lip to chin.

Morning pans, and we see Longwei half buried in mud. Jazzy is folded over him like an abandoned chair. Alex sits against a distant stone, his shoulders slumped and chin lolling. There's no sign of their fifth teammate, Noor.

Before any of us can think of something to say, laughter bursts through the audio. Loud and obnoxious laughter. The shot widens, and we watch Katsu double over, his chin shaking as he raises his arms in triumph. Like revenants called back from graves, the entire crew starts to move. We're all staring helplessly when Bally's wide face appears. He's laughing too.

"Katsu has taught me the art of a practical joke. Were we successful?"

"Jesus in heaven," Anton hisses. "What is wrong with you people?"

Bally frowns. "You look upset. In that case, it was not my idea."

Katsu shoulders into the frame. "It was *my* idea! We've had this planned ever since we found out there was a comm system. So glad you finally called. Totally worth it!"

Morning has no words. She shakes her head and stalks off.

I see Noor edge onto the screen, her smile bursting out of the circle of her hijab.

"I did the fake blood!" she says proudly.

Longwei leans in too. "I didn't think it was a good idea."

Katsu scowls at Longwei before turning back to us. "How's my favorite crew?"

As I explain the situation, the humor fades. Their faces are a mixture of sympathy and accusation. "But she wasn't kidnapped or anything?" Noor asks.

"Nah, she went on her own. Speaker thinks she'll be . . . celebrated."

"Good for her," Katsu says. "Bad for you."

All I can do is nod. "I'm just glad you assholes aren't dead."

Bally shoulders back into the frame. "I just learned that word. It's Katsu's favorite."

I can't help rolling my eyes. It's taken Katsu all of two days to convert Bally to his particular brand of humor. "After what happened with Holly, did you really think it was time for a fake-death joke? Do I need to walk you through how stupid that is?"

Katsu just shrugs. "My humor is a little too sophisticated for some, I understand."

All I can do is shake my head. "Head back to Foundry. We'll meet you there. No more accidents or surprises today. Let's just get back so we can figure out the best move. Be safe."

Katsu gives an official-looking salute. Bally mimics him and the feed cuts. The screen reverts to maps as I turn and watch the others make preparations to head home. It feels like a wasted day for everyone except Speaker, who continues raving about the new life coming to their planet. It's clear that he has no idea just how bad this could be for me. Morning knows, though, and I can see the weight of it riding her shoulders. She sends Jaime up to the front cabin and climbs into the back of the truck with me. Her look is fire and fury.

"No matter what happens," she says, "I'll fight for you. Got that?"

The truck engine revs, and we start to rumble over the nearest hill.

"Loud and clear."

CHAPTER 13

ONE SMALL STEP

───────

Emmett Atwater

Our truck rolls back into Foundry in the middle of the afternoon. The timing of the other groups is borderline flawless. Parvin's team follows a few minutes after, and Katsu comes in right on their heels. We're early enough that we catch Kit on the far side of the facility, tending to one of Babel's freshly planted gardens. The entire group gathers as he makes his way over.

"When he takes the trucks back to the depot," Morning says, loud enough for the others to hear, "I want everyone in the main hall. We need to have a family chat."

There are nods all around. Morning puts on a smile as Kit approaches, confusion clear as day on his face. "Did I miss something?" he asks. "It's the middle of the afternoon."

"Isadora and Ida are gone," Morning answers. "Beckway went with them. You can tell Babel that we suspect Isadora is using her pregnancy to gain favor with the Adamites."

Kit's eyebrows just about jump off his forehead. "Gone? Pregnant? What?"

"You take the trucks and we'll catch you up inside," Morning suggests.

"But production . . ." Kit glances up at the sky again. "We're supposed to use every hour we can to bring nyxia into the facility. That's the job you signed on to do."

Morning nods. "And it's the job we'll continue doing once we've sorted this out. Parvin's team is down to three. Their escort is gone. We need to reorganize."

Kit looks frustrated, but he doesn't offer any solutions, either. "I'll get the trucks below, but the bosses are *not* going to be happy with this. Hope they don't dock your pay."

He walks past the group and accesses the Foundry interface again. We all move toward the entrance, trying to look as casual as we can. Morning strides at the head of the group, glancing back only once to make sure that Kit's moving in the opposite direction.

The second we're inside, all eyes turn to Morning. I don't know what she's got planned, but Anton walks beside her and I know whatever it is will be a huge first step in the right direction. She guides us out of sight of the entrance. In one sweeping gesture, she draws the nyxia from her shoulders. The substance expands, misting around us to form a translucent cube that's just big enough to fit all of us inside. I flinch at the snap of static, but it's followed by complete silence. The distant trucks, the snatches of wind, all gone. It's like we're standing in our own private room. Omar clears his throat, and the sound echoes off the nyxian walls.

Holly starts to walk toward the shared living space. I can see a pile of dishes there that has caught her eye, but Parvin puts a hand on her shoulder.

"Wait," she says. "Holly. You're still one of us. Sit, please."

Holly's empty eyes process the command. She glances back at the dishes, like she's storing the information for later, and decides to sit down. Parvin keeps a steady hand on her shoulder and nods a *go ahead* to Morning.

"It took me a while to figure out this manipulation," Morning explains. "But we can speak freely in here. We can see out of the cube, but Babel can't see in it. They can't hear in it, either. My nyxia is jamming every signal. You can all speak freely."

The group shifts uncomfortably. We all trust Morning's ability, but I think the idea of actually dissecting our employer's motivations will always feel dangerous.

"When Babel recruited me, they made a lot of promises," Morning starts. "I'll admit that I liked the idea of being rich. I liked the sound of mi abuelita getting the medical treatment she needs. I even liked the idea of exploring a new world. But I think we can all agree that Babel hasn't exactly kept their promises."

Most of the group nods. Only Parvin disagrees.

"My parents were receiving payments," she says. "I don't like how Babel set up the fights outside the escape pods, but at the end of the day, did they force you to fight? Or did people choose to fight? I think we signed on for this. If we do the job, we'll be rewarded. I see no overwhelming evidence to disbelieve Babel's ultimate promises. Not yet."

Alex takes up Morning's cause. "The girl on your ship, Emmett. What was her name?"

"Kaya," I reply softly. "Her name was Kaya."

"What about her family?" Alex asks. "Will they be paid?"

Parvin shrugs, and I've never seen a more heartless gesture. It has my pulse soaring.

"She didn't fulfill the contract," Parvin says. "I imagine Babel will send the promised salary, but we *agreed* to this. We took on the risk. We signed the papers."

I don't trust myself to speak. Azima notices my trembling and sets a hand on my shoulder to steady me. I let the words I want to say burn holes through my tongue. I'm trying to file this one away, but it has me too hot to think straight. I'm thankful when the others speak up for me, because I'm not the only one bothered by Parvin's response.

Anton says, "We didn't agree to die. We didn't agree to kill. Would your parents trade the money to get you back, Parvin? To see you safely home? Don't be heartless."

"Heartless?" Parvin replies. "I'm being logical. Did you even *read* the contract?"

"Of course I did," Anton snaps. "I don't remember anything about forced murder."

"No," Parvin replies crisply. "But there's an entire page about the risks of the venture. We decided to come anyway. We took a risk, a calculated one. Holly knew that when she signed up. Kaya knew it too. We took that risk because we wanted the money."

"Enough," Morning says. She holds out a small device, no bigger than her thumb. She makes a show of pressing play. "I know how much you like evidence, Parvin."

Audio trembles out. We all know the voice. Babel's chief of space operations—David Requin—speaks with that familiar confidence. "We chose our Adams and Eves carefully."

A muddled voice replies. Requin answers with bite.

"That's not the point. We have to keep up appearances at home until it doesn't matter. That's the point. Make the payments, supply the treatments, and put on a good show, Roman. Do that for the next year and it won't matter."

The other voice sounds again. The words mutter and rattle.

"They aren't going home," Requin answers. "If any of our top-tier plans succeed, they'll never be interviewed or interrogated by anyone on Earth. Going home was never a realistic option and you know that. They would shed too much light on our operations in space. Either the Adams and Eves can start a new world here, or they—"

His words gutter out. The truth silences everything. I've known about Babel's dark side since the day Defoe shoved Karpinski down in front of me and offered to let me execute him, but I still feel like I'm falling through worlds. This is confirmation. They aren't taking us home, and they never were.

I can see the truth hitting the entire room. It's not just Parvin, either. A few of the others have spent all this time thinking the best of Babel. Morning shoves the device back in her pocket.

"Is that enough reason to react?" she asks.

I know I should be thinking this through, analyzing it all. But my first thought jumps to the fact that Morning had this tape and never shared it with me. With Anton, but not me?

Parvin looks defeated. "I didn't know."

"No one knew," Morning replies, her voice calm and assuring. "But now that you do know, I hope you understand why we have to act. Babel intends to keep us here. For what purpose, I don't know. But they aren't gonna let us go home. As long as they control the Tower Space Station, we're stuck here. We know they're shipping nyxia back to Earth, so we know there are freighters returning that way. Problem is Babel controls everything in space right now."

I can feel the knowledge of last night burning like a hole in my chest. I glance over at Jaime. He locks eyes with me, clearly struggling with the same thing. But this is our family. Down here, these are the only people we can actually trust.

"We found one of Babel's backup plans last night," I say.

Attention swings my way.

"I was helping Jaime with his wound." He nods in confirmation. "I noticed scuffs on the floor. There was a trapdoor that led down to a secret chamber. They have about seventy marines stored in cryogenic chambers. Just waiting to be activated."

Anton whistles. The rest of the crew looks like they almost don't believe us. Azima's dark eyebrows are about through the roof. "Frozen marines? I want to see them!" she says.

"They're not an exhibit at the zoo," Katsu snarks.

Morning waves them to silence. "So they're just sleeping?"

I nod. "For now. Kit found us down there, but he didn't suspect anything. He thinks we're all Babel just like him. His dad is down there. He's one of the frozen soldiers."

"His *dad*?" It's the first time I've seen Noor speak and not smile. "This is so wrong."

"Look, we have to keep in mind that Babel's never had

a foothold on-planet." I've been thinking about the logistics ever since we found the bodies. "The Adamites have been winning this game since jump. Every one of you saw that first video. Babel got butchered, man. So what changed? We did. We're their only way onto the planet."

There are nods all around.

Morning changes directions. "So what about the Adamites? Can we trust them?"

"Trust the Adamites?" Parvin asks, like all of this is ridiculous. "I get that they've held their own against Babel, but there's no sign of them succeeding in space. Do they have a fleet of ships I've forgotten about? Fighting Babel means destroying our only way home."

The idea of not going home silences everyone again. I don't have any real answers. No one does. Both Parvin and Morning are right. Babel has us chained up pretty good. The Imago seem like our only possible ally, but there's something off there too.

"Imago," I say out loud. "Let's have enough respect to call them by their *real* name, not the one Babel made up for them. They're called the Imago."

Morning nods gratefully at the correction.

"And I'm not sure how to feel about them either." The others are listening closely. I forgot that at least a few of them respect me and see me as a leader in my own right. "I mean, you noticed how happy they were, right? When they met us for the first time? It makes sense. Babel said they don't have kids. But all this talk about restoring hope and all that . . . It just doesn't line up, you know? We know who

Babel is, but I say the jury's still out on the Imago. I don't think we can just throw this at them and expect they'll play ball."

I'm surprised when Longwei adds his voice to the conversation.

"Didn't the rest of you read through the databases?" he asks. "Babel gave us the information they gathered. Primary resources from every employee that ever spied on the Ada—the Imago. It wasn't hard to determine they were dying out."

"No kidding," Katsu fires back. "We all understand what 'no longer can reproduce' means, Longwei. We're old enough to understand sex ed. . . ."

"But did you ask *why* they can't reproduce?" Longwei replies softly. "There have been at least four recorded interactions of humans and the Imago. Babel also had satellite reports of hunting parties and maintenance crews that left Sevenset to visit other parts of their world. In every single report, the Babel employee notes there are no women present. Can you imagine? They haven't seen a woman outside of Sevenset in two decades! The only mention of women from the Imago so far are the Daughters in the Sanctum. All the facts point toward extinction, do they not? How can a society go on without women?"

Morning nods. "Parvin found some of those reports too. So what's your point? What does all that have to do with us?"

Longwei considers the others. "I am always hesitant to team with desperate people. If the Imago are on the verge of dying out, I would be cautious of partnering with them."

Everyone nods at that. The others look even more worried. Thankfully, Anton steps forward in answer. "We can only depend on ourselves. That's why I'm going up."

"Going up?" Azima echoes. "Back to space?"

He nods. "I'll launch inside the first nyxian shipment. I came up with the idea when Kit showed us the silo. Morning and I talked through the manipulations I'd need to make it work. We're pretty sure I can survive the ascent without much of a problem. Kit's going to launch the first shipment when we hit the right quotas. If it works . . . we'll at least have someone in space."

It's actually a genius plan. Babel will have charted out every detail on the surface, but I doubt they imagined a member of our crew could head back up into space. I can already imagine Anton up there, putting a torch to all their plans. Excitement snakes through the group. Every face except for Alex's. He looks helpless, furious.

"What will you do up there?" Azima asks curiously.

"I'll keep quiet," he says. "I'll learn what I can and put myself in a good position. I've been working on stealth manipulations for days. It won't be easy, but if I can get some help, we can change the game against Babel. We already have one person up there that's willing to help. The same person that got Morning that audio."

"Which brings us to the next part," Morning adds. "Can anyone else help us? I know you might not have reached out to the techies or workers, but what about your medics? Anyone that we can trust? We could use more hands on this."

We all exchange glances. A spike of sadness guts me. I've barely even thought about Vandemeer since landing. The last time he saw me, I was about to face Roathy. Does he know what happened? Did Babel tell him I survived? I hope he knows. I hope he's safe.

"Mine can be trusted," I say. "Vandy will want to know what happened to me. If Anton tells him what's been going on, I know he'll help."

"That makes one," Morning says. "Anyone else?"

Longwei shakes his head. Jaime and Azima discuss it quietly, but agree their medic would be too nervous to play the role of a spy. Quick and quiet conversations chase around the room, but the only other duo with a trustworthy caretaker is Omar and Holly.

"Andi will help," he says. "Just make sure you don't put too much pressure on her. She gets a little anxious when she's pushed outside her comfort zone."

"Very reassuring," Anton mutters.

"That's more help than we had when we started," Morning says. "All right. I don't want *anyone* going near the silo. In fact, I'd like for there to be a ton of movement right around the time that Kit sends up the first nyxian shipment. Give Babel a lot to track and a lot to watch. Anything to keep them from noticing Anton's boarding. Everybody fathom?"

The whole group nods. "What about the Imago?" I ask. "What do we tell them?"

"Nothing for now," Morning says. "Not until we get to Sevenset. But I want you to plant some rumors. The story will be that Anton got pissed off about something and left to seek an audience with the Adamites—sorry, the Imago. It's kind of perfect that Isadora did the same thing; it will make that story more plausible. We'll keep some of his gear with us so that Babel doesn't try to track him. It'll be hard, but the longer they think he's down here, the better chance he'll have to make a difference in the space station."

"What if they catch you?" Parvin asks.

Anton transforms a piece of nyxia into one of his trademark knives.

"I'll keep these nice and sharp."

"This is great," Katsu says. "Just like when the Russians landed on the moon."

Everyone looks at him. Jaime laughs for what feels like the first time since we landed.

"They didn't land on the moon, Katsu," he says.

Katsu looks skeptical. "I read about it. It happened in the 1960s."

"That was America," Anton says. "But the cosmonauts got to space first."

"Exactly." Katsu nods enthusiastically. "Send in the cosmonaut!"

"All right," Morning cuts in. "Does everyone agree that Babel's the enemy?"

There's another awkward, stretching silence. Parvin looks less stubborn, and eventually she nods. Murmured agreement echoes. If we're going to face them, it has to be together.

"And does everyone agree we'll explore our options with the Imago?"

More nods.

"Good," she says. "We're agreed. Shoulder to shoulder."

This time the whole group echoes the phrase.

There's an edge in Morning's voice that's contagious.

We're all tired of being pushed around, and it finally feels like we're ready to push back. Back in Detroit, there were basic lessons that every kid learned growing up: where to go, what to say, when to vanish. One of those rules was that a person fights hardest when they're cornered. Babel has us right where they want us, but they don't see the rush of adrenaline, the fists balled up and ready for a fight.

We all take a second to wish Anton luck. The Russian politely asks us to quit blowing smoke up his ass. Morning laughs and brings down the barrier. I watch the group drift apart, and it's not hard to see the difference:

Purpose. We walk around like we have a good reason for every single step.

CHAPTER 14

A NEW SONG

Emmett Atwater

Night comes, and it's hard not to notice that Kit's on edge, frustrated. Babel came down hard on him. He moves around the base and tries to reclaim his authority, saying we'll have to start our digs early the next morning. I can't help wondering if Babel relayed the fact that we had a secret meeting while he took care of the trucks. But I have no idea what kind of surveillance they have here.

We don't give him much reason to be suspicious. Jazzy leads the group through a game called Signs. I've never played before, but it's actually kind of fun. The group sits in a circle, passing an invisible ball with specific hand signals, while the person in the middle spins around trying to catch the right person at the right time. Morning's signal is someone pulling an arrow from a quiver and firing. I use a waffling shake of the hand.

Surprisingly, Morning is *really* terrible at the game. I can't help laughing when she finds herself in the middle of the group, struggling to get out of the circle. Kit tries to remind us to get some sleep, that we'll need our energy for the early morning. But for me there's a lightness stretching over Foundry that has everything to do with Isadora's absence. Noor was staring daggers at me two days ago, but now she doesn't even seem to care about Isadora's vendetta against me. I'm thinking about Isadora in Sevenset, trying to convince the Imago of my guilt, when Jazzy takes the seat next to me.

"I did what I could to explain," she says. "Isadora . . . I know how she's feeling, it's awful, but I know you, Emmett. If I had to trust anyone in this base to tell the truth, it'd be you. I told them that. Ida wouldn't listen. She's obsessing over the idea of getting back to Loche. But Noor and the others are coming around. We know that whatever happened wasn't your fault."

Her kindness humbles me. "Thanks, Jazzy."

She smiles. "What are friends for?"

Across the room, Katsu has unearthed a dusty game of Post-Apocalyptic Risk. He tries to drag some of the others into the fun, but I notice Morning leaning against the tunnel to Hive-3. She's changed into her tank top and sweats. Sunlight has brought back the rich color of her light-brown skin. My eyes trace the bare shoulders, her dark collarbones. The look she's giving me is enough to spin my mind back to space, to her room, to our first collision.

"I think I'm going to sleep," I tell Jazzy. "Catch you tomorrow."

Jazzy doesn't seem to notice how quickly I stand. But as Morning and I lock eyes, everything else fades. I cross the room and Morning slides ahead of me, moving into the underground. She looks back, and my heart just about slams through my rib cage.

I catch her at the door to her room. She turns, pulling me down by the collar and into a kiss. It's the opening chord. There's nothing but the taste of her, the sound of us.

A second kiss chases a third. Our hands play background music. She works my suit away from one shoulder. I reach around and lift her up. The rhythm of our song speeds up, the notes dancing faster. I let my lips graze her neck. Her fingers dig into my shoulder blades.

"We have to actually get in the room," she says.

I kiss her neck again as she reaches back for the handle and shoves her door open. She laughs when I trip my way inside, but silences my protest with the boom of kiss after kiss. I pin her on the bed, but she twists her legs around my waist, curling us, pinning me instead. Her dark hair falls over one shoulder, and she looks down at me like a queen.

She takes me back before the Tower of Babel, back to a time where there was only one word for beautiful. We walk through all the notes we like best.

The weight of each touch and the tremble of each kiss shatter me into song.

But Babel exists to ruin beautiful things.

An alarm shakes through the silence of the room. It's still nighttime. Morning's on her feet first. It takes about twenty seconds for us to get dressed and spill out into the hallway. We move as a single unit. It would be easy to feel like there's some magical spell over us, some difference that marks us as a single unit to the other Genesis members. But it's more basic than that; it's instinct. We share a quiet determination to see all of this through to the end.

There's an agreement now that we will survive this, and we'll survive it together.

Overhead we hear the unmistakable sound of gunfire. It's heavy artillery, and each shot shakes through the walls. Anton's pulling out knives, and I realize I left my claws back in my room. Morning's moving, though, so I'm moving. The rest of the Genesis crew pours out of the other two hives. We head toward the entrance, and the sound of gunfire booms louder.

Outside, light floods in every direction. An emergency system has activated, and it's like spotlights roaming a prison yard. Kit stands about thirty meters away, his gloved hand raised, the digital interface flashing red and blue in the air. He presses a finger to one of the buttons, and another round of volleys fires from above. Each boom swallows the night.

I squint past Kit and realize there are bodies on the ground. Even at a distance, we can tell they're Imago. Both forms lie motionless, staggered along the outskirts of the base. Morning tries to shout something, but the sound of the gunfire cuts her sentence in half. Kit looks almost possessed as he directs the base's defense system to fire on the last standing Imago.

The uninvited guest waits inside a nyxian cube that looks a lot like the one Morning summoned earlier. It's about the size of a shed. We watch as consecutive shots absorb into the material uselessly. The Imago fighter doesn't even flinch as shot after shot tests his defenses. He stands there, pacing inside the nyxian boundaries, waiting for Kit to come closer.

"Stand aside."

It's such a forceful command that I duck to the right before I even get a look at who said it. Speaker comes striding through our ranks. Bally stands back, watchful. We've only really seen the smiling, quiet version of Speaker. The transformation is stunning.

He lets a wicked mace drag through the air at his side. It's a threat, a promise. Kit's still jabbing at his digital display when he notices Speaker approaching. Words are exchanged, but it's too loud for us to hear them. We watch as Kit's face pales. He flips a switch to kill the gunfire. A false sense of quiet follows. My ears strain after smaller sounds. The soft crunch of grass and dirt under Speaker's feet. The distant buzz of the nyxian barrier. Seeing a new opponent approach, the Imago raises his weapon and points.

Speaker doesn't slow his stride. He walks right up to the barrier and kneels. We watch as he plucks a few strands of grass, leans forward, and tosses them at the cube.

I can just barely make them out as they cross the barrier and drop way faster than they should. Morning frowns over at me, and I almost miss Speaker's next movement. He rounds the barrier, backs up a few steps, and starts to run.

At the last second, nyxia punches down from his left hand. He uses the spring to launch himself skyward. The surprised Imago flinches as Speaker dives through the top half of the barrier. My jaw drops about as fast as Speaker does. It's an impossible speed. He jabs the mace down, and there's a disgusting crunch. The entire barrier blinks out of existence.

"Holy crap," Katsu whispers.

Speaker looks down at the motionless Imago, then back to Kit.

"Are there any more?"

Kit toggles the interface. "I only counted three bogeys coming across the barrier."

Speaker turns and kneels over the body. Most of our Genesis crew stand there, waiting for an explanation. Bally comes forward to calm us down, but I find myself drifting to Speaker's side. Morning follows. He's still kneeling there, breathing heavily. The bright spotlight makes one thing abundantly clear: all three of the unwelcome Imago are dead.

"Speak?" I ask. We stop a few feet away. He looks back, and his face is gaunt, covered with flecks of blood. He shakes his head sadly.

"It's a great shame to die this way after all we've done to preserve our kind."

Morning offers a hand. Speaker allows himself to be helped up. Nearby, I can see gaping holes in the bodies of the other two Imago. Kit's activation of the base's defense system tore through them, probably caught them by surprise. Speaker reaches down and removes a nyxian weapon from his victim that looks alien to my eyes, but more than sharp enough to do the job.

"They came here for you," he says.

His words set off alarm bells. "You mean . . . Isadora sent them?"

"Isadora?" Speaker frowns. "No, I apologize. Not you personally, Emmett. The entire group. They came here hoping to capture one of you."

"Why?" Morning asks. "We were promised safety."

He nods. "By the Daughters, by our people, and by all of Sevenset."

Morning gets to the truth just before I do. "So they're a separate group."

"After we signed the treaty with Babel," Speaker confirms, "this cult formed. They did not agree with our plans, our dreams. It was not enough for them to welcome miracles into *this* world. They wanted more than they are due. We call them slings."

"Slings?" I ask.

"Slingshots," he explains. "Our civilization's primary function is permanence. The society is placed above the individual. We act in the interest of all, rather than ourselves. The slings choose to go against that."

We watch as he reaches down and rolls back the fallen Imago's sleeve. The tattoo along the bared wrist shows two moons in orbit. Speaker looks up at us.

"They think it's their calling to go to *your* world. Slings are selfish. They actively ignore the treaty, all the progress between our species, to benefit only themselves. I believe their ultimate goal is to capture one of you and use you to launch themselves into the stars."

Morning nods. "They think if we came down from space, we know how to get back."

For a second, Speaker's face falters. There's the slightest hint of fear.

"That is how they see you. But you are not tools. You are our welcome guests. We have rejected the slings since the very beginning. But it was . . . unwise not to be more honest about the potential danger they pose. I don't think we expected them to act so early in your stay. Please accept my apologies. We will not make this mistake again."

"Speaker," Morning cuts in. "You protected us. That's all that matters."

"And if your defense system had not sensed their approach? Would I still be sleeping? Would three of you have been taken?" He sighs deeply. "Best to not think on such things."

Too fast to follow, he manipulates the nyxia. It's not a perfect match, but I can tell what he's formed is the same shape and idea as a shovel. I start to manipulate my own, but Speaker shakes his head. "We do not have many rules about death," he says. "But there are some. When one man kills another, he will be the one to bury him."

Morning and I exchange a glance and decide not to push. Their world, their rules. His spade bites into the dirt. As kind and quiet as Speaker has been to us, he makes this look like familiar work. It's not hard to figure out that he's buried men before. Morning goes back to talk with the rest of the group. Most of them are moving back inside, thankful the threat is over.

But I can't bring myself to leave Speaker. He agrees to let me help bury the other two bodies, acknowledging he wasn't actually the one who killed them. We dig a second grave, then a third. At the completion of each one, Speaker whispers a quiet prayer.

Something about the bodies has me shedding my rust. Not that we had it easy here or anything, but the mindset Babel forced on us in training kicks back into gear. We are not safe in this world. A thousand unknowns threaten to swallow me, to grind my bones into fine powder.

When Speaker finishes, we sit there together, eyeing the unmarked graves.

"What did you say to them?" I ask.

I can still see the way they looked before he put them in the ground. The slack mouths and the open eyes. My mind echoes a vision of Kaya under her dark shroud.

Speaker answers, "It's a poem. Written by a soldier who died in battle."

"Can you—I mean it's okay if you can't—but can you share it?"

He nods once. His voice deepens, almost on the edge of song:

> *What weigh those things now, that so bent you here?*
> *Much is made of men*
> *Who rise like prayers from parted lips.*

I make him repeat the poem twice. It's as perfect as it is sad. Speaker drifts back into silence. But the words remind me of a song that I love. I ask him to wait while I duck back inside Foundry. I dig through my knapsack and pull out my player. It takes a few minutes to hunt through artists, but I manage to find it. An old beat with stark lyrics. I offer

Speaker the earbud and he actually sniffs it. I hide a laugh, showing him how it works. His ears are a bit wider and he has to hold his earbud in place. Together, we listen.

The chorus comes slow, voices dropping down to the beat and lyrics center stage. Speaker nods along when we reach the bridge, as the words come quicker and a trumpet thunders in some studio background. When the song finishes, he asks me to play it again. I put it on repeat, and we listen until the sun rises, until we feel as far away from the dead as we ever will.

CHAPTER 15

THE COSMONAUT

Emmett Atwater

The days that follow are routine.

But out here that just means that no one dies, no one abandons us, and no one tries to kill us. We go about the business of completing the task Babel recruited us for, the one we thought would bring us infinite riches when we first signed on the dotted line.

We dive down into black pits and fill Babel's already over-flowing bank accounts. The wild part is that—compared to the rest of what's happened—digging feels like doing work-sheets did back in school. It's the everyday, boring stuff. We're changing the global economics of our entire world, and it amounts to vocab practice or textbook annotations. Again, I wonder how I can ever go back and reclaim any kind of normal on Earth

The routine goes like this: Arrive. Unpack. Flirt a little. Feel guilty that I'm flirting with the fate of multiple worlds on the line. Flirt some more. Drill down into darkness. Gut the planet. Get that money. Pack it in neat boxes. Sleep with one eye open. Rinse and repeat.

Only a handful of moments break through the standard routine. Beckway returns on the sixth day. He tells us that Isadora and Ida are safe. We've been rotating teams in their absence, taking larger crews to two separate sites, and getting more rest because of it. The setup was kind of nice, but the news from Beckway reminds us their absence isn't a good thing, at least not for me. They've been invited to the Sanctum by the Daughters. It's a great honor. He explains that the Daughters are the ruling queens of Sevenset. One appointed as the representative of Glacius and the other on behalf of Magness. I miss the mini-lesson on the Imago government, though, as the news drives through me like an iron spike. Isadora has been accepted by the most powerful members of Imago society. The closer she is to them, the more power she has. My life might be in her hands already, and I just don't know it yet.

One morning, our routine is thrown off when Parvin announces that Holly's gone missing. Speaker finds her a kilometer away from the base. She manipulated her nyxia into an ax and started felling trees. By the time we found her, she had enough firewood for a few days. Speaker reminds us that there is a treatment in the works, but the sight drives home just how lost Holly is to us right now.

On the eighth day of mining, we finally reach capacity. It's the day Anton has been preparing for. Kit shows us the maps of the area. We've hit just about every mine within a 150-kilometer radius. Black dots spiral around a second

Babel emblem well to the north. Kit highlights the marked tower.

"Myriad Station." He can't keep the sigh out of his voice. "It's time to send you Corporal West's way. I'll just go ahead and warn you, he's not exactly Mr. Personality, but he's serious about the job, so at least you'll feel taken care of and all that. You'll have to travel by boat. The midsection of Grimgarden gets gutted by riverways and swamps. No real alternatives there."

He swipes the screen and we all get a glimpse of the silo metrics. The entire payload has filled it to the brim, and the digital readout has all our extra nyxia labeled off to one side.

"Here's what you've gathered," Kit explains. "Want to go up and take a look?"

Everyone agrees to go. We're laughing and joking, moving out across the field, when Morning shoots Anton a look. He gives the barest nod and I feel a chill run down my spine. He's been ready to go at a moment's notice for days. It feels impossible that he might actually launch back into space. This could change *everything*. As we walk, Alex slows so he's stride for stride with Anton. He reaches out and takes Anton's hand in his. For just a second, they look like two boys walking down the streets of Bogotá. Like a touch of hands has dragged them both through space, back to the place Alex calls home. It's a glimpse of some unwritten future with Alex guiding Anton through the streets he knows best and sharing a life free of Babel's shadow.

In the here and now, all of that feels so far away. I watch, and the two of them say their silent goodbye with each step, each not knowing if the other will be safe where he's headed.

One by one, we climb the ladder of the silo. Jazzy panics halfway up, and Azima has to shove her on from behind. A catwalk circles the silo, and a command from Kit has the roof retracting. We all stare down at the endless stacks of nyxia. Just a bunch of poor kids who Babel thought they could manipulate. I try to remember that *we* did this. *We* earned this.

"So that's what thirty billion dollars looks like?" Katsu asks.

"I could buy an entire *country* with that kind of money," Jaime says.

There's this undeniable moment where we're all kids again. Smiles trace their way through the group, and everyone imagines what it would be like to be that rich.

"I would buy a football team," Omar says. "Barcelona, maybe?"

"I was going to say the same thing!" Noor exclaims, smiling wide. "Except *Barcelona*? Are you out of your mind? Come on you, Gunners! Give me Arsenal *any* day."

Longwei smiles. "I would start my own company. Move to Shanghai."

Azima leans forward excitedly. "I want to buy Victoria Falls. Once they're mine, I'll name them something else. A name that doesn't taste so much like milk."

"Can you buy waterfalls?" Jaime asks.

Azima looks confused. "I thought we were playing a game."

"We were," Parvin says kindly. "I would buy a zoo. I've always wanted a zoo. And I know Holly can't answer for herself right now. . . ."

We all glance that way. Holly's climbed the tower with us, obedient as ever, but she's staring off into the distance, seemingly unaware. Parvin takes her friend's hand in hers.

"But she always talked about using her winnings to start a boxing school in Ireland. Girls only." Parvin smiles. "So for now, let's say she'd start hundreds of boxing schools. She'd make a whole generation of girls with a right hook just like hers."

Quiet nods of agreement make their way around the circle. Beside Parvin, Alex runs a hand through his blond curls when he realizes it's his turn.

"I don't know," he says. "I'd let hungry kids eat whatever they want, I guess."

There's something about the way his jaw tightens, about the way he avoids eye contact after he says it, that crushes me. To his right, Jazzy's cheeks blossom a bright red.

"Well, I'm embarrassed. I was going to buy an amusement park."

"It's cool," Alex says. "Just let the kids from my thing have free tickets, yeah?"

She nods her agreement. That leaves Katsu, Morning, and me. I can feel the others waiting for us to say *something*, but I don't want to talk about what I want to buy. It hurts too much to know it'll never happen. Babel promised they'd make me rich, but even that prize money is starting to feel like a pipe dream.

I know Babel's given my parents a few payments, but

what happens if the money stops? What happens if we fail? I had dreams of going back and being a millionaire, sure. I wanted to help the people in my neighborhood. I wanted to go back and carve something better out of what I left behind. Why dream of that, though, if I can't even make the little dreams come true?

Morning's watching me like she knows exactly what I'm thinking. She looks down at the pile of money and shakes her head like it's just tainted treasure. We're both saved from the awkwardness of answering by Katsu, who laughs loud enough to shake the railings.

"Three words," he says. "Huge. Tower. Of Jell-O."

Azima pats his shoulder gently. "That's four words, Katsu."

"You're no longer invited. The rest of you can come."

The whole group laughs at that. I can't say how thankful I am for Katsu's jokes, for Morning's smile. Looking around the tower, I realize these faces are the only thing I'm still fighting for out here. There's Moms and Pops back home. Earth waits like some distant, guarded prize. But it's these faces that keep me breathing and fighting. It's these people who will stand shoulder to shoulder with me in whatever fight's waiting for us.

The only outsider, Kit, leads us back down the silo. No one comments, but everyone notices that one member of the Genesis crew isn't with us. We might never know what Anton would have spent all that money on. If I had to guess, I imagine he'd use it on a few good knives.

I imagine him, squirreled away somewhere inside the silo, waiting to launch back up into space right under Babel's nose. The rest of the group follows Morning's instructions. For the next hour, we create chaos. Games in the common space. Exploring the other hives. Asking Kit to walk us around the base. We force ourselves to move and move and move until the launch sequence activates. When it happens, we all stop and stare.

Except for Alex. I see him walking back to his room, his face full of grief.

No one asks if it worked. No one looks at Morning. We make sure that Anton's name stays out of our mouths. We watch as the massive pod streaks up through the atmosphere, and we offer up silent prayers that Anton can do the impossible.

I can't help smiling. Babel has no idea what's coming for them.

CHAPTER 16

THE BABEL FILES

Katherine Ford

My day begins at four in the morning and consists of thirty-minute intervals.

Review shipments. Meet executives. Phone China. Approve flight patterns. Email specifications to Roman. Memorize speeches. And then there is the current square: lunch.

A hopeful label, but lunch is rarely ever lunch. There are no signs of seared tuna or gorgonzola salad on my desk. Lunch consists, instead, of the day's fourth coffee and a buffet of reports. What didn't deserve its own square has been relegated here. A pendulum counts off the seconds as I glance through the latest analysis of media intelligence.

Approval rates are soaring. Defoe's plan effectively flipped the reporters who wrote the Babel Files. Their new documentary has been nominated for awards after making a splash on every major network. Interviews with the families of the winning contestants. How has the money already changed their lives?

Each redemptive narrative strengthens our case. Our

harshest critics are starting to sound desperate and unfeeling. When Jeremiah Atwater weeps in his interview, the nation cries with him. Poverty can be beaten. Cancer can be battled. Even the lowly can rise. To the press, we are darlings again. The bright promise of our past finally fulfilled. Thankfully, the truth of what we've done hides in wormholes only we can access.

A second report details our own leaks regarding nyxia. BBC announces it as a solution to impending epidemics. Other reports explore its uses for combating consumerism or the failing field of housing development. It is the dawn of a new age, a post-scarcity future. I sign a pair of documents that will release another leaked video documenting nyxian gravity sealants. Scientists will marvel at the endless potential.

Roman Beckett slips in halfway through my second signature.

"Ready for space?" he asks.

"All packed up. And we won't have any surprises this time?"

"One mistake and I'm the baby brother again," he laments. "No surprises. I spent all night looking through phone calls and surveillance. There's no one in on this one. Only the families know."

"Good," I say, handing him a folder. "The early reports look promising. We've been on planet for a week and the estimated take is already sixty-three billion."

"Call me when it's over one hundred," Roman replies. "How's plan A doing?"

"We have no idea. You know how our surveillance works

there. We've got eyes on the bases we built and little else. The tech helps, but the Adamites adapt quickly."

"It's the difference between billions and trillions."

"We haven't mined nyxia in twelve years. This mission is already a success."

He pauses. "Does it make sense for you to leave?"

I frown, scanning notes. It doesn't make sense. But this is the plan we set out years ago. Babel's getting ready to reach down and pluck the forbidden fruit. It's always been agreed that I should run that part of the show from the Tower. Still, leaving Roman to his own devices on Earth feels like such a glaring error. So much weight on such unsteady shoulders.

"You'll be fine. We've made the appropriate hires."

He raps both knuckles on the door frame. "Well, bon voyage, then."

I make a few final notations for Rogers to look over when he arrives. One more review of our prototypes and the amount we're dedicating to different industries. Roman's right. We sit on the precipice between billions and trillions. More than that. World could become worlds. Succeed, and one day people will identify themselves by what planet they were born on rather than which country.

I press a button. "Lydia, my suitcases please."

The door opens and my secretary gestures. Two men remove the bags from a corner and vanish. Lydia hovers after they've gone. "Good luck, Ms. Ford."

I smile. "Take care of yourself, Lydia. Rogers is a benevolent sort of overlord."

The secretary nods and exits. I stand before the mirror and make minor adjustments. My business suit is dark, like smoke threaded into formal wear. A gift from Marcus. An appropriate sort of armor for what is to come.

I take a back door out. Down three flights of stairs, through two air locks, and into the bright, futuristic room. Ten faces glance up as I cross to the front. Babel officials wait there, offering their regal and important nods. I turn to address the children.

"You all know why you're here," I say, and my words weave out in four different languages, slithering through ears and worming down into hopeful hearts. "You were chosen to be at the forefront of the most serious space exploration known to mankind. The results of your mission will change the outlook for our species. The reward for your efforts will be beyond your imagination."

PART II

THE GENESIS

CHAPTER 17

GRIMGARDEN

Emmett Atwater

The next morning we're all suited up, lined up, looking pristine. The group waits in front of a screen that's descended out of one of Foundry's interior walls. My stomach twists itself in knots as the feed statics to life. Kit presses a button and retreats to his place in the line.

Babel. Our employers, our enemies. A certain hatred snaps to life at the sight of David Requin on the screen. He smiles like he didn't try to make us murderers. I glance over at Jaime. Kid looks ready to breathe fire.

"Good afternoon," Requin says. "We've received your first shipment. The nyxian output has been beyond our early projections. Extra incentives are being sent out now. At present, each of your families has received two hundred and eighty thousand dollars. It seems your dedication is already paying off."

No one says anything; no one smiles. The money is why we came, but we have no idea if what he's saying is true or not. Every single one of us heard his voice on that recording.

We know their true intentions; we know what's beneath the crisp suits and fake smiles.

Morning replies diplomatically, "Thank you, sir."

Requin swipes the air, and we can tell he's looking at his own map of Grimgarden. His eyes trace our progress, and all the black dots that remain unconquered.

"You will continue to Myriad," Requin says. "Most of the remaining mines are concentrated in the northeastern regions of the continent. Our systems have highlighted the safest routes through the riverways, but I've no doubt you'll blaze your own trails north."

"What about Holly?" Morning asks. "Are you aware of what happened to her?"

Requin nods slowly. "It was in Kit's report to us. From what I understand, the plan is to treat her when you arrive in Sevenset?"

"It is," Morning says. "But you could push that through. A word from you, and the Ima—the Adamites would escort her now."

"She's not a danger to you, is she?"

Morning shakes her head. "I don't believe so."

"And she's still working," Requin points out. It's exactly the kind of heartless line I expected from him. "Let's not break with protocol. She'll be treated soon enough."

I can see Morning trying to swallow her anger. She's quick to move on to the next subject before she says something she'll regret. "And the Adamites?"

Requin nods. "Everything has gone as expected. They have honored the Interstellar Contract. It outlines that you will spend seven days at Myriad Station. You'll then move on to Ophelia Station for another seven days. Your stay at Foundry was slightly longer than expected, but there are provisions that address that in the contract. Please be diplomatic. You are righting the mistakes of our early negotiations. When they ask you to Sevenset, you are to accept their invitation."

"And after Sevenset?" Morning asks calmly. "How much longer will we be mining?"

Requin offers a smile. It's meant to be reassuring, but he looks more dangerous instead. It's the kind of smile that's been dredged up from the darkest corners of the ocean.

"The agreement all of you signed was for one year."

" 'Was'?" Morning emphasizes the word. "Has the agreement changed?"

"It's entirely possible you will return earlier," Requin replies.

It takes effort to keep my hands calm and at my side. I fight the instinct to bunch them into fists. Requin is lying. Every word he says drips with promises he never intends to deliver. Doesn't he get that we've scraped through the first layer of gold? All of us know now that, underneath the surface, everything Babel's offering us is just rusted treasure.

"Our people are working through the numbers," Requin continues. "In our business model, there's a sustainable intake that, if reached, would allow us to conduct operations the way we desire. If your groups can produce the right amount, going home early seems likely."

No one says a word. We've heard Babel talk like this before. I realize they can't actually expect us to believe any of it. They're smarter than that. All Requin's doing is keeping up the cat-and-mouse game they started in space. Let things unfold. Show no tells. Always keep control.

"Is there anything else, sir?" Morning asks.

"Anton." That one word cuts like a knife through our group. Requin's eyes sweep through the ranks, tracing our faces for intentions and secrets. I look steel back at him. "Where did our Anton go?"

We've worked to spread a few rumors. Kit's overheard a couple of them, and there's no telling what he took back to Babel. Morning shakes her head and puts on a playacted frustration.

"We had a difference of opinions."

"Oh?" Requin arches a silver eyebrow. "Did this happen during your *private* meeting?"

Morning doesn't even flinch at that accusation. "It did. Like Isadora and Ida, we believe it was Anton's intent to move on to Sevenset and attempt to secure better . . . partners."

"Better than you?" Requin asks. "Or better than us?"

"Both." Morning lets an embarrassed shade of red color her cheeks. "If he can't obey simple commands, follow *my* orders, he's not useful to me anyway."

Requin sifts through her words, searching for lies. After a pause, though, he nods.

"Consider his recovery a secondary mission. Isadora's and Ida's decision has already complicated our plans enough. I'd rather we continue following protocol in our relationship with the Adamites. It's paramount that they allow mining operations to continue." Requin glances through a stack of papers. "Let's get you all moving north. Godspeed."

The feed cuts. Our crew lifts knapsacks and follows Kit out into an overcast morning. Speaker and the other escorts wait at the boundary of the base. I blink my scouter back to the map setting and find our new location pinged there.

Kit stands there, looking like an awkward teenager who just got turned down for a prom date. He heaves the biggest sigh I've ever heard. "I'm totally going to miss you guys."

There's a second where no one really knows what to say, and then Kit turns to Longwei and wraps him in a hug. Longwei shoots us a *what the hell?* look over Kit's shoulder before managing to hug him gently back. It takes a few minutes for Kit to work his way down the line, saying his goodbyes to all of us like this is the end of a damn summer camp. He even tries to give Holly a hug, though she ignores him completely.

When he gets to me, he grins.

"Let's watch a few *Illuminauts* episodes when you get back."

I nod at him, feeling a little numb. How can Kit think there's a next time waiting around the corner for us? My anger at Babel flickers back to life. Did they lie to Kit the same way they lied to us? They're successfully making all the distant battlefields murkier. If our lives are on the line, we're going to fight, but it would be a lot easier if we had obvious enemies in the crosshairs.

The Imago escorts lead us away from Foundry. We walk until we reach the crooking elbow of the adjacent river. On the map I can see that this is actually a meeting point of five different rivers, which rope through the terrain like tentacles. Kit was right. For about fifty kilometers, there's not a single section of land that isn't diced into pieces by rivers and creeks and lakes. I'm surprised, though, when we spot a massive complex looming out through the trees.

Speaker gestures that way. "We are passing the site that gave this continent its name: Grimgarden."

It almost looks like a mansion. Three connected towers angle skyward, windows broken, their lowest stories consumed by ivy and underbrush. Only a few strings of bright flowers offer their color to the dark face of the long-faded building.

Speaker's quiet voice barely carries over the river's distant thunder. "Named for a general who made his home here. Back in a time when our people still warred with one another. Thousands died on this plain. Thousands more died in defense of that river crossing. The general lived in Grimgarden and dedicated the last years of his life to burying the dead. We do not know his name."

Speaker smiles at the thought.

"He did not believe he should be remembered. Too many men died at his command. So he had his name torn from every record. He succeeded in removing his name, but no one can remove the legacy of his honor. The entire continent was renamed in memoriam: Grimgarden."

We watch all three Imago stride toward the grounds, take a knee, offer a quiet word. We're all a little shocked when Holly follows them and takes a knee as well. I glance over at Morning, but she shrugs like *who the hell knows?* There's something so sacred about it all that even Katsu doesn't make any jokes.

Around the next bend, two pristine boats wait for us.

They're almost flawless copies of the ships we practiced with in the Waterway. I turn to say something to Morning and find Omar striding next to me instead. It's easy to forget how massive he is until he's right in your face.

"Absent Anton, I am forced to step in as a chaperone."

Morning smacks his arm from the other side. "Seriously, Omar?"

"You realize Anton wasn't chaperoning us."

Omar makes a two-fingered gesture, pointing at his eyes and then at me.

"I am watching your every move," he says. "Morning is . . . a delicate flower that—"

His sentence gets cut in two as Morning takes his massive arm into a painful twist behind his back. A sharp gasp escapes his lips. "A delicate *what*?" she asks.

Omar grunts his answer. ". . . warrior queen?"

She releases him, grinning. "That's more like it."

In two strides, though, he's back between us.

"She might be able to beat me up," Omar admits. "But I'm bigger than *you*. Keep that in mind. And don't forget: I'm watching you."

Morning groans. "Don't you have someone else to talk to? Someone *you* like?"

Omar shoots Morning a betrayed look, like she's just revealed one of his darkest secrets. His eyes dart toward Parvin. "I don't know what you're talking about."

Ahead of us, the front group has reached the boats. Longwei and Holly work the ropes, pulling them closer to shore. I follow Morning forward, but a question from Azima catches everyone's attention. "Speaker! Are the rivers dangerous?"

He exchanges a glance with Beckway and Bally. "No more than the land."

Azima turns back to us. "So it's safe to say we could have a small competition?"

That has the rest of the group grinning.

"Genesis 11 against Genesis 12?" Azima suggests. "Last time *we* won."

Alex wags an obnoxious finger. "And what happened the fifty times before that? We spent a whole month *crushing* you."

"Haven't you heard?" Katsu snipes. "You're only as good as your last game."

That has the Genesis 12 crew calling out insults. Morning's eyes dart from her crew to me and I realize she doesn't like the idea of splitting up out here in the unknown.

"Look," she says out loud. "We're trying to get there *safely.* It's not a competition."

I'm surprised when Longwei leans into the conversation.

"Will that be your excuse when we win?"

It's impossible to *not* laugh at the idea of Longwei talking smack. Katsu shakes him by the shoulders, like he just hit Morning with the deepest dig ever. Morning's concerns about separating from me burn to nothing as the heat of competition rises.

She takes a long look at her old team.

"To your stations," she orders. "First one to Myriad wins."

CHAPTER 18

OLD RIVALRIES

Emmett Atwater

Genesis 12 lets out a series of whoops and shouts. Following Morning is so bone-deep that even Holly boards their ship and takes her usual station. Omar lifts both of his gigantic fists into the air like they've already sealed the victory. I shake my head with surprise when the entire Genesis 11 group rallies in a circle around me.

Longwei nods to the back of the ship. "I'll take the engine again."

Katsu wraps an arm around Jaime. "Drivers."

"I'm up front," Jazzy says. "Eye on the prize, y'all."

Azima's already hoisting herself up onto the deck. "I want to hit something!"

I raise an eyebrow. "So that leaves me . . ."

"As the captain," Longwei confirms, nodding his respect. "That's what you are."

I almost laugh. "I thought I was a bad captain?"

Katsu slaps my shoulder. "You are, but don't worry, I was worse. Let's do this."

I smile and file this one under *S* for *Surprises*. Sometimes, my grandma used to say, you've gotta file the good things too. It takes a few minutes for us all to board, another few minutes to get used to the feel of the nyxian stations.

The captain's chair is linked to every station by nyxia. It runs out like a flattened web to touch the backs of each individual console. It's a powerful feeling. It's been long enough now to forget what it felt like after I handed the reins off to Katsu. The slightest attention connects me to any of the operations on the ship. I can feel Longwei firing up the engine. I sense Jazzy swiping through settings to analyze the landscape ahead. All at my fingertips.

Speaker joins our ship and takes his post at the defensive station opposite Azima.

"Bally will follow in a separate vessel and ensure our protection."

Across the way, Morning's giving orders. I can almost feel the thunder in her voice. She throws a look my way and smiles. "Thinking about boarding our ship again?"

"If I wanted to board," I say, smiling back in challenge, "I'd board."

The engines of both boats start to roar. Morning winks before turning back to crouch next to Parvin's display system. I turn my attention back to the ship, back to my crew.

"It's like day one on the Waterway," I say. "Empty scoreboard. Grudge match."

Longwei actually sighs. "I miss the scoreboard."

That has the others laughing. Over the noise, Jazzy's voice buzzes into the comm. She keeps it carefully at the volume of a whisper. "Emmett. I've got a route."

I cross the ship to stand at her shoulder. "Already?"

"Well . . ." Jazzy looks up guiltily. "I kind of cheated."

I laugh. "Cheated how?"

She shows me her screen. "I can see the route *they're* planning."

As we watch, highlighted directions start to extend through the convoluted riverway. I glance over to their ship. Morning and Parvin are bent over the screen, deep in discussion. Parvin traces a finger, and their plan continues to draw itself onto our map. I can't help laughing.

"But can't they see our screen?"

Jazzy shakes her head. "It's all in the screen-sharing interface. The two ships are linked, probably by design so we don't get too lost out here. But I've hidden our screen. So we have eyes on them and . . ." Jazzy shrugs. "They can't see us."

I laugh again. "Perfect. Hey, Speak. Can you come take a look?"

He crosses over and examines the layout. "Impressive. They traced the paths ahead and eliminated the routes that eventually choke out, or wind unnecessarily." He leans over the forming map and double taps a split in the river. "I'd follow them until this point. They're cutting back, losing time, because they think these waterfalls aren't safe. I know a way across."

Jazzy marks the location and logs the rest of their route into our system. She grins back when it's done. "Great find, Jazzy," I say with a nod. "And thanks, Speak."

A look shows Morning's back in her captain's chair. She nods over to me.

"Two minutes?"

"Sounds good."

Our crew's looking comfortable at their stations, but the sight of Morning reminds me who we're up against. This is the same Genesis 12 team that destroyed us for an entire month.

We need an edge.

"Listen up." I let my voice whisper through the nyxian connections. "I want to try something. Jazzy, I want you to start. Push your energy toward Speaker. Speak, I want you to push yours to Katsu. Katsu to Longwei. And so on. All around the ship. Understand?"

"Is this really the time to try something new?" Jaime asks.

But Speaker's voice follows. He's either curious or concerned or both.

"How do you know how to do that?"

I shrug. "Picked up a few tricks. Let's try it out."

Speaker raises a curious eyebrow as the power around us shifts. Jazzy directs her energy to him. He glances back at me before shoving the energy around. The others follow suit, and before long I can feel the rhythm of the nyxia turning in circles around me. It revolves three times before picking up its own momentum. Longwei's the first to understand.

"Power," he says. "That's a *lot* of power."

"Keep it orbiting," I whisper. "If we can sustain the rhythm, all we have to do is pull from the energy it's making to do our manipulations. Everyone fathom?"

There are nods all around. Speaker shoots me another curious look, but says nothing.

Morning cups her hands. "Ten seconds!"

The engines throw out revolutions. Longwei's eyes are wide as he prepares to use the power at his fingertips. Both crews grip the railings, leaning forward in anticipation.

"Five seconds!"

Time slows to nothing. My vision of the river narrows. It's our ship and their ship and a single streak of waiting blue. Morning shouts, and both engines roar as we fire through the water like missiles. The entire crew lurches back in their seats, but Longwei steadies the power after a few seconds. The front of our ship pushes out past Genesis 12. Morning eyes us with suspicion as the lead increases, a full length around the first curve of the river. I glance back long enough to see her eyes go wide as she realizes what I'm doing. I can hear her shouting new orders.

"Let's hear some readouts, Jazzy," I call back.

She sounds off a few warnings. Jaime and Katsu work to make adjustments as we cruise around another bend. A dense island waits in the distance. The river ropes around each side of it, each split no wider than thirty meters or so. "Taking the western split."

Katsu and Jaime swing us that way. I have half an eye on the unfolding universe of the river. The water is dark enough to hide its dangers. The banks are overgrown too. Everything in the Imago's world feels like it's at war with something else.

But the rest of the time I'm glancing back at Genesis 12. Morning's marching around, giving orders. They're moving faster, but I'm guessing she's still getting them used to the shared nyxian manipulation.

"Rocks on our right!" Jazzy calls.

Jaime's voice shakes through the comm. "We can't cut that hard at this speed."

The boat tilts the right way, but I can tell we're coming on too fast. I'm about to order Longwei to dial back the power when Azima manipulates her defense station. She forms the gigantic hand she always liked to use in the Waterway. We watch as she lowers it, cupping the water with a massive palm.

Our boat's nose pivots just enough. Everyone holds their breath as the side scrapes harmlessly past the rocks and Azima raises her station out of the water.

"Great work, Azima," I say. "Let's keep it moving."

The next few kilometers pass quickly. Morning pushes her crew within five hundred meters, but we're firing on all cylinders too.

"We're approaching the marked split," Jazzy announces.

"Let's put on a show," I say. "Make it look like we screwed up."

Jazzy nods. We glide over the water, heading directly toward the staggering stones that mark the waiting divide. Genesis 12 keeps the pace. At the last possible second, I make the call.

"Move us east."

Our boat dives that way. Genesis 12 glides the opposite. I look back and throw them my most surprised look. I try to make my voice loud enough so they'll hear every word.

"No! Back that way! Come on, Jazzy!"

The engines roar, and we catch a final glimpse of their crew before a veil of riverside trees swallows everything.

"You still have a ways to go in your acting career," Jaime snarks.

Katsu laughs. "And the award for Worst Dramatic Role as a Ship Captain goes to . . ."

I laugh. "I will throw both of you overboard. Speak is probably honor-bound to save your sorry asses because of the treaty, but that won't stop me from doing it."

They exchange a look and laugh again. I shake my head before eyeing the riverway. The sudden absence of Genesis 12 brings out the wonders of Grimgarden. It was easy to think that this was *our* river. That's what living on Earth has taught us. We can treat anything like it belongs to us. It's clear, though, that we're nothing more than guests here.

The normal inhabitants have taken note of our passing.

We see a pair of fish streak through the water on our right before breaching. Their scaled bodies spiral out, unexpected wings flung wide. Water splashes in an arc as they flap through the air and cut overhead, eager to duck back into the cover of trees.

Jazzy keeps scanning around every corner, relaying potential dangers or asking for more speed when the scans come back clear. The orbiting power of the nyxia continues to hum in startling harmony. I think about the first time Morning taught me how to do it, how our steps synched up effortlessly. The same thing is happening now.

I can sense each moment before it comes. It's like precognition. A feeling that says Longwei's about to gun the engine or Jaime's about to shift our rudders. Speaker's reaction is telling too. We have a knowledge he didn't expect us to have.

Halfway to Myriad Station, a golden glow highlights the water in front of our ship. Jazzy points out the glittering lights, and Speaker explains, "Looklocks."

Their bright pattern extends out like an arrow. Jazzy watches them long enough to notice the pattern. "They're taking all the right turns. How do they know which way we're going?"

"Intuition," Speaker answers. "The looklocks will choose correctly for a while. Twenty turns. Fifty turns. Long enough to lure you into trusting them."

"And then what happens?" Azima asks, fascinated.

"The very moment you stop attending your instruments and start trusting their lead, they will take a turn that goes nowhere. They will distract you into a bank or a sandbar. After the crash, they'll feed on the dead."

"Everything out here is so lethal," Jaime complains. "Next you'll be telling us to avoid stepping on fallen leaves or something."

"That is a sound practice," Speaker replies, missing Jaime's sarcasm. "The graya create traps beneath the larger piles. It is always better to avoid them."

Jaime looks around at us and just shakes his head.

The golden school of looklocks highlights our way for a while, but their own hunt is interrupted by another. Azima points to a nest hanging from a tree on the eastern banks. It looks just like a massive beehive, but the entryways are bigger than my head.

I'd rather not meet an insect that needs a home that big.

"A vayan nest," Speaker announces. "They're one of the—"

But movement cuts off his sentence. Three creatures—

vayans, apparently—come spiraling through the dark door-
ways of the hanging nest. The creatures' muscled bodies are
the color of steel, and they're no bigger than basketballs. All
three of them land in the water, frantic limbs fighting gravity, and then they're up.

My eyes struggle to follow their mad dash over the surface of the water. The school of looklocks either sees or hears
their approach, because the golden glow vanishes instantly.

But that doesn't stop the hunters. Silver tongues stab
down through the water like spears. Each vayan circles as
our ship passes, busy jaws crunching down on their catches
before making a path back to their nest.

For the next few kilometers, we forget we're in the middle of a race. We don't slow the pace, but all of us watch
the river in the hope of witnessing more miracles. Finally
we're getting the hang of being the first human explorers
on an alien planet. Speaker explains which distant bellows
go with what creatures. He does his best to differentiate
animals based on their splashes or by the residue they leave
along the riverbank.

Longwei spots a trio of birds wheeling in the western
sky. They're the first creatures moving slowly enough for
my scouter to actually identify. The word *dirk* dances into
view.

Speaker lets out a relieved sigh when the birds change
course, vanishing beneath the cover of clouds. "What's up,
Speak?" I ask. "Are dirks dangerous or something?"

"In a way," he answers. "They are an indicator of danger.
They know where there will be bloodshed. They feed exclu-
sively on the dead."

I nod to him. "Like vultures. They always show up when animals die on the side of the road in our world."

"Many animals eat the dead," Speaker admits. "Dirks are different. They arrive *before* the death. Their arrival is more of a prophecy. Death will visit that place. It's an unnatural quality. We believe they gain insight by imbibing on the dead. A sense of who or what will die next. I will always be glad to see them turn away from us."

Speaker guides us through the tighter passes in the river. We make good time, good enough time to feel like we have a chance at winning. I can't stop my eyes from occasionally flicking up to the west, searching for the carrion birds. A few times I think I've spotted them, wheeling through the trees, but by the time our line of sight clears, there's nothing but clouds.

CHAPTER 19

MYRIAD STATION

———

Emmett Atwater

Jazzy's the first one to spot Myriad Station in the distance.

It looks like an old man sitting on the riverbank, gray-green shoulders hunched, feet dangling in the river. Our approach sharpens all the details. There's the main building riding along the banks, then two parallel bridges that connect with another building. The second structure sits fifty meters out on the river and looks like a faded pearl.

We can see water rushing through massive intake valves at the base of the structure. My mind runs back through images from science classes, faded hydraulics charts in textbooks that were usually older than me. Jazzy pings a location near the south face of the main building. I squint through the approaching dark and spy a pair of docks waiting in the distance.

"No sign of Genesis 12?" I ask.

Jazzy smiles back. "Nothing on the scans."

Azima raises both arms in triumph. It feels *good* to win.

"Take us in."

There's a slight shift, like a passing breeze, as Jaime and Katsu direct us that way. Speaker rises from his station as we cross into Babel territory. He looks uncomfortable.

"Where did you learn to use the substance that way?" he whispers.

"Morning figured it out."

He lifts an eyebrow. "That's a unique method. Not one we thought Babel knew."

"They still don't. Do you know why it works that way? Why's it so much stronger?"

Speaker considers the question carefully. "It's a return to the substance's natural state."

"Natural state?" I ask, confused now. "But it's buried in the ground."

I can tell I've pushed Speaker to the edge of his comfort. He shakes his head.

"This is a topic best left to the experts in Sevenset. We can discuss it there."

I nod a concession as the boat bumps the docks. It's a fair request from Speaker. Why discuss trade secrets in one of the only places Babel can call a stronghold? My mind skips from the discussion back to the base. Corporal West should be waiting for us. I'm trying to imagine what he'll be like. Kit had a boundless energy, an almost innocence.

But no one comes striding down the docks. No lights flick on in the building. Instead the sun continues to set as Azima leaps down and starts tying us up, a grin on her face.

"We win again," she says. "Nice call, Emmett."

I nod back, but now my mind's racing in a few different directions. I'm not sure why West hasn't come out yet, or at

least given some sign that we should come in. And there's
the annoying itch of fear for Morning too. It's not like her to
lose, at least not by this much.

"Let's make contact with West," I say. "Then we'll come
back and check on Genesis 12."

Our approach, though, is greeted with silence. A sense
of dread snakes through my gut, and I decide to go with the
feeling. "Weapons out. Just in case."

We reach a section of the docks that runs parallel to the
river. A single arched doorway has been carved into the side
of Myriad about one hundred meters ahead. My eyes don't
stop moving. I've got that walking-on-the-wrong-street-at-
the-wrong-time feeling deep in my gut.

There's only the river, the building, our footsteps. The
dock brings us into Myriad's shadow. No signs of West. No
signs of anything.

"Inside," I order. "Let's keep close. Eyes open."

But before we can reach for the door, it shoves open.
Holly marches out and holds it in place, eyes empty, posture
rigid. We all stare at her as groans echo from inside.

"Damn it!" Alex's voice sounds from within. "She ruined
the surprise."

Our group stumbles inside, up a double-wide ramp, and
into a common room that's almost identical to the one in
Foundry. Someone flips on the lights, and we spy members
of Genesis 12 hidden around the room like they were preparing for a surprise party. Morning grins down at us from
the balcony above.

"I told you that I don't lose."

Speaker stares in confusion. Our whole crew does.

"But we didn't see your boat," Jazzy says.

Parvin adjusts her glasses. "That was kind of the point."

Morning gives her team a few moments to glory in their win before pointing out the obvious elephant in the room. "Now that that's out of the way, what do you say we go find Corporal West? I'm guessing you didn't see him on your way in?"

"No sign of him."

"We found signs of him," Morning says, nodding to the entrance. "Just didn't want to investigate until we knew you had safely arrived . . . after we arrived, of course."

I shake my head at the dig. "Lead the way, Captain."

The whole crew moves toward the doors. The land-side entrance overlooks a stretching plain. With the sun almost fully set, we can just make out another river cutting a path to the east. Morning gestures to a set of tire tracks running downhill, a little south. A standard Babel knapsack sits right where they begin. It's unzipped, half the contents spilled onto the ground.

"Corporal West went for a little joyride," Katsu says.

"Maybe," Morning admits. "I think it's worth sending a group out after him."

It takes about two seconds to figure out what she means. "Let me guess. Your prize for winning is kicking your feet up in the base while *we* investigate?"

Morning raises one eyebrow. "Do you even know me? Our prize for winning is that *we* get to go investigate. Enjoy holding down the fort while we have all the fun, second place."

It's not hard to see why Morning was such a good leader. She's smart enough to make every task seem like fun.

There's no complaint from anyone on Genesis 12. Her intensity is infectious, and in seconds the whole crew looks ready to march across the planet for her. Bally, Beckway, and Speaker have a quick discussion. They decide that Speaker will stay behind with us.

Morning takes a second to walk over and stand next to me, all smiles.

"You know, you look pretty damn cute when you're mad."

"Who said I was mad?"

"There's this thing you do with your eyebrow. . . ."

I stare blankly at her. "What thing?"

"Oh," she says, laughing to herself. "You don't even know you do it, do you?"

She gives my hip a little bump before marching off, barking orders, becoming the commander again. I stare after her. "What thing?"

It takes about two minutes for the ranks of Genesis 12 to form up. Morning hands the lead to Bally, who knows the area better than any of them. We watch as they descend into the darkening valley. One by one, their figures merge with the landscape until they're all gone.

Our group returns to Myriad. Katsu heads straight for the kitchens, while Jazzy and Azima start up a conversation with Speaker about sports in Sevenset. I'm thinking a bed sounds like a good idea when the realization strikes like lightning: Corporal West isn't in the base.

Jaime looks ready to join the others before he notices the look I'm throwing his way. I nod over to one side and shoulder my knapsack. He walks smoothly past the conversation and heads in my direction.

"What? Is something wrong?"

"West isn't here. Seems like a good time to visit the med bay and patch you up."

Understanding clicks into place. "You think there are more of them?"

"Only one way to find out."

Jaime adjusts his scouter. I watch as he blinks through a few settings and then gives the voiced command. "I need to go to the medical bay."

The visor panel of his scouter flashes with light. Jaime blinks once, and my own scouter lights up with an access request. I nod at the accept button, and an actual blue line holograms into my vision, leading us on through the base. "The hell . . . How do you know how to do that?"

"I read the instructions," Jaime says. "Didn't you?"

I shrug. "I've kind of just been winging it. How much time do we have?"

"Depends how fast your girlfriend finds West."

I raise an eyebrow at that.

"What?" he asks.

"My girlfriend?"

"Aren't you—I thought—Morning . . ."

"Next subject," I suggest.

Jaime shakes his head as we turn down the first hallway and run right into Longwei. All my red flags go up for some reason. I start to throw out an excuse, give him some reason we're wandering off through the base, when Jaime says, "Want to see the frozen soldiers?"

Longwei's eyes narrow. "How many?"

He asks it like there's a certain amount that's *really* worth his time.

"Seventy?" Jaime guesses. "Trust me, you want to see this."

Longwei takes a second before nodding. "Let's go."

And just like that the three of us are moving through the halls. I don't know why my first instinct was to exclude Longwei. I'm glad Jaime invited him, though, because maybe that was all it really took. He might have said no aboard *Genesis 11,* but now? A lot has changed.

We might not ever be close friends, but at least we're not staring at scoreboards every night before we go to bed. We're *together* down here. We need each other to survive. I need to start remembering that, even about my oldest rival.

The route takes us back to the waterside half of the building. Outside, I can hear the river churning past. It's just loud enough that I almost miss the footsteps. Jaime and Longwei *do* miss them. In less than a breath, I've got them both by the collars of their suits and I'm dragging them into a maintenance room. The footsteps echo louder and louder.

From the shadow of the room, we all watch Holly walk past. She marches toward whatever task is waiting down the hall, looking lost as hell. The second she turns the corner, we're back on the move. Jaime gives me a nod. "Nice one."

Longwei says, "You could have just told us to watch out."

I try to ignore that as the route takes us outside, across the first of the two bridges that connect Myriad with its floating counterpart. Jaime looks for signs of movement along the docks before signaling us across. We keep low, moving patiently. One left turn, up a flight of stairs, and we're standing in front of a familiar door. Jaime pushes it open and lights flick on.

It's the exact same layout as Foundry's med room. Three gurneys arranged in a half circle. A sink built into one corner. Stacks of medical supplies in a makeshift shelving system.

I cross the room and shove aside the center gurney. There are no scuff marks along the edge, but that doesn't mean the trapdoor isn't there. It just means Corporal West had less reason to visit his batch of frozen marines. Or he was more careful about it. My finger snags on an edge and I trace it up to the latch. One solid tug has the whole thing folding upward.

"We're getting good at this," Jaime says.

Longwei eyes the hidden passage. "Is it dangerous?"

"Only if you wake them up," I reply with a smile.

The stairwell leads to a familiar hatch-wheeled door. Two spins are all it takes to bring us face to face with Babel's finest. Body after body, lining the walls like toy soldiers waiting to be activated. Jaime strides forward. I can see his fists are clenched.

"More soldiers," he says. "They've got an army down here."

Longwei reaches up to touch the glass front. "It's like the terra-cotta army. I saw them when I was a child. I didn't want to go too far into the room. I was afraid they might come to life."

"I don't know about those," I reply. "But these ones require a code for activation. Come on, let's get back to the others. We needed to come down here and confirm this. We'll take it back to Morning now. This is pretty good ammunition for our negotiations with the Imago."

Longwei starts walking back toward the entrance, but Jaime holds his ground.

"It's not enough."

A hum shakes the air. He manipulates his nyxia. I can't make out the shape he's chosen until he takes a swing. His blunted crowbar lands against the glass. One swing and it almost shatters. Jaime takes a second swing and a third. I stand there, frozen, as Longwei's instincts finally kick in. Broken glass rains from overhead as Longwei reaches him.

My body finally swings into motion.

"Jaime!" I shout. "Cool it, man!"

Longwei pulls him to one side, struggling. Anger burns in Jaime's eyes. It reaches down through the veins of his neck. He tries to fight past Longwei and finish the job.

A hiss of air sounds. The damage has already been done. All three of us look up as the glowing green dot above the unlucky marine starts to flicker to red. Cracks web their way through the entire glass panel. "Get him out! Longwei, move him!"

Jaime fumbles his crowbar as Longwei stumbles with him toward the entrance. I slide past them, careful to avoid the glass. There's a matching keypad at the base of the marine's cryogenic chamber, but Kit never told us the code. West isn't even at the base.

He might die.

I snatch Jaime's fallen weapon. It takes a second to force the image forward, manipulating the substance that was responding to Jaime's touch just seconds before. I picture the same substance I used to lock Roathy out of the launch pod.

The nyxia reaches back through my thoughts, carving

itself into the right form. The black spreads in a crackling wave. I give the substance a helpful shove, glass crunching underfoot, until the whole thing suctions to the corners. It seals the dying marine inside.

I'm not sure if I'm saving him or killing him, but the second the air stabilizes, the red light flickers back to green. I wait for a minute. The light stays green. I let out a huge sigh of relief and move back to the entrance.

Jaime stands off to one side, looking like a punk kid who got caught stealing something at the mall. I do my best to channel Pops as I grab him by the collar and pull him in close.

"Use your anger the *right* way."

He tries to shrug me off, but I don't let him loose.

"I'm serious, Jaime. These might be our enemies when they wake up. Or maybe they're just people Babel hired. Maybe Babel lied to them the same way they lied to us. We can't know that when they're in a sleep-freeze and suctioned to the inside of a buried spaceship. If you want to sink down to Babel's level, take shots at people who can't defend themselves, be my guest. Just don't involve me next time, fathom?"

He shakes his head. "If it was you in there, what would they do?"

"I'm not them. I don't plan to be."

Jaime looks ready to snap back, but instead he nods.

Longwei raises an eyebrow. "This is why I usually stay in my room."

I let out a laugh. "And miss out on all the fun?"

The three of us slip quietly back outside. Jaime's still hot with it as he leads us back over the bridge. All his anger and hate for Babel keeps building. I need to put out that fire before it burns in a direction dangerous enough to get him hurt.

Halfway across the bridge, there's movement. A figure emerges from the opposite end of the bridge, coming on quickly. Long, unpanicked strides. I squint through the shadows and can tell it's not one of the Genesis kids. It's an Imago.

"Speak?"

I'm running through excuses, reasons we were down here, when the light finally finds Speaker's face. And all the features are wrong. The approaching figure has a sharper chin, more angled eyes. A nyxian implant shades one eye like a swooping shadow.

Not Speaker.

Not a friend.

Jaime's caught midstep. I watch him flinch, legs frozen, as the stranger raises a blunt, pitch-black weapon. I remember— in the space of a single breath—that he's unarmed.

It swings down at an angle.

Longwei lowers a shoulder and knocks Jaime to one side. He pays for it too. The incoming blow catches him across one eye and sends him spiraling to the ground. Momentum has Jaime smashing into the stone railing. The weapon comes back around, seeking a new target.

My nyxia reacts faster than my thoughts can shape it. From my pocket to my hands, forming the familiar off hand of my boxing claws as it moves. All in less than a heartbeat. I answer the second blow with a raised arm and a firm step.

The Imago's eyes widen when I catch the blow, but he swings a second time, and a third. Each shot comes with such quick succession that I can only block the blows, stumbling back as I do. There's no time to think, no time to draw my other glove into existence, as the Imago presses forward.

Two more testing blows, then he spins away, grasping for my control of the nyxia. It's unexpected, but Babel trained me well. The claw starts to close around my hand, threatening to break every bone. A mental shoulder shoves the Imago back.

He gives a nod of admiration, then two more jabs, a hook. I deflect all three, but I can already feel my arms getting tired. Longwei's still down. Jaime's moving but can't seem to take his feet. The Imago retreats a step.

"You're worthy." The sound of the voice shocks me. It's softer, feminine. I stare at the intruder and realize for the first time he is a *she*. "You will be my new beginning."

I can't tell if I'm exhausted or if the words just don't make any sense. I'm heaving each breath, hands up and ready, when she flicks one wrist. The nyxian weapon retreats into a section of her belt. I'm watching the substance mist through the air, thinking that somehow I managed to scare her off, when she flicks her other wrist.

And for once, I'm too slow.

I see the glint too late, feel the prick before I can pull back, and now something's crawling up my throat. I stare at the Imago's satisfied face as it blurs, as the bridge spins beneath my feet. My arm goes numb first. Then my chest feels like it's locked up, beating against the bars of a steel cage. The stranger shows me a ring on her off hand. There's a hair-thin needle attached to the end of it. "Screwbone. An effective poison, is it not?"

My tongue's too heavy to answer. I try to form a fist, to throw a punch. She just laughs. There's a grunt as Jaime tries to rise but falls. The Imago knocks him aside before lifting me up. I can feel the pressure of her hold, but only distantly, like I've already half fallen out of my body. I can't make my eyes close. I can't move my neck.

Breathe. I have to tell myself to *breathe.*

"Be calm," she warns. "Get too worked up and your lungs won't be able to sustain it. It is not my intention to kill you, but I can't keep you from killing yourself if you panic."

She's not going to kill me.

My brain lashes itself to that thought. Not going to kill me. Not going to kill me. But why? Why poison me? Light flashes across my vision. We're moving.

Down a set of stairs. I can hear the river splashing. Everything feels dark and damp and dead. I'm set down on cold stones. Something splashes over my leg, and chills snake up my spine. The stranger cleans out my pockets of the only things that will make me dangerous.

Anything with nyxia: my gloves, my player, all of it. I have a blurry view of her shoving it into my abandoned knapsack before tossing it aside. I hear it land with a thunk before sliding out of reach.

I'm lowered into a boat.

There's a muted grunt. The engine roars to life.

And then the lights of Myriad start to fade.

CHAPTER 20

LIGHT IN THE DARK

Anton Stepanov

I move through the weightless dark.

It's been two days roaming around Babel's no-grav tunnels. I keep imagining them as the space station's organs. They're dark and vital and everyone forgets about them until they start to bleed. It took gutting an artery to lure in a friend.

A single beam of light dances in the distance. I dig my fingers into the nearest panel to keep myself from floating into sight. Babel's techie has been fussing with the control panel for a few minutes. I was counting on them sending someone in to give me a good map back out. She's middle-aged, with dark red hair and quick hands.

The task took her half the amount of time I thought it would.

Wires hang down from the back of a switchboard. The techie's replaced the pieces I fried and is bunching them together neatly, preparing to close the whole thing up and start back. I'm hoping she'll lead me to the nearest maintenance closet. I'd like to snag a few gadgets and make my life behind Babel's curtain a little easier. I need eyes on the station. I need to make contact with Vandemeer and our informant—Melissa Aguilar. But it's not as easy as pushing through an exit and hoping I land in the right room. If the wrong person sees me, this whole mission was for nothing.

A soft click announces the task completed.

Noiseless, I slip my fingers free of the wall panel. The slightest push sends me floating after the techie. She's more careful than I am, pulling herself along the wall, keeping tight to the slotted panels. I land soft along one corner of the tunnel before pushing off again.

Down the rabbit hole we go.

Her light leads me through the dark. We skip two tunnels before taking a right. I count fifty panels before she fully turns her body toward a slightly indented section. I let my fingers trail quietly along the ceiling, pulling my body to a stop. If she glances the wrong way and her eyesight's any good, she'll see there are monsters in the dark with her.

She doesn't look.

The panel slides up, and light forces its way into her section of the tunnel. I flatten my body to the wall just in case, but it takes her two seconds to slide into the light and close the panel behind her. I shove down the hallway and stop myself in front of her chosen exit. I press my ear to the door and listen. There's the gasp of an air lock. Footsteps. Nothing.

I take about three minutes to listen until I'm sure she's gone.

Carefully, I slide the panel up just enough to look out.

There's a bright room with enough space for two people. One of Babel's air locks faces a perpendicular hallway.

I count off the minutes in my head. I'm about to slide the panel up when a door directly across from the air lock opens. The red-haired techie waves to someone inside before slipping a utility belt back around her waist. She thumbs one of the devices and disappears down the hallway.

Follow the leader, I think.

The door's still open a sliver. My eyes trail the equipment hanging from the walls in neat stacks. My only hesitation is the techie's parting wave. Clearly someone's inside. Wait them out? Smoke them out? After a few restless seconds, I lift the panel and slide out into the light.

It's now or never. A quick manipulation draws my nyxia into the shape of a mask. I pull the soft material overhead. If there are Babel cameras waiting for me in the supply room, I want them thinking it's some on-ship vigilante. I'd like my identity to stay a question mark for as long as possible.

I adjust the eye holes and manipulate my knife into something less Anton. The dagger widens out into blunted knuckles. I flex my fingers on the grip, feel the weight of it, and start forward. There's an air lock separating the no-grav area of the station from the corridors that have been sealed off by nyxia to create a more Earthlike environment. There's a hissing sound as the air lock gasps open and suctions. As the entrance opens, Babel's imposed gravity comes slamming down on my shoulders.

A quick glance left, a quick glance right. No movement.

It takes about twenty seconds to get used to the restored

gravity. I set my feet and take a deep breath. One, two, three . . .

My lowered shoulder opens the door. The room is stacked with goodies. Rows and rows of extra supplies. There's a single desk to my right, occupied.

"Forget someth—"

The sight of me forces the rest of the sentence back down his throat. He's too stunned to reach for an alarm or scream through a headset. He just blinks as I bring the weighted knuckles swinging across his temple. There's a nasty smack, and he spins from his chair, slumping to the floor. I cock my head back, listening, but there's no response from the hallway.

Hesitation is death. I glide through the rows, collecting conversion cables, live-feed monitors, a set of pliers, a proper flashlight. I shove them into my knapsack before turning back to his desk. I eye the documents stacked there. Just maintenance requests full of half-assed signatures. The first drawer is all standard desk supplies, but the second one's a treasure chest.

A pair of manuals.

One turn of the pages shows me station schematics and maintenance procedures. I can't help laughing to myself as I stuff them into the bag. I take a few seconds to tear random items from the shelves. I do my best to make chaos, just in case they try to inventory the room and use what I took as the first step in an investigation. I salute my fallen comrade and glance back into the hallway. Empty. I close the door and hope no one notices the unconscious body for a few more hours. That should be plenty of time to find my way to some other section of the station.

Air lock. Panel. Darkness.

I smirk my way back through the tunnels. I keep moving until I find a comfortable nook to set things up. With the flashlight between my teeth, I locate Babel's monitoring cables and get to work. It takes a little less than an hour to patch my way through. I tap the screen on and watch as the image resolves. The security feed loops through images at ten-second intervals.

A glimpse of half-empty docks.

The underbelly of the station's exterior.

An empty hallway.

The fourth image hits me like lightning. It reaches down into my chest, takes my heart in both hands, and pumps it full of forgotten life. The image brings life to every chamber, every vessel. The screen shows slumped shoulders, a familiar face.

Bilal.

He's alive.

CHAPTER 21

SLING

Emmett Atwater

I wake to the night, to wind, to two moons in a foreign sky.

There's rope coiled around my body. I try to shift my weight, but there's barely any return from still-dead muscles. We're on a boat. It's a smaller version of the ones we've always used. I can hear it in the engine, see it in the condensed deck. The river thunders around us. Moss hangs down from branches reaching out over the riverbank.

My kidnapper sits wisely out of reach.

The angles and lighting of the bridge were enough to confuse me. Now, though, the differences between her and the male Imago are plain. She's taller than they are, her chin more angled, her hair unshaven on the sides. The slight curve of her eyes is intensified by a nyxian implant. It almost looks like a dark comet with a tail spiraling toward her temple. I think of all the reasons someone would kidnap me. My mind jumps to the most frightening possibility.

"Isadora sent you."

She looks back. "No, though I have heard rumor of her offers."

The answer leaves me more confused, more afraid. She adjusts her position and I finally see the tattoo on her exposed wrist. She wears it proudly.

Moons swinging around in orbit.

She's a sling.

I force my voice through the rust. "Who are you?"

"Jerricho of—" She catches herself, though, before saying which ring.

"What? Get kicked out of your ring or something?"

"That is how *they* define me," she answers. "I will make a new name in a new world."

The confidence in her voice sends a shiver down my spine. She sounds like Isadora. She feels absolutely certain about what she's doing. She's pleased with herself.

"Especially now that I've captured a Genesis."

"Genesis?"

She nods. "You are one of the Genesis. Our people are at an end. But your people? You are a beginning. With your help, I will walk through the doors that have been closed. You will take me where I could not have gone on my own. A new beginning. Genesis," she repeats. "You are one of the Genesis."

I stare at her and finally start to understand. Understanding leads to fear. Speaker used the word *cult* when he described the slings. I see it now. There's something in the way she looks at me, the way her fingers drum restlessly. It has my heart rate rising.

I watched these shows with Moms before. Once you're in the car or on the boat or locked in the basement, you're dead. I want to shout for help, but who would hear? Even as I try to fill my lungs with air, it's like someone's parked a car on my chest. The effort shakes my body with violent tremors. Jerricho frowns.

"Do not strain," she instructs. "The poison will fade. I need you strong again if you're going to take me to the stars. It is not my intention to kill you."

It takes a minute to catch my breath.

"You keep saying that. But your tattoo . . . You're a sling, aren't you?"

The word hits her like a thrown stone. She returns a dark look.

"*They* use that word against us. As if they aren't exactly the same. It's just their political propaganda, nothing more."

Her answer doesn't make any sense. Propaganda? "I thought . . . the tattoo on your wrist. It's orbiting around, using the planet like a slingshot."

"And they said we would use you," Jerricho answers, echoing Speaker's words. "That we have betrayed our people in choosing this path. Choosing to take our lives into our own hands."

"That's what you call this? Taking your life into your own hands?"

She nods firmly. "You're a light in the dark. A new way out of the labyrinth."

I swallow again. "You're not making any sense."

She points up at the moons. "I do not accept my end. I

will go to your planet. Our rulers would have us wait on their mercy, their choosing. A lottery run by politicians." She laughs her disdain. "I'm saying no to all of that."

"Bad news. I can't get you there. As of today, I wasn't even sure I could get *myself* out. You can call me the Genesis or whatever, but I'm as stuck down here as you are."

The words push at her barriers, her dreams. I can see the war inside her head before she growls back, "Even beggars will not give up their secrets easily. You'll resist, but eventually you'll teach me the ways of your people. You'll take me where I want to go, Genesis."

She turns away, busying herself with the ship's front console. I take deep breaths, test the movement of my toes and fingers. I'm feeling slight improvements, one minute at a time. For a while we don't say anything. I watch the stars pass overhead. Both moons glare down at me. One as ghostly as a faded pearl, the other marred by those angry red scars.

After a few minutes, I finally piece together the other thing that's digging under my skin.

"You're a woman."

She turns back. "How observant of you."

"But we—I thought there were only a few left. Babel's never seen a woman outside of Sevenset. And the whole no-kids thing, I just kind of figured—"

Her eyes darken again. "More lies."

I lean back, unsure what to think about that. Who's lying? Babel or the Imago? Babel told us that was the whole point of us coming. A society without children. We were a temporary relief from the pain of that reality. Longwei said it more clearly than Babel ever did. All the reports and the facts pointed to there being no women. It's not like the other Imago have contradicted it, either. We know their people agreed to host Babel as long as they sent the young and the innocent. Those same currents ran through their negotiations over the bases too. Kit was one of the three youngest marines in space. Babel's been clear about this from jump: the Imago wanted us to come here.

I can't put the puzzle together. Someone's removed a piece on purpose, trying to keep us from seeing the whole picture. Smart money's on Babel. I'm thinking through the clues when a loud ping echoes out from Jerricho's radar. She hunches back over the console, muttering. It takes all my effort, but I push myself up into a sitting position, my back pressed against the hull.

My hands and feet are both bound. There's still a nauseating wave of terror working through my stomach. *Calm down,* I think. *Be calm.* There's enough slack in the ropes that I can draw my knees up to my chest. Jerricho notices, eyes me for a second before seeing I'm harmless, and turns back to the console. There's a blue dot hovering on the outer reaches of the radar.

Someone is coming.

All my nyxia is gone. The ship's engine sits up front, I realize. Jerricho's wisely placed me against the back railing, centered between a pair of nyxian defense stations. My mind runs back through all the ways Bilal and Azima used them aboard the ship. Nets and shields and canvas, but weapons, too. Bilal's favorite was the pulse cannon. Thinking about the bright streaks it used to launch across the Waterway, I get another idea.

My uncle always kept a flare gun inside his boat, just in case. We never had to use it, but I've held it in my hands before, felt the weight of it. If I could get my hands on the console, maybe I could manipulate the station into something like it. Send up a flare and jump overboard.

But Jerricho has made sure I'm safely out of reach of both consoles. I glance left and right. On one side, moonlight paints the riverways bright as snow. On the other is an empty plain that looks just like everything else in Grimgarden.

I shift my weight to one side and keep watching Jerricho. She's focused now, increasing our speed, sliding us down a new stretch of river. She's not watching as I dig my right heel down, searching. Old habits never die. It came in handy when Isadora and Roathy attacked, and now it might be the only thing that can save me.

I finally feel it between my heel and boot. It's the size and shape of a coin. Small, but it's always been there, waiting for a moment like this. I just have to keep her talking, distracted.

"They're chasing us."

Jerricho makes a thoughtful noise. "I doubt it's any friend of yours."

I answer without hesitation. "That's my family back there. The second you took me, you guaranteed they'd be coming for you."

"Family." Jerricho chews on the word. "You could be

right. More likely, though, it's a member of *my* family. And we're not above murdering one another for the right price. Others will want you for themselves. As I said, the Genesis are valuable."

I shift my weight again and let my eyes drag over the river. I crane my neck, hoping to draw Jerricho's attention away from the work of my boots. I can feel the piece of nyxia moving now. It's not easy work, but I manage to get it to the inside of my ankle.

I can't remember when I replaced the piece I used against Roathy and Isadora, but I know why: because there's always a threat. A sliver of nyxia for desperate times. The rhythmic ping doesn't sound. The other ship is falling behind.

"Try and keep up with me now," Jerricho whispers.

She pulls up a map of the riverways, examining it, plotting a new course. It's the distracted moment I've been waiting for. I have seconds at the most.

Quietly, I jam my left heel into my right. Pinching the boot down, I slide my left foot up as far as I can. It's hard with the ropes tight over my ankles. A second later, though, it slips the heel. The boot tips over the wrong way. I glance up in panic, but she's still tracing a route across the map. Carefully, I tilt the boot back with my foot. There's a frightening second of nothing. Then the nyxian coin tumbles out, bouncing twice and spinning to a stop. I shift my body and snatch it up with bound hands. It's a life jacket in the hands of a drowning man.

Jerricho starts to say something as I focus on my first manipulation. I'm amazed when it takes. The black coin expands, and the only image I can summon comes from those regular nights with Pops down at Snookers. I center the image of a pool cue in my mind. It stretches the substance until the opposite end smacks against the nyxian console. As soon as it makes contact, I feel the bigger connection pulse to life.

All that nyxia, all that power, all at my fingertips.

Jerricho whips around, curses flying, but I'm too fast. My second manipulation flings itself through the link: *flare gun, flare gun, flare gun.* The manipulation shivers from my brain, through the link, into the console. A familiar red-handled barrel takes form. Another thought points the thing skyward and pulls the trigger.

She lunges, but the shot is an explosion of sound and color. It cuts a path through the sky before bursting out, bright enough for anyone following us to see. Jerricho hesitates for just a second. I take the extended nyxia in both hands and pull myself to my feet. She starts forward again, but another tug brings the pool cue swinging around like a spear.

Jerricho dodges back, calling her own nyxia into its weapon form. She slips into a fighting stance before realizing she's got it all wrong. I'm not looking for a fight.

I take a deep breath and leap.

The stars spin overhead. My hands almost fumble the nyxia. My entire body braces for impact as the water backhands the air from my lungs. The force of it crushes the entire left side of my body. I almost drown as my mouth opens in forced exhale.

Dark, cold, dark, cold . . .

I wonder if I'm about to die. But an anthem beats inside

my chest. The same one that saved me from Isadora and Roathy. A bone-deep promise I make to myself every morning: *today is not the day that I die.* I come gasping out of the water. Overhead, the flare is falling. The boat's momentum took it about five hundred meters down the river. I watch as it starts to wheel.

The nyxia pulses in my left hand, feeding off my urgency. I concentrate on the image of Pops's army knife. I hold it there, front and center, before forcing the vision into the waiting substance. It shifts instantly, and the weight of his knife fills my palm. I lean my body so that I'm floating on my back and start slashing through the ropes.

The first few coils slip from my wrists. Jerricho's turned the boat around. It thunders, picking up speed again. I slip the rope from my ankles, then tuck the knife back in my belt. A spotlight skips across the water, searching, as I start swimming to shore. My world is reduced to one stroke after another after another. All of Babel's training in the tank resurfaces.

I don't pause to breathe. I am an arrow firing at the eastern bank.

A roar announces the boat's approach, but my hands slap down on mud and branches. I gasp out of the water, framed by light, and pull myself onto land. I don't risk looking back. Two stumbling steps bring me through the bank's brush and onto the plain. The spotlight follows. I'm pumping my arms, thinking about all the creatures that hunt at night, when something hits me at hip level. It takes me spinning into the taller grass, and I realize Jerricho's caught me.

She comes out on top, but my hand is tight on the grip

of my knife. I jab upward and she spins away. My blade grazes her left shoulder. I hear the hiss of pain as she backs off, towering over me, her figure backlit by the boat's light.

I try to get to my feet, but she steps forward and strikes again. It forces me onto my back. She circles, strikes, circles. My second attempt at a jab fails. She knocks the knife from my grasp and lands a dirty elbow against my nose. The blow stuns me; blood gushes. I hack a choking cough as she stands over me.

"You are a worthy opponent. You *will* take me to the stars."

"Emmett!"

The voice has us both squinting back to the river. Jerricho's boat has been joined by another. The distant figure doesn't wait for the ship to make land. She leaps from the prow and rolls to her feet. Jerricho continues to squint, but it's a voice I would recognize anywhere.

Morning.

CHAPTER 22

DUEL THROUGH THE DARK

Emmett Atwater

Blood runs down my nose. The slightest movement has my vision spinning. I groan my way onto an elbow and watch Morning's approach. Her eyes burn from me to Jerricho. The Imago takes a single step, setting herself between us, and Morning's rage doubles.

"Give him back," she says, "and I'll let you live."

Jerricho laughs. "Do you plan to fight me *alone*? I am Jerricho, once of the Seventh Ring. I have killed savoys, slayed eradakan. This mace knows its way through bone."

Morning slides out her hatchets and tilts her head. It's a familiar look. She always did it before duels, a moment of weighing her opponent, of finding them wanting.

"Last chance," she says, raising her voice. "Leave now and live."

Jerricho laughs again. "I'll take you too. A second Genesis. More beginnings."

Morning's face steels. There's a second where the *wrongness* of all this pulses through the air. I don't want Morning to do what she's about to do. I don't want her to die because of me. Before I can say anything to stop her, she's sliding forward.

Her body dips and she closes the gap between them. A false lunge. Jerricho lurches. She only gives herself away slightly, but I see Morning's eyes snap like a camera lens. She sees where Jerricho's foot would have stepped and how her mace would have swung. She takes all of that in and slides to the right. I watch her circle before flashing forward.

The metal sings. A few exchanged blows is enough to erase the smile from Jerricho's face. I wasn't a match for her, but Morning? She pushes Jerricho to the edge of her comfort. It's clear that Morning is probing the fringes of who Jerricho is as a fighter, picking up her habits. After trading a few more strikes, she clears space between them. Jerricho is breathing hard.

Morning changes tactics. The nyxian jacket lifts from her shoulders like mist. Jerricho narrows her eyes at the manipulation, then smiles.

A current cuts through the air. Jerricho is wrestling for control of the nyxia. I think about the Imago on the ship—Erone—who took hold of Kaya's necklace, how helpless we were.

But in the space of a breath, the sling's expression goes from confident to confused to worried. The nyxia in the air forms four black doors that look like they're made of smoke. One appears in front of Morning. The other three surround Jerricho. She considers Morning's creation and gives up trying to take control. The grip on her mace tightens.

Morning walks through the first door and everything

distorts. The sound of a whip cracks across the sky, and she appears behind Jerricho. Her first blow cuts across Jerricho's right calf.

The sling cries out, wheeling, but Morning is faster. A step back and she reappears in the second door. Another lunge brings her hatchet raking across a shoulder. She steps back again.

I stare as the doors draw inward, closing around the fight like a noose. Jerricho tries to guess where Morning will appear, but each of her lunges misses. Morning dips beneath every strike and tags Jerricho again, and again, and again. Each blow draws blood until Jerricho is barely on her feet, limping and struggling.

Morning shows no mercy.

The nyxian doors close until there aren't any more gaps. They narrow into a perfect cube of black *nothing*. I hear a final scream before silence thunders out.

"Morning? Morning!"

The darkness melts away. Morning comes out one side, disarmed. She's circling. I start to rise, desperate to help her, when I see Jerricho. She stumbles to a knee and collapses sideways.

Morning's hatchet is buried in her forehead.

She kicks the mace away, and the two of us watch as Jerricho takes her last breaths. Morning's chest heaves chaotically. I can tell it's not the pump of adrenaline. She's taken a life. Blood is on her hands. I start forward to help her, but she holds up a hand in warning.

"Give me space."

I stand there, watching, as she leans over Jerricho. She

closes the sling's eyes and cleans the bloodied hatchet on the grass. After a second, she transforms her nyxia into a shovel and begins to dig. When I start to manipulate mine, she shoots me a look that's made of iron.

"No," she says. "You heard Speaker. Down here, you bury them yourself."

CHAPTER 23

ACROSS THE UNIVERSE

Emmett Atwater

The sun decides to rise. Light stretches across the riverway and paints the highest branches gold. I sit there in silence as Morning buries Jerricho. A stranger in a strange land. Only when she sets aside the shovel, sweating and exhausted, do I cross the distance. Morning doesn't say a word. She lets me wrap my arms around her. I hold on until she stops crying. She rescued me. She *saved* me. But the cost of this will chain her to this place forever.

I file this one away for both of us. I put this one in the place where I've stored the darkest memories, piles upon piles of angry moments: *I* for *Injustice*. She didn't deserve this.

I can see her steeling herself, pushing the pain down far enough that she doesn't have to feel it. After a second she looks up, face carved like some beautiful ruin. She pulls me down by the collar and kisses me. I run one hand through her hair. Each following kiss softens until we're a whisper away. "I thought I lost you," she says.

"I knew it was you. The second that boat pinged on her radar, I knew it was you."

She nods once, eyes trailing the fresh grave. For the first time, she notices the blood coating her sleeves. The sight makes her tremble. "I—I told her to let you go."

"Hey, none of that. Jerricho kidnapped me, poisoned me. I have no idea what would have happened if you didn't save me. Fathom?"

Her jaw tightens but she doesn't resist. I take her by the hand and lead her back to the river. She stands there like a ghost as I sit her down and help rinse off the stains. She's not the first one to wash blood away in Magnia's rivers. She won't be the last.

I grab my knapsack, and we get into the boat. Morning sits in the back as I direct us back through the riverway. It's as easy as reversing her route and letting the boat handle the rest. I keep an eye out for creatures, other ships, but it's like we're driving through an abandoned world. I don't push the conversation, so most of the journey rolls by in silence. Near the outskirts of Myriad, she stands up and joins me by the console. After a few seconds, she takes my hand.

"You learn to defend yourself," she says. "You know?"

I nod at that. "Like a sixth sense."

"I got bullied at school. Bigger girls. I was pretty small for my age, I guess. Started figuring out how to use everything to my advantage. Reading people. Changing the fight. Most days I really hate that *this* is what I'm good at. But today? I would go back there and do it all over again. If it meant saving you, I'd go back."

"That makes you a good person. You know that, right?"

She sighs. "Why are you so nice to me?"

I look down at my feet to make sure her words haven't transformed me into something else, into a bird or the wind or something. "It's easy with you."

Sunlight strays through the branches. It's bright across her light-brown skin. She's beautiful the way a mountain is tall. I almost tell her before stopping. You don't need to tell a mountain it's tall. It already knows that.

The conversation turns. The river breeze reminds us of what we left behind. We share little pieces of our hearts, our homes. She tells me her favorite dessert. I describe my boys.

The words grow wings as we talk our way back across the universe.

CHAPTER 24

PIECES OF THE PUZZLE

Emmett Atwater

The sight of Myriad brings reality's shoulder slamming back into us. Omar waits on the dock, his wide face full of worry. Morning guides the boat in and tosses him the ropes. He sets to the task of tying us up, but it's not hard to see how angry he is.

"You should have waited," he rumbles. "Why risk going alone?"

"I ran into Jaime and Longwei on the bridge," she answers. "I saw the boat leaving with Emmett on it. I made a choice. It worked."

Omar heaves a sigh. "There were other slings in the base, but only Longwei's hurt."

I remember the way he stepped in and shoved Jaime out of the way. It might be the most unselfish thing he's done since I first met him. I can't imagine he'll go exploring with us anytime soon. "He took a pretty nasty shot on the bridge."

Omar helps us both off the boat. "One eye caught most of the damage. He's in the med bay now. Should be fine. And the plans might be changing. Speaker says there's an Imago guard making their way to us now. More security after the attack exposed Babel."

I nod at that. "You never said if you found Corporal West?"

"We found him," Morning says. "About three kilometers from the base. Dead."

"We booked it back to Myriad," Omar says. "But the attack was already happening, and you had already been taken. Come on, Speaker wants to address the whole crew. Make sure we know what happens next."

The main room is full. Beckway and Bally stand by the entrance like bodyguards. The rest of the Genesis crew sits in grim silence until they see us. They let loose a roar and come surging forward, crowding around to welcome us back.

"Always getting in trouble," Katsu says with an arm wrapped around my shoulders.

Jaime crowds in. "I'm sorry, man. I'm still not seeing straight from that shot to the head. I told Morning what happened as soon as she got here. I'm glad you survived."

We bump knuckles. "Got lucky," I say. "No sweat, man."

As the noise settles down, Speaker steps forward and clears his throat.

"Emmett, I am glad to see you alive and well. I must apologize, on behalf of our entire society, for what happened here last night. It's a mark against our hospitality that any of you were in danger." He pauses meaningfully. "However, there is a clause in the Interstellar Contract regarding this. Babel gave us the right, in the event that they failed to protect you, to accelerate the timeline of moving you to Sevenset. We need to speak with one of your leaders."

Morning nods over to Parvin. "Let's get Requin on a call."

It's a surprise to see Parvin sporting the familiar, Babel-made glove that we all watched Kit use to control the station. Genesis 12 must have found it when they located West's body. Jazzy stands at Parvin's shoulder, talking through the floating interface. It takes them a few moments to figure it out, but a wall eventually retracts near the entrance to reveal the same kind of screen Kit used in our first conversation with Requin. Parvin sends off a message before looking back our way.

"I have no idea how long it will take," she says. "For all we know, Kit put these requests in days in advance. I don't even know when they'll receive it."

"We can wait," Speaker replies. "Our guard is coming regardless, but we'll remain inside the base until we can discuss the necessity to move on to Sevenset as soon as possible."

The room takes a breath. Katsu mutters something about needing a mojito, and we all stare when Holly marches straight for the base's makeshift kitchen. Katsu's mouth hangs open.

"Wait . . . ," he says. "I didn't mean you . . . I don't think we even have ingredients!"

He pushes to his feet and heads after her. My eyes flick back to Speaker and the other Imago. I hope they really have a solution for what's happening to her. A second of eyeing Speaker is a reminder of what was so unexpected about Jerricho. I nod his way.

"My kidnapper was a woman." My voice carries around the room. "We kind of thought there weren't many women left. Based on what you've said, they live in the Sanctum, right?"

Speaker glances briefly toward the entrance. Bally and Beckway have taken an unconscious step forward, the news cracking across them like a whip. There's a second where they all silently make sure they're on the same page. Speaker takes a deep breath before looking back my way.

"Who was she? Did she give you a name?"

"Jerricho."

Speaker lowers his eyes. I realize I've seen this kind of gesture before. Jaime did it, aboard *Genesis 11*. I must have dismissed it before because Speaker's a different species— we were told the cues and the body language would be different—but he's giving himself time to think. It's the thing most people do as they dig down for the right lie to tell. When he looks up, that renewed confidence sits comfortably in his eyes. He spins gold for us.

"A staggering loss," he says. "One of a handful of women remaining in our society. It's senseless, really. Jerricho could have had whatever she wanted. I've never understood what might motivate someone to become a sling, but for a woman it is even stranger. I did not know her personally. I do remember that she was a warrior of some renown."

He looks over to the other Imago. Beckway steps forward with a nod.

"She's from the Seventh Ring," he says. "Southside Battalion, a ranked duelist."

Speaker weighs that. "Lucky, then, that the two of you

are alive. It must have taken all of your considerable skill to bring her down together."

Morning and I exchange a glance. She doesn't mention the fact that she defeated one of their ranked duelists all on her own. I decide to keep my mouth shut about that too.

Speaker says, "It is a sad day for our people. Her death will be mourned across the rings."

I watch him carefully. He's lying *again*. I don't call him out on it, because I don't understand. Why would he need to lie about this? It takes a few seconds to remember where we're standing. Myriad is one of Babel's only strongholds on Magnia. Is that why? Is he trying to mislead them? A staticky voice cuts through my thoughts.

The screen behind Parvin blinks into existence. Requin's staring out at us.

"Genesis crew," Requin says in greeting. "We just watched the footage of Corporal West's capture. Have the Adamites offered any explanation?"

Speaker steps forward. I'm watching him more closely now, looking between the lines. Since our introduction, he's been the perfect diplomat. He frames every response with a smile. The sight of Requin tests his abilities as an actor. I note the narrowed eyes and the pulsing vein at his neck, visible for just a moment before he steps into character.

"An outlying faction," Speaker says. "They exist outside of Sevenset's governance."

"They're still Adamites," Requin replies. "Will you activate the Erone Provision?"

That name *thunders* through me. Erone. I'm the only

Genesis member in the room who knows his name. Marcus Defoe let that detail slip in the discussions after Kaya's death. Erone is the captured Imago. What's the provision? What does that mean? Speaker glances back to the entrance. Beckway and Bally nod their encouragement.

"This interpretation stretches the intended purpose of that provision," he says. "But as a sign of good faith, we'll accept the provision and activate our new request: Sevenset."

Requin mulls that over. I watch as he fakes discomfort. Like Speaker, he's setting up a well-manicured lie. "That's far too soon. It's one-third of the expected timetable."

"And right now you've offered only one-third of the expected protection. Holly's mistake occurred because of inadequate training. Corporal West died, and you are fortunate none of the Genesis suffered the same. Our one core agreement still stands, the one statement present in every clause of the treaty: *the children must survive.*"

My mind races. We mean more to them than we know.

"Very well," Requin replies. "But under two conditions."

"Give them and we will decide," Speaker replies.

I'd forgotten that Speaker has another side. We've never asked him about the name he gave during his introduction: The Daughter's Sword. Occasionally, the quiet and soft-spoken version vanishes beneath something far fiercer. Right now he looks just like he did when the sling appeared outside Foundry in search of blood. It's nice to see Requin meet his match.

"They travel in our trucks," Requin says. "There are some inherent defenses that would make us more comfortable.

Feel free to accent that protection with whatever patrols you think necessary, but it allows us to extend safeguards and ensure their arrival in Sevenset."

I glance over at Morning. She's sifting through the request just like the rest of us. I see her raise one eyebrow and I know she sees what I see: using the trucks keeps Babel in the loop. Whether they have cameras on board or just some standard tracking coordinates, it allows them to stay more in the know than any Imago-provided travel would.

"We accept your request," Speaker says. "What's the second condition?"

"Ophelia Station," Requin says. "I want my teams to personally confirm that Corporal Ava Rahili hasn't been compromised. If she's not there, we have the right to pull half of our team from the planet."

He's bluffing again. They don't want to pull us from the planet. Besides, they clearly have eyes on all their bases. If what he said about West is true, they're on a delay, but they still *have* footage. Babel would know within twenty-four hours if someone was dead or alive in their base. There has to be some other reason for sending us there.

"Extending their time outside of Sevenset endangers them," Speaker says simply.

Requin smiles. "We're not the ones trying to kidnap them. The slings have attacked twice. During our last discussion, you assured *us* that they were a limited threat. How can we trust that they won't attack again once you're inside the city?"

"The odds of a successful attack decrease in Sevenset. As you are well aware, the contract between us demands a *minimal* Adamite presence while your crews work the mines. This was against our advisement. We wanted contingents of five or six soldiers with each of your teams. You denied that request. Their security details in the city will be much larger.

"We will also have control over which routes we take through the city. We will know where they are going and how to defend each location from attack. That measure of control has been lacking in Grimgarden. Sevenset will be a safe option, you have my word."

The room's quiet as Requin considers the information. After a moment, he shakes his head. "I need confirmation that Ava Rahili is alive and well at Ophelia Station. The crews do not need to stay there for longer than a few minutes. Visit the location, confirm her presence, move on to Sevenset. I suppose we can make these days up after their visit."

Speaker nods. "Agreed. So long as the trucks do not cross the barriers established in the Proximity Clause, we accept the two requests in exchange for an earlier departure date."

"We accept too," Parvin chimes in. "Not that *either* party asked our opinion."

Speaker looks a little embarrassed about that. Requin just smiles.

"You'll be the first explorers to ever enter the capital city of an alien race on a distant planet. I didn't expect you of all people to complain, Parvin."

She adjusts her glasses. "Point taken."

"On to Sevenset," Requin says. "I'll await word of Corporal Rahili. Godspeed."

The feed is killed. Speaker looks relieved as the group

starts moving around the base. Most of the crew looks exhausted. I bump Morning with an elbow. "I want to go see
Longwei."

"You should," she says. "I'm going to talk with Speaker.
Do some digging."

I lower my voice to a whisper. "He was lying. About Jer-
richo. I don't know why. Maybe he thinks Babel's listening.
If they are, maybe it's better we don't dig right now. And
Requin's lying too. He wants us in the city just as much as
Speak does."

Morning nods. "I knew Requin was lying. Didn't catch
Speaker. I'll proceed with caution."

I shoulder my knapsack and we head in opposite directions.

I hate to admit how thankful I am for silence. Other
members of the Genesis crew are moving through the halls,
but it feels like we're all in different orbits, gliding through
our own temporary universes. A shiver runs down my spine
as I think about the last time I visited the med unit. This
time the door's already open. Bright light filters out into the
hallway. Longwei is lying there with his eyes closed.

Omar was right. It's a nasty wound. The blow slashed
the spot just above his eyebrow and all the way down to his
cheekbone. Instead of sewing him up, someone packed the
wound with a liquid form of nyxia. The substance gleams
back like the surface of a black mirror. Longwei *would* have
the most badass-looking scar.

I glance right and catch my own reflection for the first
time in days. There's dried blood under one nostril. I thought

I had stubble, but it's almost worked its way into a beard. There's more of Pops in my face than ever. I've got his wide eyes and full lips.

The only difference is that time with Babel has carved a restless look into me. Pops always looks comfortable in the world around him. He has a way of blending into every backdrop. I look more dangerous. Put me back on the streets of Detroit and people would notice.

"Emmett?"

The voice is all rust. Longwei looks up with one eye. The other stays shut, even though I can see the muscles twitching around the wound.

"He's alive!" I say, walking over. "I went and got kidnapped. You found the wrong end of a weapon. We really gotta work on staying out of trouble, man."

There's the faintest hint of a smile. "How bad is it?"

"The wound? I think you're disqualified from future space travel. Stuck here, man."

This time he really does smile. "Do you think I'll see out of this eye again?"

I can only shake my head. "I wasn't the one who treated it. Maybe Speak did? They patched you up with nyxia. I'll have to ask. I'm sure you're going to be fine."

Longwei leans back and sighs.

"And hey," I continue, "it's kind of like they made you an honorary Imago. It almost looks like one of those nyxian implants they all have. Maybe you'll have superpowers."

He nods once. "I forgot to tell you that I can read minds now."

A snort slips out. Longwei telling jokes is *very* new territory.

"Yeah? What am I thinking about?"

"That's easy," he says. "You're thinking about Morning."

I laugh at that. "You came into your powers awful quick."

He smiles again, flicker and gone. It's quiet for a while. This is new for us. Most of the words we exchanged aboard *Genesis 11* were threats. That was what Babel wanted from us. Iron scraping against iron. They wanted us sharp and hard and cold.

This conversation feels right, though. Kaya offered comfort. Bilal offered kindness. Every time I offer the same, it's a whisper of a promise that I won't forget them, that they're both with me now and forever. I pull a second gurney over and adjust the back into a sitting position. Longwei glances over with a frown.

"Are you sick?"

"Nah, not sick."

His frown deepens. "Then what are you doing?"

"Hanging out with you, man."

He swallows once and closes his eyes.

It takes a few seconds to pull my player out from the bottom of my knapsack. I scroll through songs before tapping his shoulder and offering one of the earbuds. He stares at it for a few seconds before fitting it into an ear. I play a soft song. It feels like hip-hopping down a river. Longwei actually starts to nod his head after the first chorus.

"I knew you'd like it," I say.

"It's better than the first song."

I frown. "The first song?"

"You played it during our first meeting with Babel. It was so *annoying.*"

I laugh at the memory. "Sorry. I turned it up just to grind at you."

"No worries," he says, exhaustion in his voice. "I still beat you."

"You were only up by two hundred thousand points at the end. I was totally gaining on you."

That earns another smile.

We sit there, listening, until he falls asleep.

CHAPTER 25

OPHELIA STATION

Emmett Atwater

For the second time, we stand in front of a Babel stronghold and wait for the Imago to arrive. This time, though, Speaker stands formally at our side. It's a reminder that we've already been accepted and welcomed. In the distance, twelve black dots loom larger. Dirt and dust spin skyward. We watch them each unfold like the wings of strange insects. Imago pour out from the linked vehicles in smooth formation.

I recognize Thesis from the first meeting. He's smiling his too-wide smile like we weren't just attacked by some of his people. All the guards, though, are new faces. Every one of them comes armed. A short gasp leaves Speaker's lips. We watch him bow unexpectedly.

Our entire group goes rigid, unsure if we should do the same. The formation of soldiers fans out, and we finally see the reason for Speaker's reaction.

"Genesis," Thesis announces. "I present one of the Daughters of Sevenset."

Thesis takes a knee as the woman strides forward. She walks with all the grace and bearing of a queen. Her dress takes the sunlight and spins patterns out of it. Flowers, abstract shapes, curling leaves. The shapes change and slash with each step forward, dizzying to the eye. Like Jerricho, she's taller and slighter than the male Imago. Her wide-set eyes are the same color I saw as I fell from space: the deep and dangerous blue of their world's oceans.

A veil of brown hair frames a full face. Babel hadn't seen a female Adamite in decades, according to their reports. I've seen two in less than twenty-four hours. Thesis gestures to her.

"This is Ashling. Known as the Beckoning Star, the Bright Reach."

Ashling's smile is brief and stunning. "Welcome to Magnia. On behalf of the Daughters, I invite you to Sevenset. Our home is open. Our people await. Will you come?"

Parvin steps forward as our spokesperson. "Of course. Thank you."

The Daughter's smile brightens to blinding. She's just as excited to meet us as the other Imago were, but she wears it regally. "You are a gift our people will cherish for generations. I understand that one of your number has been Gripped. Will she come forward?"

Before we can answer, Holly strides out, unable to resist the beckoning of a queen.

"She will come with me," Ashling says, and it is not a question. It's a statement that becomes reality. "I will watch over her with my own life. Arrangements are being made to treat her. The process will depend on her instincts and toughness. If it is in our power to guide her back, the next time you see your friend, she will be as you knew her."

A whispered word from Ashling has Holly marching toward the nyxian carriers. Ashling eyes us for another moment, nods once in expectation, and turns. Two guards follow, protecting her flank. No one says a word as nyxia swallows them, as the vehicles become dark streaks along the distant hills. My heart beats hopefully. I have to believe Holly is tough enough to survive.

Thesis steps forward in Ashling's place with all the dramatic flair of an actor.

"If we want to start the entrance ceremony before nightfall, we should begin the journey. I believe you're providing your own transportation?"

Parvin uses Corporal West's glove to bring the trucks out of their loading bays. She's savvy enough with the tech to preset our coordinates for Ophelia Station. She tucks the glove into her knapsack when she's done. Morning gives her a look and she shrugs.

"You never know. Might be useful."

I start to follow Morning into the nearest truck, but Omar cuts me off and climbs up behind her. I raise an eyebrow and follow. We take our seats in the cab and Morning actually groans when she realizes that he's planted himself between us.

"Now this is a *proper* date," he says, smiling.

Longwei's helped into the truck in front of us. Jaime and Azima sit with him in the back of the truck bed. He actually waves at me. I grin and wave back like a little kid. It's like we've summoned some new version of Longwei into being and I don't want to lose him. Azima throws an arm around him. She whispers some joke and they laugh together.

Morning leans far enough forward that she can get a good look at me.

"We're a family now, aren't we?" she asks.

"Didn't start that way, but yeah. Those are my brothers and sisters up there. Katsu's more of a cousin, though."

"Don't forget," Omar rumbles, "we have two more sisters waiting in Sevenset."

"And a brother," Morning corrects, just in case Babel is listening. "I haven't forgotten them. Let's just hope the Imago have helped all three come to their senses."

The drive begins quietly. The rumble of the engines drowns out conversation. The hills of Grimgarden roll past. Black spheres ride in protective formations along both flanks. If the slings make another appearance, we'll meet them with force this time. I try to glance over at Morning, but Omar's broad shoulders are in the way. He shoots me a lopsided grin.

"If you want to write her a note," he suggests, "I could review it before passing it on."

I shake my head. "Back on Earth, Omar's not allowed on any dates."

Morning laughs. "Dates? You asking me out?"

"There's this restaurant in Detroit. It's where my parents went on their first date. Burgers as big as your head. I thought we could go there. And if that goes well, I could take you over to the RiverWalk."

Omar nods. "Sounds wonderful. Just send me a date and time."

Morning leans past him. She's clutching her dark braid, cheeks blushing.

"Are you asking me out? Or *asking me out?*"

I smile. "Both. You wanna go with me?"

"For burgers?"

"No. Like go with me. Dating for real. Boyfriend and girlfriend."

She deadpans. "You're seriously asking this with him right here?"

"We're on an alien planet. You saved my life. And *this* is what bothers you?"

She snorts at that, sitting back. After a few seconds, I notice Omar elbowing her.

"Well?" he whispers. "You can't just leave him hanging."

"Whatever," she says, and I can hear the smile. "Fine, I'll go with you."

The truck continues to thunder over the hills. I feel like I just launched into space again. Omar sits there looking pleased with himself. "This is nice, isn't it?"

I roll my eyes at Omar, but there's no way I could be mad now. It's like Morning's smile is the only thing that exists in the world.

It takes another hour to arrive at Ophelia Station. The building looms, identical to Foundry. We see the matching silo, the paneled tower reaching skyward. They've arranged the greenhouses differently, but otherwise it looks the same.

One noticeable change is the figure waiting by the front gates.

Corporal Ava Rahili. She flags us down as we approach.

I remember that Requin's reasons for sending us here didn't even come close to lining up. I'm hoping our exchange with Rahili will shed some light on Babel's real intentions.

Rahili sports the same glove that Kit did. As the trucks pull in across from her, she raises the digital interface and makes some adjustments. I glance around the base, looking for a response from the solar windows or the greenhouse roofs, but nothing happens.

She backhands the screen away and sweeps her other hand through dark hair. Matching eye shadow gives her a thoughtful, brooding look. She's not quite as young as Kit, but I doubt she's clear of twenty-five. It's only when we've climbed down from the trucks and started walking her way that I realize how short she is. Barely up to my shoulders. She might not be tall, but she's still plenty intimidating.

"You're here early," she says.

The veins of her robotic glove hold their blue glow, like she's ready to summon the base's systems into action at a moment's notice. She doesn't have the same automatic trust that Kit did when we first arrived. Parvin takes the lead, and Speaker and the other Imago remain safely in the background.

"We were redirected by Requin," Parvin explains. "We came here to make sure you were still alive. After checking in with you, we're supposed to head directly to Sevenset."

Rahili nods along like this is all news to her. "What happened to West?"

"He's dead," Parvin answers. "The slings came for him. You haven't had any visitors?"

"Nothing I couldn't handle," Rahili replies smoothly. "What about the trucks? Are you taking them all the way to the gates of the city?"

I hear a distant ping cut through the air. It's the same sound you hear when a program finishes downloading. Rahili ignores it, but I notice the palm of her glove flashing like she's got a new notification or something. I file it under *S* for *Suspicious as Hell.*

"We're leaving them a specific distance away," Parvin answers. "Speaker mentioned there's a rule in place because of the treaty. A line we're not allowed to cross."

"The Proximity Clause," Rahili confirms. "Here, I'll program the trucks to return to Ophelia so I can outfit them and send them back to Myriad. As you can see, I'm alive and well. Feel free to move on after I program the return sequence."

Parvin nods before taking a polite step back. Rahili brings up the interface again. Morning gives the all clear, and our crews disperse back to their trucks. I follow the order, but my eyes trail back to Rahili. She took the news of West's death easily. Maybe she's tough.

Or maybe she already knew.

The consoles inside the truck show loading symbols in the top right corner. Rahili's instructions walk our systems through their new directives. We sit there waiting until the screen finishes the upload. Morning waves down to her when it's done.

"You're all set," Rahili calls up. "Fire away."

And just like that we're leaving Ophelia Station behind. The trucks angle away from the base, heading northeast. I crane my neck to get a look back, but Rahili's already vanished inside the tower. I keep my suspicions locked away for now. I'll talk to Morning when we're not sitting inside a Babel-made truck.

I'm not sure what just happened, or why the exchange with Rahili felt so *wrong*. I just get the feeling that Babel's plans are spinning all around us like invisible webs. I can still see the faces of all the frozen marines they have buried in their hidden basements.

Genesis.

Not just the name the Imago chose for us. Babel calls us that too. I realize we're heading for a city that Babel—in spite of all their power and intelligence—has never entered. It's been over two decades, and they've been cut off at every pass by a superior species. Jerricho's not the only one who views us as a new way through the dark. Babel does too.

Genesis.

As we walk through the city's gates, is Babel walking through them with us?

CHAPTER 26
A TASTE OF HISTORY

Emmett Atwater

The outer wall of Sevenset looms darkly against the horizon. Above it, a span of blue brushstrokes. Below it, blinding green fields that look so fake I have to reach down and run my fingers through the blades of grass, just to make sure I'm not dreaming.

The wall is a study of black. Midnight spires stagger up every three hundred meters, narrowing to spikes the color of pitch. The walls look charred, like dragons have breathed fire against them for centuries. A towering, five-story gate sits at the very center of the construction.

There's a full hour between the first time we see the distant gates and the moment we stand before an older, outer gate. We leave the trucks behind. It's like throwing a huge weight off our shoulders. Babel's grasp on us is about to loosen. The Imago escorts lead us to the smaller wall, one that could only be called a ruin. Stones have fallen from their keeps. Weather has worn down the structure for what looks like centuries.

They walk us to a fragmented archway. It's thicker than I expected, and the space beneath the arch has been carved out with purpose. Thesis asks us to take seats around a pit that's been dug in the ground. We can see the actual gates looming just a football field away.

"A traditional entrance ceremony," Thesis announces, his voice taking on a dramatic weight. "Every true Imago partakes in this ceremony. It's a taste of our history."

A mouse-quiet guard named Journey moves through our ranks. There's something odd about him that I can't quite peg. He doesn't really lock eyes with us or acknowledge our thanks. He does get a fire going in no time, though.

The sun starts its descent as the flames get bolder, brighter. We watch as Journey places a triangular table over the pit and sets twenty matching alabaster cups on its flattened surface. He removes a bottle that's full of the purest, most silver-looking liquid I've ever seen and pours a measure into each cup before stepping back and letting the fire heat them from below.

"Straylight," Thesis names it. "A way to look back."

Smoke curls out from each cup. It's so quiet that I can hear the substance start to boil. Thesis uses a hand-length tool to snatch one from the tray. He sets it on the ground in front of Morning, then moves on to the next person, and the next. He instructs us not to drink until the liquid stops churning. He raises his own cup when the time is right.

"To old ways and new."

Our escorts—and the guards—echo the phrase. We all repeat the words and take our first, tentative sips. Noor almost chokes. It takes a few slaps on the back from Parvin to set her straight. The liquid curls around my tongue. It's heavy, like warmed honey, but it skips from one taste to the next as it goes down. It's like my tongue is chasing flavors it can't quite catch.

"When you finish," Thesis says, "watch the city walls."

He gestures to the distant gate. We all sit there, waiting patiently, unsure what we're supposed to see. Jazzy's the first one to let out a gasp of surprise. The noise echoes through our group. I realize that whatever the effect is, it's hitting the lighter and smaller of us first.

I'm starting to wonder if straylight is a type of alcoholic beverage when I finally *see* it.

The distant wall has vanished. The plain appears empty, just a set of cliffs that overlook a brooding ocean. It's not possible. As I watch, the plain fills with people. They're burdened, stumbling on in a huge group, setting themselves down wearily. Thesis begins his narration.

"After the March of Folly, our ancestors came here. The population had suffered a massive blow. The people you see were determined to live. It became the dominant characteristic of our kind. Come rain or fire, come plague or famine—we *survive*."

Time speeds forward. We watch buildings rise up, burn back down, and rise again. Enemies attack the edges of the makeshift village, but the survivors turn them back. The houses bloom larger; outer walls spin into existence. We watch centuries pass by in minutes.

"A village became a town. A town became a city. A city cast itself over the water."

My attention is drawn to the harbor. Boats roam the

shore as another wall flings itself skyward. Taller this time, meant to separate the land from the sea. We can see the village in front of us shrink as the wall grows.

"As various primes evolved into our natural predators, we created the first barrier. The outer ring of Sevenset began here. A queen named Marimar directed us to build out into the ocean using nyxia. She oversaw the creation of the Sixth Ring. Her granddaughter led the construction of the Fifth. And then the Fourth . . ."

My entire body becomes weightless. I feel like I'm flying. Something pulls me forward by the chest, and my vision struggles to take it all in. I hold my breath as momentum carries me right through the outer wall of Sevenset. Out over the first fledgling ring, now known as the Seventh.

Thesis's words carry us over massive stretches of ocean. To the next ring, and the next, and the next. Until finally . . . "The Sanctum."

Our bird's-eye view shows an island dominated by a single, sprawling building. It stretches over everything like the roots of a tree. One side is dominated by a vast glass window. The other shows off countless spires, all scraping their way to the clouds.

"Home of the current Daughters," Thesis explains. "Our queens. But all of this began here. As you walk each ring, as you become the first human group to grace our city, know now what went into its making. Know how our history shaped this impossible place. Know that we did whatever it took to survive a cruel and difficult world. Know this is our *home*."

I flinch back as the images reverse. We fly from the

Sanctum, crossing oceans, skipping rings, until we're sitting around the fire again. The sunlight is fading. The vision vanishes.

Thesis stands solemnly before us. He holds out his hands like he's just completed a performance on a stage. I glance to my right and realize Speaker is weeping. Many of the guards are too. They don't wipe the tears away. Maybe among their kind it's not something worthy of shame. Thesis allows us to feel the full weight of his words before smiling.

"It's also a tradition to celebrate. Pour our friends more drinks, Journey."

The transformation happens in five minutes flat. The rest of the Imago are curious and excited to be with us. Their enthusiasm is infectious. Speaker leads the cooking. He spits and roasts two animals I've never seen before. We mingle with the honorary escorts as he does.

Journey's talent for beverages has our cups filled with a drink we're told will have us dancing in no time. I stand with Speaker for a while, trying to understand the story Thesis just told us. "So the Daughters? They live in the Sanctum?"

Speaker nods. "At the very center of Sevenset."

"Why didn't Babel know about them? I don't remember learning about the Daughters from any of Babel's studies."

"We never allowed Babel to meet them," he says. "Your employers knew about the last child born on Magnia. I assume they made their own conclusions on the subject."

"So how many are there?" I ask.

"There are always two ruling Daughters." Speaker points up to the sky. "One for each moon. The Glacian queen protects and preserves and builds. Those queens are known for peace. Most will forgo the protection of a Sword like me, because they are called to rule with quiet patience, not steel and blood. She protects and preserves. Our people all agree that Ashling sits the Glacian Throne quite well."

Speaker's voice skips a little as he describes the second queen.

"The other reflects Magness. She rules with fire and passion. She's a reminder of powers we can't control. None would argue with how well Feoria fits that description."

I glance back up at the moons. Tonight, Magness and Glacia are dancing awfully close to one another. "Two queens," I repeat with a nod. "But that's not what I was really asking, Speak. How many women are in your world?"

Speaker considers me for a long time. I can't tell what he's thinking, what he's weighing. His face takes on a sadness I haven't seen since he had to bury three of his own people.

"There might be twenty remaining. The count varies."

He doesn't have to explain. Twenty women left in an entire society. We came here knowing their odds of survival were low. A society without women can't go on. Somehow the specific number makes it feel more real. There's no way they'll make it past the current generation. Their excitement in hosting us makes more sense than ever.

We are a reminder of what's been lost, a reminder of what they'll never find again.

"I'm sorry, Speak. I shouldn't have asked."

"There's nothing to forgive."

"So Feoria," I say with a knowing smile. "You like her or something?"

He looks at me like I just cussed out his mom.

"She's one of the Daughters."

"Right," I say quickly. "It's just the way you were talking about her . . ."

"I have been her personal guard for thirty-five years. I have a deep respect for her."

My brain struggles to break down all the things that are wrong with that sentence.

"Her personal guard? Why'd they send you out here, then? Isn't that a demotion?"

Speaker smiles. "Not at all. The queen values your lives. I'm here at her command."

It takes a second for my brain to skip back to the other strange thing about that sentence. The idea that Speaker's been the queen's personal guard for *thirty-five years*. Pops hasn't been working at the factory for half that long.

"Speak, how old are you?"

"I am seventy-four."

My jaw hits the floor. "You're serious?"

"I know, you must think I'm too young to be the queen's guard."

That has me laughing. "Nah, Speak. That's not what I was thinking at all."

Journey comes around to make sure our cups are full. Speaker drifts into other conversations. I slide over to watch one of the Imago guards slice roasted meat onto a stone slab. Our group crowds around eagerly. The meat's all grease and goodness. Journey's drink fizzes and fires. I overhear the guards laughing as Jazzy tries to explain a pig-pickin'. Bally

takes a wooden instrument out and surprises us with graceful fingers.

He starts us off slow before picking a song that's faster,
a song worth dancing to. He laughs when Azima is the first
one to trot circles around him. Morning agrees to an offered dance from Beckway. I raise an eyebrow, feeling a
roar forming in my chest, but she winks my way every time
he spins her around. The style looks like something out of a
history book, all wild turns and quick feet.

It's by far the strangest party I've ever been to. We dance
beneath foreign stars. Katsu drinks too much, laughs too
loud. Even Longwei summons the courage to dance with
Azima after his third round. Noor takes the instrument
from Bally after we're a dozen songs in. The Imago walks
her through the chords, and somehow Noor has a song going
just twenty minutes later.

I watch her play, fire skipping over her face, hands moving so fast and so hard that sweat starts to streak down her
forehead. Out on the dance floor, our group circles up and
cheers on Alex. Kid is actually a brilliant dancer. I watch
him match the rhythm flawlessly, each step faster than the
next. He dances like Anton might be watching him up in
space.

Omar joins an Imago drinking game that involves one
too many knives for my taste. I watch the whole scene and
feel a sudden absence in my chest. Kaya deserves to be here.
This was the world she so desperately wanted to see. And
Bilal should be here too. I can picture him smiling awkwardly, charming his way around the fire.

I shouldn't have had to say goodbye to them. It's a feeling I can't drown with a smile, or another drink. Instead I force myself to take in the crowd. There's Morning with her dark braid. She has a freckle just under her left eye that I've never told her I love.

I memorize the details of every face. There's a certain joy in forgetting who brought us here and why. Babel would take Jazzy's poise under pressure, Katsu's booming laugh, Azima's endless energy. For the right price, they'd burn away the little things that make us who we are and sell us to the highest bidder.

As the party staggers to a halt, the Imago post guards around our location. Speaker helps manipulate cots and sets them at the edge of the firelight. Parvin heads to bed first. Omar keeps glancing over at her, but never works up the courage to say anything. Only Azima doesn't stop dancing. She rings her way around Beckway until the fire's no more than sparks.

Morning eventually nestles in beside me. "You've been so quiet."

"I was thinking about how much I love this freckle." I brush the spot with my thumb. "It's my favorite one. You're my favorite one."

She bites her lip, smiles recklessly, and kisses my cheek.

"Quiet and brooding," she says. "Looks good on you."

I smile at that. She kisses my cheek again before curling up beside me. I sit there long after she falls asleep, thinking about the family we've forged, not through blood, but through steel and chaos. I never asked for any of this. At the beginning, I fought hard *against* it. But now that they're mine, now that I'm theirs, I'd do anything to keep them from being taken.

I can feel the weight of the night in the air. It's like a sixth sense. Something instinctual that says we're standing on the edge of events that will change the rest of our lives.

What happens next will change the fate of *worlds*.

We are the Genesis.

I look up at the stars and fall asleep, knowing there's no one I'd rather have at my side.

PART III

SEVENSET

CHAPTER 27

THE SEVENTH RING

Emmett Atwater

The next morning, Thesis leads our party into Sevenset.

We angle away from the main gates and to the base of the nearest spire. As we walk forward, the wall divides to reveal a finger-thin passage. Speaker asks that we remove our exterior gear first. The whole group pulls off scouters and hands them over.

"It is a part of the treaty," Speaker explains.

He doesn't understand that we're more than happy to hand them over. We've been waiting for a more private audience with the Imago ever since we landed. An Imago in full leather armor stands by the door; he beats his chest in salute as Speaker leads us past.

Strange lanterns cling to the dark walls of the tunnel. We pass through seven doors before sunlight slashes the dim. A stone balcony. Above, the sky's blue is interrupted briefly by the color of a TV screen tuned to a dead channel. It reminds me of Morning's manipulation, except the Imago have covered their entire city with it. As I watch the protective layers flicker in and out of view. So that's what Babel couldn't get past. I've never seen anything like it.

Below, the sound of five hundred fists beating five hundred chests echoes. I can't help leaning over the railing to watch. Jazzy lets out a syrup-thick "Wow."

Imago soldiers are arrayed in perfect rows with matching leather armor. They don't look up as their general leads them through a march. Groups cross the square in intricate, weaving patterns. They turn at the sound of a barked command. Somehow they slide through other groups without bumping shoulders or stepping on toes. The general conducts them, hand gestures wild and voice as grating as the sea.

Beside me, Azima observes it all with pure delight.

Thesis and the rest of the escorts watch our reactions, smiling.

The troops straighten out, taking up their original positions. The general barks more commands, and we watch as they manipulate nyxia with seamless precision. A sword, a shield, a helmet, an arrow, back to a sword. They shoulder their weapons and stop on a dime. Statues and stones, every single one. The general marches along the front lines, but he finds no fault among his men. Proudly, he climbs the stairs two at a time, graying hair swept up in a neat knot.

"Allow me to introduce General Gavelrond," Thesis announces. "He has directed operations along the Seventh Ring since the seven hundred thirty-seventh year of Magnia. There is not a soldier in Sevenset he has not trained in some form or fashion. He will be our host on the Seventh Ring."

Gavelrond bows. "It is a great pleasure to have you grace the halls of the Seventh. The men you see below are our finest soldiers. They earned the right to perform before you today. Their protection of our people has also earned them the right to be the first ones to witness your historic entrance into our city. May I permit them to look?"

We all smile at each other. Morning says, "Of course."

Gavelrond crows an order. They're not full words, but sounds. Short and crisp syllables that sound more like drumbeats than anything. As one, the soldiers look up. They do not smile or react; they stare. The general laughs to himself, proud as any father, and gives a second order.

His words release them like a spell. Every single face breaks into a grin. Some of the bolder soldiers wave up at us. There is laughter and unchecked joy. Gavelrond's eyes swivel back over our group. He has a shrewd face, an eye drawn to details.

"Your party is four short of its original number," he says. "Is that correct?"

Thesis nods. "I'm glad you've been informed, general. Will this be an issue?"

"I chose fifteen soldiers to honor," Gavelrond informs us. He gestures down to the first row of men spaced perfectly across the square. "We hoped that each would have the opportunity to sit across from a guest at dinner. As a reward for their service to Sevenset, but also as a gesture of good faith to our guests. We will simply reduce the number, so as to match the number of guests we are hosting. Not a problem, emissary."

Thesis looks satisfied, but Morning shakes her head.

"Were the men already informed of the honor?" she asks.

"They were," Gavelrond answers. "Earlier this morning."

"Then let them come," she says. "We would be honored

to have them with us, even if we are a little outnumbered. I'd hate for them to have the opportunity taken away."

It's a kind gesture, but Gavelrond's face pinches with distaste. I realize this must be some deeply inherent custom. The general's eyes dart from Thesis to Morning.

"But the numbers won't be right."

Morning falters. "We don't mind."

"Fifteen men to sit with eleven?" Gavelrond looks like he's considering some impossible math equation. "One simply cannot serve a proper dinner with such numbers. The table would be so disorganized."

The other Imago look uncomfortable, shocked even. Thesis clears his throat.

"General, a request has been made by our *honored* guests. I understand your concerns, truly I do, but it will be a small sacrifice to make for them, yes?"

Gavelrond's face pinches even tighter. "I've never heard of a table set for twenty-six. It's a travesty is what it—"

"Travesty or not," Thesis replies sharply, "it will be done."

Gavelrond sighs. "Are there any other *peculiar* requests I need to consider?"

"Yes," Thesis commands. "We'll need an outer table for ten."

At this, Gavelrond looks ready to explode. I have no idea what's happening, but it feels like one of those British dramas Moms used to watch. It's been a while since I've seen someone argue about dinner. Morning gets a word in before the general can snap off another angry reply.

"I'm sorry for complicating things," she says. "I really didn't mean to."

Gavelrond bites off his remark. After a breath, he recovers his respectful, contained manner and gives Morning half a bow. "We will make the necessary changes."

Morning nods again. "Thank you."

"Wonderful," Thesis says. "Now that it's been settled, can our guests get some rest?"

"Of course." Gavelrond whistles and a fleet of servants come pouring out of nowhere. They smile and whisper, taking knapsacks and satchels from us. Beside me, Longwei wrestles for his bag until I explain what's going on. He gives an embarrassed smile and releases the servant to his duties. The general waits for them to finish before continuing. "I have scheduled time for you to rest. Before dinner, however, we have scheduled a Gripping ceremony."

Thesis sucks in an excited breath. "They found a match for the girl?"

"The girl?" Parvin echoes. "Holly? You mean Holly?"

Gavelrond nods. "The timing was flawless. Your friend is very fortunate. We cannot guarantee perfect results, but she'll be treated and you will be witnesses. I'll be certain that you're escorted to the Maker's Claim at the appointed time. Until then, enjoy the Seventh."

The news spreads through our group. The idea of having Holly back, whole and unharmed, is like having a dark cloud lift from overhead. Smiles weave their way onto every face. I grin over at Morning and can see the relief there.

As we follow servants down the stairs, the soldiers straighten, eyes fixed on the walls behind us. Near the front of the group, I notice Alex stop. He's been quiet ever since Anton left, that playful smile of his virtually absent. Some days he barely looks like he's holding it together. His golden hair's long, so wild and curled, that he looks like a beach bum. But there's nothing ragged about the way he straightens himself before the nearest soldier.

He gives a perfect salute.

At first I think he's joking around, but he doesn't laugh or smile as he rejoins the group. He just turns and marches after our escorts. Sometimes it's easy to forget that we all had lives before Babel. We walked into their world, but that doesn't erase what we were before. Most of us are wearing our history and our memories somewhere deeper, in places Babel couldn't touch.

We're almost past the group of soldiers when Azima sweeps forward and kisses one on the cheek. The man startles, only to shiver back into a statue as she slips away.

Thesis leads us out of the square and into the Seventh proper. A salty ocean smell pours from the stones. A central street stretches ahead of us, dark and flawlessly paved. Over the shoulders of distant buildings, we can see snatches of sun-streaked ocean.

Our escorts explain the barracks to us. Fifty soldiers live in each building. They're given permanent homes in the Seventh only after their first assignment is completed. The structures are flat-faced, metallic squares. Each rises about five stories high, piling up in stacks like an abandoned Jenga tower. Pieces are missing on the second and fourth stories.

Instead of rooms, those spaces look like open-air courtyards. I can see dangling vines and comfortable chairs in each one. Thesis praises the designer, a man he claims is from the Second Ring. He also explains that the structures extend two stories underground. These basement rooms, he claims, are coveted for their easy access to the city's network of tunneled waterways.

At the main crossroads, Thesis gestures left and right. The curve of the main road is barely discernible to the eye. Thesis invites Speaker forward to share his research with us.

Our quiet escort accepts gladly. Between each ring, he tells us, there are exactly fifty kilometers of ocean. He lists the diameter of the Seventh Ring at 620 kilometers. Speaker claims that if a man started walking along the Seventh road without stopping, it would take him nearly twenty-one days to return to his starting point.

"How do you know our measurements?" Longwei asks.

Speaker smiles at the question. He explains that he was in charge of taking their system and converting everything into the one used on Earth. With a trace of pride, he tells us that the process took him nearly three years, but was entirely rewarding, as he knew it would allow him to give us a true sense of Sevenset's size and majesty.

From end to end, the width of each ring stretches only two kilometers. The Seventh follows the same standard pattern of the other rings, he informs us. Homes along each outer rim and a main street bisecting them. Here, the main street is almost always clear and empty. Occasional marches, but not the slew of street vendors and performers that Speaker predicts we'll see in the other rings.

"And it's the most dangerous ring?" Jazzy asks. "Isn't that right?"

"It's the most exposed," Thesis answers. "Several of the planet's deadliest creatures live in the sea. And while some are nastier than others, all are dangerous. Before our people rallied around Sevenset, the population fell to dangerous lows. We were unnecessarily exposed. There were a few unexpected migrations—primes entering new territories—that created even more problems in the vulnerable regions.

"Now the Seventh stands proudly as a barrier against those dangers. Our systems analyze everything that swims beneath the walls. The soldiers are quick to identify threats, within Sevenset and without. Aside from hunters, they're the only Imago who face such dangers regularly."

"Sounds exciting," Azima remarks. "I'll keep my spear ready."

Thesis replies, "And I will pray that you don't have to use it."

Our tour ends at a central barrack. We're escorted up through winding stairwells to private quarters. We're all on the same floor, but thankfully, we have our own rooms. Even if we had private rooms in Foundry—and even on *Genesis 11*—I always assumed Babel was watching. It'll be nice to have privacy for once.

The servant orients me to the room. Convinced I know where to sleep and where to shower, he leaves, and it's all I can do to collapse onto a bed that's flush with the floor. It's heaven. I don't have the energy to kick my shoes off, so I fall asleep with them on.

I wake up disoriented. Somehow I'm in only underwear. There's a freak-out moment where I think the Imago came in and undressed me before I remember waking up sweaty midnap and stripping down. The idea of someone carefully slipping off my boots makes me laugh.

I roam into the other room in search of the shower. The floor is tiled, and natural light sneaks through a wall of shuttered windows. At the back of the room, there's a slight drop to a clearly separated area. Ventilation shafts run up and down all three walls with grated drains on the floor. Stripping down to nothing, I glance around for a shower handle.

Confused, I step inside.

And flood.

It's like I fell through a magician's door and landed in a waterfall. Instead of knocking me over, the heavy blasts of water come from every direction with so much pressure I can't even move. All I can do is keep my eyes and mouth closed as it pounds over me in surprisingly satisfying torrents. There's a click, and something that smells like honeysuckle washes down with the water. I open an eye long enough to see a cloud of white suds running over my skin.

Another click and the water stops. I'm drenched and gasping and not at all ready for the blast of air that comes next. Ten seconds later I'm completely dry and remarkably clean and smelling a little too much like Moms.

Wary of setting something else off, I backpedal slowly. Everything's a threat now. Lean the wrong way and I might get flushed out to sea. I'm a few steps clear when I hear:

"Oh."

I whip my head around to see Morning, eyes wide and the deepest red fighting up her neck and her cheeks. She should look away, but she doesn't. I cover what I can, moving away from her slowly. "I think I found the shower."

She laughs, but the noise is drowned out as the shower activates, flattening me again.

CHAPTER 28

THE GRIPPING CEREMONY

Emmett Atwater

Morning sits with me on the balcony. There's no mention of the embarrassing moment in the shower, but she's still flushed and half giggling. Endless ocean stretches out below us. To our right, hundreds of ships toss at anchor.

It's beautiful, but my eyes keep finding their way back to the strap of Morning's tank top and the hip peeking past her jeans. She grins when she notices.

"Hey, I didn't come here for that," she says. "It's time to run the details. This is what I used to do with Anton. Walk through the scenarios. I want to see through your eyes, think with your brain. Let's break everything down. The less surprises the better."

"About Babel?"

"About anything."

"Right," I say, thinking back through it all. "Let's start with Rahili."

"Suspicious as hell," Morning mutters.

"Requin didn't have to send us there," I add. "He could

have confirmed she was alive on his own. The confirmation was a ruse, but to do what?"

"Plant something? Bug something?"

"Requin needed us in range of her or the base. That's all we know."

Morning chews on one nail, eyes out to sea.

"Right. How about the Imago?"

"Speak says there are only twenty women left."

Morning nods. "Which confirms Longwei's theory. It's not about physical reproduction. They can't reproduce because they're running out of women."

"And that means they're going to die out, doesn't it? Why would Babel push to get all of this done right now if they can just wait fifty years or so?"

"Defoe and Requin," Morning says simply. "Do they strike you as the kind of people who are willing to hand off the inheritance of all their hard work to the next generation?"

"Fair point."

"Back to the Imago," she says. "They're long-lived. Their average life span is way longer than ours. But you're right. No matter how you swing it, this is the last generation."

I'm still navigating through the details. "It doesn't make any sense. Why bring us?"

A knock at the door startles both of us. Morning raises one eyebrow, wondering if I was expecting someone. We step back in from the balcony as Parvin peeks inside.

"Sorry, hope you're decent, but, Morning, we need to talk."

Morning stands. "Sure, come on in."

"This is more of a show-and-tell. I need you to look at some of the readouts we're getting from Corporal West's glove. I'm mining some very *interesting* data from Corporal Rahili."

Morning glances at me. I wave her on. "Catch me up later."

She ducks out after Parvin. I stand, trying not to feel restless, and decide to find company. I take one of the lifts and roam into the second-story courtyard. We still have time before the Gripping Ceremony, so I'm thrilled to find Katsu lounging in one of the chairs. We've had time to get used to walking around without our nyxian masks, but I'm struck for the first time just how much he looks like a kid. He sits there, quiet, enchanted by the ocean waves.

I take the seat next to his. "Nothing like vacationing on an alien planet."

He smiles over. "Agreed. Too bad the service in this hotel sucks." I laugh as he rattles an empty glass and calls out to no one, "Another mojito! Now!"

"The hell is a mojito?"

"No idea," he says. "Saw it on a TV show."

We both laugh. "How are you doing, man?" I ask. "Hanging in there okay?"

He shrugs. "Better than you. I didn't get kidnapped. And I don't have a pregnant girl acting like she's a bounty hunter or something. If there was a scoreboard, I'd be a few thousand points ahead of you."

I don't want to talk about Isadora, because I don't want to think about Roathy and Bilal and Loche and Brett. "Can you imagine?" I ask. "Five million people and just twenty girls."

Katsu raises both eyebrows. "Stiff competition. I couldn't even get a date in Tokyo."

"Do you miss home?"

It's a question I ask myself every day. Detroit was beautiful, the way a flower is beautiful right before it's about to die. Some days, I wake up and don't ever want to go back. Other days, I can't figure out why I decided to leave in the first place. I wanted to make my life there better, but things haven't really worked out that way.

"Tokyo?" Katsu scoffs. "Hell no. I hated that place. Why do you think I came here?"

"For the money, I guess."

"Yeah, and that turned out well." Katsu looks down at his hands like he's never seen them before. He's quiet for a while before he says, "You think we'll make it back to Earth?"

Another question I keep asking myself. Another fear that's eating me alive.

"I don't know," I answer. "You heard Morning's recording."

"Pretty messed up."

"More than messed up," I say. "Babel's playing God."

"Playing God? Sounds about right. They have all the power, they do what they want, and they don't give two shits about us. I'd say Babel's putting on quite a convincing performance." He slams his cup down on the table. "I'm going to take a shower."

Long after he's gone, I'm still chewing on his words. At least they're honest.

Still, I don't believe them, even if I don't have much of a reason to believe in God. Too many nights without food.

Too many times taking Moms to the hospital. I can't recall extra blessings or catching breaks. There was never enough of anything. I know people had it worse, but I know a lot of people had it better too. Then my big break comes, and what has it gotten me?

Kaya's dead. Bilal too.

Even if Babel weren't lying through their teeth, I'd go home with a million dollars and still have a closet full of ghosts. It's like, no matter which planet I'm on, deity isn't all that interested in me.

But that can't be all of it. It just can't. One thing's always bothered me. My whole life's been rough, but somewhere I picked up the idea that it wasn't supposed to be that way. I don't know where I learned about justice, when I started thinking I deserved something more. There's a part of me that knows, beyond the shadow of any doubt, that the world is supposed to be better, more.

And if there isn't some God out there working behind the curtains, then I don't think I'd have much reason to hope it will ever change. I can't make heads or tails of the feeling, but I'm glad that a small part of me hasn't given up. Kaya would be quick to nurture that part. Bilal would tell me it was always there. I'm glad for any reason to hold on to hope.

"Emmett?" Speaker stands by the entryway. "The Gripping Ceremony will begin soon."

I nod and follow him down. The whole procession waits outside our barracks. We're a strange mix. The Imago in their tight tunics and showy jewels, and then all of us rocking the closest thing we have to street clothes. A bunch of

plain tees and jeans. It's been a while since we've been outside a Babel uniform, and the effect is freeing. I try to catch
Morning's eye as she walks, but she's halfway through an
animated conversation with Parvin.

Everyone's excited and talkative, well rested for once. I
end up trailing the group, walking in step with Longwei. He
doesn't turn away or march faster. He matches my stride
and nods a hello. We arrive at a columned building, and a
pair of heavy arched doors is thrown open. The room we
enter looks half courtroom, half coliseum. A gray gravel pit
surrounded by stadium seating. The Imago lead us down
the polished hardwood steps, across the first hardback pew,
and into uncomfortable seats.

Our escorts take their own seats in the row behind us.
Boots sound, and a company of soldiers files inside, filling
row after row. Longwei nudges me, and my eyes are drawn
from the forming crowd and back to the gravel pit.

At center, two nyxian boulders have punched up through
the dirt, two or three meters high. Neither has been polished or shaped, but it's impossible not to see the crude outlines of dark thrones. Around each, four hip-high columns
have been constructed. They're equidistant from the dark
chairs, connected by dusty black shackles.

My stomach turns uncomfortably as Holly is led out. A
whispered word from the guard has her taking a seat on
the throne to our left. She doesn't resist as a pair of Imago
patiently attach the shackles to her wrists and ankles.

I swallow again when I spy movement at the back of the
room. A prisoner is led forward by more soldiers, followed

by General Gavelrond. Our gracious host has donned a golden tunic that shivers with its own light.

The prisoner's skin has faded to a dead color; his ribs are carcass thin beneath a scarred chest. He stands before us and doesn't say a word as the soldiers chain him to the stone chair beside Holly. It's a slow, deliberate process. One chain for each hand. One chain for each foot.

Even before Gavelrond begins the explanation, I know I'm about to see something horrible. On my left, Alex's hands are trembling. Longwei's knuckles have gone white as he keeps a death grip on his chair. We can all feel the darkness hovering just out of sight.

Holly sits in perfect stillness. Her eyes are dark pits, her posture straight. She looks a little worn by the constant drive to do the next task, but otherwise she's healthy.

My eyes flicker back to the Imago prisoner. I realize that whatever is left of this man is about to be taken from him. I don't know how I know and I don't care why. I feel like my own hands and feet are chained to the floor. A sideways glance shows that the same horror is snaking its way through the entire group. How do we leave without offending them? Is this really something we want to see?

The chains rattle as Gavelrond steps forward. He stands before us like a lawyer would before a jury. My stomach turns again. Will we decide? Is that why they brought us here?

"You've seen our order, our discipline," Gavelrond says. "Easily one of the most important aspects of any army, any soldier. Aside from personal skill and ability, the only other aspect I teach and instill in every man I've trained is a hunger for justice. A desire to see the crooked made straight. The Daughters appointed us to be the upholders of the law in Sevenset."

The general gestures back to the chained man. If the prisoner recognizes that all eyes have swung to him, he doesn't show it. Soldiers stand sentry at each of the four columns, their palms pressed to the surfaces as if to keep them from flying away.

I do not want to be here.

A vision of Kaya's throat, streaked red. Karpinski kneeling before me and the blade at his neck, which looked more alive than he did. Bilal going cold in space.

The room feels alive with dark things.

"This man is guilty of murder," Gavelrond continues mercilessly. "For that crime, our punishment has always been the same. He must be Gripped to the Eternal Tasks. We pray that the Maker will count his final days as a first penance for committing such an unspeakable sin. We also pray that when he is unmade, the Maker sees fit to re-form him by some better part, some better moment, some stronger passion than that which caused him to take another's life.

"It is less common, but we also ask that your friend be restored. This trade has been arranged. We will hand over the guilty to restore the innocent. Send one being into shadow to bring another back into the light."

Gavelrond turns back to the prisoner, and his cloak whips around his shoulders.

"Do you have any last words, Seafind of the Third Ring?"

The name pulls the man's eyes up. They're the quietest shade of blue I've ever seen. He stares at Gavelrond. I can just barely hear the words he speaks.

"I am more than what you will make of me."

When Gavelrond doesn't reply, Seafind retreats into darkness.

"The rod and reproof bring wisdom," Gavelrond says, and the words echo to me in Defoe's voice. He was the first one to speak those words to me, to teach me what they mean. *The rod answers for past mistakes; the reproof instructs future action.*

"Before these witnesses, let the Gripping Ceremony begin."

Air is sucked out of the room. All four chains lift from the ground on their own, stirring and writhing like serpents. I can't tell if the guards are manipulating them or something else is, something deep within the nyxia. The prisoner doesn't react until all four chains go tight. His whole body goes rigid and his eyes widen. Something takes hold of him, and we watch as he tries not to let it destroy him from the inside out. The screams come. Loud and shrill and as horrible as I could ever imagine any sound being. The chains rattle and his body twists inhumanly.

On his right, Holly sits motionless. Her dark eyes do not blink. She's a statue.

A weight enters the air, a presence I can't ignore or escape. The force grows and moves and shakes the walls, hungry and aware. I almost flinch when Alex takes hold of my hand and grips it hard. I'm left breathless; so are the others.

There's a moment when Seafind's screams go silent. His

head bows, and there's a perfect stillness to the room. And then Holly gasps back to life. She takes in ragged breaths and stares down at the chains rattling around her wrists. Her eyes flick up to us. They're green again, bright and full of the life we thought she had lost. She leans back in the chair, and tears start to fall down her face. It takes her two seconds to start sobbing uncontrollably.

"I want to go home. Please, I want to go home."

Parvin and Morning are on their feet. Both look desperate to get down to Holly, but the ceremony isn't complete. One by one, the chains around Seafind release. The guards rush forward, relieved to be unstrapping the chains. We all watch as Seafind lifts his head, and it's not hard to see he's no longer Seafind. The blue has left his eyes, replaced by black pits.

"Seafind of the Third Ring has been Gripped to the Eternal Tasks of the Maker. From this day forward, he will know nothing but the justice to which he's been bound. Go and find someone to serve."

Gavelrond steps aside as a door beneath us opens. We watch Seafind walk forward, steps steady and determined. He doesn't look left or right, up or down. He goes, and the silence of the crowd devours me. The only sounds are Holly's quiet sobs, and retreating footsteps on gravel. We listen until we can't hear them any longer.

Gavelrond looks up at us, hoping for signs that we're pleased, but what he finds in our faces has him worried. Morning and Parvin leap the barrier, land hard in the gravel pit. Both of them help Holly out of her chains, sweeping arms around the terrified girl.

The rest of our group looks lost.

Our possible allies have shown a darker side. We wanted Holly back, but we didn't know it would happen this way. They call this justice, but it's still a reminder that every blade has a side that's sharp. We were hoping to wield the Imago like a weapon against Babel. Today is a reminder that we forgot to inspect what kind of weapon we had in hand.

I file it away under *D* for *Double-Edged Sword.*

It takes a second, but I'm the first one to rise. Longwei's face is a nightmare. I've never seen so much emotion from him. Alex wipes away tears. I look down the long row of friends and family. I force my voice to be loud enough for all of us.

"Let's go," I say. "Come on. Everyone up."

Morning and Parvin guide Holly out of the pit. One by one, the Genesis crew follows my command. An entire procession of Imago watch us carefully. Speaker stands near the back, looking concerned. Gavelrond's watching from the arena, speechless.

They realize they've made their first miscalculation.

I lead our march through the dark halls.

Outside, the sea smells like it's dying.

CHAPTER 29

STRIKE THE SLIGHT

Emmett Atwater

Speaker tries to understand. "I thought you wanted Holly returned to you."

"We did," I reply. "We just didn't know what it would cost. I mean, do you do that to people on the regular? Send them into the same darkness Holly had to live through?"

"Seafind will move through Sevenset in service to all," Speaker explains. "If someone asks him to perform a repair, he will attempt it. If a soldier asks for his help in lifting supplies into a boat, he will attempt it. The Gripping punishment is reserved for those who will not choose redemption on their own. He will live the better life he refused to choose for himself."

The entire group stands together in the streets of the Seventh.

"He's forced into it," I say. "It's not real redemption if he can't choose it."

That answer frustrates Speaker. "The Gripped are all around us. Less on the Seventh than elsewhere, but they're a pivotal part of our society. Imagine the cruelest in your world transformed. A man who would have chosen to murder again will help build homes, repair bridges, sweep floors. Even you have been helped by them and did not notice."

I stare back at him. "Who?"

"Journey," he says. "The guard who served drinks before we entered Sevenset."

The thought turns my stomach. There was something strange about him, an absence.

"I thought he felt wrong."

"Nyxia claims their spirit," Speaker explains. "Have you not wondered at your ability to form new materials? The speed at which they're created? It is—at least in part—a credit to those who have been Gripped. Where your hands would fumble, their collective work steadies."

That realization thunders. All the times we've used nyxia. The forces that push and pull. The faces I've seen floating in that dark, on the edge of form. They're all prisoners? Slaves? Speaker sees my mind turning those truths over and is quick to make a correction.

"They're not alone," he says. "At the end of a well-lived life, most of our kind will commit their spirit to the substance as well. Remember what I told you? We believe in the collective good above all else. Do you see now? It is not a mark of shame. It is a way forward. When you use the nyxia, you're interacting with our weak and wounded, but also our proud and precious. To enter those shadow lands is a mercy for men such as Seafind."

I want to push back, tell him it doesn't feel fair. But I

realize I have no idea how long it took the Imago to decide on this punishment, or how it actually works in their society. After all, how long did it take humanity to understand that executions did nothing? Nothing for the guilty or for the innocent, but we still used those methods for centuries.

And if Speaker really pushed me, would I be able to defend our prison system versus their Grippings? The crowded jails full of boys my age? What makes our way any better?

Gavelrond returns and asks a miracle of us.

After watching Seafind's punishment, we're to attend dinner.

It's life-giving to have Holly back. Parvin walks with her, arm in arm, but all of a sudden the Imago feel like shaky ground. I'm feeling recovered enough to not throw up as we take our seats across from the honored soldiers. A first course of breaded fish steams its way onto the tables.

The soldier across from me is mercifully talkative and excited about everything. His name is Myan. He says he's young by army standards, only thirty-seven years old. I hide inside questions, asking as many as I can and hoping to speak as little as possible. In my mind, it's Seafind across from me. The fish tastes like a black hole.

"Our average life span?" Myan muses across the table. "I read a study recently that listed it at two hundred and twenty years. The eldest member of our society at present is two hundred and sixty-four. From what I understand, our race is longer-lived than yours?"

I nod, searching for easy facts to throw back at him, simple thoughts.

"I'm sixteen."

Just sixteen and a witness for the dead and dying. Just sixteen years old.

Myan smiles curiously. "How strange. I can scarcely remember being so young."

"No?" I ask quietly, then glance down at my plate. "What's this again?"

And Myan launches into another lengthy explanation. I nod along. I'm not trying to be rude, but I feel like my shadow's been ripped away, taken to the same place Seafind was taken. It doesn't help that Myan's nyxian implant sits in the pit of his right eye. The whole socket looks pitch-black, an echo of Seafind's empty irises. I can't help glancing at it as he explains the fish the chefs have chosen and how it adds necessary proteins to a soldier's diet.

"An army marches on its stomach, so we treat every food like medicine."

"Your eye," I ask suddenly. "Is that an implant?"

Myan stiffens slightly. "It is."

"Speaker said it's a reminder . . ."

"Of our ancestors," Myan confirms. "We're all connected through the substance. It's a reminder of those who came before us. And it's a promise to those who will come after. Once, our people thought it protected us from Magness."

I frown at that. "From the moon?"

"Surely you've seen her in the sky? Magness has the red rivers streaking her surface."

"They look like scars."

He nods. "Were the moons explained to you?"

I trace back through our first introduction. So much was

happening. Isadora had just threatened me. The emissaries came to greet us, and yeah, they corrected Parvin on the names of their world. "Thesis said one was Glacius and one was Magness."

"Correct," Myan says. "In the early years of Magness's reign, fire showers down from the sky. Those red rivers are volcanic. I do not fully understand the science, but when she's close enough to our world, the material shakes loose? It falls to our world."

"So . . . how does a nyxian implant protect you?"

Myan smiles. "It doesn't. Research disproved that, but you can see the mysticism behind the choice. A piece of nyxia implanted like a charm to protect you from the falling nyxia."

Realization slams into me. "Nyxia comes from the *moon*?"

"Of course," Myan answers. "It has rained down for centuries. The largest meteors strike the planet, tunneling their way into the ground. The substance cools and becomes nyxia. I suppose it's logical that you don't know this. Your kind first came here some twenty or thirty years ago, did they not? The last activity from Magness was nearly a decade before."

I'm still stunned. All this time Babel could have been tapping the actual *source* of the nyxia. My brain's scrambling through a million questions, but one realization hits harder than the rest. Speaker gave me the clue days ago. "It's returning to its natural form."

Myan lifts an eyebrow. "I am not sure I understand."

Moving in a circle, in orbit. Before I can explain, Gavelrond stands. The general raises a glass, and all the corner conversations die away. "I'm very pleased to host this group," Gavelrond says. "It has been nearly twenty-five years since I last met someone from Earth. To see you walking the streets of the Seventh is a wonder. To old ways and to new."

We all raise our glasses and tentatively tip them toward one another, filling the room with soft clinks. The Imago repeat Gavelrond's phrase, and I wonder again if it's a common saying, a common hope for them. Before we've even set our glasses down, servants bustle into the room and deliver plates with the kind of classic silver covers I've only ever seen in episodes of *The Fresh Prince of Ganymede.* The general holds up both hands to stop us from lifting our lids.

"I planned this dinner in the hope of displaying the life of a soldier here on our world. Eating is only another form of training. What enters the body will either make it stronger or weaker. I teach my men to understand what they are building out of themselves. There is no dish more healthy and *competitive* as the one that's been placed before you. It's the most time-honored tradition of ours here on the Seventh."

By some signal, the soldiers across from us all stand. They snatch sharp, hand-length skewers and shift into combat stances. I notice that the silver dish covers have started to move, rattling against plates and even lifting briefly from the tabletop.

Straining, I hear a soft fluttering sound like silk. Gavelrond holds up his right fist and the soldiers each pinch the handle of their dish cover between thumb and forefinger. Some smile. Some are so focused they don't seem to be breathing.

"The game is called Strike the Slight." Gavelrond looks giddy. "Strike!"

We watch a sequence of fast-forwarded movements blur across a single breath. Every soldier flashes his silver dish cover sideways. There's a burst of bright color and wing-beats and a dart of vague movement. The soldiers lunge forward with their skewers, and it's like someone hit the pause button.

Of the fifteen Imago, fourteen have each speared a small, delicate bird on the end of his skewer. The only escapee flutters to a corner. Before the servants can get there, it triple taps the glass window with a sharp beak and slips through a hole the size of my thumb. It vanishes in a dash of pink.

The only failed soldier takes his seat first, cheeks blushing with embarrassment. The other soldiers take their seats, and the nearest elbow him playfully. The way they're joking around reminds me of PJ and the Most Excellent Brothers. Gavelrond explains.

"Per pound, slights are the fastest creatures in our world. One in every ten Imago can do what these soldiers just did. They are trained to be quick, to be deadly. And their reward?" He gestures down the ranks of his men. Each of the successful hunters has slipped the little bird from his skewer. The slights look small and bright on the stone plates. As we watch, smoke curls out of black-dot eyes and narrow beaks. The men use little knives to strip away the feathers, and Myan holds his out, showing me the exposed meat beneath. Somehow it's cooked perfectly.

Gavelrond answers before we can ask. "The final attempt to escape accelerates the heart rate. When the slight is properly skewered, its heart bursts. The energy explodes into the bird and you're left with roasted perfection. It is one of the most tender and delicious meats that exist, I dare say, in our world or yours. Not only is it delicious, but it provides an unparalleled increase in energy and adrenaline. A lot of gravs eat them before their ranked matches."

I find myself wondering what a *grav* is as the soldiers dig into their meals. Steam ushers out, and the sharp scent of smoked meat crosses the table. Myan cuts his own meat into two pieces no bigger than bottle caps. He eats them slowly, savoring each bite and closing his eyes like the world has quietly come to an end. Gavelrond laughs when he sees our faces and gestures for us to stand.

"Come now," he says encouragingly. "It's your turn."

We glance down the rows, exchanging nervous looks and laughter. Everyone stands and grabs a skewer. I pinch the handle and try to mimic the way Myan stood. A glance shows he and the other soldiers are loving this.

I take a deep breath and think about the birds. They're really fast. If I'm going to snag mine, I have to make a good guess. Find the color, the direction, and aim high.

"Strike!" Gavelrond shouts, and the room descends into a chaos of moments.

Bright pink. Up and to the right. I stab my skewer out and am stunned when the blow lands. My slight's wings spasm and stop. Overhead, a handful of birds flutter to the ceiling. They're just as smart as they are fast. We watch them dart to the same corner as the first and escape through the ready-made exit. Laughter fills the room and I glance around at the others. On my left, no birds. On my right, only one. Morning offers me a little wink as she slides a red-nosed slight onto her plate. We're the only winners.

"Ah, man," Jazzy says. "I was looking forward to that."

Gavelrond signals to a corner and servants enter bearing uncovered plates with prepared slights on display. Little sauces are splashed brightly around the birds, and everyone looks relieved that they won't be missing out.

The taste flattens me. For a second, I forget the world exists. Myan laughs at my reaction, and for the rest of the night we trade descriptions of other foods and favorite cuisines. Katsu spends a long time describing chocolate cake to the Imago, who've never heard of it before. A little more research and we discover the worst: the Imago live in a world without chocolate.

Katsu jumps to his feet when he's told. He delivers a long and ridiculous speech about how insulted he is to not be eating chocolate in this new world. With dramatic flair, he exits.

At first they're not sure if he's serious. Then Bally stands. The Imago escort gives his own supposedly serious speech about his new mission to fly to Earth and bring back chocolate for his people. He refuses to stop until every Imago has tasted the divine mystery. He makes a show of marching out, calling after Katsu. We all laugh and drink and lose ourselves in the taste of good things, in the comfort of good company. It feels like the first step in a necessary partnership with their people.

When I'm finally back in the quiet of the barracks, I shrug out of my clothes and collapse into bed. I reach over to shove open a slatted window, and the sound of water and wave crashes into the room, each withdrawing roar quieter than the next. Before I can fall asleep, Morning slips into my room. Moonlight washes over her face.

She curls up next to me, head pressed against my chest, arm draped across my hips.

I kiss her forehead. She kisses one of my ribs.

At dawn, shutters beat back the rising sun.

CHAPTER 30

THE SIXTH RING

―――――

Emmett Atwater

Speaker chooses to split our group onto three separate boats. The Imago claim it's just a precaution, but it's not hard to see how nervous they are today. Word reached Gavelrond during the night. Soldiers and citizens have heard dark rumors, all of them about me.

Emmett Atwater is in every whisper.

Isadora has made her first move against me and it isn't subtle. She's calling for my head. Jazzy says it's just like John the Baptist. I'm thankful when she doesn't explain the comparison.

I thought I'd be safe in Sevenset, but when I mention that to Speaker, he shakes his head.

"We will obviously do everything in our power to protect you, but reports are conflicting. Isadora and Ida are with the Daughters in the Sanctum. I would have expected them to manage the situation before it skipped across the water and found the ears of other rings. You have to understand, Emmett, that the bonds of women in our world are very powerful. I'm afraid she might wield more influence than we could have guessed."

I take my seat on the ship and try to pretend I'm not terrified of dying. There's a difference between pretending to be tough and ignoring the truth, though. Pops has always told me ignorance is the most dangerous thing in the world. Fools, he used to say, will ignore whispers until they become shouts. And by the time a whisper is a shout, it's usually too late to make a difference. The only problem is that I don't know what to do with these whispers.

Our boats unmoor. The engines thunder to life. These Imago vessels look almost identical to the ones we worked with on the Waterway, but with some slight advancements. All the technology Babel hasn't had the time to copy yet. They're a little bigger, with a series of inner cabins for sleeping. A few of us help work the boats into the water, but our Imago escorts step in as captains. Even with the dark news, Speaker is confident we'll reach the Sixth Ring with ease.

"What about the Sixth Ring?" I ask. "Will it be dangerous there?"

His explanations had me thinking the Sixth Ring was like my neighborhood. Detroit is the only home I've ever known, but that doesn't mean it isn't dangerous. The opposite, really. I can't help wondering if the Sixth has the same reputation. Maybe it's a place where Imago from the inner rings keep a hand over their pocket as they pass through.

Speaker shakes his head. "It is unlikely. A successful attack would require intense organization and high-performing operatives. That is not the hallmark of the Sixth."

I'm surprised how harsh he sounds. He's worried, I know,

but it sounds like he's forgotten that all of us come from the Sixth Rings of Earth. We're not wealthy or high class, not even close. The unfairness of it roots deeper inside me.

I thank him mechanically before joining the others at the back of the ship. Morning slides over to make room, and I take deep, steadying breaths as Beckway shoves the ship into a higher gear. A few kilometers later, the wind whips across us with such force that I have to close my eyes to keep them from watering. We cross the fifty-kilometer stretch of ocean in half an hour.

"How's Holly?" I ask.

Morning glances that way. Holly is still looking pale, staring off most of the time, but at least she's not a walking zombie. "Just keeps saying she wants to go home. Her memories of what it was like are kind of fuzzy. She just—she just wants to go home."

"She's not the only one."

A few minutes later, Morning nudges me and nods to shore. A crowd has gathered around the docks. Thousands of faces dot the landscape. They fill every street and alley, every window and rooftop. Speaker whispers a command to Beckway, and seconds later the ship's submarine cover emerges. We watch the nyxia stretch and seal before the vessel dives. Blue swallows everything. One hundred meters later, blue gives way to black as we plunge into the tunnels. It's a narrow underbelly, marked by distorted light and roller-coaster twists.

Beckway attaches our ship to a bright air lock. We're led up and out, passing through a dimly lit basement, up stairwells, and into a room of domed ceilings and vast arches.

It reminds me of an old, empty church. The rooms are far larger than I would have expected in Sevenset's poorest district. The other crews join us in the same open hall, though by different routes and led by other captains.

Once everyone's gathered and settled, Thesis raises a hand to get our attention.

"Welcome to the Sixth. We hope you will find your stay comfortable and educational. Though these are the least esteemed among our people, of all the rings, this might be the one that needs you the most. They need the hope you offer. Please, let us know if you lack for anything, and we will attempt to accommodate you. We'd encourage you not to give gifts to the beggars you see."

His words fall like lashes from a whip. The others stiffen too, but I can't tell what they're thinking. Is this how people talked about me when I lived in Detroit? Am I like the beggars? Don't give me too much of a handout or I'll be encouraged, I think darkly. Babel should be taking notes.

"We do think you'll be pleased to hear," Thesis continues, "that the finest chef in Sevenset has agreed to host you for a meal during your time here. In his care, you will lack for nothing. He has cooked for every famous citizen in Sevenset. His renown is well noted by all."

The other Imago smile. In their eyes, this seems to redeem the fact that we have to see their poor and lowly. It takes effort to unclench my fists as Thesis dismisses us to our rooms, hopeful we'll find the meager spaces comfortable. I end up sharing a room with Longwei.

Based on their talk, I'm expecting something the size of a closet. But it's almost four times the size of my room in

Detroit. A servant explains that the water pouring from a fountain in one corner of the room is entirely drinkable. He shows us a nyxian converter that takes in salt water and transforms it into fresh. The technology reminds me of Babel. Finer than anything I had on Earth, and yet the Imago are worried we'll think them poorer for it.

Before we can see the waiting crowds, Speaker reminds us not to give anything to anyone, not to separate from the group, and not to pet the stray half-hounds. His voice drips with disdain. I decide to show them how wrong they are, to treat these people like royalty.

We move through the first gates and into an open square. Outside a second gate, the crowd is waiting for us. The faces there look no different. I see nothing to mark them as poor or less. They have bright, wide-set eyes on even wider faces, and they're built with the typically sturdy frames common in Imago people. They're all smiling.

Their clothes look a little shabbier, maybe, but you have to look close to notice the difference between them and our escorts. A missing button here, a makeshift belt there. As we march forward, hands reach out for us; excited murmurs follow our steps.

"Genesis," they call. "Welcome!"

Many in the crowd are older. I wonder if life has slowly demoted them here, leaving them to live out the last of their days on the very outer reaches of society. The descriptions from our escorts had me expecting dirty and ragged, but they're not that. Mostly they're clean, with sharp beards and styled haircuts. I look as many of them in the eye as I can. I shake the hands that reach out from the crowd. I smile because these are my people, more than Speaker and Thesis could ever know or understand.

The buildings too are as pristine as any on the Seventh. They're stacked a little higher and hunched a little tighter, but otherwise they're the same. Clothes hang over alleys and under brightly colored awnings. When we finally make it to the main road, the crowd parts to reveal a series of street entertainers staggered as far as the eye can see.

A group of gold-painted men dances, their movements weaving a story or a song or both. On one corner, a juggler manipulates objects in midair as he works to keep them up. I get drawn over to a group of deep-voiced singers who sound like beatboxers. One invites me into the rhythm and I can't even dream of saying no. I offer up some of my favorite stop-and-go snares and they listen for a while before joining in. Seconds later, they're weaving their song around my beat.

I finish breathless and smiling so wide my face feels broken. Our group is spread out along the main drag now. Everyone's drawn to different exhibitions, and it feels like a county fair. Speaker and the other escorts stand to the side, mocking smiles on their faces. A passing man asks something and Thesis dismisses him coldly.

I forget for a second that they've treated us well so far. I forget how I could have built any affection for them as the man stumbles away, empty-handed.

On Earth, I was never the welcome guest. I got the sideways looks; I saw the hands drifting toward purses. Feared or dismissed, I got used to living my life as both.

So I seek out the next entertainer with my biggest smile.

I try to lose myself in appreciation for these people. They greet us warmly, making room for me to watch.

Longwei and I stand together, watching two men with painted faces trying to climb the same ladder. It's some kind of silent humor show, the kind of thing Pops would find hilarious while Moms and I rolled our eyes at each other.

They pretend that neither one knows the other person is trying to climb the ladder too, so they keep accidentally knocking each other down the wooden rungs. The ladder spins and wobbles, and the crowd gasps at all the right moments. The act ends when they both make it to the top, only to finally see the other person and pass out backward in shock. Each of them twists into a graceful tuck, rolls on the landing, and offers a series of sweeping bows.

One of them pulls Longwei out of the crowd and tries to get him to climb the ladder. I'm amazed when he agrees to it. He's never liked fun or games, but maybe he sees them as his people too. The performer makes a show of offering Longwei his most prized possession if he can get all the way to the top. Longwei actually laughs with the crowd and starts climbing. We watch as some trick keeps him just a few feet off the ground. He's climbing fast—scrambling, almost—but the rungs are rotating somehow, keeping him from making any progress.

The man calls out laughing encouragement until Longwei starts climbing down. It looks illogical, but the new motion has him vaulting toward the top of the ladder. The man's eyes go wide, but Longwei stops short of the top rung and smiles down theatrically.

"My arm cramped," he says. "I suppose I can't reach the last one."

The performer grins and the crowd cheers as Longwei reaches the bottom and clasps the entertainer's forearm. There are a few whistles and catcalls for the blushing performer, but most of the crowd is quick to move on to the other attractions.

I spot Katsu diagonal from us, laughing as an artist paints his face with bright colors. Moving closer, I see that it's some kind of predatory cat. The artist puts his final touches on the design and whispers to Katsu. My friend laughs and lets out an absurd roar. The colors flash to life, leaving his face and manifesting in the air. The cat's about the size of a tiger, but colored snow-white with silver streaks. It rubs an imaginary head against Katsu and sits beside him.

It's all so amazing and eye-catching that I almost lose sight of Morning. Turning, I find her standing at the edge of the crowd, speaking with a shopkeeper. The man is surrounded by hanging silks and beaded scarves.

Morning's shaking her head, but the man stands up and offers her the nearest bloom of bright orange. He gestures for her to hold it tightly in her hand. She nods. Then he lurches into movement. Holding the other end of the winding cloth, he dances around her. The cloth dives under arms and swathes around Morning's neck and crosses over her stomach. Twenty seconds is enough to have her fully draped, as bright as an angel from some other world.

I stand off to one side until I catch her eye.

"How do I look?" she asks.

"Beautiful," I say without thinking. "You're the most beautiful person I've ever seen."

The smile she gives me back is something no one can ever take from me. A burst of cheers pulls us both down the street. I notice a pair of hounds slinking off in one direction, looking as much a part of the crowd as anyone else there. We find ourselves staring into the same kind of translucent cube the sling used to ward off the defensive fire of Foundry. It's bigger than that one—and the one Morning conjured—but not by much. Boxers stand outside the barrier, their trainers wrapping gloves around fists. Morning edges closer and asks the nearest Imago what's going on.

"Gravs," he explains. "Three rounds."

The word echoes from our dinner with Gavelrond. He used that term too.

Morning tilts her head. "How does it work?"

"One of them is the lead. The other is the chase. Both enter the arena. The lead can change the gravity whenever he wants. Heavier or lighter with a thought. They'll trade off for the second round. Watch."

The shorter of the two boxers enters the arena first. There's a snatch of static, and then our vision of him briefly blurs. He cracks his neck inside the translucent cube, sets his feet, and invites the other fighter in. Like Speaker, the man circles the arena, looking for an entry point. I admire their footwork, the movement of their eyes.

After a few seconds of probing, the second fighter ducks inside the cube.

Gravity slams down on his shoulders. The first fighter

pounces. He lands a jab but misses the second swing. When he dances back, I gasp. Both fighters are floating upward through the air. The nearby Imago nods at Morning. "See? Changed the gravity."

They exchange blows, pushing down from the ceiling, launching up from the ground. Right before they tangle near the center of the arena, the lead switches the gravity again. He lands first and catches the other one's quick descent. Another flick to no-grav gives him the chance to toss his opponent out the side of the arena.

"Point goes to the lead!"

Cheers follow as both trainers dance around their fighters, giving instructions. My eyes drift over the faces of the crowd. I want to take all of it in.

Before the second round begins, I see a familiar face. Not familiar because I've seen the person before, but because I've seen the *features*. It's a narrow face, and though the figure is stooping, this particular Imago still looks taller than the others. A lock of hair has escaped the protective hood and hangs down over slanting eyebrows.

It's a woman.

I start that way, squinting, but the crowds are roaring and shouting again. I duck under arms and catch a few glances as I go. The shifting of the crowd blurs the faces, though. I weave back toward Morning and find the spot where the woman was standing. She's gone.

"What's up?" Morning asks.

"I thought I saw a woman over there."

She makes a thoughtful noise. "Speaker said there weren't any on the Sixth."

The moment slips through my fingers. It keeps nagging at me for a few minutes, but there's too much fun swirling in the air to not enjoy it. We spend the rest of the afternoon with the Sixth. To the surprise of our escorts, every single one of us falls in love with the place.

It could be the welcome they've given us, or the skill of their entertainers, or the bright delight written on every face in the crowd. But I think it's more than all of that. It was Roathy who said Babel picked us because we're poor, and it was Kaya who said Babel picked us because we're broken.

We fall in love with the Sixth Ring because they're our people, and we're theirs. Outcasts, we dance in the streets and sing songs and laugh loudly. Looking around the vibrant square, I know we've found the first true bridge that crosses from our culture to theirs. Even if it's paved in poverty and brokenness, it's the path we've all been looking for since we left home.

It's a way to go back, a way to remember.

CHAPTER 31

GUESTS

Emmett Atwater

I'm not surprised that the festivities and the fun can't last. Since I first boarded *Genesis 11*, everything's had a dark twist to it. Why would life be any different in Sevenset?

I walk back through the crowd and get a solid dose of déjà vu.

The same man who Thesis dismissed so coldly before has circled back around. He stands before Thesis, hands out and begging. It's a sight I've seen before. There are beggars on every other corner in Detroit, so I know the look. We were never that poor, but there's no point in comparing it. Hungry is hungry. Sick is sick. Broke is broke.

There's something about a beggar that either pushes you away or pulls you forward. I'm ashamed to admit the truth, but most of the time I can't stand the sight. It's a creeping feeling that rushes in and tells you to go, be anywhere but here, see anything but the hand reaching out for help. It's a part of me that I don't like and never will.

So as I watch the beggar reach out to Thesis, all these billions of kilometers from Earth, the opposite feeling takes over for once. I start walking forward.

Thesis lifts his chin. The other escorts laugh as the man drops to his knees. A shuffle brings him to the feet of our assigned emissary. He reaches out and pulls at the hem of Thesis's shirt. Time slows to nothing as I cross the distance. One foot after another.

Halfway there, black blossoms. Thesis shoves the beggar away with a burst of nyxia. I'm still walking when the beggar staggers to a stop, falls to one knee, and looks up.

Thesis looks down. I can see pride fill every feature. His face contorts, his arms flex, and he pulls the nyxia from his hip like a sword. His arm arches back and the black snickers out, forming a thin sort of whip. There's nothing I can do but keep my feet moving.

They are the bravest twenty steps I've ever walked.

As Thesis's hand comes slashing forward, the whip scores a dark arch through the air. I'm fast, though, faster than I've ever been. The beggar flinches, but it's on my shoulder that the whip lands. Shards of glass bite through my suit and skin before ripping their way back to Thesis. I cry out into the silence. Blood spurts up, runs down. The whip falls limp in Thesis's hand. The pain of the blow takes me to a knee. Every eye turns to us, hungry for spectacle.

I rise. "You won't hurt him."

Alex is closest. He pushes through the crowd, blond curls tossing. I stand defiant as he manipulates nyxia and works to bandage my wound. Morning and the others are making their way to us now too. Thesis stares, horrified by what he's done. Before hundreds of his own people, he's attacked a beloved guest. He struggles to find the words.

"Emmett," he says. "I did not—"

"Mean to hurt me? I know you didn't," I say. I nod to the beggar. "But you meant to hurt him, didn't you?"

The emissary's face twists. "But he's just—"

"Poor?" I finish, voice raised and dark and double-edged. "From the Sixth Ring? A beggar? Go ahead, Thesis, what can you call him that gives you the right? 'Cause whatever you think he deserves, I deserve it too. We come from the Sixth Ring of our world."

Speaker and the rest of our escorts look lost, confused. But it doesn't matter if they understand or not. That's not the point. Alex finishes the bandage on my shoulder and I turn to the beggar. He takes my extended hand and I nearly buckle. Holly's there, though. The redhead helps me get him to his feet and doesn't say a word. When the Imago starts to apologize, I cut him off. It pisses me off that he thinks he should be sorry for anything.

"It's not your fault," I say, firm and loud. "What's your name?"

He smiles a broken smile. "Axis."

I nod. What a great name. It sounds like something old, strong. A name that shouldn't be begging on the streets. "How long have you lived here on the Sixth?"

Axis swallows, his eyes darting to the escorts, but I shake my head.

"No, not over there," I say. "Here, with me. How long?"

"For the last seventeen years," he says. He pulls up a

pant leg and we get a glimpse of metalwork in the place of flesh and bone. "Fell from the Third to the Sixth when it happened."

I don't want to ask him why he's poor or why he's reduced to begging, because it's bad enough that a person has to do it, without explaining the why and the how and the hurt.

As the crowd watches, I offer my forearm and Axis clasps it. Shock snakes through the crowd. I turn back to Thesis. "I'll have Axis as my guest tonight."

The escorts look horrified. Thesis even more than the rest.

"But we've already made plans. . . ."

"Then give Axis my place at dinner. And he can sleep in my room and use my shower. I'll find somewhere else while I'm on the Sixth."

The emissary's jaw tightens. "We can't allow you to sleep in the streets. We'll make arrangements for Axis, but only for tonight."

I nod, but I'm not done yet. Not even close.

"And all of my friends. They want to choose guests as well."

Another shock ripples through the gathered crowd. Murmurs struggle their way to us. The escorts are all too easy to read. Thesis has narrowed his eyes. Bally smiles, like he finds what I'm doing amusing. Speaker and Beckway are throwing dark looks in Thesis's direction. I glance over at the rest of the crew, hoping they'll back me.

It's uncomfortably quiet until Alex steps forward.

"Who will join me for dinner?" he asks, eyes searching the crowd.

After that, the floodgates open. Longwei picks the man on the ladder. Morning asks the poor shopkeeper. Everyone chooses a guest. Whatever honors the Imago intended to give us, they'll give the least of theirs now too. It's small—a part of me knows this might change nothing in the end—but it's better than doing nothing.

I walk with Axis once everything's been settled. The others, even Morning, follow my lead as we make our way back. Thesis strides on ahead of us, giving the command for the servants to prepare more empty rooms.

"It will be nice," Axis says, "to have a proper bath, to eat a proper meal."

"Thanks for coming with us," I reply.

I'm not foolish enough to miss the look Thesis gives me as I pass through the archway. Confusion has bled into anger. I didn't mean to humiliate him in front of his people, but there are some things that a person should never stand by and watch. What he wanted to do to Axis is one of them. Pops taught me that much. The others nod at me before they head to their rooms. Morning actually sweeps forward and kisses me on the cheek.

"You're an easy person to love," she whispers.

That word catches me by surprise. She sweeps past, though, like she didn't just cast a spell on me. Once I'm certain that Axis is being looked after, Longwei and I return to our room to get dressed. I'm showered and toweling off when Longwei's voice drifts through the cracked bathroom doorway. "Why did you do that?"

I stare at myself through the steam on the mirror. Why did I do that?

"Because it was the right thing to do."

He's quiet for a few seconds.

"Teach me."

"Teach you what?"

"The right things," he says. "I want to know."

I laugh, because I've never really thought of myself that way. Far from it. But it starts a conversation, at least. Longwei and I trade details about our lives back home. Nearly a year in space and he told us nothing. The details he shares feel like missing puzzle pieces. He makes so much more sense. He explains he is the second son of a poor Chinese family. He tells me that his birth was unexpected, and that it cost his family precious government stipends.

I nod my understanding. I'm an only child. Always wanted a brother, but America put rules in place before I was born. A second child comes at a cost in most countries these days, and China was the first to lead the global push to curb overgrowth.

Longwei explains he couldn't avoid the stain of his birth. Before he had even taken his first breath, he had condemned his family to poverty. And they'd been thanking him for it ever since. I end up talking a lot about Pops, and I realize he's the one who taught me how to live a certain way, how to be a person who does the right thing. I learned some of it on my own, but I could have gone in a lot of different directions if he and Moms hadn't given me a good shove from the start. But Longwei, he never got pushed forward. Only pushed back, held at arm's length, left to figure it out on his own.

"My brother was very good at things," he says. "They always told him that."

"You're very good at things," I remind him. "You were first on our ship."

"Yes," Longwei says. "But I was first in many things at home too. My family didn't really notice, because I was always second to them. No matter what grades I received, no matter what scholarships I won. I was the second. I was the family curse."

"You're not a curse," I say. "Longwei, you're not a curse."

He looks up at me. "That's why I came. When Babel chose me, I thought it would finally be a demonstration to my parents. I was chosen. I promised myself I would succeed and restore my family's wealth. And when I came home, they wouldn't see me as the second son. But then I heard Roathy talking in the first days of the competition. Do you remember?"

"Of course. It's hard to forget."

"They didn't choose me because I was better than my brother," Longwei says, voice tight. "They chose me because I was poor. I was the second-place son. I was broken, and they knew they could control me because of it."

"That's why they chose all of us. You're not the only one."

Longwei smiles at that. His eye looks like a kaleidoscope staring out from the pit of nyxian black. It's healed well. I watch as he runs a determined hand through his front sweep of hair. "Would you agree that Babel sees me as loyal to them and not you?"

"After everything on *Genesis 11,* yeah, they probably think that."

"So would it be a surprise to Babel or Defoe if I joined them, when the time comes?"

I shrug. "No, they'd expect it."

"Good," Longwei says. "They will make war. I'm certain. So I will join them when it begins. It's easier to kill something the closer you are to it. Just remember this conversation. If the time comes, I will go with them. I will lie to them. But you will know the truth."

Longwei is trusting me with his secrets. It makes me uncomfortable. Not because I have someone's secret to keep, but because someone thinks to trust me at all.

"Why me?"

Longwei looks at me. "You are a man of honor."

His words humble me. "What will you do? Once you're with them?"

Longwei's eyes narrow seriously. "I will blow things up from the inside."

CHAPTER 32

SCARVING

Emmett Atwater

Longwei walks with a new confidence now. It's not the cocky pride he had on *Genesis 11*. It's more of an assurance, a destiny. I walk beside him and feel the same thing. When the time comes, we know who our enemies are. We're not helpless, either, because Babel gave us tools to fight with. They made us into weapons. It will be their downfall.

It takes a while to gather the entire crew back in the main reception area, but by the time we're all walking down the stairs, our chosen guests have already arrived. Axis finds me in the crowd. He didn't look noticeably dirty before, but a shower's still done him some favors. He's even combed his thinning hair stylishly to one side.

"Genesis," he says in greeting. "Good to see you again."

I nod back to him. "Emmett. My name is Emmett."

"A good name," he says. "A strong name."

"Thanks. The escorts said something about a famous chef. Do you know who it is?"

Axis looks offended. "Scarving! Only *the* best chef in
Sevenset. And a better soul than he is a cook too. Every
month he holds lotteries. No charge to enter, just the effort
of putting your name in the selection. The chosen eat at
his restaurant free of charge. Even if he's busy hosting the
wealthiest in Sevenset, he makes time for us too. He's not
one to stand on ceremony."

Axis nods in the direction of Thesis. I can't help laughing. I know it's not right to forget how they've treated us
so far. Speaker, especially, has risked his life to protect us.
But for tonight? I'll celebrate Axis and my lowly friends. I'll
celebrate the Sixth.

"So you've eaten at Scarving's before?" I ask Axis.

"No, I haven't," he answers. "Never won the lottery. What
you did, that's the only time I've ever felt like I've won anything. Thank you again for helping me."

"It's nothing. I was glad to do it."

The escorts lead us to a square building with an open-air
entryway. A light breeze follows us into the wood-smoked
interior. Everything is dark engravings and thick stones.
Chairs gather around a circular table so that it looks like the
whole restaurant consists of campfires. Unfamiliar, enticing
smells rush forward before we're three steps inside. Axis
doesn't bother with manners. He inhales, rubs his belly,
and nudges me with an excited elbow.

Our escorts keep their promises. What we receive, our
guests receive too. But Thesis sends the guests to their own
table, asking that we sit around the one at the center of the
room. The escorts take a table to our right. They've honored

our request, but still refuse to soil their reputations in the process. Axis doesn't seem to notice as he clasps my forearm and pulls me close. "Tonight, I am the richest of men."

He grins and follows the other guests. Our table's a massive circle of tiered stones, centered around an empty pit. Longwei sticks to my side, and I end up with Alex on my other.

I'm reminded that Alex is missing the one person he actually wants to sit with. He smiles politely but looks tired, like sleep has been more fight than rest these days. It's not hard to see how worried he is about Anton. We have no idea what's happening up in space, which only makes things worse. As we take our seats, I make a silent promise to pull him aside at some point and talk to him. He's my blood brother too, a kinship Babel forced on us.

Morning sees that the spots beside me are taken and snags the seat directly across from me. One wink from her has me grinning like a fool. The table's unlike any I've ever seen. Tiered and sleek. There's a thin outer layer of stone right against our stomachs. It can't be for anything but elbows. The second cut of stone rises a few centimeters and is about the length of my forearm. A third stretches to the center, running off the circular cliff cut out of the middle of the stones. We're glancing around when a man steps out of thin air, head and shoulders the only thing visible within the pit.

"Welcome to Scarving's," he says. "I, of course, am Scarving."

Unlike most Imago, he's completely bald. His head is shaved and wide, accented by a series of tattoos under his neck. A slash of heat rises, and we watch a flickering red fill the circle around him. "I've been informed," Scarving continues, "that you are accustomed to *ordering* food at the restaurants you visit on Earth. Government secrets, I know, but I am a man who knows things. So I've taken the liberty of printing menus. Please, take a look."

A trio of servants whips around the table, dropping off miniature menus. But the slightest touch shatters them. Thousands of little crystals dance across the tables in front of us, glittering under the bright. Azima trails a finger through and gives it a taste.

"It's like sugar," she says, delighted.

"Apologies!" Scarving exclaims. "I suppose you'll just have to eat whatever I make you. I am not like your cooks back home, I'm afraid. They ask what you want, take your order, and make it. Not here, not at Scarving's. That is not art. Art is making what you feel and giving it to the audience as it is. So tonight, I will make art. Be my witnesses."

With a smile, he begins. I can hear pots banging and knives sharpening. Light leaps and slashes over his face. He spins and turns, dancing around stovetops we can't see.

"I like to think of this first dish as an invitation."

Smoke has started to drift up. He leans to the left and presses something, and we hear a suction sound. The smoke vanishes, and he continues to work. Turning and talking.

"I'm a stranger to you, but a meal is an invitation, isn't it?" He looks up briefly and smiles. "Are you willing to let me lead you into the tastes of our world?"

He snatches a towel, wipes away sweat, and shoulders it. We watch as he plunks down little saucers and spoons for each of us. He flips another switch inside the walls of his pit, and the stone tables grind to life. The third tier rotates forward as the second rotates beneath it and away. We all lean in to get a look, and end up laughing. Inside the fist-sized saucers, there's nothing but smoke. It hovers there, hiding what's beneath.

"Our first test." Scarving claps his hands excitedly. "Do you trust me?"

Alex pokes at his. Longwei spoons down into the saucer and lifts up, hoping to remove whatever is inside from the smoke. That doesn't work. The mist follows, gathering around the spoon, keeping its secrets. We all smile, and Longwei shrugs, then takes a bite.

His eyes close like the world's just ended. He hammers a fist against the table.

"Wow," he finally says. "Wow."

Laughing, we follow his lead. Scarving salutes Longwei's service, and we all decide to trust him for the rest of our lives. It tastes like a strawberry, filled with some kind of cream and dipped into some sort of hardened caramel.

"Very good," Scarving says. "Two points to my friend over here. He's in the lead."

Longwei nods his approval at being in first place. We watch the chef move like a storm within the pit. The work of his hands isn't in our line of sight, but he twists and turns and dances, describing the next dish while he prepares it.

"I love to make *choices*," he says. "I like to think that every choice depends on the choice before it. And even the choices of others. Our next dish will force you to make difficult choices."

He spins to face me. It's startling, the gray of his eyes and the directness of his stare.

"I was in the square today," he says quietly. "I saw what you did."

Heat creeps up my neck. A few eyes flicker over to the table of Imago guests. They're starting courses, laughing like we are. Scarving angles his body to lift a massive block of wood up and out. He sets it down and rotates the stone tiers so the whole thing sits in front of me. There are countless little dishes sitting on the wooden block. Smoked meats, fine cheeses, and seasoned slices of fruits and vegetables I've never seen. The smells race upward.

"As a gesture of my gratitude," he says, "I give you my highest honor. You may begin the game." He points down the rows. "Spicy, salted, sweet, and bitter. Enjoy!"

I eye the offering and end up picking the thing that most looks like bacon. Grinning, I hold it up so the others can see what they're missing out on. Then I dig in. The meat's crunchier than bacon, with hints of something sweet in the aftertaste.

Before I finish chewing, Scarving hits a switch, and the second stone tier begins rotating to the left. Alex startles as the tray of food heads his direction.

"The rest of you have to think on your feet," Scarving explains. "Pick one and only one! If someone chooses the food you had your eye on, you absolutely must say, 'I wanted that!'"

Alex plucks up a thin-stringed vegetable and takes a bite.

Jazzy makes a face. "Well, I definitely didn't want that."

The table goes round and round, and the wooden block

slowly empties with each revolution. Azima's the first one to try the spicy food. A waiter knowingly rushes forward, setting a cup beside her and pouring some kind of milky water. Azima gulps it down and grins.

"Tastes like home," she says.

I notice that Morning always goes for bitter and Holly only eats meat. Parvin becomes the token sufferer in the game, struggling to make her choice when Jaime picks the food she wanted three times in a row. We each get four bites before the game comes to a close.

By then, Scarving's got the next dish ready. Waiters set a pile of black flame-lashed rocks in front of each of us. We're told not to touch them until the end of the meal. The next dish is seared, with strange crablike claws thrusting up out of the meat. Longwei's actually snaps at him when he gets too close with his spoon.

Then there are vegetable trays paired with little translucent balloons. Scarving instructs us to set them over our plates and pop them. Something like helium has us laughing and singing songs in absurd voices. When the balloons run out of air, they pop and splash down over the vegetables. My vanquished balloon tastes like barbeque sauce. Scarving laughs and cooks the whole time, answering questions and making conversation as he creates ten, then twenty, then forty different dishes. Somehow I never feel too full.

Every new dish is no more than a taste, no less than perfect. At the end of the meal, we're each given a pair of tongs and a wooden straw. The flame-lashed rocks have sat to the side all evening, burning and flickering. Scarving has us lift the top rock.

"Now you'll take the straw and suck in the smoke," he says. "But slowly."

Using tongs, we set the charred hunk to one side. Smoke pools in the empty space, and we all feel a little foolish as we set the ends of our straws in the ring and breathe. Something like mint floods and burns through our mouths. I cough a little, then turn to pat Longwei on the back as he nearly chokes. It feels like I've been chewing thirty pieces of gum.

"Refreshing, yes?" Scarving asks. "It makes the canvas blank again."

He's right. I can't taste a thing. We all sip at the minty smoke, and Parvin raises a few eyebrows with a joke about getting high. Scarving inquires what she means and looks horrified at the suggestion. "I'm a purist," he claims. "I want you tasting more, not less."

After, Scarving turns to each person and asks their name. He's kind and serious. He repeats each name like he's engraving it into a tree inside his head. He asks favorite dishes, notes what worked and what didn't, nods his thanks. I'm the last one he speaks with.

"And you?" he asks.

"My name's Emmett."

Scarving smiles. "And what was your favorite dish?"

"I liked the balloons," I say. "Never seen anything like that."

"Good," Scarving replies. "And let me thank you again. It has long been the practice of my restaurant to ignore the rings. I do not care where one comes from, so long as they have a stomach for my food. Everyone deserves to eat, to taste the best thing this world can offer."

At the other tables, meals are still being served. I catch sight of Axis, and he raises his cup in salute. I raise mine in return. On our other side, Thesis has a piece of skewered meat held up for Bally's inspection. The two of them laugh together. I look back at Scarving.

"You see? It gives me hope," Scarving says. "Food can give a man back his dignity. So can treating him with honor and respect. In the days to come, this will be our measure. Do we treat others with the dignity they deserve, regardless of where they come from? It will surprise our people to learn lessons from one as young as you, but keep teaching them, so long as you are here."

I walk back to our rooms beside Axis and Morning. I keep looking down as we go, because it feels like I'm floating, like my feet are lifting off the ground. I've shrugged off some burden I can't name. Morning hooks her arm into mine, and I forget where we are and why we're here, if only for a night.

CHAPTER 33

THE COSMONAUT
AND THE ALIEN

Anton Stepanov

My dark is broken by the fine golden edges of a distant square. The color gold always briefly summons Alex's face to mind. The long curls, the easy smile. I have not prayed for him up here in space, but I have threatened whichever gods are listening.

Keep him safe, or I will come for you too.

My vision settles. I glance down at the watch on my wrist. Vandemeer is late. Hands scratch and scrape. There's a soft curse, then a click. The panel swivels, and light floods into the dark. A narrow face waits there, backlit.

"Anton?" Vandemeer whispers. "Are you there?"

I made contact three days ago. I'm glad Emmett spoke up about him; otherwise the mission would have been far more difficult. Our entire plan depended on my main contact, Melissa Aguilar. We hadn't touched base with her since she handed Morning the sound clip of Requin, right before we launched.

She managed to get herself promoted, though. I searched the ship logs to get a read on her maintenance routes before realizing she'd been pulled up to the executive communication team. Right next to Requin. That kind of proximity made her an impossible contact. Enter Vandemeer.

I tap my knife twice on the nearest tube. The sound echoes. I wait in the dark for him to tap back. Five seconds, ten seconds. Three taps sound. It's clear, then. I let myself drift over to the light. "Vandemeer. Good to see you again."

His face is a shadow. "Hello, Anton."

Careful to avoid the exposed wires, he shoves two sacks through the gap in the detached panels. I tuck them into the straps of my suit. Vandemeer looks nervous, as always.

"Is it in here?" I ask.

"The identification card came from one of the lead pilots. Sorry it took so long. I needed to figure out which one of them was the most careless with their things. They're all pretty savvy, though, Anton. He'll notice it's gone before long. Why do you need it?"

I grin out at him. "I'm expanding the territory of our game."

"Just be careful." Vandemeer glances down the hallway. "I need to go."

"No news?"

"Very little," Vandemeer says in a rush. "The Genesis crews entered Sevenset. I overheard some of the techies discussing it. They have a hard time surveilling anything in the city. Two decades and they've only had a few, temporary windows. But they've apparently had better luck now that Emmett and the others are inside the city. Something about dual signals? They seem excited by the new access."

I consider that. It makes sense. Babel might have used the invitation to smuggle their tech into the city. Get the right programs and devices *behind* the city's barrier and it could be just the thing they need to poke holes big enough for a good long look.

"Bilal and Roathy?"

"I don't have access to them. I—I'm trying."

It would have been easy to fight my way to Bilal after I saw him on the video monitor. Easy and stupid. Walk into a detention block, trip a few alarms, and I'd just join him inside the cell. I want to get to him before Babel changes their mind, but it requires more firepower.

"What about the ships?" I ask. "What's going on with the personnel?"

"A lot of preparation," he answers. "It's very busy in the Tower. They're keeping the skeleton crews of each ship in the dark, but it's not hard to see that something is in the works. It will happen within the next few days, I'd guess. Maybe sooner than that."

"Good," I say. "Time to find a queen for our game."

Vandemeer hesitates. "There are food rations for the rest of the week in there. Be careful. The crew's taken note of you. They think there's a ghost on board."

"There is a ghost on board."

"I'd like the ghost to stay alive," he replies softly. "Stay safe."

He slides the panel back in place. It takes a good ear, but

I listen closely as he moves down the hallway and toward the nearest air lock. I listen for any other twitches, rustles. There's nothing. Only the empty drone of Babel's equipment. He's alone, unfollowed.

Eventually they'll peg him. Defoe and Requin must know that something is afoot in the dark underbelly of their space station. They might not know that it's me, but they'll flush the vents before long or send someone after me who's not a gadget techie. I need to make my first move *before* they march out the heavies.

I weave past wires and through the ghostly ways. I tap the flashlight on and let its light spill over the stolen manual. It takes some looking, but I find what I need at the back. *The red wire must be plugged in for sensors to detect movement within the room.* Two turns, up through the tight pipes, down into another strangled room. I find my wires, and snip-snip goes the red one.

Shoving the flashlight between my teeth, I run a finger down the page. No cameras in this room. Every other location has pages of instruction, but this one has only three sentences. They read like afterthoughts. It's a purposeful obscurity. What's inside? Toys for Anton? I smile.

The room requires black security access.

Up through the access chamber. I give myself a shove and catch the door's handle. Turn and click. It's a bright corridor. Just like the others, so why no cameras, Babel?

Gravity establishes itself and I sag to a knee. Deep breaths. Start walking. Twenty meters and a turn. Twenty meters and a turn. I press my back to a wall and proceed with a little more caution. It won't do to get caught now. There's still so much fun to be had.

I dig into the second sack and remove Vandemeer's prize. An identification card hangs from a black lanyard. "That's quite a smile, Commander Allen Crocker."

The card scans. The door releases.

Blinding brightness. Spend too long in the dark and every bulb's the sun. I stand there blinking until shapes form in the white. Sharp things, bright screens, and a man.

He hangs from the wall, held down by straps. His face is half hooded, and he's breathing quick and ragged. Tubes run in and out of body parts. Babel has taken from him like they've taken from us. Stolen his future, his freedom, his everything.

I cross the distance carefully. There are burns and scars and more missing things. I drag over the nearest med table, ignoring the awful grinding noise. It takes a second, but I climb up and snatch the hood from his head. A dark face snaps to life, and he struggles against his ropes. Bloodshot eyes blink, then stare.

I ask, "What's your name?"

He starts to pull again. I can feel invisible fingers itching for my nyxia.

"Hey, none of that." I hold the knife to his throat.

He stops, face twisting. "Erone. My name is Erone."

"Erone. Look at what they've done to you. It's the worst kind of pride. They can't imagine a world in which you're not in their control. It's what they did to us too. I'm not with Babel. Understand? I'm here to help you."

Five slips of the knife and his bindings fall. He sags down to his knees, chest heaving. He's been hanging for a while. He's weak, but at least they've been feeding him, giving him fluids. I can tell he's made of iron. It won't take long to get him up and running.

I watch as he gets used to his freedom, his movement. I drop the rations on the floor beside him. "You should eat. You'll need your strength."

He does. We sit quietly for a while. I can see the gears turning in his head, but I've got a few questions of my own. "How did they capture you? A trick?"

He throws a broken smile at me.

"A trick, but not theirs."

"One of the other Imago helped them?"

Erone shakes his head. "They captured me because I let them capture me."

I expect him to laugh. He doesn't. "But they tortured you."

"As we knew they would," Erone says. "But the possibilities were worth the risk. I have lost a great deal. I will admit their security surprised me. I pretended to be weak and expected them to treat me that way. I thought my escape would be easy. It has been . . . a long journey."

I can't help chasing all the rabbits he's putting in front of me. Erone came here willingly. He let Babel capture him on purpose. He's been tortured—maybe for years—all for a reason. It's the first time Babel looks like they're a step behind. I find it refreshing.

"What's your name?" Erone asks.

"Anton."

"Why did you free me? What do you want?"

"Babel. I want to put an end to Babel."

Erone swallows a final bite of food and stumbles to his feet.

"I get to kill Requin."

"We'll flip a coin for it."

Erone nods. "Fair enough."

"We need to keep the ships intact," I say. "My friends and I need at least one of them. We're not with Babel, but none of us agreed to live here forever."

He nods again. "Do you have more of it?"

"More of what?"

He points at my daggers. Of course, he wants nyxia. I pull open my knapsack and hand him two pieces I swiped from the silo cargo.

"No more than this?"

"That's all I can spare."

His hands shape what's there. God, he's fast. He cracks his neck and holds up a sword that's bigger than I am. Stepping forward, he hacks through the first mechanical arm dangling down from the ceiling. It shears through, and the metal collapses with a booming crash. He stares at the mess and nods to himself. Without a word, he starts toward the door.

"Wait," I say. "We can't just go storming over to the station. There are alarms, breach points, access codes. We have to have a plan."

Erone turns that twisted smile back to me.

"Plan?" he asks. "My plan is simple. I will kill every single one of them."

PART IV

MAGNIA

PART IV

CHAPTER 34

THE OTHER REQUIN

Emmett Atwater

It's difficult to say goodbye to the Sixth.

I walk the streets outside our building with Axis before leaving. He talks about the night before like it changed his life. I don't think he understands the reminder he's been. The past few days have been a rallying cry to rise above what Babel wants to make me.

We turn back through an alleyway and I actually stop dead in my tracks. The walls between the buildings are painted. Colorful advertisements reach across a strained canvas. One image is more familiar than the rest. "That looks just like Thesis."

Axis looks up with obvious discomfort. "The emissary?"

I point to the spot. Thesis has been painted elegantly. His features look exaggerated to a degree, but there's no denying that it looks *just* like him. The artist drew him with some kind of old-fashioned robe on. The image is framed by a repeating word that I can't decipher.

"What does it say?"

It takes Axis a second to reply. "It's an old advertisement. Thesis . . ." And now my guest hesitates, glancing down the alleyway like Thesis might come walking down it any second. "He was an actor once. A long time ago. This was one of his famous plays."

I glance back up. I guess it does kind of look like an old movie poster.

"We should return," Axis offers.

Nodding, I follow him. I don't want to call him out on the one thing that doesn't line up about his explanation. I'm always surprised when people expect me to not notice the little details. So many lies are like badly buried bodies, just waiting for a little rain to unearth them.

The painting on the wall was *fresh*. It was painted sometime in the last week or two. My mind races through the clues. Axis lied about something so small. And what's weirder is that he did it to protect Thesis, a man who almost whipped him the day before.

More importantly, Thesis is an actor. It's strange. From jump, I noticed how much smaller he was than our other escorts. I guessed he was a politician, but actor makes a lot more sense. It explains the way he performs. The narration outside the city gate. The smiles he throws us before each speech.

Outside the entrance to our makeshift hotel, Axis clasps my forearm. He thanks me, and I decide to overlook the lie, thanking him in return. I have the same on-edge feeling I always get with Babel. Like there's something waiting ahead of us we never expected.

Our crew is gathering inside. Other rings are waiting to

see us. Hundreds of thousands of Imago people. Like last time, we're loaded into boats and ushered out to sea. I can't help noticing that Thesis is absent. Speaker's assumed his role for the time being. I wonder if his slipup in the public square cost him his job. I doubt I'll feel bad if it did.

The nyxian roof stretches over the ship, sealing us inside, and we dive under the waiting waves. Morning takes the seat beside me and whispers, "We need to talk."

I glance around. Speaker's the closest Imago, but he's busy commanding the ship.

"Parvin figured out the command Rahili used. It's a simple code, repeated over and over again for some reason. It boils down to: *uplink complete.*"

"Uplink to what?" I ask, frowning.

"Our best guess was the scouters. It's the only tech we had."

"And they were confiscated at the gate. Genius plan, Babel."

Morning shrugs. "Or they've uplinked it to nyxia somehow? I have no idea. That sounds too risky. The Imago have way more control over nyxia than Babel does."

I've got no answers for her. Only more questions. "Earlier I saw—it was really strange—did you know Thesis is an actor?"

"An actor?" Morning says. "I had him pegged as a politician."

"Me too, but there was an advertisement up for a play or something? I have no idea."

Morning thinks about that for a second. Her eyes slowly widen. "Emmett. They could have chosen *anyone* in their society to send to us. It's easy to see why they sent Speaker. He called himself the Daughter's Sword. He's a guard, one of their best. I'd be willing to bet Bally and Beckway are on par with him. But their chosen emissary is an actor?"

"Only reason to choose an actor is if you want to put on a show."

She looks worried. "Exactly."

Another hour passes in brooding silence. We make our way through dark tunnels before linking up to another air lock. Light leaks from above. I shoulder my knapsack and follow the others up through the basement. The high of last night hasn't fully faded: helping people and eating good food. Existence outside Babel's reach suits us well.

The talk with Morning echoes. I can feel something coming. The dark clouds before a storm. Our passage spills into a high-ceilinged room. It's all smoked wood and dark cushions. I almost stumble right into Morning as she notices what I missed. The room is occupied.

Twenty guards circle the interior. Directly opposite, two women are waiting. One is an Imago, a Daughter. Like Ashling's, her eyes are wide set in an even wider face. She doesn't look as graceful or queenly, but she has an intense focus to her stare. Wherever her eyes settle, it seems like holes should be burning. I startle at the sight of a hound sitting to her left. It sits with perfect stillness. Compared to the hounds I saw on the Sixth—and any dog I've seen back home—the thing is massive. Its coat is dusty gray with splotches of black. The Imago strokes its unmoving head with a delicate hand.

The other woman is more shocking because she's human.

Her hair's blond, slicked back, with the sides buzzed. She wears thick-framed glasses that glint a classic nyxian black. She sports the same tight clothes and bright colors as the Imago, but her boots look straight out of a New York boutique. It's impossible to look at her and not see the familiar features of David Requin.

There's only one person she could be.

"Remove their bags," the Daughter orders.

Guards close in around us. Our own ranks tighten, disorganized but together.

"It's a temporary precaution," she says loudly. "Trust us."

All eyes turn back to Morning. She has a hand on the grip of one hatchet. She takes a long second and decides better of it. These are our most likely allies. I guess they're taking the initiative to begin negotiations. Morning makes a show of unshouldering her knapsack. She tosses it to the nearest guard. The rest of us follow her lead.

Before we can move forward, the Daughter raises another hand. We all feel the stirring of power around us. My stomach turns as our nyxia starts to rise through the air. I don't struggle, because I remember what happened to Kaya, but some of the others do. The Daughter's power leaves them helpless. Every single piece of nyxia flings itself to the ceiling.

Loud thunks sound as the pieces latch on like magnets.

The Imago guard spreads around the room. Disarmed, we stare at our weapons before moving forward and taking seats. It's impossible to feel good about what's happening.

When everyone settles in, the Daughter steps forward. Her voice is iron.

"I am Feoria, ruling Daughter of Sevenset. Welcome."

As usual, Parvin takes on the role of spokesperson.

"It's an honor," she says.

The other woman steps forward. Her sharp voice carries to every corner of the room. We all know her name before she says it. "I am Jacquelyn Requin."

She has sharp eyes, an athletic frame. We all look at her like we're seeing a ghost. Every one of us remembers the vids. She's the little girl the Imago spared.

Feoria doesn't bother easing us into the conversation. Instead her first question cuts right to the bone. "Do you know why you're here?"

When no one answers, Jacquelyn turns and clicks something. A screen unfolds behind them. It's the first technology I've seen like it in Sevenset. The images load, cycling through faces and landscapes. We see shots of Defoe, Requin, Babel marines. There are overheads of the three bases Babel has since established. Jacquelyn pauses the series on a picture of Imago people standing across from Babel on an open plain. It's a glimpse of negotiations.

"The Interstellar Contract," Feoria says. "I'll ask again: do *you* know why you are here?"

"We came to mine nyxia," Parvin answers.

"That was one part of the treaty," Feoria agrees. "You would be given safe passage to our city. You would be permitted to access mining deposits of nyxia during your stay. But were you told what we were to receive in return?"

Feoria's question chills the room. We all know Babel's promises are dangerous things. I can feel worlds spinning in and out of existence. This moment could change everything.

"We were told our presence here was wanted as a blessing to you."

"A blessing," Feoria repeats. "To a people on the verge of extinction?"

Parvin frowns, but has no answers to that.

"You were promised to us," Feoria corrects. "All of you."

My mind is lightning; my heart is thunder. Babel's lies taint everything.

"Promised how?" Parvin asks.

"Babel believes the Imago are dying out."

Her words gust through the room like a cold wind. It's a horrible thought, the idea that they might go extinct, but I have a feeling we're about to be invited into the horror somehow.

"You still haven't answered the question," Parvin notes. "Promised how?"

"The contract promised you would help extend the existence of our people. We were told that you had agreed to come here, willingly, to participate in Jacquelyn's fertilization program."

Fertilization is a word that leapfrogs to other ones. Genetics, pregnancy, babies. Parvin glances her horror back at us. Morning has to speak up on her behalf. "We were never told."

"So we expected," Feoria replies. "Babel operates a certain way. They prefer to leave their own in the dark, especially when it suits their overall purposes and goals. We've found this to be a very valuable space in which to combat them."

Jazzy sits up straighter. "So wait," she says, accent thick. "You want us to have *babies*?"

"That's not why we came." Morning raises her voice. "That's not Babel's to offer and it's not yours to take. We never agreed to *anything* like that."

"You can't possibly expect—" Parvin starts.

"This is wrong," Katsu calls out. "This is *so* wrong."

"Completely messed up," Noor agrees.

Jacquelyn holds up a hand for silence. It takes a few seconds for the entire group to hit the pause button. Our anger is a pulsing, living thing.

"We would *never* ask that of you," Jacquelyn clarifies. "We needed to see your reaction. It's been unclear to us how you stand with Babel. We've waited until now to tell you this, because we needed to be certain you would join us in the war to come. Babel signed you away without consent. They promised each of you to us forever. That was their intention."

Her words don't make any sense. The Imago arranged a treaty. They invited us to their planet with a purpose in mind. But Jacquelyn is talking as if that was all . . .

"A ruse," she says. "We told Babel what they wanted to hear. We carved them a road into our capital. We've been waiting for them to walk down it ever since."

Parvin struggles to find her voice. "But what do you *really* want? Why are we here?"

Jacquelyn and Feoria exchange a smile.

The Daughter answers simply.

"You are the Genesis. You're here to create a new beginning for us."

CHAPTER 35

COLLISION

Emmett Atwater

I expected the puzzle to get clearer. I wanted to understand which pieces fit where, but Jacquelyn's revelation just took the box and shook it. None of this makes any sense.

"Why go to all that trouble?" Morning asks. "Why bring *us*?"

"You were the reasonable lie," Jacquelyn explains. "We have successfully kept Sevenset off Babel's radar for a long time. They don't know our population breakdowns. It was easy to hide our women and come to Babel with a problem we knew they would be all too eager to solve. We needed children.

"More importantly, we knew *how* they would handle the issue. We expected lies and deception. Babel delivered both. We assumed the group they sent would desire an alliance. We also assumed Babel would bring more of their ships across space if we gave them a new window of opportunity. We were correct on both counts."

I find myself nodding along with the explanation. All

this time I've feared how far ahead of us Babel could plan, how extensive their reach seemed. But the Imago clearly won't be outdueled on that front. They have a far better read on Babel than Babel does on them.

"So your population, your women . . ." Morning looks lost.

"Both have been at normal rates for decades," Jacquelyn says. "There's no shortage, no need for you to provide more children. Thesis and the other emissaries have done a brilliant job selling the story. We assume Babel's been watching the entire time. It was our way of luring them closer."

That explains Jerricho's presence outside the gates. And the woman I saw in the crowds of the Sixth. There's no shortage of women; they've just kept them out of sight. It also explains having Thesis as their emissary. Hire an actor to make sure the show leads the audience in the right direction. He was chosen as much for Babel's eyes as for ours.

The clues lead to one conclusion.

"There must be something else threatening you," I say.

Feoria offers me a look of approval. "Show them, Jacquelyn."

With another click, images load on the screen behind her. Statistical data, star charts. We're all eyeing the bright screen when Jacquelyn presses her thumb to an icon in the corner. A video widens until it fills the whole screen. It's like something out of an astronomy class.

"You've seen our moons," she says. "Glacius and Magness."

The screen shows them revolving in their separate orbits. It follows their paths, dancing in and out, as the entire planet rotates on an axis. Parvin's the first one to see where this is going. Her response isn't elegant, but it hammers the point home just fine.

"Shit."

I translate that for her. "A collision."

We watch the orbits strangle one another. The two moons dance too close, and there's an inevitable crash. The simulation shows the probable debris. Massive chunks escape out into space, but even larger pieces find their way into the atmosphere. The simulation stops there, but words like *cataclysm* and *apocalypse* and *extinction* come to mind.

Jacquelyn says what we can't. "Our world is coming to an end."

It's like someone keeps pressing a defibrillator to our chests and lighting us up with electricity, not realizing the shocks to our system are already too much to handle.

Morning asks the million-dollar question. "How long have you known?"

"It was discovered six years ago. Every historical record in our archives mentions a world with two moons. The references can even be found in the oldest poems. Our scientists believe they have orbited for millennia. According to my—to Erone, a two-moon system can survive for a very long time, but the moons statistically *have* to collide at some point. We just happen to be the generation who will see the inevitable come to pass."

Erone. That name again. It's so distracting that I almost miss the anger in Morning's expression. "Six years. So you invited us here even though you knew this was going to happen."

Jacquelyn and Feoria look away for the first time. This

must have been the one potential flaw in their plan. An understanding that they've done the same thing that Babel did. The Imago saw an opportunity and took it. They willingly invited us into danger so that they could attach themselves to us. We are the genesis, whether we want to be or not.

I file it right where it belongs: *U* for *Unforgivable*.

"And you call people like Jerricho slings?" I ask. "How are you *any* different?"

Feoria shakes her head. "A sling works for himself. We work for all of our people. Do you think everyone in this room will survive what's coming? I made these decisions for my people knowing I would die beneath the only two moons I have ever known."

I ignore all of that, almost shouting. "If you never lie to Babel, they never recruit us. If they never recruit us, we never go into space. Do you know how much this has already cost us? Bilal, Kaya, Brett, Loche. They're all dead. And that's not just on Babel's head anymore. It's on yours too. How many more names will we add to that list before all this is over?"

An unbelievable sadness crosses Feoria's features.

"Should I have let my people die?"

I shake my head, because I can't answer that. The hardest thing is that I damn well get it: she did what any of us would have done. But it's getting harder and harder to feel like we're anything more than pieces on a game board. Just playthings at the mercy of enormous forces.

"You're here now," Jacquelyn answers quietly. "We can't change that. The choice is simple: you're with us or you're with Babel. We plan to move on to the Sanctum now. There are necessary preparations to make sure we take advantage of Babel's attack. We'll return your personal effects and let you discuss the decision among yourselves, but remember we have more to show you. About who we are, about who Babel is. I'm sorry that it had to happen this way, but understand: you are our *only* hope."

CHAPTER 36

A HOUSE DIVIDED

Emmett Atwater

As the boats prepare for departure, Morning drags the entire Genesis crew into an empty sunroom. She casts her nyxia to the walls and we all hear the sharp crackle, the silence that follows. Creaking doors and distant footsteps vanish. It's just us now. Just family.

"Thoughts?" Morning asks.

"This is bullshit," Katsu says. "That's the main thought."

"I just want to go home." Holly repeats her tired refrain. "I hate it here."

"Babel makes the most sense," Parvin adds unexpectedly. "We go back to Babel."

Everyone stares at her. Jaime's been quiet so far, but his anger breaks through now.

"I thought you were supposed to be the smart one," he says. "Go back to Babel? They lied to us about *everything*. I mean, were you even in that room with us? You realize their plan was for you to come here and be a host for alien *babies*."

Parvin fires back, "We're sitting on a planet that is scheduled for destruction. Remind me again, how many space-ships do the Imago have?"

Jaime looks helpless. "None."

"Exactly," she snaps. "And when we show up and tell Babel, 'Oh by the way, the entire planet's about to *explode*,' don't you think they'll accept us back into their good graces?"

"Sure they will," Jaime says, shaking his head. "And then halfway home they'll politely float us into space so no one ever knows what their real plans were out here."

This time it's Parvin who doesn't have an answer. Morning uses the pause to jump in. "Let's take a step back," she says. "I told my team when we landed and I'm going to tell you all again so you don't forget it: we have *each other*. We can't count on Babel. We can't count on the Imago. We have each other. Shoulder to shoulder. Fathom?"

No one repeats the phrase, but there are nods all around.

That logic leaves me frustrated. "All that means is we're stuck in this room. I'm not trying to kibosh the team-spirit thing, but we're gonna have to choose one side or the other. We need to figure out what the best-case scenario is for each one."

Morning nods to Parvin. "How do you imagine it going with Babel?"

She adjusts her glasses. "We escape Sevenset. We get back to Babel. We use our information as a bargaining chip to return to the Tower Space Station. Once we're up there, we would just have to position ourselves so that Babel can't get rid of us."

Morning gestures to Jaime. "And the Imago?"

He looks uncertain. "They have to have a plan. They knew the moons were going to collide. So there has to be a reason why they're luring Babel in. We just have to find out why."

"Scenarios don't matter," I say, the realization thundering. "We're thinking about it all wrong. The answer is obvious. There's only one choice. Who actually needs us?"

The entire group considers that. Longwei's the first to answer.

"The Imago."

"The Imago," I agree. "Can we carve a way home with Babel? Maybe, but at the end of the day they've already shown us that we're expendable. If they return to Earth, they'll weave some story about our tragic deaths and not think twice about it. But the Imago can't do that."

Morning is nodding now. "If they show up in Babel's ships . . ."

"People will call it an alien invasion. A hostile takeover. No way that goes well. If they have a real plan to fight Babel, they're the side I want to be on. They actually *need* us to make things work on Earth. Always pick the side that can't get rid of you."

It's quiet for a few seconds before Katsu starts laughing hysterically.

"I'm sorry," he says between each burst. "I just . . . Babel's trying so damn hard to get down on this planet . . . and it's literally about to explode. The irony is just . . ."

Parvin raises her voice, annoyed. "So we go to the Sanctum?"

Morning looks around like there's no other choice.

"We go to the Sanctum."

CHAPTER 37

THE SANCTUM

———

Emmett Atwater

The escort boats are waiting. Feoria traveled ahead of us with her guards, but Jacquelyn Requin waits on the docks. Wind tosses her cloak as we all pile aboard the escort vessels. I end up on board with her and a handful of others. Speaker steps in as captain.

We should be overwhelmed, but all the little details keep spinning back to the surface. I slide past the rest of the crew and nod an introduction to Jacquelyn.

"You said the name Erone, didn't you?"

Her attention sharpens on me. "I did."

"I've heard his name a few times. The Erone Provision."

Jacquelyn nods. "The rule was named for him. He was kidnapped."

"I know."

She frowns now. "You know what?"

I've shoved the memory of that bright room down into the darkest corners of my mind. Sometimes, though, details thunder back without warning. I can still see Erone's arm rising in the air like a drawbridge. The scars running over his skin.

"He was on our ship."

Jacquelyn's cool exterior vanishes. It's replaced with a desperation I've only seen at funerals. It's clear that Erone was more than a colleague to her. "He's alive?"

"I'm not sure. He was—they were torturing him." I can see how that information guts her. "I'm sorry. There was an accident. I'm not sure what Babel did with him after it happened. He was alive, though. A few months ago."

It takes a second for her to steady herself. Speaker is sounding commands as the crew prepares for our descent. Jacquelyn nods once. "Thank you for telling me."

Nyxia starts to stretch overhead, sealing the boat. I slip back to Morning's side. Waves rock the boat as we start to nose-dive. Seats unfold from the railings, and Speaker calls for all of us to strap in. "We're taking the Quick. It's going to be a little jolt to your systems."

"The Quick?" Morning asks.

"Just strap in," Speaker replies. "You'll see."

We take our seats as the light fades overhead. Through the front windows, I can just make out the looming mouth of a massive tunnel. We've been through the waterways before, but everything was tight and winding. This one's three times the size of our ship. Ahead of us, the other escort ship reaches the entryway. We watch the dark water spiral and bubble. A whirlpool rotates the ship twice before it launches into the black.

"It's like a roller coaster," Jazzy says excitedly.

"Don't look left," Speaker suggests. "Or right, for that matter."

The crew eases us over the threshold and we can hear turbines humming around us. There's a suction noise, a distant groan, and then our boat starts to drift. All of us tighten up as the revolutions start. Before we're fully upright, the air in the ship compresses and we shoot into the darkness. Speed eats at the edges of our vision. In seconds, my stomach is in my throat.

Someone lets out a whoop, but I keep my mouth clamped shut. It's not worth losing my cookies to act tough. The race through the tunnel lasts fifteen hellish minutes. Finally the speed drops. I hear the engines stall, and our pace goes down notch by notch. Everything is still blacked out except for the radar and equipment. I swallow back the rising bile, but not everyone's so lucky. There are a lot of queasy faces in the group.

"Two minutes to the first checkpoint," Speaker announces. "Everyone all right?"

"Oh, just peachy," Jazzy complains.

The tunnel forks in three different directions. Speaker guides the vessel up, cutting engines and letting us drift. There's a rumble overhead as our nyxian stations attach us to a slotted ceiling. A glance through the portholes shows weaponry on every wall. Each gun glows blue, and they're all trained on our boat. I eye them curiously.

"What are those, Speak?"

"Security," he replies. "This is the only underwater entry into the Sanctum."

The ceiling grinds open. Water bubbles rush up and Speaker lets us drift into the next space. The wall snaps closed and we're in a new chamber, with new guns along the walls. They wheel in our direction. This time, I spy a flash of white scanning the side of the ship.

"What are they scanning for?" I ask.

"Unwelcome guests," Speaker says.

"And if they find one?"

He glances back. "Then it was a pleasure meeting all of you."

Fortunately, we're not harboring fugitives. We pass through the final checkpoint, and sunlight beats at the windows. Speaker lowers our nyxian covering and we're all forced to shield our eyes from the brightness. The platform rises into an open room, water dripping and draining from our ship's exterior. We blink out at pristine gardens, an arching glass dome.

"Welcome to the Sanctum," Speaker says.

A glass-paneled dome arches overhead, casting squares of light down on everything. Rows of flowers extend in every direction. Trees tower overhead, draped by ivy or dangling fruits. The garden's architect shows off on the path to our right. Great ivy buckets have been turned over by ivy hands. Bright flowers spill from the buckets and across the paths like water. Speaker leads us forward, allowing us to take in the majesty of it all.

We pass by a tree with millions of delicate white petals. The lowest branches are speckled with little red dots. Of course Azima runs a finger across one of them. We all smile when she jumps back. "It bit me," she says, licking the blood on her fingertip.

Speaker smiles. "You're not the first. Look."

We watch another red dot sink and solidify into the petal. One blink and I lose it among the endless speckles. Wonder leads us to wonder, and Speaker regretfully forces us out of the gardens and deeper into the Sanctum. Posted guards stare out from the hidden nooks and corners. They move constantly, cycling past us, eyes curious but hands ready on weapons.

"The Sanctum was founded three hundred years ago," Speaker explains. "The ancient queens were more likely to associate with the Seventh back then. Many were renowned warriors. Their decision to center themselves in Sevenset created new orbits. Our entire world shifted."

"Have your rulers always been women?" Jazzy asks.

Speaker nods. "Almost without exception."

"I like this," Azima says with satisfaction. "Women are better rulers than men."

Speaker smiles. "You will hear no argument from me."

"But anyone can become a tyrant." I didn't mean to say it out loud. Speaker and the others glance back. "Sorry. Just . . . that's how it goes, right? Power corrupts? You know, more money, more problems."

"More money, more problems." Speaker looks dumbfounded. "A strange concept."

Omar laughs. "Emmett, you can't just quote 50 Cent as a universal truth, man."

I grin back at him. "Correction: Diddy said it first. I'm

just trying to keep the legends alive. Sorry, Speak. Must be an Earth thing."

He shakes off the confusion and leads us forward. The Sanctum consists of what the Imago call sanctuaries. After the first was built, each successive generation of rulers wrapped a newly styled sanctuary around it, echoing the already built rings of Sevenset.

Speaker informs us that we've already passed through the outer sanctuary. The gardens were constructed by the youngest generation, the current rulers of Sevenset. We all gasp as we cross the threshold into the next sanctuary.

Walls stretch thirty meters high, all lined with books. The dark wood shelves curl around every corner, tower to every ceiling. Even the floor beneath our feet shows faded spines through glass.

"Nearly every book ever published in our history," Speaker reveals. "The Daughters of that generation valued reading and education. Some won their favor by hunting down the rarest volumes. The Imago who recovered the first translation of the *Parables of the Maker* ended up marrying one of the queens."

We wind through the endless library and pass into the third sanctuary. Speaker gathers us on a stone platform that overlooks a floorless hall. "The Daughters responsible for the third sanctuary were fond of clockwork and mechanisms. It's the most famous. Even after all these years, all of their inventions and workings have not been discovered. They built something they claimed was as complicated and unique as any living creation. Most historians agree."

He tugs the nearest lever, and our platform grinds to

life. Gears spin and chains rattle as we're lifted into the air. We go up about ten meters before our platform tracks with something in the walls and glides smoothly across the gaping black below. Speaker gestures to Jazzy.

"Go ahead and tap one of the stones."

She grins at him and reaches out, then knocks twice on a granite square.

We all wait and watch, but movement stirs along the wall directly opposite. The stone splits on an invisible seam, opening like a cuckoo clock. A miniature rope unfolds over the side. As our platform passes, we have to turn to watch a pair of wooden soldiers lower a bucket. At first we can't see what's inside, but then little heads peek out from blankets, identical to the half-hounds we've seen around Sevenset.

"The Parable of Bane and Bless," Speaker remarks. "I've only seen it once before."

Our platform continues its grinding way, and we watch as the rope retracts back into the walls and the stone clamps shut. Jazzy can't stop talking about it as the platform kisses the edges of a second landing. There's a lot of nervous laughter as the floor shakes, then quiets. Speaker leads us away, turning yet another corner. "And the oldest sanctuary," he announces. "The first queens created calm with word and deed. You'll see their desires for simplicity and comfort here."

It's a vast room of fountains and cushions and distant light. The roof is open to the elements, coloring the room with gold. We cross to the nearest fountain, and Speaker has us press our hands to the stones. They're impossibly soft, almost like feathers.

"Not an easy manipulation," Speaker says. "To the water, the substance is unyielding. To flesh, it is giving and comfortable. Every stone here boasts unique properties. You just have to make sure you don't roll into the fountain while you sleep."

On cue, Azima leans too far forward and goes splashing into the water. A hilarious chaos follows as Speaker and Longwei try to help her out, but she grins and splashes away from them.

"Come in," she calls. "The water is warm!"

The revolution starts that easily.

Speaker's eyes widen as everyone strips off shoes and socks and clothes. Jaime's the first one to figure out that all the fountains are separated by little underpasses. Speaker gives up his efforts to get us out and agrees to oversee a game of freeze tag instead. Maybe he realizes this is what a sanctuary is supposed to be. For thirty eternal minutes, we're children again.

It's a nice surprise to discover that Alex is the best swimmer instead of Morning. We set up our teams, splashing wildly, calling fish out of water, and cheating, because pool games aren't fun if you don't cheat a little. Alex weaves his way through a drainpipe to make the final tag on a flailing Parvin. He smiles for what feels like the first time since Anton launched into space. The whole thing feels like a regained paradise.

The game ends and we climb out of fountains, dripping and splashing, almost untouched by the burdens that brought us here. While the others pull clothes back on, laughing and complaining, I walk over to where Speaker is standing.

"Why'd you show us all this? Why show us the rings? Any of it?"

"We wanted you to see what we stand to lose," he says quietly. "Our entire world, Emmett. Thousands of our kind will not make the voyage through space. I am one of them."

He notes the shock on my face.

"I volunteered to stay with my queen. It was an easy choice," he says. "But remember that none of what we built will travel across the universe either. If our plan works, we'll leave behind our histories, our legacies, our everything."

He smiles sadly before slipping away. My eyes trail him. He's not putting on a show like he did in the early days of our time together. I can only imagine what it was like when they discovered what was about to happen. How long have they spent counting down the hours until the day their entire world would be destroyed?

I look around at the paradise they've carved into this place. Each stone so precise. The fountains formed with such delicate care. How long before all of it vanishes in fire and smoke?

CHAPTER 38

BROTHERS BY FORCE

Emmett Atwater

The rooms we're given are simple. Bright balconies overlook the distant ocean. We split off into sections designed for three. Jaime claims a bed in the first room. I'm about to follow him in when I spy Alex glancing down the hallway, looking unsure where he belongs.

"This way, man." I wave to him. "We've got an open bed in here."

I've wanted to talk to him for a while. Jaime, Anton, Alex, and me, we are brothers by force. Babel's final experiment bonded us in some dark, impossible way. It's kind of unfair that three of us landed together. We got to work and talk through the pain. But Alex landed alone. I'm guessing he talked with Anton here or there, but when Anton launched into space, it left Alex alone again.

Alex is all polite nods. His golden curls toss whenever he walks. He's got light brown skin that the otherworldly sun has darkened since landing. It doesn't take us long to start exploring the room like we're staying at some fancy hotel.

We kick our feet up on the balcony right around sun-
set. It takes a few minutes of awkward conversation to get
where I promised I'd go. I force myself to talk about those
dark minutes before we launched down from space.

"I've been meaning to talk with you," I say, sounding
more like Pops than I ever thought I could. "I know what
Babel put you through. With Loche."

In a breath he goes distant. His smile retreats. He cracks
a knuckle, lips sealed. I know the feeling. "You don't have
to talk about it," I say. "I get it, you know? But if you haven't
talked to anyone about it, you should. Jaime and I talked
about it after we landed." I nod over to him. "Anton too. He
was there. We actually got to talk it out."

Alex looks up. The bright color of his eyes seems to be
fading.

"No one else in my landing party went through it," he finally says. "I saw their faces after. I thought—I don't know—
that maybe I was the only one shaken by it. Took a few
minutes to figure out that none of them had to fight. None of
them even *knew* there were fights."

"So you didn't bring it up?"

"With Katsu in my group? Hell no, man."

I nod. "He makes everything into a joke."

Jaime grunts at that. He's been on the end of Katsu's
jokes more than most.

"Not this," Alex says.

"No, never this."

He looks down at his hands.

"The worst part is that I wanted to do it in the end."

"Because you had to do it."

"No," Alex cuts back. "They put me with Loche on purpose."

I shake my head. "Why Loche?"

"We had a history."

I cock an eyebrow. "Before you launched?"

"Nah, nothing like that." Alex glances nervously at Jaime. "I'm—well, Anton and I . . ."

"You go together."

He nods his thanks for putting it that simply. "Early on. I just . . . I like him, you know? We got along so easily. He thinks I'm a little too much sometimes, but let's be honest, Anton needs a little *too much* in his life. Loche was the first one who picked up on the fact that it was more than a friendship. Anton didn't like talking about it. He's from Russia, so I understood. I grew up near Bogotá. It was easier there. You didn't have to jump through hoops because of who you were. You could just be yourself.

"Anyway, Loche noticed and he kind of dug into us about it. Never anything crude, you know, but he outed us to the rest of Genesis 12. He said he thought they knew, that he'd be the last one to notice. That's how he was. This tough rugby guy, always so macho about things. Anton and I would be hanging out at breakfast and I'd glance up, catch him smirking at us."

"I'm guessing Anton fixed that."

Alex nods. "I told him not to, but that's Anton. Cornered him one night, and we didn't see too many smirks from Loche after that. I got over it."

"Until Babel put you two together," I say, piecing it all together.

"In the room, he tried to use it against me. Told me that

Anton and I weren't like him and Ida. We didn't have the connection that *they* had. He told me that he and Ida talked about having kids. All he really meant was that their relationship was *normal*."

I shake my head. "That's so messed up."

"He ranted about it," Alex says. "And the second I let my guard down, he went for me."

Alex lifts up his shirt. His skin is tan, but slashed white beneath his ribs is a sharp, winding scar that's healed all kinds of crooked. He lets the shirt drop and shakes his head.

"Gutted me," he says. "Made it easier to gut him back as he fumbled through my pockets for the key. The part that gets me, man, is that Ida still doesn't know. She doesn't know that he's dead, and she doesn't know that I'm the one who killed him."

I shake my head. "Knowing wouldn't do anything but make her aim at the wrong target. Give her time. She'll realize Babel is behind all of this. Not you or me or Jaime. It's Babel."

"Maybe," Alex hedges. "But it was easy in the end. Easier than I expected it to be. I know Babel set it up and all that, but I'm the one who did it. My hand drove the knife in. In the end, it wasn't even hard to do."

"Except it was," I say after a few seconds. "Listen to yourself. The fact that it's eating you up is proof enough. You didn't want to do it. If you had the choice, you never would have done it. But you didn't have a choice 'cause Babel took it away. That's not your fault."

Alex nods, but his eyes are proof he doesn't completely buy what I'm saying.

"Still. I killed him."

It's the simplest, cruelest truth. *Still. I killed him.* Beneath all the justifications and rage, beneath Babel's forceful hand and their own desire to stay alive, is the simple fact: Alex, Jaime, and Anton are killers now. It's a clean, twisted kind of truth. I glance over at Jaime.

"They made us this way," he says simply. "They can face the consequences now."

It's a brutal stance, but it's talk I've heard before. In the hallways of my school. On the streets of my neighborhood. Answering like for like, taking blood for blood. Travel across the universe and some things just don't seem to change.

"My pops used to tell me to be good."

Alex looks up. "Huh?"

"I don't know. Whenever I messed up—and man, I messed up all the time—he wouldn't even talk about the bad thing. He'd just tell me to be good. Like, hey, next time, be good."

"I like that," Alex says.

"Maybe we can be good. The next time. Maybe there will be a way to be good again."

He runs a hand through his golden locks. The motion makes him look twenty years older, twenty years a wanderer. "You mean like what you did for that beggar, Axis."

"You were the first one to join me," I remind him.

"So what, we just keep doing that? And maybe one day all the little things will take away the big thing." He hitches on the thought. "Doubt it, but hey, it's worth a shot."

"It's worth a shot," I agree.

I reach out and offer him a handshake. He clasps my forearm, and just like that, he sees me as a brother too. More than what Babel would make us. We both glance over at Jaime, but he waves the idea away. "They're the ones who changed the rules. Now that I know what game they're playing, I'm going to make my own moves. I'm going to take what they took from me."

Alex nods his respect at that. It's such a dark promise. I decide to keep working on Jaime, to keep pulling him back to something better.

Speaker interrupts, knocking on our door to remind us we should sleep. He tells us the Daughters will host us in the throne room early the next day. We start claiming beds around the room, but Morning appears in the entrance and waves me over. "Isadora," she whispers. "She's here, you know?"

"She wanted to use the Daughters against me," I remind her. "But the whole pregnancy thing. It's not worth as much as she thought it was, is it? I guess if I'm in danger, we'll know tomorrow when we meet with them."

Morning frowns. "I'm nailing your door shut."

"Seriously?"

"Just for tonight."

She squeezes my hand before closing the door behind her. I can hear her messing with the lock as Jaime turns the lights off and we settle in for the night. We talk a little bit about home, a little bit about nothing. It has the taste of a normal conversation, the kind we would have after school or eating burgers on a Friday night.

It's almost enough to forget the dead, and all those we've left behind.

CHAPTER 39

KING DAVID

———

Emmett Atwater

But the dead rise sometimes. Revenants from graves.

I wake to pressure. Just a hand on my chest. I confuse it for Morning, but the face that looms in the darkness doesn't belong to her. It's not Jaime needing to be helped to the med bay, either. This face has walked out of my nightmares and into real life: Isadora.

"Do not move," she whispers. "Do not speak."

One hand is on my chest. The other dangles a knife over my throat. My eyes roam to the door. It's closed, sealed. But another glance shows the curtains by our balcony entrance rustling in the wind. We actually left it open. I can't believe I left it open.

"Have you ever read the Bible?" she whispers. "There's one story I *always* hated. King David? You know him?"

I nod carefully.

"He's being chased by Saul. What an awful king. He promises David a good life but betrays him, then hunts him across the wilderness. Do you know the story?"

A whisper shakes through my lips. "No."

"David hides in a cave. It just so happens that Saul goes to that same cave and falls asleep outside of it." Her eyes glint down at me. Moonlight frames her. *I am about to die.* "And I hated this story, because it was the perfect moment for David. His greatest enemy made weak. Delivered at his feet like a gift. But what does David do?"

Isadora's off hand moves down to my waist. She pinches the fabric of my shirt up. I swallow as she slides the knife away from my throat and starts to saw through the hem.

"He cuts off a piece of Saul's robe," Isadora says. "He doesn't gut him like he should have. I always thought, 'What a fool.' If I had the chance, I would punish my enemy. But now I understand. David needed proof of who he was. Later he took the piece of robe to Saul and explained. He could have killed him, but he didn't. Saul was in his hands, but he showed mercy."

Isadora finishes sawing. She rips at the dangling threads before holding up a patch of fabric no bigger than a fist. I can see her jaw clenched, her eyes narrowed.

"If I kill you, Morning will come for me," she says. "If I hurt you, the group will turn on me. I can't afford this. My baby needs to go back to Earth. So tomorrow I'll show this to Morning and you'll explain to her what happened. This fabric is a promise that you won't come to harm. When I attempt to rejoin the group tomorrow, you will support me."

It takes me a second to realize she's waiting for me to agree. I nod in disbelief.

"I will not be left behind in this world," Isadora says softly. "My baby will go home."

She waves the fabric once before retreating into the shadows. I watch as she heads for the balcony. I follow her movements until she disappears down one side. It's all I can do to roll out of bed. My legs aren't working. My lungs won't take in oxygen. I gasp my way to the balcony entrance and slam the doors shut. Jaime rolls over in his bed. Alex groans awake.

"Anton?" he asks. "Is it already time to go?"

For a while, I don't respond. My back is pressed against the glass. My mind is racing through the details. Isadora. We let down our guards for a night, and she could have killed me for it. But she didn't. She spared me. Alex rustles again, sitting up.

"Emmett?"

"It's nothing," I say. "Get some sleep."

He nods those golden curls and turns back over. At some point, I force myself to walk back to my bed. I lie back down, but sleep never comes.

CHAPTER 40

THE BEST-LAID PLANS OF IMAGO AND MEN

Emmett Atwater

The next morning we gather in the main sanctuary. Morning winks at me, but I'm still lost in a dream state. Did last night even happen? Is there more to Isadora's plan?

Speaker enters. Isadora and Ida trail him.

Their presence echoes through our ranks. Morning reacts immediately. She cuts across the group until she's standing between Isadora and the rest of us. I have to crane my neck to get a look at the piece of torn white fabric Isadora is holding in her hands. It's proof that last night wasn't just a dream. She waves it like a white flag.

"We come in peace."

"No," Morning says. "You don't get to walk in there with us. You left *this* behind. You promised one of ours harm. We don't forget that easily."

Isadora just waves the shirt again. "Take this as a token of my new intentions."

"It's fine," I say, startling Morning. "Let her come with us."

Morning stares back at me. "Fine? She—"

"Could have killed me last night."

Those words ice the room. Everyone except Morning. She stares her fury at me before whipping it back in Isadora's direction. I take a step forward and set a hand on her shoulder. She tries to shrug it off, but I pull her closer, doing my best to be a calming presence.

"She didn't, though," I explain. "Last night she could have killed me, but she didn't."

Isadora shows the fabric again. "I don't have to like him to know you're my best way out of here. If I wanted him dead, he'd be dead. Keep the fabric if it helps you remember that."

"He's alive for now," Morning says. "Right? As long as it serves your purposes, but what about twenty days from now? Or two years from now?"

"If there's a two years from now," Isadora replies, "we'll all be thankful to be alive."

Morning's not convinced. "I don't believe you."

"That's your right." Isadora sets a protective hand on her stomach. "But I started feeling kicks last week. It's a boy, I think. Just a feeling. I've had morning sickness too. Some cramps. The more the baby—I don't know, the more *real* the baby gets, the less I care about Emmett. I don't like him and I don't like you, but I'm going to get my baby back to Earth. If that means swallowing my pride and my hate, go ahead and pass the bottle."

There's a second where Morning looks ready to fire back, but I squeeze her shoulder. She looks up at me, and Parvin takes advantage of the hesitation.

"I'm convinced," she says. "Welcome back. Speaker? We were heading somewhere?"

He nods. "The Daughters wait in the throne room."

And just like that we're back on the move. Morning stays tight at my side, but I think these are the first steps toward something necessary. We have one less thing to fear.

Everything around us is old stone. Absurdly wide and absurdly high, as if monsters made the castle so they could slouch through every door and into every hall. A basic slate colors the walls and floors, accented only by an occasional painting. I stop short as we pass by a vase of sunflowers etched against a baby-blue backdrop. The piece almost looks like a Van Gogh. My mind skips back to middle school art classes, most of which were spent pretending I wasn't looking at Sherry Taylor. Everything about Earth feels like it happened in another life, to someone else.

The real masterpieces wait in the next hallway, speckled by light from stained-glass windows. Speaker pauses us before the series of portraits. Fifteen of them hang from the walls.

Our own portraits stare back at us. Rendered with delicate precision. Our features look a little exaggerated, even a little heroic. I find mine and smile. My eyes look harder than I remember, like they're carved out of stone. The painter took my skin a shade too dark, but also left my hair looking a lot neater than it's ever looked. I couldn't ever afford the twenty-dollar artists at the fair, so to see myself in a portrait is stunning, unimaginable.

"Who painted these?" Azima asks, standing before her own.

"Feoria's work," Speaker answers. "She has quite an eye, doesn't she?"

I glance over. Red flushes up his neck. I smile at him and he can't even hold the look. Feoria must be his favorite. She's one hell of a painter. Anton grins down at us from the far right. He looks like he's causing trouble, and I say a silent prayer that he is, that he's still alive and an unpleasant thorn in Babel's side. Longwei's looks the most badass, of course. Somehow Feoria's adjusted the painting so his right eye glows out from the black nyxian scar.

I tap his shoulder and nod to it. "That's a framer."

He shakes his head and smiles.

"How'd she paint these?" Alex asks, staring up at his own face. "The other day was the first time she saw us, wasn't it?"

Speaker smiles. "Thesis captured an image of you all waiting in line at our first encounter. It was a moment our people wanted to remember. Feoria decided to take things a step further. She wanted to complete these portraits before you arrived. I believe yesterday's meeting with you was the first time she's left her studio."

We stand in front of our portraits a while longer, long enough for me to start thinking about the faces that aren't there. Kaya and Bilal and Loche and Brett and Roathy. Faces the Imago will never see because Babel chose to play God. They deserved portraits too, every single one of them. A darker thought follows that one: the Imago started *all* of this.

Katsu nods up at his portrait and grins. "She got my good side."

Morning rolls her eyes before turning to Speaker. "Thank you. These are wonderful."

"Come. The Daughters await."

We follow him through the endless halls. Our path wraps back around the building, descending a generous staircase, and directing us toward a gaping hole in the distant wall. Only when we're twenty meters away do we notice that the hole is actually a mouth. Flaming eyes hover above the black. Scales ripple out from the gleaming pits, forming a long snout above twisting teeth. Speaker gestures to the doorway.

"Emmett, this is the creature you saw your first night in Grimgarden. A century."

The yawning jaw stretches from floor to ceiling, ten meters. Maybe bigger.

"Why are they called that?" Jazzy asks.

Speaker answers, "If they survive for one hundred years, they transform."

"Into what?" Azima asks curiously.

"Something bigger," Speaker replies. "Something *much* bigger."

Teeth scythe down like swords. Speaker leads us through the maw of the beast like it's not the most terrifying decoration we've ever seen. There's ten meters of pure dark. On both sides, something swallows the light before we burst back into a room filled with sunshine.

There's no roof overhead. The covering of static flickers in the distant sky. A bridge leads us over a man-made river and onto a wide marble platform. Every five meters, the marble rises by a step. It also narrows, a single meter at a time. We climb thirty or forty steps before getting our first sighting of the Daughters.

Ten thrones ring a final marble platform. The Daughters watch us ascend. I walk on the far right, putting Ashling straight ahead of me. The queen who greeted us on the open plains has her veil of thick hair pinned aside. She wears a deep ocean-blue dress that matches her eyes.

Feoria sits on her left. Her gaze is still burning holes in everything.

But the real surprise is Jacquelyn. She doesn't stand off to the side like an adviser would. Instead she sits in one of the thrones. A queen in her own right. It was easy to think of her as more human than Imago, but her position in one of the thrones sends a strong statement.

Feoria begins. "Ashling and I have invited you here in confidence. The plan we share with you today is no small matter. Please respect the nature of these secrets, and understand we spent years working through this with our very best advisers."

Ashling nods at that. "We're sympathetic with your position. We assume your cooperation depends on our plan's viability. We're confident we can find common ground."

Parvin steps forward. "We just want to know whose hand we're shaking."

With a nod from the Daughters, Jacquelyn stands. She lifts one of our confiscated knapsacks, putting it on display. After she's sure we've all had a good look, she flips the pack and unsheathes a knife. We all watch as she works away the bottom padding. There's a few seconds of fabric giving way before her blade strikes metal. Jacquelyn widens the hole and lets a small silver device fall to the floor.

"Have any of you seen these before?"

The entire group offers her blank stares.

"We knew you were Babel's way into the city," she explains. "We assumed they would use your entrance to undermine our current defenses. Each one of your packs came with one of these built into the lining. Babel calls them vanguard devices. It's multifunctioning tech. They're designed to go into a territory before actual troops do. They scan for population and movement. Babel's always wanted a look behind our veil. Now they have it. Full readouts of our population for each of your ring visits.

"Each of these devices will also ping strategic locations back to Babel. Their coordinates act as homing beacons. Babel will launch their attack on our city, and these are designed to disable our defenses from within." Jacquelyn directs our attention to the static in the sky overhead. "Their plan is to remove the exterior shield and use that open window to drop missiles on each of Sevenset's rings. Missiles that are coordinating with these devices."

Another piece fits into the puzzle. The intercepted information Parvin decoded: *uplink complete.* Rahili's quick work must have synched her base up with the devices hidden in our bags. David Requin's reasons for sending us to Ophelia Station make more sense now.

"If you know all this," Parvin asks, "why did you let us enter the city at all?"

"Our fishing boats will bloody the water sometimes,"

Jacquelyn says. "Blood is a sign of weakness. Something is vulnerable. Fishermen use it to lure in bigger catches. Our entire plan depends on the destruction of Sevenset. If Babel thinks we're wounded and weak and on the run, what do you predict they'll do?"

Parvin is nodding now. "Come down in force."

"Sevenset destroyed. Our society on the run. How could Babel resist?"

It's not hard to trace that to the next logical conclusion.

"Empty ships," I say.

"Empty ships," Jacquelyn confirms. "Babel will sweep down for the kill. And we will let them. They've always wanted to be our conquerors, so we'll let them conquer a land they don't know is already doomed. While that happens? We take to the skies."

"They're already down here," I reply. "We saw marines in cryogenic chambers under the bases."

"Of course," Jacquelyn says with a smile.

Parvin cuts back in. "And you're just going to let your people die on the rings?"

"Of course not," Feoria replies fiercely. "We have a plan for *all* of this."

Jacquelyn removes a nyxian device from her pocket. She sets it down on the tiered step in front of us. An image is cast into the air. Blue light resolves into a map.

We all recognize Magnia. Sevenset sits northeast of center, its rings linking three separate continents. A word from Jacquelyn brings up eight marks scattered across the different regions. I can see faint lines tracing their way from Sevenset to the marked points.

"Each of these represents a launch station," she says. "I cannot express the immense difficulty of developing these centers without alerting Babel. Every measure of stealth technology we possess was necessary. Thousands of our people labored in secret. Many died to achieve this. Each launch bay holds thirty shuttles. Each shuttle holds two passengers. It was the best we could do in the time span Erone gave us. Two hundred and forty ships, ready to launch into space."

As we watch the layers of their plan unfold, it's impossible to ignore how *genius* this is. The Imago have thought of everything. Azima's curious voice overrides Parvin's.

"So why not just fly to Earth?" she asks.

Jacquelyn shakes her head. "We have many technological advantages over Babel. Space travel isn't one of them. The Imago aren't a people who have ever reached for the stars. There haven't been any space races. No fears of overpopulation, either."

Azima pushes back. "But you have nyxia, right? How hard can it be?"

"The mechanics and the science are beyond us," Jacquelyn answers. "But we *are* using nyxia to our advantage. The craft we built work simply. They'll launch through the atmosphere. Once they're in orbit, they're designed to seek out other nyxian objects."

"Babel's ships," I think aloud. "Genius."

Jacquelyn blushes. "It was Erone's idea. Once they find the ships, they'll operate on a standard seek-and-attach program. Our individual ships are designed to function as air locks. Attaching and sealing onto the hull of their ships. Babel comes down. We go up."

Katsu actually bursts into laughter.

"I'm sorry," he says. "I was just imagining the look on Defoe's face."

I hear Jaime whisper, "It's literally perfect."

Parvin glances back at Morning, who nods her approval.

"I think we can work with this," she says.

Jacquelyn strides forward. "So you agree to an alliance?"

Parvin nods. "Like I said, we just wanted to know whose hand we were shaking."

She holds out both fists. Jacquelyn smiles at the familiar gesture. They dap up in agreement, twist their wrists, and bump fists again. Smiles sweep through the entire group. It's not hard to see why Isadora came to us. She made the smart decision. I'm guessing the Imago shared their plan with her already. If she knew all this, there were two options: join us or fight her way back to Babel. This was the right choice.

Feoria holds up a hand for silence. "We have one more thing to show you."

Both Daughters stand and march past us. Jacquelyn gestures for us to follow. They lead us halfway down the queenly staircase before turning to the right.

There's a hidden ledge there, slipping through the stone walls, leading outside. We file after them until we're in the bright of day, looking down on an open-air courtyard.

It's full of Imago. The ranks aren't as tight and precise as they were on the Seventh, but there's still something majestic about them. The gathered crowd has dressed in their finest. It takes a few seconds to realize what connects them: they're all so young.

My eyes trace down the rows. A handful of them look like teenagers. At the top end, there might be some in their thirties. Beckway and Bally stand in the front row, their faces full of pride. "The Remnant," Jacquelyn says. "Fifty of our youngest, brightest citizens."

Some whistle up. Others wave. It finally hits home. This is their only plan for avoiding extinction. Launch into space. Defeat their sworn enemy. Cross the universe. Land on Earth.

We do what we have to do to survive.

"What about the other rings?" Morning asks.

"Seven other stations," Jacquelyn answers. "One assigned to each ring. The name of every citizen has been entered in a lottery. Sixty names from every ring will be chosen. We've already started evacuating. We expect Babel's attack to come tomorrow."

"Do you see now?" Feoria asks, sweeping out one hand. "The difference between our way and the slings? We've forged our best path forward. This is our future. They can't go without your help. You are the Genesis. We place our fate in your hands."

I look back at the rest of the crew, more sure than ever.

"We're going home," I say firmly. "And we're taking them with us."

CHAPTER 41

I FORGET THE REST

Emmett Atwater

The world is reduced to tutorial and preparation. It's amazing that the Imago think they've predicted Babel's attack down to the hour. Jacquelyn tries to run us through the tech side of things, but only Parvin and a few others can actually keep up.

Morning hammers out the details of our agreement. The Daughters argue back and forth with her, making sure there's an understanding of how this alliance will extend from the second we leave the Sanctum to when—if all goes well—we land back on Earth. It's smart. Pops would call it CYA: cover your ass. I stand by as they negotiate. Morning is forceful about keeping our crews together from start to finish.

"We'll man our own boat," she says. "Babel trained us for it. We work best as a crew."

Jacquelyn shakes her head. "And risk losing all of you?"

"That's my point," Morning argues back. "We survive together. Shoulder to shoulder."

Jacquelyn starts to protest, but Feoria cuts her off.

"Let them. We owe them the right to choose."

Jacquelyn heaves a sigh. "Only if I come with you. I don't have time to run you through the schematics, the break-away formations we're using on the surface, the rendezvous points. Either I'm on board with you or it doesn't happen at all."

Morning accepts that. "That's fine."

Feoria laughs. "Going back to the humans, Jackie?"

Jacquelyn almost snorts. "It was your plan, not mine."

We're all escorted back through the sanctuaries. Jacquelyn runs us through the unloading process. Our ship will be seventh in the lineup. She walks us through the basics of the tunnel, emphasizing the necessity for stealth. After that she describes our exit point, our route from the northern shoreline, and the coordinates of the launch bay reserved for the Sanctum. Only when we've recited the whole plan forward and backward does she release us.

"Now go eat. Go rest. Be dressed to leave at a moment's notice."

I should feel lighter, more at ease. The threat of Isadora has gone quiet. The current plan is far better than we could have ever hoped. Even the distant possibility of Anton already working behind the curtains in space should have us believing this can actually happen.

But I've always had a hard time with hope. The word has a habit of slipping through my outstretched fingers. I'm not sure if I'll be able to sit back and breathe until we land on Earth.

We take seats around a circular table. Speaker explains

SCOTT REINTGEN

that our meal is fuel for the days to come. Everything we've had up to this point was made with taste in mind.

"These might not taste as good," he says. "But they were handpicked. There is food here that will steady your hands, focus your minds, increase your awareness. A soldier's diet."

Jazzy asks, "Are y'all expecting a fight?"

"In the end," Speaker replies, "what we expect does not matter. What happens will."

"I wouldn't mind a fight," Jaime says. "Get a few shots in on Babel before we go."

Speaker frowns at that. "I would rather a quiet walk to a ready launch station. There are fights in our future. That much I can promise. It is so likely, in fact, that I would rather not wish more into existence."

Jaime shrugs before focusing on his plate. The rest of us are quiet. That calm-before-the-storm kind of feeling. Next to me, Morning actually looks a little nervous.

"It's a good plan," I whisper to her.

She nods. "It's just the waiting. I hate waiting."

"You know, I was thinking, they mentioned the pods have room for two." I throw her a playacted look of nervousness, biting my fingernails with exaggeration. "I was— I mean, if you're not busy or whatever—I was wondering if maybe you'd launch into space with me."

She smirks. "We gonna go to the movies after?"

"Of course. No popcorn, though. Too pricey around here."

"My parents always snuck stuff in," she says.

"Moms does that too."

She looks at me for a long second. "You think I'll get to meet them?"

"Whoa, whoa, whoa," I say, smiling wide. "Slow *down,* girl."

I laugh again when she smacks my shoulder.

"This is just like the cold-hands thing," she says, shaking her head. "Yeah. That's right. I didn't forget. First time you *ever* talked to me. Told me I had cold hands. Who does that?"

I'm still smiling when Omar leans over.

"I'm starting to think you two need a chaperone again."

Morning throws him an eyebrow. "These are your last days on an alien planet, Omar. Isn't there someone else you would prefer spending them with than us?"

I almost laugh when his eyes dart *directly* over to Parvin. He starts to blush.

"I don't know what you're talking about."

"Neither does she," Morning replies. "But she should. Before we risk our lives and launch ourselves back into space. She should know how you feel."

Omar somehow turns a deeper shade of red as Morning stands.

"Come on," she says to me. "I want to go look at the ocean."

It's easy to follow her outside, kick our feet up in the air, and pretend the world belongs to us. Even in the bright of day, we can make out the faintest traces of both moons in the sky.

The truth has changed how I see them. Bright and beckoning has become dark and deadly. We've talked this whole time about forging alliances. One force being joined to a second. I have this deep, unspoken fear that our alliance might be more like the two moons colliding in the sky. Bright, brief, and the end of everything.

So we steal what we can from what little time remains.

Wind at our backs, sun on our faces, we lie there together; I forget the rest.

CHAPTER 42

BABEL REVEALED

Emmett Atwater

We work our way back through the halls of the sanctuary, looking for the rest of the crew. Morning leads us toward the kitchens and we run smack into Isadora.

I see Isadora's jaw tighten before she takes a meaningful step back, holding the door open for us to pass through. But Morning answers by reaching out for the other half of the door and wedging it open with her own strength. "We're good. Thanks."

Isadora just shakes her head. "You're wasting your time with this."

"I don't trust you," Morning returns. "It's that simple."

"We're exactly the same," Isadora says. "Whether you want to admit it or not."

Morning flinches at that accusation. "I'm nothing like you."

"Please," Isadora says with sarcasm. "In every situation, you'll work to keep this team safe. You're going to fight like hell to get the group home, right? But if you had to choose between Emmett or us, which one would you choose?"

Whatever ready comeback was sitting on Morning's lips goes silent. She glances back at me, then at Isadora. "Well?" Isadora asks. "You'd choose him, wouldn't you?"

Morning nods. "Every time."

The truth has my heart skipping beats. Isadora just smiles.

"If Roathy's actually alive, I'm going to choose him over you *every single time.* Otherwise? I'll do what I can to make this plan work. I'm no different than you—"

A single bell tolls through the Sanctum, cutting off Isadora's sentence. It rings its way through stone, shakes the halls, and gutters out. It takes two seconds to leave the rivalry in the hallway. Jacquelyn's trained us to know the rendezvous point. Morning is careful to let Isadora walk ahead of us, but we make our way through the halls together all the same.

The rest of the Genesis crew is waiting, but instead of leading us down to the escape route, Speaker has us moving up the building's southern tower. Jacquelyn waits on the building's roof. It's not the tallest tower, but it offers a 360-degree view of the surrounding ocean. We stand in nervous formation. Jacquelyn folds her arms, counting off the beats with a tapping foot.

Our group flinches as the sound of a whip cracks overhead. A static discharge sounds, followed by a thundering boom. The sky clears completely. The protective dome falls away. We all shield our eyes as the extra brightness floods down, reflecting harshly over the surface of the water. "We're still protected," Jacquelyn says. "I designed a secondary system to activate above the Sanctum. We felt it was important to witness this. For us and for you. Know your enemy."

A long minute passes. Jacquelyn eventually points south.

"We've shown you who we are," she says. "Now we'll show you who Babel is."

It takes thirty seconds for the bombs to start falling.

Great booms color the horizon with light. We watch as the First Ring goes up in flames. In every direction, explosions rake into the blue. Babel leaves nothing to chance. Sharper whines sound overhead. We all flinch, but Jacquelyn's secondary system wards the dangers away. We watch the translucent layers catch a first and then a second and then a third missile. The explosions tongue skyward, ineffective.

"Genocide. That was their plan in the end." Jacquelyn's whisper carries. "Do you see why the Imago kept them at a distance? They always feared *this*."

Jaime's muttering darkly, his fists clenched. All that rage that's boiling inside him is threatening to surface again. I can see him pounding the frozen marine with the nyxian crowbar. Parvin stands beside Omar. He sets a heavy hand on her shoulder as she covers her mouth in horror. It's the first time I've ever seen his size look gentle.

Isadora grips the edge of the railing, a familiar desperation written across her features. Every fear we've had about Babel since day one has built to this moment.

Hundreds of thousands of deaths. It would have happened that way if not for the Imago's plans. Babel has nowhere left to hide now. The truth is an ugly thing.

"Time to go," Jacquelyn says. "The trap's been set."

They lead us back through the sanctuaries. Our equipment is already packed neatly aboard our ship. We move with purpose through the halls. We're not afraid as bombs drop on distant buildings, but confident. I can feel Babel's end hanging in the air like a promise.

Servants rush through the halls, running twenty ways, hands full of last-minute supplies. By every other measure, practice has resulted in perfection for the Imago.

As we enter the gardens, we find the chosen Remnant arranged in columned lines according to rank and station. They wait in their patient formation by the loading docks as the pressurized escape route opens up. The first boat drops, and there's not even a second of hesitation as the first crew of Imago file on board. Guards take up the defensive stations as the chosen passengers march belowdecks. Captains are barking orders from every direction.

After the first ship vanishes, there's a noticeable staggering. One military boat followed by a passenger ship followed by more soldiers. Jacquelyn shouts orders, pulling my attention to the nearest techie. "Make sure you disable every security measure and flush our radiation signatures. I want green lights for all ships all the way out to the coast. Last time we wasted oxygen and time—let's not repeat that mistake, okay?"

I watch as he wheels back to the control panel. Our Genesis crew waits impatiently. Only Isadora and Ida aren't with us. The Daughters invited them, as a matter of custom, into their boat. They framed it as a tradition for more honored guests, but I'm guessing it was their way of defusing whatever situations might come up. We need Morning fully focused.

A ship splashes into the water tank as another rotates through the hangar, waiting to be dropped. Jacquelyn continues sounding commands.

"Double-check your pressurized suits," she shouts. "No radio contact when we reach the ocean floor. Preserve your oxygen at all costs. Keep the ascent slow; follow the models in the readouts. We'll move to Cadence Point for our surface location, off the northern coast. We have four separate breakaway packs. Remnant and Genesis ships will prioritize reaching the coast. Military boats will patrol the surrounding waters. Understand?"

We give an answering shout of affirmation.

"Next ship is Genesis crew," Jacquelyn calls out. "Let's load it up."

Pressurized suits are passed back through our ranks as the boat splashes into place. We only practiced putting them on once, so it's still a slight struggle to pull the bulky suits over clothes and boots. The suit hangs loose until I find the button on the shoulder that compresses the lining. A second button pops helmets up from shoulders. There are a few buddy checks before everyone begins the boarding process.

As the glass visor closes, a robotic voice runs through calibrations inside my helmet.

"Vitals: normal. Depth: sea level. Pressure: normal. Establishing link to communications network."

Jacquelyn's voice pipes through the comm. A few others

sound, affirming they're linked up. I echo the confirmation as Morning takes her place at the center of the ship.

Back on the platform, we see Isadora and Ida huddling beside the Daughters. Feoria and Ashling stand as regally as a pair of queens ever have. I remember that—at least for Feoria—this is a death march.

She will stay behind as her people reach across the universe.

"Morning." Jacquelyn's voice. "Assign stations. Let's get moving."

Morning nods in answer. She sends Omar to the back of the ship, with Longwei in reserve. It takes two seconds to fire up the massive engines. Katsu and Alex are placed on the hips for steering. I can feel the tremble of nyxia as they establish their link.

"Parvin up front," Morning commands. "Jazzy, be a second set of eyes, please. I want Jaime, Holly, Jacquelyn, and Noor on the defensive stations. Let's drop in."

Morning takes her captain's chair, and for a second all I can do is stare. Is she really benching me? The others are snapping into action, obeying her directives.

A long stride brings me to her side. "What about me? You know I can help."

She locks eyes with me. "If I get hurt, who captains the ship?"

I swallow my anger. "Me."

"You," she says firmly. "So sit back and trust me."

I reach down and squeeze her shoulder, lowering my voice. "You've got this."

I cross to the back of the ship and take a seat between

Omar's and Holly's stations. Jacquelyn roams the deck, inspecting our arrangement. There's chatter across the nyxian link as the familiar dome stretches up, knitting overhead, sealing us in. One look is enough to see that these walls are thicker than normal, meant for deep-sea diving.

Parvin throws a thumbs-up to confirm we're fully cocooned.

"Genesis, how do we stand?" Morning shouts.

The answer bellows out of us, all instinct. "Shoulder to shoulder!"

Morning releases the supports and we drop in.

"All right," Jacquelyn says through the comm. "Quarter power. Let us drift. I'll direct you to the tunnels we take for our evac route. Nice and steady for now."

Morning echoes her command. Everyone's quiet as the windows go dark and the natural overhead light is replaced by occasional ticks of red or green. The emergency lights mark our descent until the tunnel ends and we're left in the black.

"Take this right tunnel for another five hundred meters," Jacquelyn orders.

I watch our progress patiently, feeling helpless. Morning's the right person for the commander's chair, but I still wish I could do *something*. Parvin relays the radar reading as Katsu and Alex guide us down a maintenance shaft. It's tight, so the going is slow and steady. When the tunnel finally widens out, Jacquelyn orders us to dive.

"Parvin, check your third screen. You can double down with an exo layer on our outer shell. It will keep us from feeling like we're being stomped by ironhides."

Metal groans as we dive deeper and deeper.

"Everyone," Jacquelyn calls. "If you haven't popped helmets, do it now."

The boat plunges into deeper dark. Our helmet readouts tick from one atmosphere to two. Morning notices the indicator. "What's that mean?" she asks.

"It means we're really deep and we're in trouble if anything goes wrong," Jacquelyn answers.

Our course straightens out, though, and the numbers hover in equilibrium. When we've found the final evacuation tunnel, Jacquelyn has us lock onto the ships ahead and behind us.

"No radio communication between ships," she explains. "We don't want signatures being logged as we head to the surface. I'm going to walk you back through this, okay? There are four queens and four guards. We're one of the queens. It's our job to get to shore. Understand? No matter what happens, the rendezvous point is where we're going.

"This ship is my invention. Dual-engine, with sound-speed capability when she peaks. She's the fastest thing on this planet, and nothing even comes close. So as long as we can get up to full speed, we're going to be where we want to be before Babel's radar even picks up our signal."

Parvin pipes in. "But we're not expecting contact, are we?"

"No," Jacquelyn says simply. "Right now there are thousands of people going through hundreds of underground tunnels. Babel's about to come down and start sifting through the wreckage. As soon as they figure out there aren't any bodies, they'll run their scans again and see that we've al-

ready moved all over the map. Good luck targeting us before we launch."

There's another groan followed by another pop. Our
crew's attention flickers to the radar, but nothing is flashing
red. Darkness dominates the windows. The readouts look
clean. A ship ahead, a ship behind. "How do you know the
lotteries will work?" Morning asks.

Jacquelyn is quiet for a second. "I'm not sure what you
mean."

"Sixty people survive," Morning says. "Out of what? Fifty
thousand on each ring?"

"We know the odds," Jacquelyn replies stiffly.

"I just mean . . . the slings. They chose their own way.
What if others do the same?"

Jacquelyn's voice is quiet but steady. "Feoria chose to believe the best about their people. Every generation that's
ever existed has understood: the fate of the society comes
before personal interests. Ultimately, that's why I chose to
become one of them. When Feoria decided this was the best
way forward, it became the best way forward for all of us.
That's how things in our world work. Those we leave behind? They'll make the sacrifice for the good of all. It helps
to have a queen willing to do the same."

I glance over. Her suit mask frames the determined look
on her face. I haven't given the other stations much thought.
If it was humanity, there's no way their plan would work.
People would be eating each other alive outside the stations
the second they didn't win a ticket out.

"We should conserve oxygen and resources," Jacquelyn

announces. "Let's keep things quiet until we're through the tunnel, at least."

Her words leave us in the quiet, in the dark, to our thoughts. Hours of silence stretch out. Morning glances back a few times, winking once or twice. I have to remind myself to breathe.

I try to imagine the surface. The rings that the Imago have called home for generations, all destroyed. Babel ships sweeping out of the sky. The marines from the bases activating. I can picture Kit thinking it's the coolest thing he's ever seen. I have to swallow back the guilt that tries to edge up my throat then. Kit and his dad and his mom.

Did they cross the universe just to die?

It helps to imagine Defoe instead. The conqueror coming down to a world that will be his long enough to see it go up in flames. Pops would tell me to never wish the worst on someone. I feel like maybe he'd make an exception for a man who masterminded a failed genocide.

Eventually we reach the end of the buried ocean-floor tunnel.

It dumps us out into a wider, emptier darkness. The boats detach and start their ascents. The front ship marks our destination on the radar, and we all watch the progress, the frightening inevitability of light. I'm trying to imagine us crossing the rest of the ocean, landing on another foreign shore, heading for the launch station.

How many Imago will make it? What happens if we succeed?

I haven't forgotten that both sides gambled on *us*. The Imago put on an act for years to bring us here and lure Babel in. We're supposed to be their emissaries in a new world. I think of the show Speaker and Thesis acted out for us. It was convincing. It was supposed to be.

Babel's guilty of the same. Like magicians, they were always brilliant at drawing our eyes to the bright ribbon in their left hand as they fumbled through our pockets with their right.

I'm starting to realize that our training was plan B. The nyxian mining, the Rabbit Room, all of it. Babel needed us on planet. They needed us to reach Sevenset. They trained us to be survivors and then used those final duels to push us toward the Imago. It was one more reason to distrust them, and it guaranteed we would move where they wanted us on the game board.

"First boat preparing to surface," Parvin says. "Radar looks empty."

"How long until we breach?" Morning asks.

"Five hundred meters."

"Let's get the nyxian link orbiting," she says. "Just like we did on the river."

The entire crew sits up straighter. Jacquelyn gives us an appraising look as the familiar nyxian rhythm establishes itself, rotating and circling. Myan and Speaker described it as the substance returning to its natural state. The power builds as we rise to the surface. I grip the arms of my chair and feel my stomach doing backflips. My eyes are pinned to Parvin's radar. We all watch the first beacon ping as it breaches. Then it vanishes.

"First ship surfaced," Parvin says. "And their signature's gone."

"It happens sometimes," Jacquelyn says. "If they're converting from deep-sea mode to open sailing, the signature changes."

Morning doesn't buy it. "Fist stations get your shields up. Omar, triple the power."

A deep hum shakes and rattles the ship. I hold on tighter as Holly forms a nyxian shield against the already-thick walls of our submarine covering. Longwei sits on the other side of Omar, waiting to add his strength if necessary.

"One hundred meters," Parvin announces. "Four ships up and out."

I catch a glimpse of the dots starting to spread. One edges to the west.

There's a burst of white light against the porthole windows, then a loud plunk, and Morning retracts the walls. Air rushes in through the overhead and the sky plunges like a bright knife. We blink, and blink, and take in the scene.

To the west, one of the Remnant ships bleeds into the horizon. I spy a smaller ship trailing behind it and realize it's not one of ours. An unwelcome guest.

There's a breath of a second as we take in the strange debris floating all around us. The details start to solidify. Imago bodies. Snapped boards. Enemy ships.

A Babel ambush.

CHAPTER 43

THE AMBUSH

Emmett Atwater

It's all chaos.

A circle of Babel boats converges around us, but the Imago military vessels are already moving through their formations, causing trouble. On the distant shore, we see a flash of bright blue light curling to life.

"Cut left!" Morning shouts. "Let's get outside their formation. All power to engines and shields. Right flank, get 'em up!"

Katsu and Alex jerk the ship that way, but too sharply. Our speed cuts, and Omar struggles to get us back into a higher gear. The waiting Babel ships respond better than we do. Pulse cannons flash to life aboard the middle one. We watch the bolts cross the distance. Some miss overhead, but a few deflect off Jacquelyn's summoned shield.

The nyxia shivers and cracks, barely holding.

An Imago ship engages the first one to blast us, but we have other concerns. There's a vessel running diagonally to our left. It's arching out, reading our movements. The angle they're taking sets up a flawless intercept. I whip my head back as more of our boats surface from below. Two military vessels will follow, and the Daughters will surface last.

The world lurches with blinding light.

Our entire right side gets lit up. Jacquelyn's shield suffers the blow before going up in smoke, but Noor's not nearly as strong as she is. Her shield shatters, and fire lashes over that side of the ship. Instinct kicks in. I lunge forward as the tongues of flame spread, a manipulation thundering out from my fingertips and into the nyxia. A thought, a breath: smother. I catch Noor, wrapping her inside the nyxian blanket. Smoke gushes out as we roll to the ground.

"What the hell was that?" Morning shouts.

Longwei's at my side. I leave Noor with him and barely get my hands on her station as a new round of volleys comes flying from a flanking ship. The Babel vessel nearest to shore has engaged with Imago reinforcements. Another is still moving to outflank us. The air brightens as a third particle blast scorches out. I get my shield up just as it makes contact.

Our ship almost capsizes, but Morning's commands keep us floating, moving.

"They're in position," she announces. "We *have* to get outside the circle they're forming. Full power to shields on the front and right. Omar, we'll take it into a dive and go beneath them."

A glance shows the massive tower on the shore reloading, gathering and harnessing energy for a fourth blast. Thankfully, one of the Imago boats has veered away from the action and toward the glowing tower. The ship enclosing our group from behind gives chase as the others fire, closing more cautiously. Each second tightens the noose around our necks. Our boat leaps forward as Morning adds her strength to Omar's.

We hurtle through the water, course set for the nearest ship.

"Let's dive beneath them," Morning commands. "You know what to do, Parvin."

The Babel captain tries to adjust as we keep our nose aimed at the side of their ship, looking like we're ready to T-bone them. One hundred meters away we can make out the faces on board. Babel marines man every station. In between the nyxian consoles, a handful of soldiers raise their weapons and take aim. Morning calls it out and our shields barely survive the first thundering spray of bullets. We're fifty meters away, knifing right at them.

Anger pulses through me at the sight of the Babel insignia. I reach back and pull Noor to her defensive station. "I need you to take over for a second."

She nods as I stumble forward. The rocking of the boat threatens to send me into the railing, but I steady myself and keep moving. I take a deep breath and focus. I have to get the manipulation right. The nyxia shivers with movement. I heft up one of Jazzy's long poles, the same ones we used in the Rabbit Room. It feels good, like an old friend.

"Hold!" Morning shouts. "Hold!"

On shore, the laser tower misses the approaching Imago boat. We might be outnumbered, but the tide is clearly turning, the Imago clearly outmaneuvering Babel. We need the tide to turn faster, though, if we want to survive. Another round of bullets lights us up, and cracks form in our frontal shield. Bullets swipe over heads and shoulders; a few tag the front of the ship.

Morning's about to submarine us beneath the Babel ship when I start running. The ship nose-dives, but not before I plant my pole just left of Parvin's front station. A scream echoes behind me as the shaft flexes and I launch myself over our front shields and into the air.

I descend on Babel like a demigod, cloaked in fury. Adrenaline shields me from the impact of the landing. I manipulate the nyxia as I roll, coming up on one knee and casting it out in a protective sphere. Every gun on board turns and fires.

A thought adjusts the manipulation just before the flash and bang. Bullets fracture the air, lodge in the black shield I've summoned. I flinch as they come, but the nyxia works flawlessly.

Dozens of bullets hover around me, silver-tipped, floating in the air. There's a pulse as the shield threatens to give way, but I shove a second burst of power into it and somehow everything *holds*. The crew stares with wide eyes. All of them scramble to reload.

But it's too late for that.

I drop one knee and shove the shield out with as much force as I can give it. Bullets hiss back through the air, hammer-struck. I watch shards of wood snap as they hit. Blood spatters. One of the soldiers throws up his own nyxian shield, but the rest of the crew slumps or falls. Screams split the silence and I rise.

Over the nearest railing, a massive splash shows the

Genesis ship breaching the surface about fifty kilometers away. Morning's face is the first one I see as their nyxian walls retract. Her eyes go wide when she sees I'm the only one still standing.

But the soldiers aren't dead. I hear groans. The marine with the best instincts is still crouched behind his shield. Some of the bullets didn't strike home. Others didn't have the velocity to do more than ding or skim or concuss. I scramble over stretching legs and past reaching hands. The captain slumps in his chair, blood spilling out of a gut shot.

His eyes go wide as I reach him. I ignore his weak, struggling hands and unclip the grenade on his utility belt. "For Kaya," I whisper. "For Bilal and Loche and Brett."

The pin springs, the grenade thuds onto the deck, and I dive over the railing.

I count eight strokes before fire rips into the air. Wooden shards come slashing overhead. Morning's crew swings past, and I wave my arms to get their attention. Jacquelyn keeps her station in its shield form, but manipulates a second piece of nyxia into netting. As soon as I grab hold of it, she starts reeling me in. I scramble on board, soaked to the bone, feeling like an angel of death. There's no time to process what I just did. No time to count the bodies.

We veer right of their smoking carcass of a ship as a new fight forms on the other side. A distant explosion follows mine. On shore, the tower ignites.

Our crew throws out a cheer as the structure leans left, then collapses into the waiting flames. The Imago soldiers scramble around the base of the tower but are cut off from their ship now. My eyes dart left. The other Imago are boarding one of the Babel ships as their own boat goes up in flames. I realize we're winning. Babel's losing.

"Morning!" Longwei's voice thunders through the comm. "Omar's hurt!"

All eyes whip back. He's slumping in his seat, still shoving whatever energy he has left into the ship's engines. But there are three rips in his suit, and red gushes from each of them.

Parvin screams. Morning lunges out of her seat too.

"Emmett," she snaps. "Captain's seat."

I watch both of them hurdle past, sliding to their knees to catch Omar as he falls. Without them, the entire boat starts to power down. Instinct kicks in again.

"Jazzy on the eyes!" I shout. "Longwei full power."

Jazzy takes a single breath—always so composed—and steps into action. I take my position in the captain's seat, trying to draw from her calm. Longwei has the engines rolling in seconds. Jazzy reports back, like we're tackling another task on the Waterway.

I can still hear Omar gasping for air. Morning and Parvin are pleading with him. *Don't die. Please don't die.* I force my mind back to the water, to the fight still unfolding all around us.

"Can we help these final ships?" I ask. "Let's convert front stations to pulse cannons."

But before the command fully registers, Jazzy is shouting.

"Returning from the west! Two ships."

"Us or Babel?" I ask.

Our eyes scan the distance. Jacquelyn's the first to sight it.

"Babel," she says. "Emmett, we need to leave. It's our job

to get to the rendezvous point. Babel's going to keep coming. Our other ships know their directives. Time to go."

I squint into the distance. We have a minute at the most. Another glance shows that the Imago military boats aren't leaving. They're circling, snapping at the heels of enemy ships. On shore, the stranded Imago have started launching their own attacks at a fleeing Babel vessel. I want to stay and fight and carry our weight.

"Emmett!" Jacquelyn shouts. "Our plan is to get into space. Get *moving.*"

I nod to myself, to the others. "Convert everything to engines. Jazzy, ping the rendezvous point. Let's get the hell out of here."

All the strength passing through the nyxian links gets thrown back to Longwei. Together we have the boat thundering through the smoke and chaos, forging a path north. The Imago on shore throw salutes and start making their own way through the forest, moving to their assigned check-points on foot.

We leave the noise and death behind. Babel's incoming boats split. One pursues us, but Jacquelyn was right. We're way faster than they are. A head start has us leaving them behind.

"Jacquelyn," I ask through the link. "Once we land on shore, how far do we have to go?"

"There's a converted repository seven kilometers north," she replies. "We have to get there and seal the door behind us. Underground tunnels link it with a cove to the west. From there, we'll have transports waiting to take us upriver. Then to the launch station."

It's quiet as our boat skips over the water. We're moving far faster than we ever did in the Waterway. I can hear shuffling behind me. "Omar?" I ask quietly.

"Didn't make it," Longwei whispers back.

I bow my head and close my eyes. I'm back in that bright room, watching Kaya's oxygen run out. I'm standing in front of Roathy as he rages against my air lock. How much more do we have to lose for all of this to finally come to an end?

We keep picking up speed. The engines roar louder and louder, but I can still hear the sound of Parvin and Morning crying: Morning for her brother-in-arms, Parvin for the man who finally found the courage to say how he felt. No one says anything; no one can.

Babel's death count keeps growing.

Our ship knifes through the endless blue.

CHAPTER 44

THE OTHER GENESIS

Emmett Atwater

"How far back are Babel's boats, Jazzy?"

"They'll land in five minutes," she says. "We have to keep moving."

Everyone unloads. Sloshing through knee-deep water and onto a pebble-laced shore. Forest hovers, dark and strangling. Behind us, a single white streak makes a line for our location. Babel is coming. Longwei helps Morning carry Omar to shore. We set him down and get our bearings.

I'm wondering how we're possibly going to carry him seven kilometers when Jacquelyn offers to help. "I'll make a carrier for him."

She manipulates her nyxia into a black sphere. It's the same kind we've seen the Imago use whenever they've traveled overland. I stand at Morning's side as she and Longwei lift Omar into the unfolding sphere. Once his body is safely inside, the black petals fold back together like a wilting flower. Parvin's still crying as the darkness closes around him.

SCOTT REINTGEN

Noor puts an arm around her and starts walking her away. Jacquelyn directs the carrier overland as Morning snaps back into motion. I can see her shoving the grief as far down as possible. I can see it threatening to rise up and choke her.

"I'm back on command," she says. "Let's move."

The group follows her through the forest. Jazzy's voice echoes through our ranks.

"That group was five minutes behind," she says. "We need to jog."

Jacquelyn agrees. "I'd like to get into the tunnel *before* they sight us. It'd be nice to slip through a few doors and leave them wondering which way we ended up going."

There aren't really trails through these forests, but Morning guides us down the paths of least resistance. She jogs at the front, pushing us to move faster. Jacquelyn keeps our pace, mentally guiding Omar's coffin as she runs. Forest sounds rush in from all sides.

"Keep an eye out," Jacquelyn warns. "This isn't Grimgarden. There are some dangerous animals that call this place home."

We catch a few glimpses to go with the strange noises. A dark spread of wings. Broad shoulders slouching into a creek. Morning tightens our formation and asks for an update.

"Four more kilometers," Jazzy answers.

It's a blessing when the forest breaks. Fields wind their way to an empty valley. Jacquelyn has us veer left, taking the easiest slopes down. At the far end of the plain, a huge cement structure is wedged into the hillside.

"That's the repository," Jacquelyn says, breathing heavily.

"Let's keep going," Morning pushes.

We cross the fields together. There's no sunlight overhead, just a gathering of thick clouds, pressed together to keep anything golden out of the world. Wind has the field of knee-high grass swaying darkly, and we're halfway across it when Morning signals for a stop.

Everyone goes down to one knee. In the distant gray, our eyes trace little shifts of movement. We all watch and wait as figures cross the scene. It's hard to tell from this distance, but they must be a Babel crew. They don't move or look like the Imago.

"Is that the crew that was chasing us?" Morning hisses through the comm.

"Has to be," Jazzy whispers. "If they set an ambush in the water, why have a crew randomly roaming around on land? They must have landed north of us."

We watch the group slink past the repository building. There's a long conversation in front of it before they move on. We wait and watch as they vanish into a northern forest that flanks the building. "And we're just going inside?" Morning asks.

"There's a code," Jacquelyn replies. "It will take me a minute, maybe two."

"Then we need to give her a minute, maybe two," Morning says to the rest of us. "Shoulder to shoulder. Stay alive. Let's use those weapons Babel gave us. If that crew turns back and looks for a fight, don't give them a second. Fathom?"

Nyxian manipulations fill the air with vibration. It takes me a few seconds to get my boxing claws fitted right. I'm feeling sluggish from the run, but my hands are eager. I'm starting to tap into the anger Jaime's shown all along. I wouldn't mind punishing a few Babel marines.

The others look ready too. Silent Holly has her boxing gloves raised. Longwei has his sword, Katsu his ax. Morning's hatchets look like they're already covered in blood. Outfitted for war, we keep low and press on to the edge of the field. Morning pauses us again.

"Keep tight to the trees," she says. "Emmett and Longwei, you see the trail off to the right over there? Take that, but be quiet about it. If they're waiting to ambush us, our approach will draw them back to the repository doors and you two can come in from behind. If no one bites, just circle back and meet us at the gate. Be safe."

She shoots me a look that's pure fire. *Be safe. Do not die. I love you.* I nod as much of that back as I can and she leads the others forward. Longwei and I trickle off to the side, crossing the distance in a crouching run. He follows me to the edge of the forest, and we put our backs smack against trees.

Glancing around, we watch Morning and the others cross the opening. They reach the first gate, shields up and out, and the whole forest is silent.

"Emmett," Longwei whispers. "Now is a good time."

I shoot him a look. "What?"

"Babel," he says simply. "I need to go now. I will pretend to betray you all."

"Whoa, whoa, whoa," I whisper. "But—the Imago's plan— what if it all works perfectly? What if we launch up to space and you get left behind?"

He shakes his head. "Babel will have vessels that can launch into space too."

I'm feeling that nervous dread in my stomach. I'm afraid that if I say goodbye to him now, I'll never see him again. "Just wait, okay? That crew might be digging into the forest north of here. I'm not going to let you go wandering off to get shot. Let's figure things out first. Get our bearings and decide then, fathom?"

Longwei hesitates. "Are you sure?"

I nod. "Let me check the path. Just wait here for a second."

He presses his back to the nearest tree. I push myself up against it slowly, get a better grip on my gloves, and ease beneath the branches. Careful not to make a sound, I turn the corner.

And she's there. A dark braid drapes over one shoulder. The familiar nyxian mask covers her jaw; a gunmetal suit hugs her hips. We see each other and the world *pauses*. She is Kaya. She looks just like Kaya. But then our eyes meet, and I know that's a lie. She's got the wrong eyes. They're angrier, darker, storms. She's someone else entirely.

The second ends and the girl lunges at me.

I lean back just enough to catch the blade across my shoulder, to hear the rip of my suit, to feel the spurt of hot blood. She twists to plant her second knife in my stomach, but I parry and absolutely crush her wrist. The pain pulls a strangled noise from her throat, and the next second comes in a lightning strike, a half-taken breath.

Pause and I die; hesitate and I lose; wait and it's over.

I bring my left hand around and crush her. There's

something horrible about how her body drops, but I take my stance and backpedal, searching for the next target, body trembling with fear and adrenaline. Who was that? What is going on?

A boy shoots through a gap in the trees. He's all Iowa. Blond and bleached and freckled, but he strikes like he was born with a sword in his hand. I get my off hand up, manage another parry, and a third blow jars my footing. He shoves nyxia forward like a wave and I'm knocked back by the force of it, flattened and breathless. The only thing that stops his sword from cutting me in two is Longwei.

A hand's length of nyxia punches through the kid's back, and I roll right as he collapses in a bloody heap. Longwei and I stare at the fallen teens—both gasping—before we remember there are more; there are others. No one appears down the path, so we ease back around the corner, hoping to call out a warning. But it's too late.

Back in the opening, warfare surrounds the tunnel entrance. Our crews have formed a tight circle to protect Jacquelyn. I can see the dark circle of Omar's tomb hovering beside her as she works. Morning and the others stand shoulder to shoulder, their nyxian shields looming in front of them. Seven unfamiliar faces harass the edges.

It's clear they've been trained. They are Genesis, just like us. Longwei and I watch as one of them jabs a spear forward to weaken the nyxian shield between Noor and Parvin. The blow strikes true. Nyxia shudders, blinks, and the hole in the armor widens.

Noor stares out, wide-eyed and openmouthed.

Parvin's hand slaps down on the shoulder of Noor's hijab.

She tugs hard, and Noor's whole body dips just as an ax comes flying forward. It skims her temple, a glancing blow. She drops and the circle reforms as Jaime steps in to help them shore up the line.

Their summoned shields flicker dangerously. I can hear Morning scream in fury. I start forward, but duck back again when a familiar face appears to our right.

Marcus Defoe strides out of the forest.

"Stand down, Genesis 13."

The angry circle backs off. Weapons are kept at the ready, but they put some distance between Morning and the rest of our team. Genesis 13. A third Genesis, a third ship. Babel's secrets keep expanding and evolving. A girl slips out of the forest to join the others.

That makes eight.

Eight because we killed the other two. I bury that thought.

"Genesis 11 and 12," he announces. "I am going to offer this once."

Inside the circle, there's so much anger that a section of the nyxian shield actually lashes out at him. Defoe throws up a forearm and deflects the blow with ease. I narrow my eyes and take note of Jacquelyn at the door, continuing to work on the entrance code. She said two minutes and it's already been three. She has to be close to opening it, but how the hell do we get to them?

"The Adamite population has just been significantly reduced," Defoe says. "We also found the fallout shelter. That aircraft station was quite clever. I wonder how much time and effort went into it. We needed about five minutes to burn the facility to the ground.

"You have a choice. Go through that door with Jacquelyn Requin, and you become enemy number one. You will be hunted. You will lose. But put your weapons down and join us now, and we'll take you back. You can be a part of our work here. You can be on the winning side of history. We will only offer this once."

One of the black links in the shield breaks. Jaime pushes through the opening, and for a heartbreaking second I think that he's going to take Defoe's offer, that he's actually giving up. But then I remember the hatred that's burned in him for weeks now.

A new fear whispers through me. He's not thinking straight. He's trading all of his caution and carefully followed rules for rage and fury, and he's aiming all that he is at Defoe.

Jaime confirms his intention by hefting a sword up and closing the gap between them. His eyes are set. His hands do not shake. My heart breaks, though, because I know without a doubt that Jaime is about to die.

"You made me kill him, you bastard!" Jaime shouts. "Do *they* know what you are? Do they know what you did to us?"

Without breaking his stride, Jaime swings. It's a moment frozen in time. I see his green eyes narrow. His high cheekbones sharpen as he shouts in rage. It's a massive, sweeping blow.

And Defoe turns it away with a flick of his wrist. Then he slides forward with such savage grace that I fall to my knees in horror. Jaime gasps as the blade slips in and out of his chest, but his hands keep reaching, so desperate to punish for so long. Somehow he gets a hold on Defoe's collar before he falls.

He smiles up. "You're shorter than I remember."

And he cracks his forehead into Defoe's nose.

All hell breaks loose. Jaime drops. Our Genesis crew comes flying out from behind the nyxian shield. Defoe is stumbling back, blood gushing from his nose, eyes darting from opponent to opponent. Longwei and I don't even hesitate. I push back to my feet and we both go running forward. Their back line turns just in time to catch claws and swords.

Blood spills with frightening ease. The nightmare is all around us. I turn away a spear, spinning around Longwei to jab a claw at someone else. Together we press a kid who looks just like me but with a flat-top. A blow catches his wrist and he falls. There's a quick second where he considers kicking his way out, but a slash from Longwei has him screaming surrender.

A brief step back offers a highlight of the chaos. Alex is standing protectively over Jaime, blood streaking one cheek, shouting a dare for anyone to challenge him. Azima doesn't need to shout. She moves through their ranks with frightening ease, spear lashing out, finding a home in the weakest places of their defenses.

Holly lands a perfect hook before ducking the swing of someone's ax. Jacquelyn comes flying out of nowhere and lands a brutal blow with a nyxian weapon I've never seen before.

Longwei and I start to turn our fury elsewhere, but then I catch a glimpse of Morning.

She's slipped through the lines. Her hatchets are seeking a home in Defoe. The sight of them freezes me on the edge of the battle. Longwei backs away, ready to fend off attackers, but my entire body locks up as Morning's movement becomes *music*.

Defoe blocks a sideswipe, and another, but she ducks inside and lures him in with the most beautiful feint I've ever seen. His footing stumbles. She forces him to block downward or get gutted, and the movement leaves his bad hand hanging, completely exposed.

Morning shows no mercy.

Her next blow takes his hand at the wrist, clean through.

He screams, dropping to a knee. She presses to finish, but his nyxian armor lashes out like lightning. She barely shields herself in time. The dark tendrils snake through the air, hitting a few of his own soldiers. We watch them drop as a violent current trembles to life.

Everything around Defoe gets forced back by a blast of power. Defoe's nyxia blooms out, and I barely spy him sprinting through a back door in his swirling creation.

Several Genesis 13 fighters have to dive out of his way. He's twenty meters clear before he turns, manipulating nyxia, his eyes bright and dangerous. We see him drop something on the ground as he continues sprinting the other way.

Morning's pursuit almost gets her blown in two. She dives left as an explosion rips through the air. The concussive blast takes us all off our feet.

By the time the smoke starts to clear, Defoe's a dark and distant shadow. Longwei squeezes my elbow before pursuing. I can hear the others calling after him, shouting, but he doesn't look back. A few surviving Genesis 13 soldiers surrender in seconds.

I ignore them as I run to help Morning to her feet. She's on her back, eyes a little wide. Blood is slipping down the side of one ear. "Are you okay?" I shout. "Morning, are you okay?"

She gives me a dazed look, takes a ragged breath, and flashes a thumbs-up.

"Jaime," she says, too loud. "Help Jaime."

Nodding, I stumble back to my feet and cross the bloody field. The survivors are almost all on our side. Three of the Genesis 13 crew have surrendered. Holly's carefully tying hands behind backs and checking pockets for extra nyxia. She's got a gash across one cheek. Noor's sitting up, and Parvin's there, holding a bandage to her head.

Jaime's on his back, staring up at the blue. He looks more pale than ever. I kneel at his side, feeling for a pulse. It's barely there. He's lost a lot of blood. His eyes find mine.

"Emmett—" A bloody cough cuts him off. "I feel so much better now."

He smiles at that, but it doesn't reach his eyes. There's a final gasp and then his mouth goes slack. My face falls and there's nothing to do but cry.

CHAPTER 45

THE GARDEN OF EDEN

Emmett Atwater

We bury the dead in beauty.

The garden we walk through shouldn't exist, it shouldn't be allowed. How can something be so beautiful after all that's happened? Shouldn't the darkness twist and kill things that look like this? We walk past slick trunks and over dark soil. Above us, the branches form a strangling canopy. Clouds and hills reduce the sun to a few slashes of faded gold.

In that impossible place, in that endless, inhuman beauty, we bury the ones we loved.

Parvin manipulates a little spoon and sets it on Omar's grave. I have no idea what it's supposed to mean, but her hand trembles as she pulls away, eyes lost to tears. Holly and Noor wrap their arms around her. Morning says her own goodbye, leaning quietly over the grave of her friend and brother-in-arms.

I walk forward next. There's only one song Jaime ever asked me to play for him. It's one of those songs I forgot was even on my player. The kind of song a white boy like Jaime *would* love. It wasn't until I listened to the lyrics that I understood.

The song's all about the family he never had. Not until he found us.

I put the song on repeat and set it next to his grave. I use the cord Vandemeer gave me to plug into the nyxia. I step back and imagine the song playing forever, just for him. Morning stands beside me, a tear running down one cheek, her jaw clenched tight.

A glance down our ranks shows gaps in the line. Omar usually stood there; Jaime usually stood here. Longwei's gone too. I fight back the tears and take Morning's hand in mine. She looks up at me—fierce and heartbroken—before gripping tightly back.

I clear my throat. "Shoulder to shoulder."

It takes a few seconds for the rest of them to figure it out, but the others close the remaining gaps. Azima wraps a lanky arm around Jazzy's shoulder. Katsu presses in next to Alex, and we make the saddest half-moon I've ever seen. We stand there—a dysfunctional family at a funeral—and everyone joins hands up and down the lines. Morning lifts mine and kisses the back of it, a wordless thank-you, as the entire group circles the fresh graves.

"Shoulder to shoulder," she calls.

Our whole group echoes the words.

I give Morning's hand another squeeze as we move apart. We move on to other sections of the garden and start helping to bury the fallen Imago victims. The surviving military boats didn't leave their dead behind. It takes hours, but we work hard, knowing all of them put their lives on the line to see us safely to shore.

Grave after grave, we turn a place of beauty into a lost paradise.

We bury our enemies too. The Imago don't help us dig the graves of the fallen members of *Genesis 13*. We killed them. The task belongs to us. And even though the Imago have the survivors in chains, they're merciful enough to let them stand over each grave and say a quiet word for the departed. I watch until I can't stand the sight any longer.

I'm so tired of counting ghosts.

Jacquelyn returns as the camp starts preparing to march. After the showdown with Defoe, she took scouts through the tunnels to try to confirm his claims about the launch station. We all listen with dread as she delivers her report to the Imago leadership council. It takes a few minutes for her to move on to us, gathering the whole Genesis crew around.

"Defoe was telling the truth," she says. "The launch station was destroyed."

The truth hits our group hard. We all know the station was our way off-planet.

"Was it Longwei?" Jacquelyn asks. "Did he clue them in to where we were heading? I saw him run off after Defoe when the fight finished."

I take a quick step forward. "It wasn't him. Longwei and I talked in Sevenset. He was kind of an asshole in space. Always took things too seriously. Never hung out with any of us. He's been coming around lately, though. He suggested going to Babel and working from the inside out. Figured they would expect him to take their side."

Jacquelyn frowns. "And you really believe that?"

I nod. "He made the decision before he knew any of this would happen. He was willing to risk his chance to escape to make sure we got into space. I believe him."

"Right," Jacquelyn says. "Well, someone or something gave us away to Babel. We're monitoring *all* communications from here on out. If we catch even a whisper of an unauthorized signal, there will be consequences. Understood?"

Our entire group nods.

"You're smart enough to understand that this changes everything." Jacquelyn eyes the group, like she's trying to figure out how much fight we have left. "Our launch station is gone. We will divert the survivors toward other stations. We have to figure out how extensive the damage is first. How many stations has Babel destroyed? Have the other rings successfully reached their launch centers? Babel hit us where it counted. We're a long way from home now."

"So what happens now?" Parvin asks.

"We still don't know what Babel knows," Jacquelyn says. "We have no idea if they figured out what the launch station was or why it was built. Our plan is to move on to a secondary base, assess readouts of the other launch stations, and form a plan from there. Half of the Remnant survived. They are our priority. You are our priority. I speak for the rest of our group when I say that we will do everything in our power—we will bleed and sweat and fight—to get you home. Are you with us?"

Morning looks around our group before looking back at Jacquelyn.

"Babel has no idea what's coming."

. . .

The Imago lead us out of the garden, away from a paradise we never knew. We walk for hours, and I feel bound to this place, chained and six feet deep already. I'm an angel without wings. I'm a demon without fire. It's such a horrible feeling that I mistake it for emptiness.

But as we make camp for the night, I know I'm not empty. Morning curls up beside me. I hold her close enough that I can hear her heartbeat. It's a rhythm that I want to listen to forever. It says we are still alive, still here. But as night comes, I can feel a darker rhythm beating in my own chest. It's a song I thought I'd buried a long time ago, beneath prettier chords.

We've lost too much. We've been pushed too far.

The darker song stretches and grows and fills the gaping holes in my chest. It is broken bones and black eyes, dropped bombs and endless lies. A lifetime of injustices burn their way to an inferno. Anger rises from it all like smoke. There's only one truth left in my world:

Babel *will* burn.

CHAPTER 46

THE FIRST RECKONING

Anton Stepanov

I'm marched, hands tied, to the command center of the Tower Space Station.

Out the bone-thick windows, stars. *Count them,* Father always commanded. His favorite drinking game. He liked seeing how the constellations changed after a drink, or five.

But I have more important things to count, Father. Better games to play too. A pair of guards flank me, my unsuspecting captors. As they switched shifts, one of them saw me slipping inside a maintenance closet. The ghost haunting their halls manifested in plain sight. It was their chance to play the hero. It still took them five minutes to crack the door open and bravely toss a stun grenade inside. Spineless, but effective.

This is the classic movie scene. The captive led before the king. I learned all this long ago. The kind of men who wear imaginary crowns always enjoy a stage. My capture will be made into a spectacle. Requin will make the conversation into a show. Erone and I are counting on it. Getting captured was just the first part of the plan. As we walk, I do my best to shake off the effects of the smoke. I'd like to be sharp, remember my lines, when the time comes to face him.

I play Morning's games to wake myself up. Case the rooms. Weigh the situation. Measure the odds. I'm flanked by two guards. The one at my left shoulder walks with a gentle limp. Something in his right knee, some issue nyxian surgery couldn't fix. The guard on my right is probably the oldest person on the ship. He looks healthy enough, but I can hear the gaps in his labored breathing. These are a far cry from the physical elites Babel usually boasts.

And the halls, they echo. The little antibodies usually running through the winding, technological stomach are mostly gone. They're left vulnerable. A week ago, I'd never have dared these halls. Too much foot traffic. Random checkpoints and roaming guards.

Where are they now?

Vandemeer was right. Something big was in motion. It's already happened.

My elder captor swipes open a doorway. Beneath the automated hiss, I hear a faint echo. The guards don't notice it because they're not listening for it. The sound is ethereal, like the groan of an automated ghost. It's the second step in Erone's plan.

I swallow a smile as we move through the ringed defenses that guard the central command deck. We pass only three workers. All mechanics. We also pass two bays of escape pods, both emptied. Finally we reach the seventh and final door. The elder guard punches a button and announces our arrival. Both men straighten shoulders, trying to stand tall.

This is their moment of glory.

The doors open. The command room is a series of sleek, circling desks. Holographic readouts color the air, and headsets glow like rave lights. It takes me two seconds to pick out Melissa Aguilar in the crowd. She's off to my right. Our informant aboard *Genesis 12*. She's buried in the light of her screen. She doesn't notice my entrance.

Unintelligible murmurs fill the air with data. Requin broods over it all, and I steal a glimpse of him before he sees it's me. The weight of an imaginary crown has bent and grayed him. Something rotten in the state of Denmark. I smirk.

Seeing me, the wear vanishes. He lets out a laugh.

"Anton? It was you all this time? Good God, how did you even get up here?"

The random activity ceases. Every eye turns to watch the king's play.

I know all my lines. "A cargo shipment."

Requin laughs again. "Morning's idea?"

"She's the brain and I'm the body."

"And in a fitting poetic end, the body has failed the mind. Your reign of terror is over." Requin stands, gesturing to the nearest techie. At his command, our sprawling view of space is replaced by video footage. "You're just in time for an update on our progress in Eden."

We get a bird's-eye view of shattered cities. The ocean has swallowed fallen buildings. Boats move through the wreckage, manned by Babel marines. Requin signals again, and we see another ring, another atrocity. Requin turns back to me, no longer smiling.

"We've won," he says. "The war is over."

War. We've brought our taste for destruction across the galaxy. I eye the wreckage, thinking about how familiar it all looks. I've seen buildings like these before, billions of kilometers away. I'm thankful when Requin turns off the screens. Images of a destroyed Sevenset could ruin our plans. If Erone sees them . . .

"They call it Magnia."

Requin shrugs. "What they call it doesn't matter anymore."

I survey the damage again. "Morning? The Genesis teams?"

Alex? Is Alex alive? Please let him be alive.

Requin says, "Alive for now."

"Send us home."

I feel guilty trying to make it work this way. It's a selfish route, one that ignores the Imago. "Send us back to Earth, and I'll let you live, Requin."

"*You* will let *me* live?" He laughs. "It's over. We're waiting for the count, but I'd guess there will be ten thousand Adamites left. Their armies will be scattered and broken. You and your friends will remain here, as was agreed upon."

"We never agreed to that."

"It's in the contracts," Requin answers. "Tricky clauses, but it's all in there. You signed them, remember? You've agreed to stay here for the long haul."

"That's a lie," I say, nodding at the nearest techie. "And

he's going to die for it. It was just going to be you, but now he dies too. Every time you lie, I pick another one."

The techie looks shocked, but Requin only laughs. "Enough with the games, Anton."

"I'll give you one more chance. Arrange my flight home, or die."

Requin shakes his head. "No, Anton. I'm afraid that's not going to happen."

"Two chances. I gave you two chances. Now I'll extend the opportunity to your friends here. Anyone who wants to live, give up your weapons right now. Set them on the floor and you'll be spared. Fight back, and you will die. I'm telling you this up front so you know the rules."

The blow lands hard and sends me to a knee. I don't have to look up to know it was the guard with the limp. He steps back into position, and Requin sighs theatrically.

"Must you always make things difficult, Anton?"

"I found him," I say, lifting myself up. "Down in the belly of the ship."

The words scrape the humor away. Requin stares at me, eyes narrowed. I have him now.

"His plan was to kill everyone," I say, laughing. "Which is fair. I'd want the same thing if I were him. How long did you torture him? A year? Longer? He's *very* angry, Requin."

"Seal the command bay," Requin thunders. "Seal the bay!"

"Sir, some of our units are still patrolling—"

"I said seal it!"

I ignore the scrambling techies, knowing they're far too late to make a difference. I keep my eyes locked on Requin as I speak. "Not to worry, Requin, cooler heads prevailed.

He agreed not to kill everyone. It's only sensible. We need the astronauts, the mechanics. Well, not all of them. Some of them. So they'll be spared. But you, Requin? He *really* hates you."

"Do you have any idea what you've done?" Requin hisses at me. "Guards, to the doors."

My captors leave my side, retreating. There are three entrances, spread at perfect intervals around the circular exterior. Guards wait at each, weapons drawn. All roads lead to Requin. The thought makes me smile. A techie pipes in. "The bay is sealed, sir."

Requin nods, but I can see the fear coiling around him, choking the air he's breathing.

"Cage is locked," I say, clapping tied hands. "I hope the monster's not already inside."

"You think this is a game," Requin snaps. "You're a fool, Anton. Erone is not a sword for hire. He will not do what you ask, take his reward, and return to Eden. He's a natural disaster, a *reckoning*. You can't control him. This will not work out the way you think it will."

I smile, even though he's speaking my fears out loud for me. Erone has acted reasonably so far, but there have been times when that side of him vanishes. The bondage and torture have reduced him to animal instincts. We moved through the dark no-gravity chambers for nearly a week. Plotting and planning. His moods swung from curious to obsessive to deadly.

I know he's dangerous, but right now I need dangerous.

"He's an inventor," I say loudly. "But you knew that when you took him, didn't you? He was working with your niece,

Jacquelyn. I didn't get to meet her, but you should have heard Erone singing her praises. If I didn't know better, I'd say he has a little crush on her. They worked together. Taking nyxia and inventing new technologies, new defenses. He's brilliant.

"So naturally, when I showed him my copy of the ship's blueprints, he had a few ideas. Really good ideas. We noticed the layer of checkpoints and access doors around this room. He pointed out some of the circuitry, said this room was the command center. He thought you'd be here. So, we just had to figure out . . . how do we get in there? How do we get past all those checkpoints?"

The silence fills with gasping doors. All three entrances open on their own. A few of the techies scramble at their desks, but they're helpless. The doors are nyxian. The walls are nyxian. They're in Erone's kingdom now. They always have been. The second they let me inside, this was already over.

The guards tense, waiting for one of the gaping holes to fill with movement, with some threat. Nothing comes, and I smile. Erone's sense of drama is right up there with Requin's.

"And then it was obvious," I say into the quiet. "We just have your people bring us through the checkpoints. Your clever guards *finally* caught me. They brought me waltzing through your defense system, which gave Erone the access he needed. And, well, you see where this is going, don't you?"

There's a snaking whisper. My eyes leave Requin long enough to see a black substance ghosting through the air. It settles in the space between each set of guards like a float-ing, shimmering mirror.

The guards turn toward each other, and their eyes widen in fear. I'm not sure what they see reflected, but all of them lift their weapons immediately and fire. Six guards drop. I stare in shock at the pooling blood, the wounds, unsure how Erone forced their hands.

The entire room flinches in terror. A shiver runs down my spine.

"Look what you've done," Requin mutters, backing away.

Erone walks through the nearest entrance with savage grace. His great two-handed sword swings with the rhythm of each pounding step. His eyes are for Requin alone.

I step aside. Erone walks past me.

He doesn't give a speech. He doesn't play with his food or boast his revenge like a character in the movies. He shoves Requin to his knees and plunges the sword through his back.

Blood bursts out with the sword tip, dribbles up his throat, runs from the corners of his lips. I watch him die and remind myself that kings aren't innocent in war. When you put on the crown and order troops to kill, you invite the judgment of an enemy's sword.

Erone breaks from his reveling long enough to cut my bindings. He returns my knives. I shake my arms loose before considering the silent techies in the room. My eyes swing directly to Aguilar. "Do me a favor and shut down outgoing communications. Wouldn't want any of your bril-liant colleagues panicking and setting off the alarms."

Aguilar grins up at me. "They've been shut down for two minutes now."

"Always a few steps ahead."

The nearest techies stare at her like a traitor, but she's always been one of ours. Aboard *Genesis 12* she started slipping Morning information just a few weeks into the voyage. She saw what Babel was doing. She saw what they were planning for us and decided to do whatever she could to keep it from happening. That was always the risk when Requin decided to play God. Push too hard and the lowly will push back.

"How many marines left on the ship?" I ask.

Aguilar glances back at her screen, runs through a few interfaces, and looks back up.

"Nineteen."

"Great. Connect me with the ship's communication system."

Erone has taken a seat in his would-be throne. His bloodied blade lies across his lap, and Requin's body is crumpled at his feet. I wait for his confirmation, a sign that I can take command of this part of the plan. I know what he can do now; I don't want to overstep my boundaries. Taking Requin and the ship was the easy part. Reining the storm back in will be much, much harder. Erone gestures idly, as if the details bore him.

Nodding, I turn back to Aguilar. She hooks me up to a glowing headset, switches the outputs, and gives me a thumbs-up.

"Tower Space Station, this is Anton Stepanov of *Genesis 12*. I am joined by an Adamite named Erone. We have taken control of the ship. Requin is dead, along with every guard who had the misfortune of being posted in the command center today. You have thirty minutes to turn in your weapons before we resort to using some of the ship's built-in defense mechanisms. Hide somewhere and you might be safe, or you might be in the part of the ship we choose to jettison. Your safety is up to you. I would prefer no more blood be shed. But test his patience, and Erone will show you just how much he'd prefer if the blooding continued. All surrendering parties should gather in the third protective ring outside the command center. Enter the second ring prematurely and you'll see what kind of fun toys we've left there for you."

I release the output button, and the faint sound of beeping echoes louder.

I nod to Aguilar. "What is that *god*-awful noise?"

"Incoming message, sir."

Some of her colleagues flinch at the use of the word *sir*. I note which ones before turning back to her. "A message from who?"

"Babel's fourth ship: *Genesis 14*. They want permission to dock."

ACKNOWLEDGMENTS

A planet-sized thank-you to the team at Crown BFYR. The past few months have given me opportunities to meet many of you and spend time with you. I've seen how hard you work and how easy you try to make the lives of your authors. These books couldn't take off without all the tireless energy you pour into the process. Thank you.

To Emily Easton for challenging me to be a better writer and pushing this story to its best possible version. To Samantha Gentry for being a correspondence goddess. And special thanks to Josh Redlich for his ability to snap his fingers and make anything happen. Someone should probably look into Josh's illegal use of magic? I'd also like to thank my agent, Kristin Nelson, and the entire team at Nelson Literary Agency, for their continual support in this and so much else.

I'd like to thank the brilliant authors who've taken time to read my work: Marie Lu, Nic Stone, Fonda Lee, V. E. Schwab, Jason Hough, Jay Kristoff, Jay Coles, Vic James, and Tomi Adeyemi. I'd like to thank Pierce Brown for allowing

Nyxia to grace his kitchen table. May all my books make it there one day.

I will always be indebted to my wife, Katie. While I was writing this book, she was literally making a human being. So we were both working on sequels, and—spoiler alert—I'm proud of this book, but I greatly prefer the one she and I wrote together. Which reminds me: Henry. Eat your vegetables, buddy. That's an order.

I would not have completed this draft without the help of longtime critiquing partner Keith Dupuis. While I tore through early edits, yours was the calmest voice in my head. I also want to thank Neil F. Comins, author of *What If the Earth Had Two Moons?* Thank you for taking the time to answer all my questions, and with such enthusiasm.

Finally, I wrote this one for my momma. There's no one who has put more time into making me a decent human being. I do not have to look far to find your love threaded through my life. If I know anything of forgiveness, grace, compassion, and presence, I learned it at your elbow. Thank you for loving us toward our dreams.

Final shout-out to Luna for being a good dog.

IT'S WISE TO LOSE A BATTLE
TO WIN A WAR.

NYXIA
UPRISING

WIN AND GO HOME,
OR LOSE AND DIE TRYING.

SCOTT REINTGEN

TURN THE PAGE TO START READING!

THE KING

Longwei Yu

18 days 12 hours 11 minutes

Babel's king bleeds.

For a moment, I think I've lost the trail. But I double back and find his blood painted across moonlit leaves. A great streak of scarlet marks the body of a swollen trunk. If I squinted any longer, I might have been able to convince myself the mark looked like the Chinese characters for *dying*.

I need this king alive.

Moonlight dominates the clearing. A creek angles west. It forks, and just there, I see where Defoe must have gone. There are no footprints, not in this ghostly place, but it's the most reasonable decision. A massive tree has been exposed at the roots. They curl above and around a hollow. It's the kind of burrow a deer might sleep in. I watch the shadows for several minutes.

No movement.

I follow the creek forward. The trees sway, their branches and leaves grasping at the light of the nearest moon. It almost feels as if the entire forest is flinching away from where Defoe is hidden. Fifty meters. I lift both hands innocently into the air. My eyes trace over the landscape, through the shadows. I'm not eager to die just because some creature has picked up our scent.

Twenty-five meters. I pause, hands still raised, awaiting an invitation. The shadows are too deep to see anything. Breathing. I can hear breathing. One shallow breath after another.

Reaching up, I tap the light on my shoulder. A beam flashes out—like a third moon—and highlights the make-shift cavern. Defoe is there. His eyes take in the sight of me before closing in pain. I can feel him grasping, the subtle trace of nyxia in the air. Clearly, he's far too weak to do much with the substance. I have a choice to make. The consequences will echo.

The first choice ends here and now. How painfully simple it would be to finish him. One of Babel's greatest threats, erased. It would eliminate any opportunity for him to hurt the others.

It would also eliminate any opportunity to infiltrate Babel. Show up on their doorstep without him and I become a prisoner. The other choice: Save him. Rescue. Subvert. Wait.

When I strike, I want to make sure I hit an artery. My two choices and their consequences play out in less than a breath. "Mr. Defoe." I make my voice calm. "I came to help you."

He wheezes. It's almost a laugh. It is clear what he thinks of me.

"Longwei—of course you did. . . ."

I watch as he leans his head back. Hidden at his hip, an explosive. Identical to the one he used on the battlefield. The same device that nearly ripped my friends apart with a single blast. Defoe lifts the device so I can see it more clearly.

"I thought—well, never mind what I thought." A cough shakes his body. "Take this. Replace my fingers on the pin and get rid of it. Three-second charge. Throw it as far as you can."

His arm shakes, but I am steady. I replace his fingers quickly, device secured, and turn. Twenty paces bring me back to the edge of the creek. With a deep breath, I throw the grenade as far as I can. Moonlight dances across its spiraling surface; then the grenade falls below the tree line and vanishes briefly from sight. A second passes before an explosion tears the darkness in two.

Bright and loud. A pair of birds take to the air. Something massive stirs deeper in the forest. I move back to Defoe's side. "I can't—stop the bleeding," he gasps. "The nyxia won't take."

I kneel so that my shoulder light is centered on the curled, covered stump of his arm. He has a soiled towel wrapped around it. Ineffective. I set down my own pack and start digging.

A new bandage, gauze, a plastic bag.

"I need to unwrap your current bandage."

Defoe nods once. I pinch the gauze between two fingers, carefully avoiding the blood, and lift one corner. The folds unravel. Defoe doesn't protest as the material rips and snags.

The wound exposes the bloody interior of his arm. Babel's king. How human he seems now. For too long I thought him a god. Seeing him this way will help in all that is to come.

I pack the gauze in tight around the exposed areas before wrapping the bandage tightly. Layer after layer. I use a piece of nyxia to seal it to his arm. Defoe lets out a groan as I pull the plastic bag over the entire wrapping, cinching it on his forearm, closing everything within.

"It needs to be iced," I say.

"It needs a lot more than ice," he replies. "I haven't slept. I've forced myself to keep moving. I need you to seal us in here. Keep us safe. Do you know how to do the manipulation?"

In answer, I reach for my nyxia. The substance pulses. A firm thought casts it out like a curtain, big enough to drape over the entrance of the hollow. "Like this?"

"Adjust it," Defoe gasps back. "So we can see out, but nothing can see in."

The change takes a few attempts. Defoe worms his way deeper into the hollow so there's room for me. I reach up, tucking the top of the nyxian drape between a set of exposed roots. I test it with a tug and it holds. The fabric stretches as I adjust the flaps and enclose us. There are gaps to let oxygen in, but we're hidden from prying eyes now. Defoe turns his back to me, injured arm balanced delicately on his hip.

"Sleep. I need sleep."

For the second time, I consider killing him.

The moment slips by like a long, slithering snake. Understanding shivers down my spine. I can feel the goose bumps run down my neck and arms. I know what keeping him alive will mean. Someone will die. A friend of mine, perhaps. Defoe is formidable. He can turn the tides in a single battle with ease. His intelligence will also give Babel the upper hand in the coming days.

Who will die because I let him live? What will the cost be?

I force myself to swallow those fears. I chase the dark thoughts away and remember that it's wise to lose a battle if it means we can win the war.

Unbidden, my eyes roam up to the distant moons. Glacius looks like an unpolished pearl; Magness like a bloodshot eye. The two moons appear hammer-struck into the sky. It's hard to remember they are moving, spinning, spiraling. I know their paths are drawing them inevitably toward one another. I keep the thought quiet—almost afraid Defoe might hear it if I think about it for too long. But no matter how much I try to bury it, the truth is impossible to ignore.

This world is coming to an end.

At dawn, we march through the forest and onto an open plain. The first continent was marked by creeks and rivers. This one is dotted instead with old ruins. Stone buildings long abandoned, the patterns they carved into the hills all but faded.

For all his faults, I admire Defoe's sense of efficiency. He breathes and walks and uses every ounce of what he has left to move toward safety. He speaks rarely and I follow his lead.

Our silence is interrupted once: a loud, droning beep. It's sharp and ear-piercing. Defoe stares down at his watch as the noise winds to a more bearable volume. I glance over in time to see four blue lights, arranged like cardinal directions. The northern one flickers and vanishes.

Defoe considers the watch long after it goes silent. His expression is telling, dark.

It takes us seven hours and forty-eight minutes to find a roaming unit of Babel marines. They emerge from the cover of the nearest hill like ghosts dressed in black. Their weapons are drawn and raised until they realize it's Defoe. In a breath their original directive is abandoned. They transform into escorts. We're directed to an elevated ruin just south of the location.

There's enough light to see a sprawl of vehicles packed into the abandoned courtyard. Everything bears Babel's signature designs: nyxian, sleek, deadly. Even injured, Defoe straightens his shoulders and marches into camp like a king. I am less revered. One of the marines stops me. I'm briefly frisked, my weapons removed. I take a deep breath and wonder if my chance to strike just slipped through my fingers.

But Defoe waits. Once my weapons have been removed, he signals for me to join him. I might be defanged, but I'm still in the right position. A marine leads us around an armored truck and directly to a team of techies. Holoscreens display satellite imagery, live-feed camera shots, and landscape views. Defoe doesn't hesitate. "Give me a full status update."

There's confusion as the techies turn to take in the scene.

Every eye settles on the bleeding stump I treated the night before. In the day's failing light, it looks like a poor excuse for medical treatment. One of his men arrives at the same conclusion.

"Mr. Defoe," he says. "We need to treat your arm. You're bleeding, sir."

He glances at his bandages. "In a minute. I want a status update. Now."

One of the other techies takes the lead. I note he has the same glove that Kit Gander wore. When he swipes a finger through the air, one of the smaller screens migrates to the central monitor. The image resolves into a massive map of Magnia. We all watch as the empty outlines of continents begin to populate. Lines—like the migratory patterns of birds—color the screen.

"Blue lines are likely escape routes for each ring," the techie explains. "Our teams are working through the wreckage of Sevenset. The reported casualties are far lower than expected, sir. After discovering the first deep-sea tunnel, our crews ran scans as directed. We have a general idea of where the evacuees would have gone, but there's still no explanation for how they evacuated so quickly. The amount of time between when we disabled the defenses and launched the attack was less than five minutes."

"And each ring has its own evacuation tunnel?" Defoe asks.

"There are hundreds of tunnels, sir," the techie answers. "But there do appear to be tunnels specifically designated for leaving Sevenset. They're all buried far more deeply than the rest."

"Seven exit points that connect to four different continents." Defoe considers that. I can see him trying to figure out where they went wrong, how the strike could have come too slow. I'm thankful that he doesn't look at me. "The facility we destroyed to the north was designed for aircraft warfare. The designs were pedestrian compared to our tech, but it was the clear destination for the group leaving the Sanctum. Are there matching bases near the other exit points?"

The techie shakes his head. "We have no visuals."

Those words draw Defoe's attention more sharply. He doesn't look surprised. Rather, it's a confirmation of something he already suspected. He glances down at the missing light on his watch.

"When were the last satellite images sent from the Tower Space Station?"

"Four or five hours ago?" The head techie frowns. "We weren't sure what to make of it. Command was directing us away from the crews that escaped our initial attack. But every single soldier on this mission knows the Adamite leadership was our primary objective. We hesitated to pull troops until we had confirmation from you."

Defoe nods. "Did you receive any distress signals?"

The techies exchange glances. "None, sir."

"Send a request for verbal confirmation. Ask for a Code Four Update."

There's a brief pause. "You suspect casualties?"

"Just send it."

The room grows tense as the techies scramble to complete the request. I listen as they carefully pronounce each word. The message vaults through atmospheres, corrects for orbiting patterns, and glows green upon delivery. Everyone takes their cues from Mr. Defoe. Silence is held sacred until a response appears in front of the central techie. He leans forward, squinting, and reads.

"All-clear response. No casualties."

Defoe clinches his good fist. "So the Tower Space Station is compromised."

The entire group stares back at him. Only the lead techie manages to find his voice.

"But they're reporting no casualties. . . ."

He holds up his watch. Three of the lights are still glowing blue. The fourth light is gone. Defoe decides to pull back the curtains and explain the mystery. "And yet this tells me that David Requin is dead. Combine that information with their desire to redirect you from our priority target, and we can make the reasonable assumption. Let's keep lines open, but treat all communication with them as tainted. I'd like to start gathering as much intelligence on the ground as possible. Falsify any reports you send back to them. Let's go ahead and get working on action plans for recovering the space station."

When the others don't move, Defoe raises an eyebrow. The look transforms hesitation into action. The techies busy themselves, and a handful of marines retreat to discuss strategies.

Defoe looks deep in thought. "Wait. The *Genesis 14*. When is it scheduled to arrive?"

"Any day now, sir."

"And can we communicate directly with them?"

The techie shakes his head. "We didn't diversify our

outbound communications from the planet. All our messages have to go through the Tower Space Station."

Defoe looks briefly disappointed by that. "Get to work. Action items to me within the hour. I'm going to have this arm treated, and by the time I'm finished, I want a debriefing session with strategies for every outcome."

I stand there—a forgotten shadow—as the others begin to work. Defoe pulls one of the techies aside. He speaks, and it's clear that he's forgotten I'm there. Either he's forgotten, or he truly trusts me. As the camp spirals into chaos, Defoe offers me a single insight into his next plan.

He says, "Activate the Prodigal."

EXPLORERS AND SURVIVORS

Morning Rodriguez
15 days 08 hours 12 minutes

We are the first human explorers of this world. The first and the last.

No one will find our footsteps. No one will see the hills we see now. This world is about to come to an end. Our group can't stop looking up. Both moons hang in the sky. Glacius is almost full, but the angles and light have narrowed Magness down to a curving blade that's edged by a single, fiery streak. It's an ax waiting to fall on the exposed neck of the planet.

Fifteen days. The moons will collide in just fifteen days.

"Base ahead," the call echoes down the lines. "Base ahead."

I glance at Emmett. When he thinks no one's watching, his shoulders always slump now. The weight of all of this. That's one of the fundamental differences I've learned between the two of us. Emmett draws his strength from what has happened. I draw mine from what comes next. One isn't better than the other, but it does mean we come to each problem from different angles.

A quick survey shows the whole group is heavy shoulders and empty hearts. I haven't seen many smiles since we started marching. The threat finally feels real, because this time Babel wrote the words in blood: Jaime, Omar, Loche, Brett, Bilal, Kaya. Emmett whispers their names in his sleep. I'm glad that he does. Babel wants to erase those names, but we're fighting for a different end to their story. We want a history where their names are remembered and the people who killed them are brought to justice. I'm not sure how we're going to pull it off, but we will, we have to.

A second shout works its way down the lines.

"Units Three, Seven, and Eight on patrol!"

No surprise Genesis isn't involved. The Imago leadership intentionally keeps us out of the action. We haven't seen Babel troops in days, but the Imago don't want to lose their lifeline to Earth. We're the ones who promised to represent them. They'll do anything to keep us safe.

Or maybe they're worried we'll explore other options.

The crew looks happy to take a seat in the shade of the run-down compound. Jacquelyn and Speaker disappear inside, followed by the Daughters and a handful of guards. We pass a few canteens around, heaving sighs as we sprawl in the swaying grass. I imagine Feoria painting this scene—using the same colors she used for our portraits. A landscape dotted with young soldiers marching into a war they never asked to fight.

"What are we doing?" Katsu complains. "What the hell are we doing out here?"

I don't think he's actually looking for an answer, but Parvin offers one. The two of them have been digging under each other's skin the whole march. "They're running scans for activity in the launch stations. You know that, Katsu."

He lets out a laugh. "Can't wait to see the video footage of all those Imago waving down at us as they launch into space and leave us here to die."

And now he's digging under my skin. "No one's gonna die."

Katsu doesn't even look at me. He just leans back and waves up at the sky.

"You up there, Anton?" he calls. "If you can hear me, send down a pair of sunglasses. I'd like to at least watch the world end in style. You guys heard Jacquelyn talking about what will happen after the moons hit, right? We don't even get the badass one-shot meteor that just vaporizes everything. It's a bunch of *little* meteors. Boring stuff at first. But the bigger pieces will cause chain earthquakes, so that's cool. Maybe a few continent-consuming fires. And she said all that debris will eventually choke out the atmosphere. I always thought air quality was bad in Tokyo, but this?" He looks back up into the sky. "Anton! Send down oxygen masks too!"

I shoot a look over at Emmett. His whole face unlocks, like he's realizing for the first time that Katsu is under *his* command. I raise an eyebrow that would make mi abuelita proud and he finally intervenes. "Cool it, Katsu."

Katsu looks over at Emmett. I watch as he takes in the group and realizes it's not the right time for his standard comedy routine. He finally shuts his mouth, and I take advantage of the silence. Leading is all about momentum. Time to rally the crew.

"One way or another," I say, "we're going home."

No one responds. For the first time, I'm promising something I'm not sure I can deliver. Azima slips off to talk with Beckway. I'm not the only one who has noticed the two of them marching together. It has the taste of a doomed romance. I glance back and catch Parvin watching them. Noor sets a comforting hand on her best friend's shoulder. Omar died right after he told Parvin how much he liked her. Our days might be numbered down here, but I still hate Babel for taking those final weeks from them.

The thought drags my attention back to Emmett. He's leaned against the building with his eyes closed. The soldier's marching beard suits him. It frames perfect lips and softens the carved jaw. This damn boy. The boy who let me listen to his favorite song. The boy who tackled me into the water. I want to take this boy back to Earth so bad it hurts. I want to meet his mom and eat burgers and dance at parties. . . .

I let out a sigh. We have to survive today before I can think about tomorrow.

It takes an hour for Jacquelyn to resurface. She makes a line for our group.

"We've got news," she says. "You'll all want to be inside for this one."

At some point, I learned to read a voice. Life with mi abuelita taught me that much. How she used to come back from the hospital and say everything with mother was fine. Just fine. Those two words had a little piece of everything in them. Hope that it really might be fine. Fear that it never could be. Anger that we were going to lose her too. A quiet determination to beat an endless cycle. Jacquelyn's voice splits the same way.

I can hear doubt and love and fear and hope. It takes us all a few seconds to stand up, shake the dust, and trudge toward the entrance. I fall in beside Emmett. Our shoulders touch briefly as we both set our eyes on the next obstacle. Our romance isn't about kissing and holding hands now. It's about carving a path home, together.

On our left, the *Genesis 13* crew is huddled together. Guards circle, even though they're all chained up. Emmett's gone over and talked to them a few times. He's got the biggest heart I've ever seen. I can't force myself to extend an olive branch. The sight of the survivors takes me back to the first time we met outside the repository building. All the blood spilled there.

I'm not the only one who notices them.

"I feel bad for them," Alex mutters.

Katsu shakes his head. "If Jaime missed that head butt on Defoe, we'd be the ones marching in chains. If you ask me, we're wasting time dragging them across this godforsaken continent."

"Good thing no one is asking you," Parvin cuts back.

The crew goes silent after that. I realize some of them agree with Katsu. It's the first potential divide. The first small step away from *we* to words like *us versus them*.

Jacquelyn guides us inside and surprise echoes through our ranks. Outside, the building looked abandoned: faded stones and warped railings. But two steps inside pulls back the curtain. There are Imago guards manning a handful of technological consoles. Analytics roll down the screens alongside complicated maps of the entire planet.

"We gutted these old shelters," Jacquelyn explains. "Built a few fallout bases just in case our plans didn't work as intended. It wasn't easy to keep the construction off of Babel's radars."

I resist pointing out that the reason we're here is that they didn't keep their *real* base off Babel's radars. We still have no idea what gave us away. Maybe Babel just got lucky.

She leads us into a wider room. There's a table full of Imago generals, all waiting on us. Feoria stands. A casual sweep of the queen's hand brings a digital screen to life. The images resolve into a map as we take our seats. My mind skips back to the first time we saw a map of this new world. David Requin—Jacquelyn's uncle—walked us into a lie that would change our lives forever. He did it with a damn smile on his face too.

"We will not waste your time," Feoria begins. "We have enough data to make decisions about what we do next. Babel presented you with partial truths. Time is too precious for us to make the same mistakes they did. We want you to know everything that we know."